SEE YOU NEXT MONTH

JAMEY MOODY

See You Next Month

©2024 by Jamey Moody. All rights reserved

Edited: Kat Jackson

Cover: Anita Hallam

This is a work of fiction. Names, characters, places, and incidents are the product of the author's imagination or are used fictitiously. Any resemblance to an actual person, living or dead, business establishments, events, or locales is entirely coincidental. This book, or part thereof, may not be reproduced in any form without permission.

Visit my website or sign up for my mailing list here: www.jameymoodyauthor.com.

I'd love to hear from you! Email me at jameymoodyauthor@gmail.com.

As an independent author, reviews are greatly appreciated.

❋ Created with Vellum

ALSO BY JAMEY MOODY

Live This Love

One Little Yes

Who I Believe

* What Now

See You Next Month

The Your Way Series:

* Finding Home

*Finding Family

*Finding Forever

The Lovers Landing Series

*Where Secrets Are Safe

*No More Secrets

*And The Truth Is ...

*Instead Of Happy

The Second Chance Series

*The Woman at the Top of the Stairs

*The Woman Who Climbed A Mountain

*The Woman I Found In Me

Sloan Sisters' Romance Series

*CeCe Sloan is Swooning

*Cory Sloan is Swearing

*Cat Sloan is Swirling

Christmas Novellas

*It Takes A Miracle

The Great Christmas Tree Mystery

With One Look

*Also available as an audiobook

1

"Welcome to paradise," Kelsey Kenny muttered morosely as she stepped off the plane and walked through the long hallway into the airport. She looked around as people smiled at familiar faces or hugged. No one was there for her, so she strolled through the airport to baggage claim.

Passengers were already plucking pieces of luggage off the rotating table like they were precious prizes. Then, just as quickly, they turned to hurry out of the airport in search of their tropical vacation in paradise or perhaps some of them even lived here.

Ah, the Virgin Islands. Kelsey couldn't imagine living there—then again, she could work from anywhere.

Kelsey was in no hurry. Yes, she guessed this could be considered a vacation for her, but it simply didn't feel very festive. As she walked to the end of the baggage claim and found a place to wait, she spied her bright blue hard-sided suitcase beginning its trek around the sliding tabletop. She hadn't packed much, just a few swimsuits, some shorts, and a couple of cute dresses that she could dress up for dinner or dress down for a casual day at the resort.

A woman hurried towards where Kelsey stood. She was having trouble corralling her oversized purse and what looked like a computer satchel as she reached for one of the bags.

"Dammit," she huffed as the bag passed her by.

Kelsey watched this playing out and could see how frustrated the woman was, so she reached down and easily plucked the bag off the carousel.

"Here you go," Kelsey said as she rolled the heavy suitcase towards the woman.

The woman gasped. "Thank you so much! I missed it."

Kelsey smiled. "Glad I could help."

"I've got another one and you'd think they'd be together," the woman said, staring at the opening where the bags tumbled onto the table.

Kelsey smiled at the woman's Southern accent. It reminded her of syrup, sweet and slow. She turned back to the table only to realize she'd let her own bag pass by.

"Way to go, Kelsey," she mumbled.

"Excuse me?" the woman asked.

Kelsey chuckled. "I let my bag get by me. I'll just have to wait until it comes around again."

"Oh, I'm sorry."

"It's okay. I'm in no hurry."

The woman sighed. "I just want to get to my room. I hope there's a shuttle waiting outside."

Kelsey nodded and kept her eye on her bag as it came into view once again.

"Oh good, there's my other bag," the woman said happily.

A bag matching the suitcase Kelsey had taken off the

carousel for the woman was directly behind Kelsey's blue suitcase. This bag looked even larger than the first one. *She must be staying for several weeks*, Kelsey thought.

Kelsey reached for her bag and easily pulled it off the table. She could see the woman was having trouble lifting the large suitcase over the short rail, so Kelsey reached under the bag and gave it a push.

"Thank you!" the woman exclaimed. "I've done this before, but maybe I packed too much."

"You think," Kelsey said under her breath.

"I promise you, I handled both bags with no problems when I boarded in Charlotte. Just watch," the woman said.

Once she had both bags on their wheels and their handles pulled up, she slipped the satchel over one handle and her purse over the other. She rolled the bags away a short distance and spun each bag to do a little pirouette.

"See what I mean." She smiled and did a slight curtsey.

Kelsey chuckled. "You are skilled." She rolled her bag near the woman and smiled. "I can only manage one bag, so I have to cram everything inside."

The woman smiled. "I doubt that. I think you're just being nice."

Kelsey raised her eyebrows in surprise, and then smiled. "Let's see if we can find a shuttle."

They fell in step next to each other and rolled their bags the short distance to the exit. Outside, Kelsey looked both ways and then saw the shuttle for her resort.

"Thank God!" the woman exclaimed as she started towards the small bus. She turned back to Kelsey and smiled. "Thanks again for the help."

Kelsey returned her smile. "I think we may be going to the same resort." She nodded towards the bus and followed the woman.

"I'm going to The Coral Bay Resort," the woman said.

Kelsey nodded. "Me too. Let me get on the bus and I'll help you with your bags." She didn't wait for the woman to reply. Instead, she stepped onto the bus, smiled at the driver, and rolled her bag into the empty space in front of the first seat.

She turned back just as the woman was lifting her first bag onto the bus.

"Here, I've got it," the bus driver said, quickly getting up from his seat.

He took the first bag and rolled it in front of an empty seat then took the second bag and rolled it into the space across from where Kelsey had left her bag.

"Thank you," the woman said, taking her seat next to the bag.

Kelsey sat down and smiled.

The woman leaned over, extended her hand, and said, "I'm Isabella Burns."

At that moment the driver revved the bus and Kelsey barely heard the woman's name.

"I'm Kelsey Kenny." She took her hand and shook it.

"Thank you again for your help, Kelsey." Isabella smiled.

"You're welcome, Bella." Kelsey appreciated her nice, firm handshake.

The driver pulled away from the curb and Kelsey leaned back to glance out the window. What a beautiful place. If her girls didn't want to be with her at Christmas then surely this little piece of paradise would keep her from missing them.

She sighed and shook her head. It wasn't necessarily that her girls didn't want to be with her; they just wanted to do their own thing, which didn't include her. They knew she wanted to spend Christmas at a beach somewhere instead of skiing in the mountains like they'd always done in the past. But this wasn't what she'd had in mind; she wanted her daughters to be with her.

Kelsey had planned to stay home and work, but she knew the girls would feel guilty. When the opportunity arose to spend Christmas at one of her client's resorts, it seemed like a good idea. The folks at Coral Bay were so excited she was coming so that she could see and experience the resort at its best.

Once she was in her room, she'd give each of her daughters a call, and then try to enjoy the experience. She watched as the palm trees whizzed by.

Kelsey sighed, then glanced over at Isabella and saw her gazing out the window as well. She wondered if she was meeting her family here. Surely she wasn't traveling alone with all that luggage. Just then Isabella looked over at her and smiled.

"It's gorgeous," Isabella said, gesturing towards the window.

"Yeah, it is," Kelsey replied.

"It feels a little strange to be spending Christmas on a tropical island," Isabella remarked.

"It does to me, too," Kelsey agreed. "I noticed a Christmas tree in the airport, though."

"Oh, I missed that." Isabella chuckled. "I was hurrying to baggage claim. Maybe that's a sign I need to slow down and enjoy this beautiful paradise."

Kelsey nodded and smiled. Perhaps Isabella was right. It shouldn't be hard to enjoy these beautiful views, the crystal clear water, and island breeze. She'd wanted to spend Christmas at the beach and here she was, only minutes away.

This was an opportunity to get to know her client and

their product better, so it was a plus for her work life. As far as her personal life, she was at a beach resort on a tropical island. *Come on, Kelsey!* she chided herself.

"Are you okay?" Isabella asked, drawing Kelsey's attention back to her.

Kelsey grinned. "You're right. What's not to enjoy? Merry Christmas."

Isabella chuckled. "Merry Christmas to you, Kelsey."

The driver pulled up to the front door and Kelsey noticed Isabella stayed in her seat. She looked over at her and furrowed her brow. "Do you need any help?"

"With all the trouble my bags have caused since deplaning in St. Thomas, it's best for me to wait and let the other people get off first." Isabella chuckled.

"Are you sure? I don't mind helping you."

"I can get it," Isabella assured her. "I don't want to get in anyone's way."

Kelsey nodded. "It was nice meeting you."

"You too, Kelsey. Maybe I'll see you around."

"Maybe," Kelsey said, then exited the bus. At least Isabella would be a familiar face since she didn't know anyone else at Coral Bay.

"Can I help you with that?" an eager attendant asked her as he held open the front door to the reception area.

"No, but there's a woman on the bus with two large bags that could use your assistance," Kelsey said with a smile.

"I'm on it," the young man said, walking towards the bus.

Kelsey chuckled. She figured Isabella could handle her bags, but a little help was always nice.

"Welcome to Coral Bay," a woman with a cheerful smile said from behind the counter.

"Hi, I'm Kelsey Kenny. Carmen Oliver said to ask for her when I check in," Kelsey explained.

"Oh, Ms. Kenny, right this way."

Kelsey followed the woman down a hallway. There were a couple of meeting rooms on either side and executive offices at the end.

The desk clerk stopped in the doorway of a large office. "Carmen, this is Kelsey Kenny."

"Kelsey!" Carmen exclaimed, coming out from behind her desk. "You made it."

Kelsey shook Carmen's hand and smiled. "It's nice to meet you face to face."

"You as well. How was your trip?"

"It was uneventful, just the way I like it when I'm flying."

"Isn't that the truth? I have you all set up in one of the bungalows right on the water," Carmen said.

"Shouldn't you be using that for your paying guests?"

"You're a special guest. Let us spoil you a little. After all, it's Christmas."

"I can't wait to see everything. The pictures you've shared with me don't do it justice."

"I've told you to come see for yourself and I'm happy you finally have," Carmen said.

"I already have ideas for updates on the website," Kelsey said.

"Our website is as beautiful as our resort, but I trust you to make whatever changes it needs," Carmen said. "We've just gone through a branding change and thought it would be a good idea for you to meet the new team while you're here."

"That sounds great. I want Coral Bay to be successful and am happy to do anything I can to help," Kelsey said.

"I know you're a team player. That's why you've been our web designer all these years."

"You are a valued client," Kelsey said.

"That's enough business talk for today. Terese will take you to your bungalow so you can get settled in. I'd like to have a short meeting with you and the brand designer in the morning," Carmen said. "Don't worry, it won't be early. Everything moves a little slower on the islands."

"Sounds great. I'll see you in the morning," Kelsey said.

Terese, the desk clerk, took Kelsey's bag and she followed her out the back of the building down a path that went by an inviting swimming pool, and then opened up to the most beautiful beach.

"This is incredible," Kelsey said.

"I know. I've lived here all my life and the view never gets old," Terese said.

They left the path to walk over to a private bungalow. It had a small front deck with two chairs for lounging. Terese opened the front door and Kelsey was immediately drawn to the floor to ceiling windows that framed her own private view of the water.

Kelsey gasped. "This truly is paradise."

Terese chuckled. "You have a deck through those doors. Sapphire Beach runs along the entire resort. It's not too crowded this time of year, so it's kind of like a private beach for you, especially after sunset."

"Thank you, Terese," Kelsey said, reaching into her purse.

"Oh, no, Ms. Kenny. It's my pleasure," Terese said, holding up both hands.

"Will you at least call me Kelsey?"

Terese smiled. "I can do that. If you're hungry, I recommend the fine dining in the restaurant we passed when we exited the main building. The seafood is always fresh. If you need anything, please let me know."

"I can't imagine needing anything," Kelsey said, looking around the room.

"Enjoy your stay. I'm always nearby if you need anything." Terese laid the key card on the table and closed the door.

Kelsey opened the door onto her back deck and inhaled deeply. "Hello, paradise," she said with a touch of optimism in her voice.

2

Isabella walked into her bungalow and gasped. "Wow, this is incredible."

"I'm glad you like it," Nadia said. "Where would you like me to leave your luggage?"

"Let's see," Isabella said, looking around the large room. "How about over there?"

Nadia rolled the bags in front of the closet. "Carmen has assigned me to be your assistant while you're here. If you need anything at all, simply call the front desk."

"Don't you get to go home at night?"

Nadia chuckled. "I'm here a lot, but yes, I go home at night. Someone will always be at reception if you need anything while I'm not here."

"Thank you," Isabella said. "Do you do this for all your guests?"

Nadia smiled. "Well, not everyone, but we try to be extra available to our guests in the bungalows since you're not in the main building of the resort."

"Carmen didn't have to do that for me. I'm supposed to be working," Isabella said.

"I hope you'll be able to enjoy the resort as well."

"Oh, I plan to," Isabella said. "Let me get something for you."

"No, ma'am. I'm here for you. It's all part of our service," Nadia said.

Isabella tilted her head. "Are you sure? I don't feel right not giving you something."

"Believe me, I'm glad to do it," Nadia said, walking towards the door. "All of our restaurants are exceptional. I suggest the fine dining restaurant tonight. The chef is always doing something special."

"Thanks for the suggestion."

"I'll see you later." Nadia left, quietly closing the door behind her.

Isabella turned back to the beautiful view out her back deck and took a deep breath.

This would be her first Christmas away from the boys and she wasn't handling it well. When her ex-husband told her he was taking them to New York for Christmas, she was upset. They had always spent Christmas at home in Charlotte. This was the second year they'd been divorced and it was his turn to have them for Christmas, so she couldn't really do anything about it.

Christmas wasn't the same without them. To keep from ruining Christmas for the people around her, she'd decided to work instead. A small smile played across her lips. It just so happened that her current client was a resort on St. Thomas in the Virgin Islands. Isabella had hoped the sun and sand would keep her mind off Christmas.

She planned to try to call the boys, but figured they'd be out doing something fun with her ex-husband's family. Isabella ambled over to the mini refrigerator and took out a bottle of water.

Once she opened the glass door onto the back deck, the rhythmic lapping of the waves called to her. She settled into one of the chaise lounges and drank deeply from the bottle.

Her thoughts drifted back to meeting Kelsey Kenny. Isabella furrowed her brow. *Did she call me Bella?* No one called her Bella and if they did, she usually corrected them. She tilted her head and smiled. There was no need to correct the kind woman. Isabella probably wouldn't see her again anyway. Just because they were staying at the same resort didn't mean their paths would cross. It was a big place.

When the attendant had appeared at the shuttle to help her with her luggage, she wondered if Kelsey had sent him her way once she'd gone inside the resort. Of course, the resort offered top-notch service, but she wouldn't be surprised if Kelsey had a hand in it.

Once she'd made it to the reception desk, she looked around and didn't see Kelsey anywhere. A few minutes later the resort's executive director, Carmen Oliver, appeared to welcome her and then Nadia led her to the bungalow, pointing out amenities along the way.

She wondered if Kelsey was traveling alone, just as she was. When they were on the drive from the airport to the resort, Isabella had glanced over at Kelsey as she gazed out the window. Something about the woman's face made Isabella think she wasn't exactly happy to be there.

Isabella sighed, closing her eyes and letting the island breeze waft over her travel weary body. She hopped up and decided to take a quick shower and change her clothes. Isabella didn't care for dining alone, but she was hungry and fresh seafood sounded delicious.

* * *

Kelsey strolled down the path back towards the main building. It was so peaceful and hard to believe there were so many other people at the resort. She walked past the bar and over to the entrance of the restaurant. Her eyes scanned the room, seeing mostly couples with a few families already seated and enjoying their meal.

She thought about going back to the bar and ordering dinner there.

"I knew it," a familiar voice said from behind her. "This place is full of couples and families."

Kelsey turned and looked right into Isabella's smiling face. "Hey," she said with a friendly smile.

"Shall we sit together? I hate eating alone," Isabella said.

"I do, too. I was about to go back to the bar," Kelsey said.

"Maybe we'll hit it after dinner." Isabella winked.

As they followed an attendant who took them to a table, Kelsey noticed Isabella's large purse on her shoulder. Kelsey smiled and couldn't keep from laughing as she remembered her looping the purse onto her bag and giving it a spin.

"What's funny?" Isabella asked as she sat down at the table for two. She hooked her purse over the chair.

"Your purse reminded me of your little dance with your luggage earlier today," Kelsey explained.

Isabella stared at Kelsey as she put the strap to her small crossbody bag, barely big enough to hold a phone and not much more, over the back of her chair.

Kelsey raised her eyebrows. "What?"

"You bring one bag and have a small purse and here I am with two large suitcases, my computer satchel, and a huge tote. Perhaps I could learn something from you."

Kelsey raised her eyebrows. "How long are you staying?"

"A week or so," Isabella said, resting her chin in her hand.

Kelsey laughed. "We'll see about that when you observe me repeating outfits later in the week."

"I don't know, the idea of not lugging all this around is appealing in this relaxed environment," Isabella said.

"The fewer things I have to carry with me, the better," Kelsey said as their server appeared with menus.

"Could you bring us two delicious fruity drinks fit for this paradise?" Isabella asked, looking over at Kelsey.

She nodded and the server disappeared to get their drinks, letting them peruse the menu.

"I have two boys," Isabella said, leaning over the small table. "I'm never without snacks or maybe a dinosaur or two in my purse."

Kelsey chuckled. "I remember those days."

Isabella studied Kelsey again and tilted her head. "Do you have kids?"

Kelsey nodded. "Two daughters, but they are in their twenties now."

"What!" Isabella exclaimed, surprised. "You must have been a teenager when you had them."

Kelsey thought for a moment. "My oldest, Dana, is twenty-four and Emma is twenty-two. Your comment made me realize that I was Dana's age when I had her."

"Really? I thought we were the same age," Isabella said.

"How old are your boys?"

"Wyatt, my oldest, is thirteen and Gus is ten," Isabella said.

"Oh, you're getting to the fun stuff then—teenagers," Kelsey said, widening her eyes. "I think you're a lot younger than I am."

Isabella shook her head. "I'm forty. That's not far behind forty-eight, but I swear, Kelsey, you don't look it."

Their server set two drinks down that were the color of

the sunset. Each had a skewer with a piece of pineapple and a cherry.

"Oh, these look delicious," Isabella said, holding up her glass. "To my first Christmas without my boys and no, I'm not taking it well."

Kelsey clinked her glass to Isabella's. "I get it. My girls didn't want to have Christmas with me."

They both sipped from their drinks and nodded in approval.

"What do you mean they didn't want to have Christmas with you?"

Kelsey paused. "Are you sure you want to hear this?"

"Yes, it might make me feel better about my situation."

"Okay, here goes. I'm from Denver. Dana is in nursing school and has been a patrol and rescue skier since she was a teenager. She stays on the mountain during the holidays, but usually makes it down for Christmas Day. Emma, my youngest, is in the last year of her political science degree and got the opportunity to go to California with her roommate whose mother happens to be a congresswoman. She's in heaven right now. So..." Kelsey paused to take another sip of her drink.

"So?"

"The girls know I've always wanted to spend Christmas at the beach. Be careful what you tell your kids," Kelsey said, leaning over the table. "They thought it would be a great idea for me to come on this beach getaway while they're doing their own thing for Christmas. I don't think either of them realized I wanted to spend Christmas at the beach as a family."

"Oh, okay. I'll remember that. Be specific," Isabella said, narrowing her eyes.

"Exactly." Kelsey nodded. "Now, what about you? You said this was your first Christmas without your boys?"

Just then their server came back to take their orders.

"Would you want to order the seafood sampler and split it?" Isabella asked. "We can try everything that way."

"That sounds good," Kelsey replied.

"And bring us another round of these drinks, please," Isabella said.

When the server left the table and after another sip of their drinks, Kelsey said, "Okay, Bella. It's your turn."

Isabella scoffed. "You called me Bella."

Kelsey furrowed her brow. "Isn't that your name?"

Isabella shrugged. "My name is Isabella."

Kelsey sighed. "I barely heard your name on the bus. The traffic was kind of loud until we left the airport. I'm sorry."

"It's okay. You can call me Bella. I kind of like it."

"Are you sure?"

Isabella nodded.

"I like your Southern accent," Kelsey said with a smile. "Now, about your boys?"

"I've been divorced for two years. We alternate holidays. I had the boys last Christmas and it's my ex-husband's turn. I didn't think it would be a big deal because we both live in Charlotte, but he decided to take them to New York to be with his family."

"I'm sorry. That must be hard," Kelsey said compassionately.

"I started to work over the holidays, but decided getting out of town would keep me from bringing my friends down. Can you imagine how awful it would be to spend Christmas with my friends and their kids? Anyway, I can work from anywhere, so here I am."

"So we're both single moms spending Christmas without our kids," Kelsey said with a frown.

"Yep. Hey wait, what about your girls' father?"

Kelsey raised her eyebrows and noticed their server coming towards their table. "That's a whole other story."

Isabella tilted her head and furrowed her brow.

Their server set the large platter of food in the middle of the table and gave them each a plate. Another server was right behind him with their second round of drinks. Once they had everything on the table and the servers were gone, Isabella raised her eyebrows.

"I'm all ears."

3

Kelsey smiled and put an oyster, a shrimp, and a piece of fish on her plate. "Well, when I first got out of college I worked at a fertility clinic. I hadn't had much luck in the love game and I wanted to have kids." She paused, picked up the oyster in the shell, added a few drops of hot sauce, and slid it into her mouth.

"Good?"

"Mmm." Kelsey nodded and widened her eyes. "Do you like them?"

"I do," Isabella said, then ate the oyster on her plate. "So?"

"So, I decided not to wait to find the right partner and went through IVF. When Dana was a little over a year old, I used the same donor and was able to get pregnant again. I had Emma and became a single mom of two."

Kelsey looked over and saw Isabella staring at her.

"You are so brave," Isabella finally said.

Kelsey shrugged. "I had help. My brother and his family live nearby, so the girls have grown up with their cousins. My mom and dad also helped."

"Still, you were so young. God, when I was twenty-four there was no way I could've had a kid," Isabella said.

"Parenthood is different for everyone," Kelsey said. "Hey, what's this?"

"What?"

"This." Kelsey pointed with her fork to a piece of fried food.

"Oh, that's conch. It's kind of like crab. Dip it in this sauce, it's yummy," Isabella said.

Kelsey followed Isabella's lead and tasted the fried food. "Mmm, that is good."

Isabella grinned. "Here, have a piece of this fish. It's delicious. What am I saying, it's all delicious." She giggled.

"It is." Kelsey smiled at Isabella and was suddenly glad she'd grabbed her bag off the luggage carousel. She hadn't expected to meet anyone on this trip, and thought she would be doing most things by herself.

Isabella returned her smile. "Thanks for having dinner with me. This is much better than eating at the bar."

"I was just thinking the same thing."

"Now, tell me what else I need to watch for since you made it through the teenage years with your girls."

Kelsey laughed. They continued eating, talking about their kids.

Their server came back to check on them as they were finishing up. "I wanted to let you know that the breeze off the water tonight is very nice. A moonlit walk along the beach would be lovely."

"Oh, thanks," Kelsey said, giving him a smile.

When he walked away, Isabella leaned over the table. "Oh, my God!" she said in an excited whisper. "He thinks we're a couple."

Kelsey chuckled. "Look around us, Bella. It's all couples. It wouldn't be a stretch to think we're together."

Isabella surveyed the restaurant and looked back at Kelsey with a smirk. "Okay, I guess I see what you mean."

"I was going to walk along the beach after dinner anyway. Would you like to join me?" Kelsey asked with a grin.

The corners of Isabella's mouth turned up. "Well, I can't let you go alone since we're a couple now."

Kelsey laughed.

Just then the server came back with their ticket. "Let me have that," Isabella said, taking it from his hands. "I'll put it on my room. My deal is all-inclusive."

"Mine is, too. Let me at least get the drinks," Kelsey said.

"You can get it tomorrow," Isabella winked.

Kelsey dropped her head and smiled. *I may have found someone to hang out with while I'm here.*

* * *

They left the restaurant and walked down the path to the beach. With her sandals dangling from one hand, Isabella could feel the cool sand between her toes. She gazed over at Kelsey and thought back to all they'd talked about at dinner.

"Why do you keep looking at me and looking away?" Kelsey asked.

"I was wondering..."

"Yes?"

"Did you date while the girls were growing up?"

"Not really. They kept me pretty busy and there wasn't much time for going out or meeting new people," Kelsey replied.

"Oh, wait!" Isabella said, stopping in the sand.

"What?"

"Were you hoping to have a little vacation fling? Am I messing that up for you?"

Kelsey turned to Isabella and laughed. "No! You probably didn't notice, but I haven't seen any single gay women roaming around the resort. So, I don't see a fling in my future."

"Oh, you're gay," Isabella said quietly, narrowing her eyes.

"Yes, I am. Is that a problem?"

"Not at all. I wondered when you said you hadn't found a partner." Isabella smiled and couldn't quite believe Kelsey didn't at least have a girlfriend. They may have just met, but Isabella could tell Kelsey was a nice person. Her dark brown hair was thick and curls fell at her shoulders. Then there were her eyes. Isabella had noticed at dinner they were hazel, a light brown, but she had a feeling they might look green or blue depending on what she was wearing.

"Maybe someday." Kelsey shrugged.

They began walking again and Isabella saw the bungalows coming into view. "It really is nice out tonight. Thanks again for having dinner with me."

"I had a great time. Thanks for taking a walk with me, especially after our server thought we were a couple," Kelsey replied.

"It didn't bother me."

"It seemed to."

"Not at all. It's just funny to me how we assume things about people just by looking at them and who they are with," Isabella explained.

"Do you mean how I thought you were staying for weeks when I saw your luggage?" Kelsey said, amused.

"Or how I thought after seeing you with one bag and

your small purse that maybe you could teach me a few things about letting go," Isabella said.

"Letting go?"

"Yeah, maybe I don't need all this stuff, just a few things will do," Isabella said. She was hoping that instead of sulking about Christmas without her boys, maybe this could be a kind of reset for her life. Being a divorced mom was not going so well.

"Hmm, that may be true, but I don't know what all you have. Maybe you need everything," Kelsey said. "We're all different people."

Isabella nodded. "But we all learn from each other, too."

"I'm sure there are a few things you could teach me as well," Kelsey replied.

Isabella stopped and smiled. "You're just being nice again."

Kelsey chuckled. "You don't know that. I tried conch and I probably wouldn't have ordered it if we hadn't shared that platter."

"You're welcome, then." Isabella grinned.

Kelsey smiled as they neared the bungalows. "I think this is where I'm staying."

"You think? You don't know?"

"It's dark and I haven't seen it from the beach," Kelsey explained.

"I may be staying right next door." Isabella chuckled, looking at the row of bungalows. "Since we're both here alone, would you want to do something together tomorrow afternoon? I mean, we are a couple now."

Kelsey laughed. "Sure. I have a meeting in the morning but I'm free after that."

"You're not just here for Christmas at the beach then. Okay, well, I have to work in the morning, so…"

"So I'm not the only one working. Will you give me your phone number, so I can text you?" Kelsey asked, pulling out her phone.

"Of course." Isabella took the phone and entered her number then sent herself a text. "There you go."

Kelsey looked at her phone and chuckled. "You put your name in as Bella."

"That's what you call me." Isabella shrugged. "Look," she said, showing Kelsey her phone.

Kelsey threw her head back and laughed. What a nice laugh, Isabella thought. She hoped to hear it again.

"My other half?" Kelsey asked, handing the phone back to Isabella.

"Sure, we're a couple while we're here and you're the other half." Isabella chuckled.

"You're funny, Bella Burns. I'm so glad we ended up here together."

"Me, too."

* * *

The next morning Kelsey knocked on Carmen's open office door. "Good morning."

"Hey," Carmen said, getting up from behind her desk and taking a notebook with her. "Let's go in here."

Kelsey followed her into one of the meeting rooms.

"Our new brand consultant is meeting with us," Carmen said, sitting down at the table. "How was your night?"

Kelsey sat down across from Carmen and smiled. Once she was back in her bungalow last night, she'd thought back over her day. Isabella Burns had made what could've been a rather bittersweet day into a delightful one instead. She was glad to be at the beach, but she wasn't sure how much she'd enjoy it without her girls.

"I had a delicious dinner where I tried conch and then had a lovely walk on the beach," Kelsey said.

"Was the conch fried? You've got to have it sautéed in this scrumptious sauce our chef created," Carmen said.

"I'll try it," Kelsey replied.

"We're in here," Carmen said as someone walked past the door.

"Hi," Isabella said, walking into the room.

"Bella!" Kelsey exclaimed.

"Hey, Kelsey. Am I your meeting?"

"You two know each other?" Carmen asked.

Kelsey chuckled. "We met at the airport and had dinner last night," she said with a smile.

"*Met* might not be the right word." Isabella laughed. "Kelsey helped me with my luggage, but we had a wonderful dinner last night and a nice walk on the beach."

"Oh good. Your bungalows are right next to each other because I knew you both wanted to work while you're here," Carmen said. "Have a seat."

Isabella sat at the table next to Kelsey and took her computer out of her purse. "Sometimes a big purse comes in handy."

Kelsey chuckled and lifted her satchel from the floor and took out her computer as well. "I know."

Isabella laughed and hit Kelsey on the arm. "You were holding out on me."

"Not really. It was in my bag." Kelsey noticed the confused look on Carmen's face. "We were comparing luggage yesterday."

"Oh, okay," Carmen said. "I wanted the two of you to

meet because Isabella has redesigned our brand and we want it on the website."

"You're the brand designer?" Kelsey said, turning to Isabella.

"Yeah. You're the web designer?"

Kelsey nodded. "I love what you've done with the brand."

"Thank you," Isabella said with a smile. "I love what you've done with the website."

"We think you're both the best," Carmen said. "That's why we wanted you both to experience the resort and see what other ideas you come up with while being here. We want to make Coral Bay the go-to resort in the Virgin Islands."

"From what I've seen so far, we have plenty to work with," Kelsey said, glancing over at Isabella.

"There's so much I want you to see," Carmen said. "St. John is a short ferry ride away and is home to one of my favorite bars in the islands as well as a beautiful national park. You can hike or ride bikes around the island. I also want you to go on one of our catamarans that offers day trips with snorkeling and other water adventures."

"That sounds wonderful. Is there anything better than a bar on the beach?" Isabella said.

"Hmm, I know the resort offers to set up excursions for their guests," Kelsey said. "Maybe you could offer packages for different types of guests."

"Oh yeah," Isabella said excitedly. "One for families, maybe something for couples or even for friends' trips."

"We offer destination wedding packages, but we could do something for bachelor or bachelorette parties as well. These are great ideas," Carmen said, quickly scribbling in her notebook.

"What about a guest blog or a travel blog by someone who gives a review on their stay at Coral Bay? They could write a daily post on each experience in a certain package," Kelsey said.

"Oh, I like that," Carmen said.

"I do, too, but I don't think you want a professional blogger. Hmm, I'm thinking," Isabella said, putting her finger to her chin.

"Right," Kelsey said, following Isabella's thought. "We need someone who has a following."

"What about an influencer?" Carmen asked.

Isabella raised her eyebrows at Kelsey. "I have an idea."

4

"How about highlighting different packages throughout the year?" Isabella said.

"Okay," Carmen said. "I'm listening."

"You could start in January and call it Winter at Coral Bay," Kelsey said excitedly.

"Yeah, and they can come back and do Valentine's Day," Isabella said.

"Oh, then spring break," Kelsey added.

"I see. That's interesting," Carmen said.

"You could come up with a different package for each month," Kelsey said.

"We already do something for Mother's Day and Father's Day," Carmen said.

"Oh, that's good," Kelsey said.

"Then you could have a family vacation, something for fall, then in November you can start the holidays," Isabella said.

"And it all culminates with Christmas at Coral Bay," Kelsey said. She could imagine all the things she could do with the website, highlighting each month and the special excursion packages.

"But who do we get to blog about it?" Carmen asked them both.

"Hmm," Kelsey murmured. She noticed Isabella was giving her a big smile.

"How about: Two Single Moms Do Coral Bay?" Isabella said with a twinkle in her eye.

"Two single moms?" Carmen asked.

"What are you thinking, Bella?" Kelsey raised her brows.

"Why not have us do it?" Isabella said.

Carmen gasped. "You two would be perfect. Isabella already has a significant following."

Kelsey tapped on her keyboard, pulling up Isabella's social media. "You do have a following, Bella!"

"So do you, Kelsey. Once people know you're the web designer they will take notice," Isabella said.

"Wait," Kelsey said. "You want us to come back every month and experience one of the packages?"

"Why not us?" Isabella said.

"We could do one on a budget and one with our kids," Kelsey said.

"Exactly." Isabella nodded.

"What about the couples package?" Kelsey said, lifting one eyebrow.

Isabella laughed. "We can do the couples' package, too. We're showing the options. Maybe we can bring some of our friends or—oh, I know! Your girls could bring their friends for the girls trip package. We can do this, Kels," Isabella said.

"I guess we could try some of the excursions while we're here this time and see if we can pull it off," Kelsey suggested.

"I'll get my staff started on what kind of excursions to

put in different packages. You two can report back to me each day and give us an idea of what you think would work well together for each occasion," Carmen said. "I love this idea. You two are going to make Coral Bay the place to go in the Virgin Islands!"

"I thought we were supposed to do that with the website and brand," Kelsey said.

"What better way to show people!" Isabella exclaimed. "We can blog and do videos. People will see us actually living the experience."

"I think they would trust you more than an influencer," Carmen said.

"Yeah, we're just two single moms raising our kids and helping people find the perfect place for every occasion." Isabella sat back in her chair, smiling.

"Hmm, it could also show that it doesn't matter what time of year or what the occasion might be. Plus, you want your guests to return year after year. It could keep the resort fresh and make vacation plans easy because they already have the destination," Kelsey explained.

"Why go someplace else? You know what you're going to get at Coral Bay and there's no place better," Isabella added.

"I knew there was a reason we hired you two. You *are* the best!" Carmen exclaimed.

"Let's take a few days, do a few excursions, and see what we come up with before you get too excited," Kelsey said. "Bella, can you come back every month?"

Isabella nodded. "I can if you can."

Kelsey took a deep breath and slowly let it out. "I think I can make it work."

"You know, one thing you haven't thought of is that these places we partner with may want to use your talents as well. This could bring you new clients," Carmen said.

"Hmm, I hadn't thought of that," Isabella said.

"Me either. I thought our focus was on Coral Bay," Kelsey said.

"It is, but the bars, boats, and other adventure businesses are private companies that need websites and brands, too," Carmen said. "You're free to recruit new clients."

"What do you think?" Isabella asked.

Kelsey stared into Isabella's eyes. "What did you want to do this afternoon?"

Isabella furrowed her brow. "I don't know. Sitting at the beach enjoying the sun, shade, and drinks sounds good."

Kelsey nodded. "Let's do that and we can talk more about this."

"Okay. You'll learn I can be a bit spontaneous. It's good that you like to think things through," Isabella said.

"Perfect. You can take the ferry to St. John tomorrow and spend all day on the island. I'll get together a few places for you to visit while you're there," Carmen said, getting up from the table. "I'll talk to you later as I get things going on my end."

Isabella and Kelsey got up and started to walk back through the building.

"How about we stop off at the bar?" Kelsey said.

"Yeah, I could use a drink after all that."

* * *

After they were seated at the bar and had ordered their drinks Kelsey turned to Isabella. "Now, let me get this straight."

"I thought you were gay," Isabella said with a grin.

"Very funny, Bella. You know what I mean," Kelsey said.

Isabella giggled. "You were saying."

"You want us to come back here each month and experience one of these packages. We'll write about it—"

"And video," Isabella added.

"And video ourselves doing the various things, then we'll post it on the website," Kelsey said.

Isabella nodded. "I'll also post it on all our social media accounts and other vacation travel sites."

The bartender served their drinks and Kelsey reached for hers, taking a long sip.

"Do you not want to meet me back here every month?" Isabella asked.

"It's not that. It's just..."

"It's just what?"

"Are we interesting enough for people to want to follow our antics?"

"Sure we are!"

Kelsey looked at Isabella and studied her for a moment. She had the most beautiful blond hair with mischievous blue eyes and a vitality that came across when she smiled. Then there was her cute accent. People would fall in love with her. "So we'd come back next month and do winter in Coral Bay."

"Right. You've always wanted to go to the beach for Christmas to get out of the cold. It's the same idea."

"But what about next month? It's Valentine's Day," Kelsey said.

Isabella nodded. "Just because we don't have, uh, partners or boyfriends," Isabella said with a smile, "doesn't mean we can't show what the resort has to offer. There are a lot of single women that do 'Galentine's Day' where they get together with their other single friends."

Kelsey chuckled. "I've heard about it. Maybe we could

get a couple that's already here to do the romantic Valentine's thing with us while we do Galentine's."

"That's a great idea," Isabella said. "See there, we can do this, Kels."

Kelsey smiled at Isabella and took another sip of her drink. That was the second time today that Isabella had shortened her name to make her point... Or was she trying to convince Kelsey to do this?

"How about we change into our swimsuits and find ourselves a nice little spot under an umbrella on the beach?" Isabella suggested. "We can figure out what we want to do over the next few days and plan this epic year of adventure."

Kelsey smirked and then smiled. "As long as we're near the bar. I'm going to need several more of these if you want me to agree to this outrageous undertaking. Do you have any idea how far out of my comfort zone this is?"

Isabella laughed. "You're the one that travels light and is supposed to be showing me how to let go. Oh, that's another thing we can highlight on these trips. The ideas just keep coming." She clinked her glass to Kelsey's.

"Oh, man. I'd better hold on."

"I've got you, babe. Don't forget, we're a couple," Isabella said with a wink.

Kelsey laughed and slid off her bar stool. She held out her arm. "Come on, other half, let's go."

Isabella giggled and put her arm through Kelsey's as they started back to their bungalows.

"I can tell you're unsure about this," Isabella said as they walked past the pool. "Give me the afternoon to convince you."

"You seem to be quite sure we're up to this and that people will want to see what we do here," Kelsey said. "Coral Bay isn't one of the big resorts. You know they're counting on us to make them a better fit than the larger and more popular destinations."

"I realize that," Isabella said.

Kelsey stopped outside her bungalow and looked at Isabella. "Don't you have a friend you'd rather do this with?"

Isabella smiled. "Go change and I'll meet you at the chairs and umbrella outside our back doors."

Kelsey sighed.

"I'll explain to you why I'd rather do this with you than anyone else."

"Okay," Kelsey said and went inside her bungalow.

So many thoughts were flowing through her mind. The idea of coming back to Coral Bay every month was a bit daunting. However, Kelsey traveled for work from time to time, so that wasn't a problem. Carmen was right that they would have the opportunity to secure new clients and that was good for her business.

She opened the drawer where she'd stored her swimsuits and selected a sapphire blue one piece swimsuit with a long sleeve oversized sheer cover-up. Once she'd changed, she found the canvas tote bag she'd packed to take on the beach. Inside she threw sunscreen, a towel, and a hat. Kelsey had brought along all her electronics on the trip, including her laptop and her tablet.

She chuckled to herself. At one point she had envisioned sitting on the beach and reading a book or two on her tablet. "I'm not sure I'll have time to do that now," she mumbled. Kelsey still put the tablet in her bag in case she needed to take notes or look something up while she and Isabella discussed this crazy idea.

Did she want to come back every month and do something new with Isabella? The thought made her smile. She barely knew this woman, but they did have several things in common. This led her to ask the question: Was there anyone in her friend group she would want to take a trip with every month? *Probably not.*

Since she and Isabella were doing this for a client it gave them both a shared responsibility of working together and doing a job. They shared the same goal of showing the resort in the best light possible in order to gain new guests. These monthly adventures were more than just a vacation.

When Kelsey thought about the idea in this way it made sense for her and Isabella to be the ones to not only go on the excursions, but also to promote them. Potential guests would know they didn't work directly for the resort or the companies providing the excursions, so their opinions would be more valuable.

Kelsey smiled. Maybe this could work. The idea of seeing the islands with Isabella could actually be fun. It gave a whole new meaning to the phrase *I love my job.*

She chuckled again, slung her bag over her shoulder, grabbed a bottle of water from her refrigerator, and opened the back door.

"Well, paradise. What do you have in store for me today?"

Kelsey put on her sunshades and walked out onto the sand with a smile on her face.

5

"Kelsey, look at you," Isabella said, sitting in the lounge chair next to her. "That swimsuit. The color is perfect for you. How has some lesbian not snatched you up?"

Kelsey chuckled and took off her sunglasses. "What about you with that blond hair, those sparkling blue eyes, and that winning smile?"

Isabella gave her a cheesy smile. "But is this smile good enough to win you over to this grand idea?"

"We'll see. What about my earlier question? Do you have a friend you'd rather do this with?"

"I've been thinking about it," Isabella said seriously. She looked into Kelsey's eyes and noticed they had a blue-green tint reflecting the nearby water. They were beautiful and serious, but she also saw a hint of amusement.

"I don't have a friend I would want to come back here with every month. I only want you. What better way to get to know each other and make a new friend?" Isabella said honestly.

Kelsey smiled. "I thought about it, too, and you're right. There's no one I want to do this with but you."

Isabella's smile was brighter than the sun. "Does that mean you'll do it?"

Kelsey nodded. "We both know that our responsibility is to Coral Bay. I don't think our friends would understand that the way we do."

"I agree, but we can have some fun along the way. Can't we?"

Kelsey laughed. "We'd better. That's the whole idea, isn't it?"

Isabella leaned back and released a relieved breath. "Do we need a drink to toast to our new partnership?"

"I brought you a bottle of water," Kelsey said, reaching into her bag and handing the bottle to Isabella. "I have to pace myself if I'm going to make it all day."

"Oh, this is going to be a beautiful friendship," Isabella said, opening the bottle. "You will keep us on task and semi-clear headed."

"I'm glad you think that, but honestly, I love these drinks so much that if I didn't pace myself, I'd be drunk and asleep before the sun sets."

Isabella chuckled. "I'd be right there with you."

Kelsey held her bottle to Isabella's. "Let's have the time of our lives and show the world what a jewel Coral Bay truly is."

"To the time of our lives," Isabella said, touching her bottle to Kelsey's then taking a big gulp.

"So tell me, Bella," Kelsey said with an inquisitive tone, "why has someone not snatched you up?"

"Oh, God, Kels," Isabella groaned. How could she tell her she hadn't even thought about a man since the problems began with her husband?

"Come on. Have you dated since your divorce?"

"I haven't nor have I had the desire to," Isabella said. "I wouldn't even know how to go on a date." She looked over at Kelsey and saw a compassionate smile; then she furrowed her brow. "What is it?"

"Uh oh. I'm rethinking our marketability. I haven't been on a date in forever."

Isabella chuckled. "So what? We didn't sign up to find love on these excursions. We're just out for a little adventure."

Kelsey raised her eyebrows. "That might be an angle we could explore."

Isabella dropped her chin and stared at Kelsey. "Are you saying we should look for love interests while we're on these little rendezvous?"

"Not for me. For you!" Kelsey exclaimed.

"Why not you? Why not both of us?" Isabella shrugged.

"I thought you had no desire," Kelsey said, lowering her voice.

Isabella smiled. "I don't want to be single for the rest of my life. Eventually I want to find someone who is more than a friend."

Kelsey smiled and took a drink from her water bottle. "I am patiently waiting for you to continue."

Isabella chuckled. "So this is the getting to know each other part, I guess."

"Well, since we are a couple I think it would be a good idea, don't you?"

Isabella saw the kind smile on Kelsey's face and realized how easy she was to talk to. They may not have known each other long, but she got the idea that Kelsey was not one to judge.

"Spencer, that's my ex-husband, and I had very different

ideas of marriage. How we didn't know this before we got married still baffles me. He wanted the traditional Southern marriage where the wife stays at home and raises the kids. To put it mildly, I did not want that."

Kelsey furrowed her brow. "I don't see you as the stay at home type."

"Exactly. So I found something I was good at and could do around raising my boys. That meant we shared responsibilities of the family and even though I worked mainly from home, sometimes he had to do his part."

"And he didn't like that?"

"No, he liked the idea of me being home and handling most of the day to day things. But we're great at co-parenting so far." Isabella looked over at Kelsey and tilted her head. "You had to do everything, didn't you?"

"I'm kind of like you. I found something I was good at and could do from home while the girls were younger. I did most of my work while they were in school and scheduled their activities around the rest of my workday. It was quite a balancing act at times and it meant some late nights for me after they went to bed," Kelsey explained.

"Did you wish you had a partner to help?"

Kelsey sighed. "There were times when I wished I had a partner to share things with. Sure, it would be easy to want help when they didn't want to do homework, take a bath, or were just generally cranky. But for me, it would've been nice to have someone when they did things I was proud of. Like when they took their first steps or did well in school. It would've been nice to turn to someone and be excited for them together. It was a lot of little things."

Isabella couldn't keep from reaching over and squeezing Kelsey's hand. "And now?"

Kelsey smiled. "They will both graduate soon and begin their careers. I know Emma will likely end up in the D.C. area immersed in politics and I wouldn't be surprised if Dana moved after she finishes her nursing degree. I get the feeling she's ready to leave the mountains, which is a big deal for her."

Isabella smiled. "You really know your daughters."

Kelsey shrugged. "I hope so. I want them to always know they can come to me with anything. We all need someone we can count on."

"A partner would be nice for that," Isabella said as she looked out over the water.

"Yeah," Kelsey replied wistfully.

Isabella sat up and turned to Kelsey with a warm smile and extended her hand. "Well, Kels, you can count on me for the next year to be right here, by your side, doing all kinds of crazy adventures."

Kelsey met Isabella's eyes and took her hand. "Okay, then. You can count on me as well, Bella."

They shook hands and both chuckled.

"I think it's time for a drink," Isabella said.

"Would you look at that, here comes an attendant. Make a note of how they appear just when you need them," Kelsey said with a grin.

Isabella took out her computer and began to tap the keyboard. "I'm making a document we can share for notes. We may as well start now. Oh wait, I have an email from Carmen. I think it's our itinerary for tomorrow."

"Good afternoon, ladies. I'm Luis," the attendant said with a smile. "Is there anything I can get you?"

"Hi, Luis. You are here just when we need you," Isabella said.

"That's my job," he replied with a grin.

Kelsey chuckled. "Do you have a nice frozen cocktail that's perfect for the beach?"

"I have a frozen mango or pineapple daiquiri that is delicious. Or there's always the classic margarita," he replied.

"Oh, the frozen mango for me, please," Isabella said.

"I'll have the pineapple," Kelsey added. "We can share," she said to Isabella.

"I'll be right back," Luis said.

"I like how we've settled on this sharing thing," Isabella said.

"It'll make our reviews more interesting." Kelsey winked at her.

Isabella laughed. "Have we already started the job?"

"We're simply taking notes, right?" Kelsey grinned.

"Right." Isabella nodded and looked back at her computer. "Here's our itinerary for tomorrow. She sent this to both of us. First, we have breakfast here then we take the ferry to St. John."

"Hold on," Kelsey said, taking her tablet from her bag. "I'll follow along."

Isabella waited so she could pull the email up then continued. "Once there, they'll provide us with snorkeling gear and we'll hike to Honeymoon Beach," she said excitedly.

"Hmm, it's about a one mile hike. We'll have to carry the snorkeling gear and they'll also provide lunch to take with us. We can do that, right?" Kelsey asked.

"Yes, it can't be too difficult or they wouldn't suggest it," Isabella said.

"We'll spend the morning and part of the afternoon on the beach. They have the leaning palms and we might even see sea turtles. Then we go back to the trailhead where we can rent bikes to pedal around the island," Kelsey read from the email. Her phone began to ring and she fished it out of her bag. "Oh, that's Dana, my oldest," she said to Isabella.

"Go ahead and take it."

"Hi, honey," Kelsey said, connecting the call on speakerphone.

"Hi, Mom. I just got off the mountain and my face is frozen. I knew you could warm me up," Dana said.

Kelsey chuckled. "I'm sitting under an umbrella on the beach watching the waves roll in. I just ordered a frozen pineapple daiquiri."

"Mom!"

"I told you that you and Emma should have come with me."

"Which swimsuit are you wearing today?"

"The girls helped me pack," Kelsey said to Isabella.

"Of course they did." Isabella laughed.

"Who are you talking to?" Dana asked.

"My new friend, Bella. I'm wearing the blue one piece," Kelsey said.

"She looks amazing!" Isabella said loudly.

"I knew you would!" Dana exclaimed. "I won't ask if you're having fun because the beach and a frozen drink sound heavenly right about now."

"I'll tell you all about it when I get home," Kelsey said.

"Thanks, Mom. I'm warmer already. Have fun. I miss you," Dana said.

"I love you, sweetie," Kelsey said.

"Love you, too."

Isabella smiled at Kelsey. She'd enjoyed watching their conversation unfold. It was easy to hear the love in Kelsey's voice and see the joy on her face. "Show me their pictures," she said to Kelsey once the call ended.

Kelsey opened the photo app on her phone. "This is

Dana," she said, leaning over to show Isabella. "And this is Emma."

"They both have your pretty eyes," Isabella said. "Yours are a beautiful shade of blue-green today."

"Thank you," Kelsey said shyly. "Let me see pictures of your boys."

Isabella took out her phone and pulled up a photo. "This is Wyatt and that's Gus. His name is Augustus and we call him Auggie sometimes, but he's our Gus."

"They are beautiful," Kelsey said. "Their hair is a little darker than yours, but they have those blue eyes."

"I guess we both passed along our gorgeous eyes," Isabella said with a grin.

Kelsey chuckled. "I like your confidence, Bella."

Isabella smiled. She wished she felt as confident as she sounded on most things. "That's not confidence, it's fact. We both have nice eyes."

"We do!" Kelsey nodded. "Perhaps you're teaching me to be a bit more factual."

Isabella laughed. "Honey, if you've got it, own it."

Kelsey laughed with her. "Okay, let's go back to St. John. What's next?"

Isabella turned back to her computer but noted Kelsey's shyness when talking about her beauty. She stole a glance towards Kelsey and wondered if she realized just how beautiful she was. Isabella knew she had been turning heads all her life. There was something about blond hair and blue eyes coupled with her Southern accent that made people notice her. But Kelsey had more than just good looks. She had a presence about her that was inviting and friendly.

"You're staring at me, not the itinerary," Kelsey said.

Isabella snapped her attention back to her computer.

6

Kelsey looked away from her tablet as Isabella stared at her computer. Before she could say anything, Luis walked up with their drinks.

"Here you go," he said, handing each of them a large glass full of their chosen frozen concoctions.

"Thanks," they both said.

"Can I bring you anything else?"

"I don't think so," Kelsey said, glancing at Isabella.

"If you need anything, I'm right over there," he said, pointing to a small bar nestled between several palm trees. "Just wave. I'll come around to check on you in a little while."

"Thanks, Luis," Isabella said.

"Mmm, this is good," Kelsey moaned, taking a sip of her drink.

Isabella tried hers and nodded.

"What were you thinking while you were staring at me?" Kelsey asked.

Isabella eyed her and sipped from her straw. "After another one of these I might tell you."

Kelsey raised her brows and couldn't help wondering what was going through Isabella's head. *Was she thinking about me?*

"I think it would be fun to ride bikes around the island," Isabella said, turning back to her computer.

"We could do that then stop at the bar Carmen told us about. Oh my God!" Kelsey exclaimed. "The name of the bar is Peaches. That's so gay."

"It is?"

"Yes. Take it from your new lesbian friend," Kelsey said, chuckling. She watched as Isabella furrowed her brows, thinking how cute the little line that formed between them was.

"Well, new lesbian friend, would you care to explain it to your new straight friend?" Isabella said.

"Are you?" Kelsey couldn't stop herself from teasing Isabella just a little.

"Am I what? Straight? Or your friend?"

"Oh, you're definitely my friend," Kelsey said. "Have you ever thought about a woman as a partner?"

"Honestly, Kels, I've never really thought about a partner other than Spence," Isabella admitted.

"But now that you've met me, maybe you should give women a thought or two," Kelsey said with a grin.

"Oh, you're teasing me," Isabella said.

"No, I'm not. I'm not saying give *me* a thought," Kelsey clarified. "I'm just saying maybe you should keep your options open."

"Hmm, my options," Isabella said, glancing at Kelsey. "I do have options, don't I?"

"Sure you do."

"If I have options then you do, too."

"Let me put that in our notes," Kelsey said, turning back

to her tablet. "We have options," she said as she typed. "Don't get caught up in the adventure, notice everything."

"I'm not sure what that means, but okay," Isabella said.

"It's just a reminder to keep our eyes and hearts open. You never know what you'll find," Kelsey said. "Or what will find you."

"Okay. I can do that," Isabella said. "Now, why are peaches a lesbian thing?"

"Uh—um," Kelsey stuttered. She could feel the heat in her cheeks and hoped Isabella would think it was because of the sun. *Oh shit, we're under an umbrella!*

"Come on. You started it," Isabella said.

"Okay, okay," Kelsey muttered. "The peach and its juiciness have been compared to..."

Isabella raised her brows but didn't say anything.

If Kelsey didn't know any better she'd think Isabella was messing with her and it was obvious she was enjoying Kelsey's sudden discomfort.

Kelsey widened her eyes. "Compared to the loveliest parts of a woman," she said with a smile and delight that maybe she'd gotten herself out of this embarrassing moment.

Isabella giggled. "You're awfully cute when you get flustered. Good save, Kels."

"My, how quickly that turned," Kelsey said, shaking her head.

"Just imagine what all I'll learn from you after a few more drinks. Let's get another round," Isabella said, chuckling and waving at Luis.

"I'm going swimming first. Why are we just sitting here when we can be in this gorgeous water?" Kelsey said, getting up and taking her shirt off. "Come on!"

Isabella laughed and hopped up. "Wait for me!"

Kelsey held out her hand and Isabella grabbed it. They ran towards the water and fiercely stepped into the surf. Once the water was about mid-thigh, Kelsey dove under and surfaced but couldn't see Isabella anywhere. She looked around and felt a moment of panic when suddenly Isabella grabbed her shoulders from behind and pushed her back under the water.

Kelsey shot out of the water laughing.

"You have the best laugh," Isabella said.

"We'll see about that." Kelsey lunged at Isabella and wrapped her arms around her, picking her up then crashing back into the water, taking Isabella under with her.

They both came up for air laughing.

"Okay, okay. We're even," Isabella said, taking a few quick breaths. "You still have a great laugh."

"Thanks. I hope you get to hear it often the rest of the week," Kelsey said.

"I'll make that a goal." Isabella grinned.

They floated in the water, enjoying the coolness. Kelsey looked back at the resort and let her gaze follow along the sand until she was looking at Isabella. She was a little sad that her girls didn't come with her, but how could she not feel lucky? Here she was in this beautiful place, floating in the water with a gorgeous woman. This might be a merry Christmas after all.

"What are you thinking, Kels?" Isabella asked, meeting Kelsey's gaze.

"Oh, no you don't," Kelsey said, wading over closer to Isabella. "You never told me what you were thinking about when I caught you staring at me earlier."

Isabella grinned. "Okay. I was wondering if you knew just how beautiful you are because, Kelsey, there's more to you than those curly locks and mesmerizing eyes."

Kelsey couldn't hide the shock on her face, then she laughed. "You think I'm beautiful?"

"Don't do that," Isabella said.

"Do what?"

"Laugh and make light of yourself. You are an interesting woman, and I can't wait to find out more about my new friend."

Kelsey smiled and sighed. "I laughed because a statement like that coming from such a beautiful woman made me want to tell you to look in the mirror, Bella. But..."

"But what?"

"I have to be careful because if I tell you you're beautiful, you might take it the wrong way," Kelsey explained.

Isabella tilted her head. "Why?" Kelsey saw realization dawn on her face. "Oh, because you're gay?"

"Yeah."

"Hmm, so how could I take it the wrong way? Surely you have better moves than just telling me I'm beautiful. Don't you think I'd know if you were coming on to me?"

"Oh, God," Kelsey muttered. "I need that drink now." She started walking out of the water as the red tint on her cheeks deepened.

"Hold it," Isabella said, grabbing Kelsey's hand. "I didn't mean to embarrass you."

Kelsey kept walking because she couldn't imagine looking in Isabella's eyes at that moment.

"Stop walking, Kels," Isabella said, pulling her hand.

Kelsey winced and slowly looked at Isabella.

"I would take it as the compliment you meant it to be. You don't have to choose your words carefully around me. I thought we were becoming friends. I want you to be able to be honest and open with me."

Kelsey smiled and nodded. "When we were in the water,

I gazed around this beautiful setting and then my eyes stopped on you. I thought to myself how lucky I am to be here with you. Wait... I take that back. I thought how lucky I am to be here with a gorgeous woman and it might be a merry Christmas after all."

The smile that spread across Isabella's face rid Kelsey of any of the remaining embarrassment from earlier.

"Thank you. That wasn't so hard, was it?"

Kelsey chuckled.

"I'm lucky to be here with you, too. We are going to have a merry Christmas, Kelsey. You'll see," Isabella said as they began to walk back to their chairs.

They sat down and both reached for their new drinks.

Kelsey took a big slurp through the straw and immediately groaned. "Brain freeze!"

Isabella laughed. "Oh, I hate that."

"I'm going to try one of those fruity drinks from last night next," Kelsey said.

* * *

After finishing their drinks they took another quick dip in the water then plopped down on their chairs.

"Luis just keeps bringing drinks," Isabella said. "We have to put that in our notes. Beware of the efficient bar staff."

Kelsey chuckled and took a sip of her fruity cocktail. "This is even better than last night's drink." She lounged back on her chair. "Oh, Bella, this has been the perfect way to spend our first afternoon, don't you think?"

Isabella glanced over at Kelsey and grinned. "It has, but I'll be ready for dinner after this drink."

"Oh, good. I thought you were trying to get me drunk."

Isabella laughed. "You only brought one bottle of water

for us. We have to drink something."

Kelsey giggled. "I think I'm already a little drunk."

Isabella looked over at Kelsey and smiled. She couldn't remember when she'd felt this relaxed and had this much fun.

"You're staring at me again."

"I'm having fun. Can't I look at you?" Isabella giggled.

Kelsey met her gaze and they both began to giggle.

"It sounds like you two are getting to know each other and enjoying the beach," Carmen said, walking up. She moved their things to an empty chair and joined them.

"We're having a wonderful time," Kelsey said, straightening up. "Luis keeps bringing us drinks and it's caused a bout of giggles."

"I think we both needed this though," Isabella said. "I haven't been this relaxed and carefree in ages."

"Tomorrow will be a full day depending on how long you stay at Peaches," Carmen said.

Kelsey giggled. "I love that name."

Carmen furrowed her brow and looked from Kelsey to Isabella.

"Big ol' lesbian sitting right here," Isabella said, snickering. "Come on! Peaches, get it?"

Kelsey laughed, but Isabella realized what she'd just said and gasped. "Oh, my God, Kelsey! I'm so sorry!"

"It's okay," Kelsey said, stifling a laugh. "I'm not ashamed of who I am."

"Uh, big lesbian sitting right here, too," Carmen said, pointing to herself with a smile. "How many drinks have you two had this afternoon?"

"Luis just kept bringing them," Kelsey said. "We may have lost count."

Carmen chuckled. "You're both tipsy and funny."

"I promise we are professionals," Isabella said. She looked at Kelsey and mouthed, "I'm sorry."

Kelsey shook her head and mouthed back, "It's okay."

"I know you're professionals and neither one of you has probably been on a vacation in a long time. That happens to single moms," Carmen said. "That's another reason I think you'll be perfect for this campaign."

"Don't you have kids?" Kelsey asked.

Carmen smiled. "I do. I have a son and a daughter who are both off doing their own thing. They're a little older than your girls, Kelsey. My son followed me into hotel management and my daughter is a teacher. They are both in the states. However, I am not a single mom. I don't know how you two do it. My wife and I live here in St. Thomas."

"Maybe we can get them to do the Valentine thing," Isabella said, widening her eyes.

"Good idea," Kelsey said.

"So you haven't just been lazing on the beach and drinking all day," Carmen said. "You've been talking about the coming year?"

"We have," Isabella said. "We're already making notes."

Carmen leaned forward and rested her arms on her knees. "You don't have to start now. I want you to have a good time while you're here. I don't expect you to go through the excursions we have planned and start working. They're for you to see what I'm talking about and we'll go from there. We can start planning the January trip before you go back, but for now..." Carmen stopped and looked around. "Please enjoy this."

"Oh, we are," Kelsey said. "Can't you tell!"

Carmen chuckled. "I can and I'm glad to see it."

Isabella looked over at Kelsey and smiled. *This has been the best day.*

7

They talked over a few other things with Carmen then decided to watch the sunset on the beach after another swim. Carmen suggested they have dinner so they'd feel peachy in the morning. This brought on another round of giggles.

"Let's change for dinner," Isabella suggested. "Are you tired?"

"Nope. I feel great. Taking a swim after each drink was a good idea. I was a little tipsy and our fit of giggles would've probably happened no matter if we'd had one or no drinks." Kelsey chuckled.

"We did laugh a lot, but that's a good thing," Isabella said. "I love your laugh."

"We should try one of the other restaurants for dinner," Kelsey said. "I'll have my small purse again," she added as they made the short walk to their bungalows.

"Got it." Isabella chuckled. "What are you going to wear tomorrow?"

"Hmm, probably my board shorts with a swim top and

shirt. They're comfortable and I can wear them all day. Oh, I'll also wear my hiking sandals. I'm glad I threw them in my bag at the last minute," Kelsey said.

"You're going to have to show me how you got all of that in one bag," Isabella said.

"I'm telling you, I'll be repeating outfits. Don't be judgy," Kelsey said with a laugh.

"Me? Surely you can tell by now that I'm not like that."

"You wouldn't judge me because now I'm your friend," Kelsey said. "I'm going to take a quick shower. I'll see you in a few."

"Okay," Isabella said, walking in her back door.

Kelsey threw her bag on the bed and took her swimsuit off before stepping into the shower. The water felt glorious, washing away all the sand and sweat that had accumulated over the afternoon. She washed her hair and thought about what Isabella had said earlier. Was she beautiful? Kelsey would never say that about herself. She knew her eyes were interesting because of the way they changed colors depending on what she was wearing or her surroundings, like being near the water today.

It was nice the way Isabella had said there was more to her than her looks. But to be called beautiful still made her feel good and it did make her heart skip a beat. She stepped out of the shower and towel-dried her hair. As she looked in the mirror she started to pull it up and away from her face, but decided to leave it free to curl at her shoulders.

Kelsey slipped into a pair of wide-legged pants and put on a sleeveless top. She decided to apply a little mascara and lipstick. Her phone pinged with a text message just as she slipped her feet into her sandals. Isabella was ready and waiting on her front deck.

Kelsey smiled, slipped her phone into her small purse, and took one more look in the mirror. She nodded and opened the front door.

"Hey," Isabella said. "Don't you look fresh and lovely. Your hair looks great like that."

"Thanks, so do you. Did that shower feel amazing or what?" Kelsey said, falling into step next to her.

"God, yes. I didn't think I tracked in that much sand, but it was *everywhere*." Isabella knocked her shoulder into Kelsey's.

"Oh, I know." Kelsey chuckled.

They had dinner in the casual restaurant and Kelsey tried the conch that Carmen had told her about that morning. When they finished eating, Kelsey reached for the ticket and signed it with her bungalow number then looked up at Isabella.

"I guess it doesn't matter who gets this because Carmen's paying our way." Kelsey shrugged.

"I know, but it's still fun to take turns," Isabella said. "Are we walking on the beach?"

"I think we should. It's a nice way to end the day," Kelsey said. She held out her arm and chuckled when Isabella looped her arm through it.

"We need to try the swimming pool while we're here," Isabella said as they walked past it.

"I'm hoping we can try the spa, too."

"That might be good after our big day tomorrow," Isabella suggested.

"Listen to us planning our time like we're experienced travelers," Kelsey said.

Isabella laughed. "I don't know about you, but I haven't really traveled that much."

"Me either. We took vacations, but they were during the summer and not that far away," Kelsey said.

They stepped onto the beach and walked along in silence. Kelsey didn't feel the need to say anything and she guessed Isabella didn't either.

"The breeze feels lovely," Isabella said as they neared their bungalows.

"It does," Kelsey agreed.

"I wonder if Luis will miss us tomorrow?" Isabella quipped.

Kelsey laughed. "Of course he will. How many different drinks did we sample? I can't imagine anyone being more fun than you and I."

As they stopped at Kelsey's back deck, Isabella turned to her. "Thank you for such a nice day, Kels." She surprised Kelsey by hugging her tightly.

"I don't have anyone that I can do this with back home" Isabella said after she pulled away. "The divorce made it awkward for our friends and most of them are busy with their own families anyway."

"I understand. I get together with my friends, but we usually end up talking about our kids. We don't laugh like we did today, that's for sure."

Isabella smiled. "I told you that you have a nice laugh. And I like hearing it."

"Isabella Burns, I don't think you give yourself enough credit. I only know a little about you so far, but what I know is wonderful. There is so much more to you that I get to find out in the coming days and months."

Isabella started to say something and Kelsey put her finger over her lips. "Don't do that. You're going to say something like, I hope you're not disappointed."

Isabella giggled. "You know me so well already."

Kelsey smiled. "Good night, Bella. See you in the morning."

"Night, Kels," Isabella said, walking the few steps to her back door.

Kelsey watched her close her back door and wondered how much laughter they'd share tomorrow.

A little later as Kelsey got ready for bed, her phone pinged with a text. It was a link and when she clicked on it, she saw that Isabella had written up a little summary of their day. Kelsey thought maybe she was getting ready for the daily blogs they would do on their monthly visits.

The post was titled "Our Day at Sapphire Beach." Isabella had included photos. Kelsey thought back and remembered them taking a few pictures of their drinks, the water, and each other, along with a few selfies.

But one photo caught her attention. It was a picture of her sitting in her lounge chair, gazing out over the water. Her face was relaxed and she looked pensive. Kelsey studied the photo. She didn't remember Isabella taking any pictures of her. As she stared at the photo, she was surprised because she realized she looked beautiful, just as Isabella had said.

Kelsey smiled because she knew what she'd been thinking when the photo was taken. She was thinking about Bella and how glad she was that they were on the beach together.

* * *

The next morning Isabella decided to wear her two-piece swimsuit and slipped on a pair of shorts with a long sleeve button down shirt over it. She would be comfortable hiking to the beach and could easily take them off for swimming and snorkeling. Next, she gathered her sunscreen, phone, and a towel. She paused, contemplating taking her laptop. Once they were at the bar they might want to add a few notes about their adventure.

She sighed as she looked at what all she wanted to take and thought that maybe she and Kelsey could take one bag packed with all of their stuff. They'd have to carry snorkeling gear as well as their lunch to the beach and she didn't want to add to their load.

Isabella grabbed her phone to text Kelsey and saw the pictures from yesterday still opened in a window. She scrolled through the selfies they'd taken and their happy faces made her smile. Then she stopped at the picture of Kelsey gazing at the water.

How could Kelsey not have a partner? They had so much fun yesterday and to be honest, Isabella thought Kelsey was interesting. She wondered if Kelsey didn't have time to date or maybe she wouldn't let herself. From their conversations Isabella could tell Kelsey was devoted to her daughters. Maybe this was Kelsey's chance to let go and enjoy herself for a change.

Isabella smiled and couldn't think of anyone she'd rather have fun with. She texted Kelsey and a few moments later there was a knock on her door.

"How much stuff do you want to take with you today? Please don't tell me you're taking one of your suitcases," Kelsey teased when Isabella opened the door.

"Good morning to you, too." Isabella grinned.

Kelsey chuckled. "Good morning, Bella. I'm ready for adventure, are you?"

Isabella laughed. "I am, but I'm thinking ahead about all the stuff we have to carry today."

"Look at you learning to travel light," Kelsey teased.

"We'll see about that," Isabella mumbled.

They were able to combine their items into one bag and agreed to take turns carrying it along with the other things they'd have once they made it to St. John.

"I was afraid we'd lost this new job on the same day we got it after Carmen showed up on the beach yesterday," Kelsey said. "You wouldn't stop making me laugh."

"Me?" Isabella exclaimed. "You were the one with the giggles."

Kelsey chuckled. "Oh, God! I know. I haven't had that much fun in..."

"In?"

"I don't know! It's been a long time," Kelsey admitted.

"Hey," Isabella said, putting her hand on Kelsey's arm. "I want to apologize again for telling Carmen you're gay. I am so sorry."

"It's okay. I told you yesterday not to worry about it," Kelsey said.

"I know you did and I know you're proud of who you are, but I shouldn't have said anything. That's your story to tell," Isabella said.

"I'm not necessarily proud, Bella. It's who I am. It's just me." Kelsey shrugged.

"There's nothing 'just' about you, Kelsey Kenny." Isabella smiled at her. "I'm glad we're doing this together."

Kelsey smiled. "You are good for my self-worth. Now, let's go have breakfast and please don't give what you said another thought. I'm not."

Isabella let out a relieved breath. "Oh wait," she said, widening her eyes. "What if you find someone at Peaches? Does that mean we're not a couple anymore?"

"Oh my God," Kelsey said under her breath. She put

both her hands on Isabella's upper arms and stared into her eyes. "You are my ride or die on this trip, Bella. We're a couple."

Isabella smiled. "Good to know."

"For two people who came on this trip solo we have certainly latched onto each other," Kelsey said.

"I'm glad," Isabella replied.

"Me, too." Kelsey winked. "Now let's go eat breakfast. I'm starving."

"One more thing," Isabella said. "This isn't a job, Kelsey."

Kelsey grinned. "I know."

* * *

They stood on the top deck of the ferry, their arms resting on the railing as they gazed at their surroundings.

"My God, it is beautiful here. Everywhere I look it's just gorgeous," Isabella said with amazement in her voice.

"Do you ever think it gets old? I mean, do the people who live here ever think it's ordinary?" Kelsey mused.

"We'll find out. Ask me again in December," Isabella said. "Oh wait, it's December now. Ask me next December."

"It's still hard for me to believe we'll be coming back here every month or so for the next year," Kelsey said.

Isabella linked her arm through Kelsey's and looked into her eyes. "Oh wow, your eyes are green today."

Kelsey smiled.

Isabella shook her head. "You're not having second thoughts about this, are you? Do I need to give you my winning smile?"

Kelsey chuckled and leaned into Isabella. "No, I'm not having second thoughts. It's just hard to believe." She smiled at Isabella and narrowed her gaze. "Now let me see that winning smile."

Isabella gave Kelsey her cheesiest grin, but then it settled into a genuine smile.

"Yep, you've still got it," Kelsey said with a grin.

8

A short time later they got off the ferry and were met by one of the island's outfitters.

"Kelsey and Isabella?" a woman asked, walking up to them with a smile.

"That's us," Isabella said.

"I'm Sylvie," she said. "I'll be taking you to the trailhead."

They followed her to a Jeep with the doors off. Once they were settled inside, she put the Jeep in gear and off they went.

"I have your snorkeling equipment," Sylvie said. "You brought your lunch from Coral Bay, right?"

"Yep," Kelsey said. "We have that and a few other things here."

"Great. Spend as much time as you'd like on Honeymoon Beach. I'm going to give you my number. If you text me when you start the hike back, I'll be waiting for you when you get to the trailhead. From there you can decide what you want to do next."

"Carmen mentioned something about biking around the

island and then we're going to a bar," Isabella explained.

"You're not going to just any bar." Sylvie grinned. "You're going to Peaches. The owners are friends of mine and you won't find a better place on all the islands."

Kelsey turned around from the front seat and exchanged a look with Isabella.

"Maybe we'll skip the bikes and go to Peaches after the beach," Isabella said with a chuckle.

"You're my kind of people." Sylvie laughed.

It was a quick ride to the trailhead and Sylvie helped them to manage their gear. The snorkeling equipment was in a backpack that Kelsey slipped her arms into.

"Let me have our lunch bag. I can sling it over my shoulder, too," Kelsey said.

"Wait," Sylvie said. "I think it will fit in the backpack."

Kelsey stood still while Sylvie opened the backpack and pushed the lunch bag inside. "Just right," Sylvie said. "Is it too heavy?"

"Not at all," Kelsey said.

"I'll wear it on the way back," Isabella said. She put their bag with the other items over her shoulder. "Are you ready?"

"Text me when you leave the beach and I'll be waiting for you," Sylvie reminded them with a smile.

"Let's go," Kelsey said as she started down the trail.

It took them about twenty minutes to make the hike over the trail. There were a few rocky places here and there, but it was mostly easy going.

"Oh my God, Kelsey!" Isabella exclaimed. "Look at this!"

The path opened up to a white sandy beach that met the most beautiful bluish-green water Kelsey had ever seen.

"Look at those leaning palm trees!" Kelsey looked around, amazed. "It's like a postcard, but better."

"Let's go down this way," Isabella said, walking along the

sand past a few other people who had their things spread out on the beach.

"No wonder they call it Honeymoon Beach. Wouldn't this be a great place to begin your honeymoon?" Kelsey said, letting the backpack slide down her shoulders.

Isabella took a large towel out of the backpack and spread it on the sand near one of the leaning palm trees. Kelsey helped her set up their area and reached into the lunch bag for two bottles of water. She handed one to Isabella and smiled.

"What do you want to do first?" Kelsey asked, taking a drink.

"Can we sit and just enjoy this for a while?" Isabella asked, raising her eyebrows.

"Absolutely." Kelsey sat down on her side of the towel.

Isabella shimmied out of her shorts and took her shirt off then sat next to Kelsey.

"You didn't answer my question," Kelsey said once Isabella was settled. "Don't you think this would be a great place to honeymoon?"

"Oh, I didn't know it was a question. Yes, this is another slice of paradise." Isabella nodded, gazing at their surroundings.

"Where did you go on your honeymoon?" Kelsey asked. "Did you go to a beach?"

"No, we went to Las Vegas. Neither one of us had been and there was a lot to do," Isabella said flatly. "It wasn't the greatest trip."

"Oh, sorry."

"What about you? Have you ever thought about where you'd go on your honeymoon?"

"I've never even thought about it," Kelsey said.

"Oh, come on. Surely you dreamed of a wedding and a honeymoon at some time or another," Isabella said.

Kelsey sighed. "People in love have dreams like that."

Isabella looked over at Kelsey. "Are you saying you've never been in love?"

"Hmm, I had a girlfriend in college. I loved her, but I'm not sure we were in love. At least we weren't in love enough to have a life together after graduation. We were in different places in our lives, I guess. I was ready to start my career and have kids, but she wasn't."

"And there hasn't been anyone since then?"

Kelsey looked over at Isabella and gave her a sad smile. "I've dated several women, but honestly most of the time it led to a date or two and then sex. After a few of those kinds of—you can't even call them relationships—I thought, what's the use." Kelsey looked back over the water. "I'm not one to have casual sex. It's not for me."

Isabella ran her hand over Kelsey's back. "I'm not surprised, Kels. I bet you're an attentive partner and that your love language is doing nice things for the woman you love."

Kelsey looked over at her and furrowed her brow. "My love language?"

"There are like five love languages and one is doing things. I think it's called acts of service."

"Why do you think that's me?"

"Because," Isabella said.

"Because?" Kelsey watched Isabella as she looked away.

"Because you've done nice things for me. Like helping me with my luggage and other things. You probably don't even notice you're doing it," Isabella said.

"What about you? What's your love language?"

"For me, it's quality time. When I care about someone, I love spending time with them," Isabella said.

"What are the others?"

Isabella looked back at Kelsey and smiled. "Let's see, there's physical touch, saying nice things, and I forget... Oh, gifts."

"Like giving gifts?" Kelsey asked.

"Or receiving. You know how it makes you feel when you receive a gift."

Kelsey leaned back on her elbows. "Well, I may like to do things for others, but there's nothing wrong with nice words and touching."

Isabella looked at her and chuckled. "You're not wrong."

"You say nice words to me, Bella. Quality time isn't your only love language."

"It's easy to say nice things to you. I love to see the surprise on your face then the shyness that usually follows," Isabella said.

Kelsey chuckled. "I guess I'm not used to it." She paused. "And it's nice. It feels nice."

Isabella nodded. "I know. It feels nice when you do things for me."

They sat in silence for a few moments, enjoying the breeze and listening to the gentle waves.

"Were you in love with Spencer?" Kelsey asked quietly.

Isabella let out a deep breath. "I loved Spencer and I still do as a friend, but you know, I'm not sure I was ever in love with him. I suppose I thought I was or I wouldn't have married him." Isabella turned to Kelsey. "What is being in love like to you?"

Kelsey took a moment to ponder Isabella's question. "I think she would be the last person I thought of at night and the first person I thought of each morning. You know, not having to consciously think of them. Thoughts of them would always be there, in my head and in my heart," Kelsey said softly. A smile crossed her face just thinking about ever feeling that way about someone. "What about you?"

"It would be feeling the other person's heartbeat. Not just with your hand over their chest, but you could feel their love beating inside of you and your love beating inside of them. You could feel their love in a look, a touch, or even a thought. Not so much knowing what they're thinking, but I would hope they could feel the love in my heart for them. I know that sounds dumb, but I think when I fall in love, my heart will know their heart."

"That's not dumb at all!" Kelsey exclaimed. "I get it. My heart knew my girlfriend didn't want the same things I did and those other women were not forever for me. I could feel it in my heart, just as you explained." She reached over and squeezed Isabella's hand. "Honeymoon Beach has turned us introspective, I think."

Isabella chuckled. "Yeah, what's wrong with us? We should be snorkeling and laughing."

"Let's go," Kelsey said, getting up and holding out her hand to Isabella.

"Wait, Kelsey, look at me," Isabella said, holding onto her hand.

"What?"

Isabella smiled. "Your eyes are blue now."

"They aren't as blue as yours."

Isabella furrowed her brow. "What?"

"Yours are as pretty as the water. Mine aren't the only ones that change. Yours get brighter blue and then other times they're a little darker."

"Damn, we are beautiful women," Isabella said.

Kelsey laughed. "Own it!"

They got their snorkels and fins then waded into the water. Kelsey held Isabella's mask and snorkel while she put her fins on then Isabella did the same for Kelsey.

"I'm not sure about this, but let's see what it's like," Kelsey said.

They put their faces in the water and off they paddled. From time to time they'd stop and excitedly talk about what they'd seen.

"Let's turn around and go back," Isabella said after a while.

It didn't take them long to get back to where they'd started and they traipsed back to their towel, both breathing hard.

"That was incredible," Isabella said.

"I can't believe we actually saw a sea turtle," Kelsey said, pulling the lunch bag out of her backpack.

"This has been the best day and we haven't even been to Peaches yet!" Isabella exclaimed then laughed.

They dug into the food the resort had packed for them and talked about all they'd discovered in the water.

"Let's go again," Kelsey said. "Only this time we'll go the other direction."

"Okay. I'm ready when you are," Isabella said. "I can't stop smiling."

Kelsey chuckled. "Why would you?" She watched Isabella for a few moments and it struck her how free and alive she felt. For so long Kelsey had done what her girls needed, but right now she could do what she needed. As she gazed at Isabella she couldn't help but wonder if she felt the same way.

"You look so beautiful," Kelsey said quietly.

Isabella looked over at her and laughed. "Oh, I'm sure I

do. My hair is plastered to my head and there are marks on my face where my mask rested."

"That doesn't matter. You should see how radiant your smile is and how bright your eyes are."

"Thanks, Kels," Isabella said. "Now that I look at you..."

"What?"

"You're right. We may look a mess in some ways, but it's just us. We have no real responsibilities except to enjoy this day. That's what's on our face. It's joy," Isabella said.

Kelsey nodded. "It's joy," she said, staring at Isabella.

They stayed like that for a moment, simply staring at each other and smiling.

"Are you ready to go again?" Isabella asked.

"Let's go," Kelsey replied, getting up and reaching for her snorkel and fins.

They waded back into the water and, feeling more confident this time, they swam in the other direction. There were so many brightly colored fish and another sea turtle.

Once they were back at their place on the beach Isabella said, "We have to take a picture in our masks and snorkels."

"We're not working on the blog yet," Kelsey said.

"I know that. We have to take a picture for us!" Isabella exclaimed.

Kelsey put the mask back on and sidled up next to Isabella. She took several selfies then put their gear into the backpack.

"Stand by the leaning palm, Kels. I want a picture of you," Isabella said.

"We both should be in it. Maybe we could get one of them to take a picture of us," Kelsey said, pointing to a small group walking down the beach.

Isabella waved them over and a woman was happy to snap a few pictures of them by the leaning palm.

"I don't know about you, but I'm ready for a cold beer," Kelsey said, sitting back on the towel.

"Oh, that sounds heavenly. Should I text Sylvie and tell her to come get us?"

"Let's lie back and soak in this beautiful place for a few minutes. Then we can go," Kelsey said.

"I want to remember everything," Isabella said, leaning back on the towel next to Kelsey.

9

It didn't take them long to gather their things and start back up the trail. Sylvie was true to her word and was waiting for them once they arrived at the trailhead.

They decided to come back to St. John another day and do the bike ride around the island. The desire for a cold beer at Peaches was too great.

Sylvie pulled into a parking space on the street and they all got out of the Jeep.

"They have a back patio that opens up to the beach," Sylvie told them as they walked to the front door. "It's a great place to laze away the afternoon. You're on island time now."

Isabella followed Kelsey into the bar while Sylvie held the door open for them.

"Oh, this is perfect," Kelsey said.

"This is what I imagined the quintessential beach bar should look like," Isabella added.

"You must be Kelsey and Isabella," a woman said as she approached them with a wide smile. "I'm Liz. Welcome to Peaches."

Isabella saw Kelsey give her a quick warning look and she almost burst into laughter. "Hi, Liz. I'm Isabella and this is Kelsey," Isabella said. "We love the name of your bar and can't wait to experience it all."

"That's what I like to hear. Let's get you a table," Liz said, leading them to the back of the bar. "Do you want to sit on the patio?"

"How can we not?" Kelsey said. "That view is incredible."

Once they'd sat at a table where they had a view of both the inside of the bar and the beach, Liz asked, "What can I get you to drink?"

"A cold beer would be heavenly," Kelsey said.

"Me, too," Isabella agreed.

"I'll be right back," Liz said, walking to the long bar that took up the opposite wall of the space.

"Aren't you joining us?" Kelsey asked Sylvie.

"I can't right now. I'll pick you up and take you back to the ferry whenever you're ready. Text me." Sylvie smiled. "Enjoy."

Isabella sat back in her chair and sighed happily. Music played in the background and several tables were full of happy tourists. She could see Liz fill their glasses with beer on tap and figured the woman was in her mid-sixties.

"I bet she could tell us a few stories," Isabella commented.

Kelsey nodded. "Those beers look wonderful right about now."

Liz walked over with three beers on a tray. "I hope you don't mind if I join you for a bit."

"We'd love it," Isabella said.

They all took a deep drink from their glasses and Kelsey moaned. "Oh, that's good."

"Carmen told me a little about this grand plan of yours," Liz said.

Isabella raised her eyebrows. "Oh, it's Carmen's plan, too."

Liz chuckled. "I hope you'll make Peaches a regular stop on these trips."

"Oh, we will," Kelsey said, smiling at Isabella. "We just got here and I already love it."

"We have a very relaxed vibe, but there are times when we turn the music up and dance," Liz said.

"That sounds like fun," Isabella said.

"Oh, there's Alex," Liz said, waving at a woman inside the bar. "She's my business partner."

They sipped from their beers as Alex walked over to their table.

"Alex, this is Isabella and Kelsey," Liz said, introducing them.

"Oh, you're the women Carmen told us about. Welcome to Peaches," Alex said, sitting in an empty chair.

"That makes me wonder just what Carmen said about us," Kelsey said, looking over at Isabella.

Alex chuckled. "How did she explain it... Oh, you're highlighting island adventures to bring us more business."

"We hope so," Isabella said.

"Are most of these people tourists?" Kelsey asked.

"Oh, yeah," Liz said. "Just watch them. We get a lot of girls trip groups, like those two tables over there. Several of them are looking for a vacation fling in the islands."

"We aren't the fling kind of people," Kelsey said.

Liz looked at Kelsey then at Isabella. "You're not together?"

"We are on this trip," Kelsey muttered.

Isabella chuckled. "Do we look like a couple?"

"Yeah, you do," Liz said. "Am I missing something?"

"We only met a couple of days ago," Kelsey said with a grin.

"We had dinner the first night we were here," Isabella explained, "and our server thought we were a couple, so it's kind of been a joke between us since then."

"Really? Well, you look like you belong together," Liz stated. "Some people you can tell, just by looking at them, that they're together. I can see the spark."

"The spark?" Kelsey scoffed. "It's been so long, I wouldn't know a spark if it singed me. I would think it was sunburn."

Isabella laughed. "We definitely have a spark, Kels." She turned to Liz. "There are friendship sparks as well."

"Absolutely. That's how Alex and I ended up as business partners," Liz said, smiling affectionately at Alex.

Isabella took a drink of her beer and watched as Liz studied her and Kelsey.

"Are you both moms?" Liz asked.

"You can tell that, too!" Isabella exclaimed.

"Yep. I've seen a lot of people pass through here." Liz smiled. "I hope you two will stick around."

"Thank you, Liz," Isabella said. She leaned a little closer. "Is this a gay bar?"

"Bella!" Kelsey exclaimed.

Liz and Alex both laughed. "The name kind of implies that," Liz said. "But we welcome everyone and people seem to feel that when they walk through our door."

"I can see us spending a lot of time here," Isabella said, grinning at Kelsey. "Maybe someone will catch your eye, Kels."

"Bella," Kelsey said with a warning tone.

Isabella chuckled. Her gaze was drawn to a woman who

had walked into the bar. "I could see you with someone like her."

They all followed Isabella's gaze and Alex chuckled. "I hope not, because she's my wife."

Isabella saw Kelsey take a deep breath and groan. "I'm sorry, Alex, but your wife is hot."

"Don't I know it." Alex grinned.

"Hey babe, they're playing our song," the woman said as she walked onto the patio and held out her hand.

Alex immediately got up and they went to the small dance floor and began to move to the music.

Liz chuckled. "Every song is their song. I'll introduce you to Riley when they come back."

Isabella noticed how Kelsey was watching Alex and Riley dance. She had a smile on her face, but also a look of longing.

"Kelsey, dance with me," Isabella said, standing up.

"What?"

"This is a beautiful song, we're in a beautiful place, so let's dance. Let's be beautiful, too."

"Okay," Kelsey said hesitantly.

Isabella reached for her hand and led them onto the dance floor. She put her arms around Kelsey's neck and smiled up at her. Isabella felt Kelsey tentatively put her hands on her hips.

"Come on, Kels," Isabella said. "We're a couple."

Kelsey chuckled and Isabella felt her relax as she pulled Isabella a little closer. "It's all part of the adventure," Kelsey said softly.

It had been a long time since Isabella had danced with anyone, but she felt comfortable in Kelsey's arms. She looked into Kelsey's eyes and smiled.

"What are you thinking, Bella?"

Kelsey had a way of asking that question just when Isabella was thinking of her. "I was just thinking..."

"Yes?"

"I don't know how those other women let you get away," Isabella said honestly.

Kelsey sighed. "Because they weren't right for me."

Isabella nodded and let her hands fall over Kelsey's shoulders. She leaned in and could smell the salt and sand from their beach adventures. Then she realized she'd never danced with a woman before and yet it felt like the most natural thing to be in Kelsey's arms.

The song ended and Alex smiled at them. "I'd like you to meet my wife, Riley."

"Welcome to Peaches," Riley said. "It's nice to meet you both."

They walked back over to the table and all sat down.

"Let's have another beer," Liz said.

"I'll get them," Alex said, squeezing Riley's shoulder before leaving the table.

"How are you enjoying the islands?" Riley asked. "What have you done so far?"

"Well, yesterday we got drunk on the beach outside our bungalows," Isabella said.

"Tipsy!" Kelsey corrected her.

Isabella laughed. "Okay, tipsy. Today we snorkeled at Honeymoon Beach and saw the most beautiful fish."

"And a turtle," Kelsey added excitedly.

"If you'd like a little privacy, Alex and I know a spot at the park with a private beach," Riley said.

"They're not together," Liz stated.

"Oh, I'm sorry. I just assumed," Riley said.

"It's okay," Kelsey said with a chuckle. "We've been

together since we landed at the airport; however, I'm the only gay one in our little couple."

Isabella shrugged. "I'm divorced and we're both single moms."

Riley nodded. "Carmen mentioned that one of you creates websites."

Kelsey held up her hand. "I do the websites. Bella is the brand expert."

"I'd love to get your take on our website," Riley said. "I try to help with the business."

"I'd be happy to look at it," Kelsey said.

"My computer is at the bar," Riley said, raising her eyebrows.

"Let's take a look," Kelsey said.

Isabella watched them walk away and couldn't keep her eyes off Kelsey. A few minutes ago they'd been dancing, much like Alex and Riley. Isabella wasn't sure what got into her, but when she saw the rather forlorn look on Kelsey's face, she hadn't thought, she'd just acted. At the time all she could think about was putting a smile back on her friend's face.

To be honest she wasn't thinking, and when she put her arms around Kelsey's neck, a wave of doubt washed over her. But when she felt Kelsey's body relax under her hands, all the nervousness went away. Kelsey said it was all part of the adventure, but she had no idea how true her statement was to Isabella.

What was it about Kelsey that was so easy one minute, then had her heart racing the next? One thing she was sure of was that she couldn't wait to spend another day with Kelsey, discovering the islands, but also she was finding out things about herself. Things she wasn't even sure she could name. Things she'd never thought of until a nice woman helped her with her luggage.

"I can see you two together," Liz said quietly.

Isabella looked over at her and widened her eyes. "Kelsey is great, but we live in different parts of the country. And besides, we just met."

"That doesn't matter."

Isabella sighed and looked over at Liz. "I've never been with a woman."

Liz scoffed. "I hadn't either. There's always a first time."

Isabella looked back over at Kelsey where she was animatedly talking with Riley. "Kelsey isn't a first. She's a forever," she said softly.

"Come back before your trip is over and spend more time here," Liz said.

"Oh, we will," Isabella said. "But it won't make any difference with me and Kelsey."

"Just come back and dance. The islands have a way of giving you a different view."

Isabella looked back at Liz and smiled. "We'll see."

"No, Isabella. I already see. Maybe in time, you will, too."

10

Once they were back on the ferry and headed to the resort, Isabella looped her arm through Kelsey's. "Liz said we have to come back before we leave. I think she likes us, plus I want to dance with you again."

Kelsey looked over at Isabella. Her eyes sparkled just like the setting sun reflecting off the water. "You liked dancing with me?"

"Yeah. Uh oh, you didn't like dancing with me. Did it make you uncomfortable?"

"No, I mean, yes, I loved dancing with you. I loved the whole day," Kelsey said.

"I did, too."

They gazed out at the water as St. Thomas got closer and closer.

"Were you able to help Riley with the website?"

"Yeah, I made a few changes and I hope it helps them."

"Do you think they'll become a client?"

Kelsey nodded. "Yep, and I think they want your expertise as well."

"I'd love to help them."

Kelsey couldn't help but lean into Isabella. She liked the closeness and neither of them seemed to mind. Why was being with Bella so easy, she wondered. There wasn't the awkwardness she felt when meeting new people.

"Liz is rather direct, isn't she?" Kelsey said.

Isabella chuckled. "Yeah, she is. She definitely knows people. Maybe she's psychic."

"What did you talk about while I was working with Riley?"

"Oh, she just kept saying to come back before we leave and spend time with them," Isabella said.

"I'd like that, would you?"

"I've never felt a place feel so familiar like Peaches did. It was like we were all friends when we first stepped through the front door."

"I know. Liz said people like it there. I can understand why."

Kelsey took a deep breath and slowly let it out. She had never connected with another person the way she had with Isabella. It didn't make sense to her. While they were at Peaches, the lines between friendship and something more had begun to blur. The last thing she wanted to do was make Isabella uncomfortable. But Isabella was the one who embraced everything. When Liz thought they were together, it hadn't seemed to bother Isabella in the least, but Kelsey's heart had sped up and her mouth went dry.

She thought back to when they'd started to spread their things out on Honeymoon Beach. When Isabella took her shorts and shirt off, Kelsey had to look away in fear of being caught staring. It had been too long since she'd thought of another woman that way. She certainly didn't want to ruin things with Isabella when their friendship was just getting started. Plus, they had a job to do for Coral Bay and Kelsey wasn't about to mess that up.

"Hey, are you all right?" Isabella asked.

"Yeah, why?"

"You keep sighing and taking deep breaths," Isabella said.

I've got to get a hold of myself. "Have you talked to your boys?"

"Uh, yes. I talked to them last night after dinner. They're having a grand time in New York," Isabella said with a less than enthusiastic tone.

"I'm looking forward to meeting them when we do the family vacation," Kelsey said. She thought talking about their families would deter these thoughts running through her head until she could get back to her bungalow and sort them all out. She was sure it was just being at the bar with other gay women that had caused it.

"I can't wait to meet your girls. We're going to have so much fun with them and their friends," Isabella said.

"They are going to love you," Kelsey said with a smile. "Dana is spontaneous like you. Who knows what we'll get into."

Isabella laughed. "It will all be good, Kels. You know that."

Kelsey smiled. *God, I hope so.*

"Hey, is that Carmen?" Isabella said, looking at the shore where they were about to dock.

"It is," Kelsey replied. "I wonder why she's here."

They both waved at her and went down the steps to the lower deck to exit the ferry.

"What are you doing here?" Isabella asked as they approached her.

"I thought I'd give you a ride back to the resort," she said with a smile.

Kelsey tilted her head and narrowed her eyes. "Shuttle services are part of your CEO duties?"

Carmen laughed as she ushered them into the car. "Get in and I'll explain. Did you have a good time at Peaches?" she asked as she pulled into traffic.

"We love it," Isabella said excitedly.

"We hope to go back before we have to go home," Kelsey added.

"Do you realize tomorrow is Christmas?"

"Oh yeah," Kelsey said. "I thought about it this morning, but we were having so much fun all day that it hadn't crossed my mind again."

"How was your day?" Carmen asked.

"It was wonderful," Isabella gushed, turning to look at Kelsey in the back seat. "I think one of our trips needs to be a long weekend getaway. We can spend a day at Honeymoon Beach then go to Peaches. After that we need to spend a day at the resort. We haven't experienced all you offer there on site."

"Let's do it in April," Kelsey suggested. "We don't have anything special for that month, do we?"

"I have ideas for most months and wanted to go over the schedule with you," Carmen said. "I thought you could spend the morning at the resort then go to Peaches with us tomorrow afternoon."

"You're going to Peaches?" Isabella asked.

"Yes, my kids are here for Christmas, and they love going to Liz and Alex's. We've had Christmas with them for several years now," Carmen said.

"We don't want to intrude on your Christmas," Kelsey said.

"You won't. We want to include you both!"

"Are you sure?" Isabella asked.

"Absolutely. We're going to be friends, don't you think?" Carmen said, glancing at Isabella then Kelsey.

"We are," Kelsey said. This trip wasn't turning out to be anything like Kelsey had expected. She thought she'd spend most of her time alone on the beach, but this was so much better. New friends coupled with fun times were just the beginning.

"Riley called me when you left the island. She wanted to invite you both over tomorrow, but she didn't have your contact information. I hope you don't mind that I shared your numbers with her," Carmen said.

"Not at all," Isabella replied.

"She wanted to invite you for Christmas tomorrow and I told her I'd meet you at the ferry. They loved the two of you as much as you liked the bar."

"This is turning out to be a very merry Christmas," Kelsey said.

"It sure is," Isabella agreed, turning around to smile at Kelsey.

"Thank you, Carmen," Kelsey said. "I wasn't too excited about this trip since my girls didn't come with me, but it's been nothing but happiness since the plane landed."

"That goes double for me. This is the first Christmas I've spent without my boys and I didn't know what to do with myself." Isabella turned around to look at Kelsey again and added, "You've not only kept my mind off the sadness of divorce and single parenthood, but you've helped me see happy times past it."

"Oh, I'm so glad. I didn't realize both of you were without your families at Christmas. I thought you'd celebrated before or would after," Carmen said.

"You'll get to meet my girls on another trip," Kelsey said. "They won't believe me when I tell them all we've done, but they'll see firsthand in March."

"I can't wait to show them," Carmen said.

"When we do the family vacation and have them all here, we may need help." Isabella chuckled.

Carmen laughed. "Won't that be a fun time." She pulled into the resort. "Okay, I'll text you tomorrow when I know what time we're leaving. Do you need anything?"

"I think all I need is a shower and dinner," Isabella said.

"That's all I need," Kelsey said. "Thank you again, Carmen."

"I'll see you both tomorrow."

Kelsey waited for Isabella to come around the car, then they walked back to their bungalows together. "What would you think of ordering room service and having dinner on one of our decks?"

"We could shower and not have to dress for dinner," Isabella said.

"Exactly," Kelsey replied. "I know we can wear anything to dinner, but wouldn't it be nice to throw on a pair of shorts and a T-shirt?" She glanced at Isabella. "You do have something casual in one of your suitcases, don't you?" Kelsey couldn't resist teasing Isabella just a little.

"Ha ha," Isabella said, knocking her shoulder into Kelsey's. "You'd be surprised to see what I packed."

Kelsey chuckled. "No I wouldn't."

Isabella laughed with her as they reached their bungalows. "I'll be over in a little while."

Kelsey went inside and took her clothes off and stepped into the shower. It felt glorious to get the sand and sweat off her body. She couldn't keep from thinking about the day as she washed her hair. Her thoughts drifted to dancing with

Isabella at Peaches. Kelsey remembered Isabella telling her she wanted to dance with her again and an idea of a little Christmas gift Kelsey could give her began to take shape in her head.

After she'd finished showering and got dressed, she was surprised to hear her phone ring. It was probably Isabella, she thought with a smile.

"Hi, Mom!" Emma's excited voice echoed through the room as Kelsey put her on speaker.

"Hi, Em." Kelsey chuckled. "You sound like you're having a good time."

"Oh, Mom, you wouldn't believe it, but I have a confession to make," Emma said then paused.

"Okay..." Kelsey's voice trailed off.

"I miss you," Emma admitted. "I didn't think it would be a big deal not having Christmas with you and Dana, but it is."

"Oh, well, honey, there's not much I can do about it from the Virgin Islands," Kelsey said. If she were in Denver, Kelsey could at least offer to fly her home.

"It's okay, Mom. I just wanted you to know and I'm happy to hear your voice," Emma said.

"Hey, how would you feel about coming to the Virgin Islands for spring break?"

"What! Are you kidding? With who?" Emma said excitedly.

"With me and your sister and some of your friends," Kelsey said.

"That would be amazing! You would do that?"

Kelsey quickly explained about the monthly trips she and Isabella were planning to do for the resort.

"Wow, that's incredible," Emma said.

"You and Dana will have to come back sometime during

the summer for a family vacation," Kelsey said. "Can you do that?"

Emma's laughter rang around the room and Kelsey felt her heart swell with love. "Let's see, vacation in the Virgin Islands for spring break and then again this summer? Yeah, Mom. I can do that."

Kelsey heard a quiet knock on the glass of her back door and saw Isabella standing there smiling. She let her in and mouthed that she was talking to Emma.

"You sound really happy, Mom, not like when I call you at home," Emma said.

Kelsey furrowed her brow. "What do you mean?"

"I don't know how to explain it," Emma said. "Is it because of this new friend you've made? Dana told me you were hanging out with a woman on the beach."

Kelsey's eyes widened as she stared at Isabella.

Isabella chuckled. "Uh, hi there, Emma. I'm the woman your mom is hanging out with. I'm Isabella."

11

"Oh, hi!" Emma exclaimed.

"You'll get to meet Isabella when we do the girls trip in March," Kelsey said.

"I can't wait," Emma said.

"Me either," Isabella said, chuckling. "So tell me, Emma. Does your mom not usually sound happy like this?"

"Not at all! She sounds so carefree now," Emma said. "She usually has several projects going and sounds kind of stressed."

"Let me remind you that those projects are paying for your education," Kelsey said.

"I know, I know," Emma droned. "Whatever you and Isabella are doing, I hope you keep doing it because you sound happy, Mom. You deserve happiness *and* a girlfriend!"

"Oh no, no, no. It's not like that, Emma!" Kelsey quickly protested. She glanced at Isabella and her grin showed how much she was enjoying this.

Emma laughed. "I was just teasing you. I can imagine your face is bright red right about now. Merry Christmas, Momma."

"You little brat," Kelsey said, realizing her daughter had teased her on purpose.

"I didn't want you to miss me too much. It's nice to meet you, Isabella. You two have fun," Emma said.

Isabella chuckled. "You, too."

"I love you, Em. Merry Christmas," Kelsey said, shaking her head and smiling at Isabella.

"Love you, too."

Kelsey ended the call. "Before you came in, Emma told me she missed me and didn't like being away from me and her sister at Christmas."

"Aww," Isabella said.

"You see how quickly she got over it. That girl loves to tease me."

Isabella chuckled. "We are going to have so much fun with them."

"They're pretty awesome kids," Kelsey said. "Well, they aren't kids any longer, but I haven't screwed them up too much."

"Give me time, my boys are still young." Isabella chuckled.

"I can tell you're a great mom. They'll be fine," Kelsey said. She took a moment to look at Isabella. She was wearing a pair of baggy shorts and a sleeveless top. "Don't you look comfy and cute."

"Thanks." Isabella smiled. "I can do casual."

Kelsey noticed she had her hair up in a messy bun and could tell it was still damp from her shower. "Yes, you can," she murmured and quickly turned away so Isabella couldn't see her cheeks turning red once again. Kelsey took a deep breath and busied herself looking for the room service menu.

They ordered their food and Kelsey found a chilled bottle of wine in her mini-refrigerator.

She raised her brows at Isabella. "Wine?"

"Oh, yes. That sounds perfect."

"Carmen thinks of everything," Kelsey said, finding two glasses on the counter next to the refrigerator.

Isabella chuckled as Kelsey poured the wine. "Let's sit on the beach. I think we can just catch the sunset if we hurry."

They watched the sun set over the water and neither said anything, simply enjoying the show.

Their food arrived and they ate dinner on Kelsey's back deck. They took turns talking about the day they'd spent together and the things they enjoyed most.

"What do you want to do in the morning?" Kelsey asked.

"Mmm, I don't know. I'll talk to the boys after they open their presents. After that how about breakfast?" Isabella suggested.

Kelsey nodded and stared at Isabella for a moment. "Are you okay? Tomorrow could be kind of rough."

Isabella smiled. "It could be just as hard for you."

"I'll call Dana sometime tomorrow, but talking to Emma tonight eased my dread somewhat. That, and you," Kelsey said with a soft smile.

"Me?"

"Yep. We've been having such a good time that I haven't thought about spending Christmas without the girls. It's not that I don't miss them. I do, but I'm not moping around about it. What good would that do?"

Isabella stared at Kelsey. "Hmm, you're right. It's up to us to have our own merry Christmas. I'll miss watching the boys open their gifts, but it's just one Christmas." Isabella shrugged. "Thanks, Kels. We're both going to have a great time tomorrow."

"We are." Kelsey finished her wine and let out a contented sigh. "I don't know how we both ended up here together and how this year-long adventure will turn out, but I'm glad we're here."

"Merry Christmas, Kels." Isabella took Kelsey's hand.

"Merry Christmas, Bella." Kelsey squeezed her hand and smiled.

Kelsey watched Isabella walk the short distance to her bungalow and go inside. She sat back down and thought about how nice it had been to hold another woman in her arms. When the girls were away at school she had dated a few times, but she hadn't been dancing. Bella had surprised her when she asked her to dance, yet once Bella's arms were around her neck, it was just the two of them and the music.

Kelsey sighed. What a strange Christmas. She'd made a new friend—make that several new friends—and now she couldn't get Bella out of her head. All those thoughts and feelings had to be caused by the events of the past few days.

She'd enjoy the rest of her stay on the islands and the time she'd spend with Isabella. Once she was at home in Denver, her life would go back to the way it always was. These once a month adventures would be something to look forward to and she'd view them as the escapes they were meant to be. After all, that's exactly what they wanted to portray: an escape from everyday life.

Kelsey went inside and got ready for bed. Now that she'd been able to put things into perspective, she looked forward to going back to Peaches tomorrow. She didn't have to worry about what was happening in her heart. It was all part of the adventure. They would have fun then go back to their lives. Everything would be just fine.

A little voice inside her made Kelsey wonder if she was

fooling herself, but she didn't have to try and silence it. She simply fell asleep instead.

* * *

The next morning Isabella heard a light knock at her back door. She tossed her phone onto the bed and slowly turned around to see Kelsey through the glass. Isabella tried to smile and knew it wasn't her best effort. She opened the back door and instead of letting Kelsey walk inside, Isabella put her arms around Kelsey's neck.

She felt Kelsey's hands splayed across her back and she pulled her close.

"Merry Christmas," Kelsey said softly.

Isabella didn't let go right away. She took a breath and was grateful that Kelsey let the hug continue. Finally, Isabella stepped back and this time her smile was genuine. "Merry Christmas." She walked back into her bungalow as Kelsey followed behind her.

"Sorry about that," Isabella said. "You caught me just as I hung up with the boys."

"There's nothing to apologize for," Kelsey said. "I'm glad I was here to give you a hug."

Isabella chuckled. "I kind of blindsided you."

"I'll always be ready from here on out." Kelsey smiled. "I can give you a minute if you want."

"Nope. What I need is to be with my merry friend."

"Um, I'm not sure merry is a word used to describe me," Kelsey said with a wince. "That would be you."

Isabella smiled. "You were merry when I needed it, so don't argue with me."

"Yes ma'am," Kelsey replied with a little salute.

Isabella chuckled. "Wyatt and Gus are having a great time, but they miss me."

"Aww, Bella."

"I know," Isabella said as tears pooled in her eyes. "I'm glad they miss me, but I don't want them to be sad."

"Have they already opened their gifts from you?"

"No, Spencer is bringing them home on New Year's Day. I explained they'd get to have two Christmases, one in New York and one at home. I think they're just ready to come home," Isabella said. "Have you already opened gifts with Dana and Emma?"

Kelsey smiled. "We're doing the same thing as you. Emma flies home New Year's Day and Dana comes off the mountain that day. They'll spend the rest of their break with me."

"I thought I'd go over to the gift shop and get the boys something from the Virgin Islands," Isabella said.

"Do you mind if I come with you? I'd like to get the girls T-shirts. I noticed a couple of cute ones the day we got here," Kelsey said.

"Would I mind?" Isabella looked at her with surprise. "We are still a couple, Kelsey Kenny. It's you and me, babe. Remember?"

Kelsey laughed and that's just what Isabella needed to raise her spirits.

"I will never mind you being with me, Kels. Just so you know."

Kelsey nodded. "How about breakfast and a little retail therapy?"

Isabella held out her arm for Kelsey. "Perfect."

They had breakfast then went to the gift shop. As they browsed the souvenir options, Kelsey held up a turtle to show Isabella. "I only know Gus from what you've told me, but what about this sea turtle for him?"

"Oh, that's cool. I think he'd like that," Isabella said.

"Didn't you tell me Wyatt plays baseball? I saw some nice caps over there. I may get one for myself," Kelsey said.

"Okay." Isabella started towards the caps and stopped to look through a rack of T-shirts. "Kelsey, take a look at these. They're cute."

"This one looks like Emma and..." Kelsey looked through the other T-shirts until she pulled out another. "This one is for Dana. Thanks, Bella."

"What about this one for you?" Isabella said, holding it up.

Kelsey grinned and reached for it. "I love it."

Isabella snatched it back. "Wait a second. I want a picture of all three of you in these on New Year's Day," Isabella said with a bright smile.

"Aren't you going to get one?" Kelsey asked. "Wait... Let me find yours."

Kelsey handed Isabella the other shirts and went to another rack. "This one's for you," she said, holding up another T-shirt.

Isabella smiled. "I'd choose that for myself."

"I know you would." Kelsey grinned.

Isabella raised her eyebrows. "So you think you know me?"

Kelsey nodded. "You know me already." She took the shirts from Isabella and held them up. "And you know my girls."

Isabella chuckled and shrugged. They went to pay for their purchases and Isabella was struck by how well they had gotten to know each other in such a short time. The shirts they had chosen for each other were totally different yet fit them individually, but that wasn't so unusual since they'd seen each other's styles from what they'd worn so far. However, it was a little surprising that they had both chosen gifts for each other's kids that they would like. *I guess we listen to each other.*

On the way back to their bungalows, Isabella slung her arm over Kelsey's shoulders. "Thanks for cheering me up this morning."

Kelsey looked over at her and smiled. "I was simply returning the favor. This entire trip has been amazing because of you, Bella. I don't have time to think about things at home when I'm gazing at these amazing views and snorkeling and dancing."

Isabella chuckled. "It's not because of me. We need to thank Carmen. She's the one who set this up for us."

"She may have set it up, but she's not hanging out with us," Kelsey said.

"Well, partner," Isabella said with a lilt to her voice. "How about putting these in our bungalows and hanging out at our favorite spot on the beach until Carmen texts us?"

"I can't think of a better way to spend Christmas, or anyone else I'd rather spend it with."

"Same for me."

"Oh, by the way. I haven't missed the mountains or snow one bit. I knew Christmas at the beach would be lovely."

Isabella chuckled. "It feels a little unreal to me."

Kelsey stopped and stared at Isabella. "I thought the same thing last night."

"It's like we're living another life while we're here, but in a good way. I think that's the concept we're trying to sell with these monthly vacations."

"I didn't know it would feel like this, but I'm embracing

it. Don't people do things on vacation they wouldn't normally do?"

"Yes," Isabella said, drawing the word out. "I think I see what you mean. Don't question so much, just do and live it."

"Yeah, live it. I like that, Bella. We should use that in our videos and blogs."

Isabella smiled as they stopped in front of the bungalows. "Meet you at our place."

Moments later, she tossed her purchases onto the bed. "Live it," she murmured.

12

"Hey," Kelsey said as Sylvie drove into the circular driveway of the resort. "You work on St. Thomas, too?"

Sylvie gave her an amused grin. "No work today, ladies. Today, we play."

Kelsey and Isabella looked through to the passenger side of the car and saw Carmen smiling.

"Merry Christmas," she said. "Hop in."

Once Kelsey and Isabella were settled in the back seat, Carmen turned around. "Did I not tell you Sylvie is my wife?" She winked at Sylvie and Kelsey heard them both chuckle.

"No wonder Sylvie knew exactly what we needed when we needed it," Isabella said.

"Not true," Sylvie said. "I gave you the same service I give all my guests."

Carmen turned to look at them. "Sylvie has her own outfitter company and I run the resort."

"Please tell me you share clients," Kelsey said.

They chuckled. "We do, but we all try to share guests on the islands," Carmen said.

"Let me guess. It's the island way," Isabella said.

"Exactly." Sylvie chuckled.

They pulled into a parking area, walked down a dock, and stopped at a boat.

"Is this yours?" Kelsey asked.

"Yep," Sylvie said, stepping onto it and holding out her hand for Carmen then Kelsey and Isabella.

"Is having a boat on the islands kind of like having a car on the mainland?" Isabella asked.

"Sort of," Carmen replied as she made sure they wouldn't hit the sides of the boat slip as Sylvie backed the boat out. "We love to spend time on the water when we're not working."

"I don't use this boat for anything but us," Sylvie said, smiling at Carmen.

"I thought you said your kids were joining us," Kelsey said.

"They are," Carmen replied. "They have gone sailing with a friend."

"They'll drop them at the beach behind Peaches and they'll ride back with us," Sylvie explained.

As they sped across the water to St. John, Kelsey leaned back, in awe of the incredible view. "I can't get over how beautiful it is. One thing we want to talk about in the video and blog is the beauty of this place. I can't imagine ever getting used to it."

"Yeah, I wonder what we'll think as the year goes along," Isabella added. "I can't imagine not being amazed, though."

"I still enjoy going to work every morning," Sylvie said. "I get to see this on my way to St. John. There are times it looks different depending on the weather, but it's always beautiful to me."

"I suspect it will be just as beautiful next December as it is now," Kelsey said. "Maybe I should think about retiring here."

"You could!" Carmen said excitedly.

"Would you miss the mountains?" Isabella asked.

"Nah, I'm a beach kind of girl." Kelsey smiled.

"You know, what's stopping you now?" Carmen asked. "You can work from anywhere. Maybe you both should think about that as you come back each month."

"Oh, I could just see the fit Spencer would throw if I tried to move the boys out of North Carolina," Isabella scoffed.

"They have two parents," Sylvie said.

"Yeah, but we put a stipulation in the divorce agreement about staying in North Carolina," Isabella explained.

"You have to stay there?" Kelsey asked.

"Not exactly. Spencer and I have an agreement if either of us want to leave the state," Isabella replied. "We did that so the boys could have a stable living environment, but if something comes along it doesn't mean we can't talk about it."

"So you have options?" Kelsey asked.

Isabella shrugged. "Kind of."

"Here we are," Carmen said, moving to the front of the boat.

"We'll tie up to this buoy, set the anchor, and walk onto the patio at Peaches," Sylvie said. "It's the back way."

Kelsey looked out over the water to the sand and saw the familiar patio. "I guess it isn't deep?"

Carmen chuckled. "It's about knee deep. Come on." She

held out her hand and helped each of them slide off the boat and into the water.

"This is awesome!" Kelsey exclaimed as they walked through the water. She reached over and grabbed Isabella's hand. "Have you ever taken a boat to a bar?"

Isabella giggled. "I don't think I have."

Liz, Alex, and Riley welcomed them as they ambled through the sand and onto the patio.

The conversation was lively and the beer flowed. Not long after they'd arrived, Carmen and Sylvie's kids walked up from the other end of the beach.

"Kelsey and Isabella," Carmen said. "This is my son, Tanner, and daughter, Mia."

"It's nice to meet you," Kelsey greeted them. She figured they were around Dana and Emma's ages, maybe a little older.

"Mom told us about this big marketing program you're planning," Tanner said.

"You don't approve?" Kelsey asked, hearing doubt in his voice.

"It's not that," he said. "It's a big undertaking."

"It is, but we're ready for it," Isabella said. "If it takes off like we hope, just imagine the traffic it can bring to the resort."

"And to Mom's business on St. John," Mia added. "Tanner thinks he knows everything about the resort business."

"No I don't, but it's different when you have something exotic like here compared to a city—" Tanner said.

"Like Denver or Charlotte?" Isabella interrupted, smiling at Kelsey.

"You have to find the thing to sell where you are," Kelsey said, looking at Tanner and Mia. "I have an idea. We're doing a spring break getaway in March. My daughters and a couple of their friends will be the focus group. Could both of you come back then and join the group?"

"You both know these islands better than we do and could give the trip a personal touch," Isabella added.

"Really? That sounds like fun," Mia said.

"Tanner, do you know about deals that maybe we don't?" Kelsey asked. "We'd love to do a long weekend on a budget, so everyone could experience this beautiful place."

Tanner smiled. "I might know of a few ways to save money and still have the island experience."

"I hope it involves your mom's resort. We are doing this for Coral Bay," Isabella pointed out.

"Coral Bay is the best place to stay," Tanner said. "My mom knows what she's doing."

Kelsey chuckled. "We think she does, too."

"Are you not going to give me a hug?" Liz asked as she held out her arms to the kids.

They both gave Liz a hug and Kelsey and Isabella went inside for another beer.

"I've got refills right here," Riley said from behind the bar.

"You know, you should really think about working from here," Isabella said, sitting on one of the bar stools.

"I don't know," Kelsey said. "It seems too good to be true for someone like me."

"Someone like you? What does that mean, Kels? You are an incredible person."

"You've only known me a few days."

"I've known you less than that and I agree with Isabella," Riley said. "If you spend a lot of time here, you get to where you can read people."

"How did you do it? Liz told us you came here for a

wedding, fell in love with Alex, and moved here in a matter of weeks," Kelsey said.

Riley smiled and set a fresh beer in front of each of them. "I had just retired. I was a teacher," she said. "I wasn't sure what I wanted to do next, but when I met Alex I knew who I wanted to do whatever with. It was scary and I had a ton of doubts."

"It's different living here than visiting, isn't it?" Isabella asked.

"Yeah, but for me everything was wide open. I didn't have to work and I could stay here long enough to see if what Alex and I shared was more than just an island fling," Riley said.

"Kelsey could work from here," Isabella said. "We both work from home."

"Then you could move here, too," Riley said.

Isabella shook her head. "My boys are in North Carolina."

"They won't always be there," Riley said. "Maybe this is an option for both of you to think about."

Kelsey looked at Isabella and widened her eyes. "That's another angle we could explore in our monthly trips. People who work from home could vacation for longer here."

"I hope you two aren't always working," Riley said.

Isabella chuckled. "We're not, but this is a big deal to us and we want to make you even more successful."

Riley chuckled. "More business is always nice, but to keep our laid-back charm we don't need too many people. However, you two will always have a place here."

"Thank you," Kelsey said, putting her arm around Isabella's shoulder.

Isabella grinned at her and they sipped their beers. Kelsey wasn't sure why, but she'd found herself reaching to put an arm around Isabella or squeezing her hand at different times during the day. She blamed the fact that it was Christmas Day and when she'd first seen Isabella this morning she was upset, but Kelsey felt closer and closer to Isabella the more time they spent together.

Kelsey followed Riley and Isabella through the back door to the patio.

"Babe, you might want to tell Kelsey that living and working here is a little different than vacationing here," Riley said, sitting down next to Alex.

"I don't know about that," Alex said. "You still get to hang out in the most beautiful place on our planet. The weather is nice most of the time. You can swim and walk along the beach every day, plus get your work done."

"You're really selling it, Alex." Isabella chuckled.

"Isabella and I were talking earlier about the things you do on vacation that you might not do in your everyday life," Kelsey said.

"Yeah, these are escapes from your everyday life and once you get back home, it's back to the real world," Isabella said.

"What you're saying is that you can't be on vacation all the time, but I think you can bring this kind of escape into your everyday life. Alex stayed and look what she got," Liz said, smiling at Alex and Riley.

"I stayed and look what I got," Riley said, nuzzling Alex's neck and kissing her on the cheek.

"That is all very tempting," Isabella said. "But it would be at least ten years before I could make the big escape to live here since my boys are younger. You all had your kids when you were kids."

Kelsey chuckled. "That doesn't mean once they're grown they don't still need you."

"Yeah, but they can need you while you live in the Virgin Islands." Carmen grinned.

Kelsey looked around the table at this group of women. She was pretty sure they had all come from different walks of life but had become friends in this magical place.

Kelsey tried to picture what it would be like to live here. She'd fit right in with this group. They had already welcomed her and Isabella. But when she thought about it, the idea of being here without Isabella didn't feel right. Kelsey chuckled when she thought: *we're a couple*.

Isabella leaned over. "What's funny?" she asked quietly while Liz told a story at the other end of the table.

Kelsey smiled. "I was trying to imagine living here. It wouldn't be the same without you, Bella, so I guess I'll have to wait until you're ready."

"What a nice thing to say," Isabella said. "But we'll see about that. You may be sick of me by the end of the year."

"No way," Kelsey said. "We're a couple."

Isabella chuckled and smiled at Kelsey. That was the winning smile that Kelsey was used to seeing and beginning to love.

"Hey, I have a Christmas present for you when we get back to our bungalows," Isabella said quietly.

Kelsey's eyes widened in surprise. "You do? You didn't buy something from the gift shop this morning, did you?"

"Nope."

Kelsey grinned. "Well, I have something for you, too."

"Merry Christmas to us," Isabella said, putting her arm around Kelsey's shoulders.

13

Isabella looked over at Kelsey as she waved goodbye to Carmen and Sylvie. The smile on her face could light up the growing darkness. They'd come back from Peaches after the sun had set but there was still enough light for Sylvie to navigate the water.

"Not bad for a Christmas Day away from home, wouldn't you say?" Isabella said to Kelsey as they turned to walk through the resort and out to their bungalows.

"It was a good day, but it isn't over yet," Kelsey said.

"Do you want to have dinner?"

"I ate enough stuff at Peaches that I'm still full. How about you?" Kelsey replied.

"Same," Isabella said. "Let's go to the bungalows, exchange gifts, then we can do our usual walk along the beach."

Kelsey nodded and Isabella saw an uncertain look on her face. "Would you rather do something else?"

"No," Kelsey said.

"Then what's wrong?" Isabella watched Kelsey give her a sideways glance.

"Nothing is wrong," Kelsey said. "I'm kind of rethinking my gift. Do you remember when you told me my love language was doing for others?"

Isabella grinned. "Of course I do." She stopped and reached for Kelsey's arm to stop her as well. "Your gift will be perfect because it came from you and you obviously thought about it, so stop worrying," Isabella said, widening her eyes.

Kelsey chuckled. "Okay."

"You are definitely the thinker in this couple," Isabella teased as they started walking again.

"Someone has to do it," Kelsey said.

Isabella scoffed. "Just because I like to do things in the moment does not mean I don't think things through." She watched Kelsey smirk and raise one eyebrow. "Most of the time."

Kelsey laughed. "Whatever our dynamic is, it seems to be working, so I'd say we're fine."

"Sometimes you need a little spontaneity and sometimes you need a plan," Isabella said.

"As a couple we have that on lock."

Isabella chuckled. "We do."

They stopped at Kelsey's front door and Isabella said, "I'll be over in a minute."

Isabella went inside her bungalow and found Kelsey's gift where she'd left it next to the TV. She walked into the bathroom and took her hair down. She'd worn it up all day, but wanted to leave it down tonight if it didn't look too bad. She fluffed it and noticed a crease where the hair tie had held it all day, but it would do.

A smile played across her lips as she walked back into the room. She couldn't help but wonder what Kelsey's gift to her was. It didn't really matter. She knew she'd love it because it was from Kelsey. Each day they had gotten to know each other better and Isabella wouldn't be surprised if they were best friends by the end of the trip.

She grabbed the gift and walked next door to Kelsey's back deck. "What's that?" she asked Kelsey while she fiddled with something.

"It's a speaker I borrowed from Riley. I'm just pairing it to my phone. We like to listen to music while we sit out here, so I thought it might sound better," Kelsey said.

"What are we drinking? I almost grabbed beer, but we drank that all afternoon," Isabella said.

"There's wine left in my fridge," Kelsey said. "How about we finish it?"

"That sounds good. Can I get it while you finish there?" Isabella asked.

"Please do. The glasses are next to the ice bucket."

Isabella went inside and found the bottle in Kelsey's refrigerator. She wasn't surprised at how neat and tidy the room looked. That was Kelsey's personality, but Isabella had discovered that she was a lot of fun, too.

"Here we go," Isabella said, pouring each of them a glass.

"Thank you." Kelsey took the glass Isabella offered her. "Merry Christmas."

They softly clinked their glasses and both took a sip then sat down at the table.

"Do you realize we're going to be here for five more days?" Isabella said. "That's a lot of adventures."

Kelsey chuckled. "Do you think we can't handle it?"

"No, but I do think we should be selective," Isabella said. "There are a lot of boats willing to take us on excursions. That doesn't include the yachts that will take us on more private tours."

"Hmm, I see what you're saying. I hope once we start

this, Carmen will have someone dedicated to do booking. I think people are going to want to do what we do," Kelsey said with a smile.

"That's confidence."

"Think about how much fun we had yesterday. Once we do a post on Honeymoon Beach, people are going to come here," Kelsey said.

Isabella furrowed her brow. "We have to make it interesting and get it out there though."

"We will," Kelsey smiled. "But we don't have to talk about that today. It's Christmas, we'll do work tomorrow."

"Right." Isabella nodded. "Here is your Christmas present," she said, handing the small bag to Kelsey.

"You even wrapped it," Kelsey said with a grin.

Isabella watched Kelsey reach into the bag. She suddenly felt her heart speed up and hoped Kelsey liked the gift.

"Oh, Bella!" Kelsey exclaimed. "I love it! When did you get this printed?"

"I have my ways." Isabella winked. "We've taken a lot of pictures since we've gotten here, but I thought that was the best one of us."

"Look at our smiles," Kelsey said, staring at the picture. "You can't tell we're drunk."

Isabella gasped. "We weren't drunk. That was before."

Kelsey laughed. "I remember you taking this."

Isabella met Kelsey's gaze and looked into her eyes. It was too dark to see what color they were, but Isabella was sure they were golden brown with a hint of green around the outside. She remembered how happy and carefree they had been that afternoon and Kelsey's eyes had sparkled.

"I printed that picture and put it in a frame because I want you to put it on your desk at home. When you're having a tough day or you're busy with work, you can take a look at us and remember the breeze, the sand, the water, and most importantly, the happiness," Isabella said with a smile.

"I'll remember you," Kelsey said softly. "Thank you, Bella."

"You're welcome, Kels."

Kelsey put the picture on the table where they both could see it then stood up and reached for her phone. Isabella watched her scroll and click then Kelsey turned to her.

"My gift to you is a dance," Kelsey said. "You mentioned wanting to dance with me again, so..." Kelsey held her hand out.

Isabella's eyes lit up with delight. When the music began to play through the speaker, she gasped. "Is that the same song we danced to at Peaches?"

Kelsey nodded. "It's called 'STRINGS' by Max."

"I'd never heard it before, but it sounded like how the beach made me feel earlier that day," Isabella said, taking Kelsey's hand. "It's hard to explain."

"I get it. This place is beautiful. I know we keep saying that, but it is and this song is beautiful as well. It's like if we could put into music how this place looks and how it makes us feel, it would sound something like this."

"You do get it!" Isabella exclaimed. "Can you start it over?"

Kelsey punched a button and when the music began, Isabella put her arms around Kelsey's neck. She felt Kelsey's hands on her hips, but they weren't tentative this time. Isabella rested her head on Kelsey's shoulder as they began to move to the music.

This gift was better than the jewelry or things her

husband had given her on various occasions because this meant something to Kelsey, too. Isabella's heart pounded and electricity flowed through her body. She could feel Kelsey's fingers on her lower back where her shirt didn't quite meet her shorts and warmth shot through her body.

Isabella moved her hands across Kelsey's back and could feel the heat of her skin through the thin shirt she wore. Suddenly, Isabella was aware of every place their bodies touched. She inhaled and could smell the sweetness of Kelsey's skin underneath the sun and sand of the day.

Isabella closed her eyes, wanting to burn this moment into her memory. She wanted to remember how it felt to have Kelsey's arms around her. She wanted to remember the scents, the cool breeze, and the music. Mostly she wanted to remember how her heart was beating *with* Kelsey's. She'd never felt this close to another soul. Is that what was happening? Was Kelsey's soul talking to Isabella's?

"Merry Christmas, Bella," Kelsey said softly.

Isabella raised her head and pulled back until she could see into Kelsey's eyes. "I'll always remember this."

"Me, too." Kelsey smiled. "This is your gift, but it's been so long since I danced with another woman I'd forgotten how much I love it, so it's a gift to me, too."

Isabella smiled. "I've never danced with a woman. Going forward, I'm not sure I want to dance with anyone else but you." She hadn't even thought about them being two women in the moment. It was Kelsey. Yes, she knew Kelsey was gay, but that didn't matter to Isabella right then. They were enjoying a dance as a Christmas gift. It didn't have to be anything other than that, did it?

Kelsey chuckled. "This can be our thing when we come to Coral Bay."

"I love that idea," Isabella said. She shook her head.

"You've got a romantic streak in you that's wider than this island."

Kelsey smiled. "I admit it."

Isabella grinned. "We're selling romance, Kels. It's a good thing."

"I hope you don't mind me being sappy and romantic from time to time," Kelsey said as the song ended. "It's so easy with you."

Isabella dropped her hands and furrowed her brow. "Easy with me?"

"Yes, it's easy to be myself with you and sometimes romance may come out. If it makes you uncomfortable—"

"It doesn't." Isabella stopped Kelsey mid-sentence. "It makes me feel special, Kels, so thank you."

"Thank you. It's nice to do something for someone else, you know?"

"No, I wouldn't know. I'm a self-centered, brand-minded influencer. We don't do for others," Isabella teased.

"Oh my God! You are not those things!" Kelsey protested then laughed.

"Watch out, Kels. You never know," Isabella said. "Let's walk."

They left their shoes on the deck and walked out onto the sand. "The moon is beautiful," Kelsey said.

"This Christmas has been much better than I expected," Isabella said, "thanks to you and our new friends."

"I don't think I'll ever forget it," Kelsey said.

"We're doing it again next year, so you'll have something to compare it to," Isabella said.

"Wow, that's something to think about," Kelsey said. "I wonder what we'll be doing this time next year."

"I hope we'll be on this beach together celebrating Christmas with our families," Isabella said.

"Let's make it happen," Kelsey said.

"Okay." Isabella stopped and took Kelsey's hands in hers. "Since we're a couple now"—she winked—"I vow to spend Christmas with you next year on this beach."

Kelsey chuckled and repeated Isabella's words. "I vow to spend Christmas with you next year on this beach."

They both laughed, then went back to Kelsey's deck to finish their wine.

Later that night as Isabella lay in bed trying to go to sleep, she thought back on her dance with Kelsey. She had never been attracted to another woman, but there was something about Kelsey. Isabella had known it the first time their eyes met at the airport.

They had done so much in just a few days and with this huge project to complete, she hadn't given herself a moment to think about Kelsey. Was something beginning between them? Surely not.

Isabella sighed. "I'm not going to think about this right now. I'm going to spend the rest of the week with Kelsey, have a great time, and then we'll see what happens when I get back home," she mumbled. "This is vacation stuff, not real-life stuff."

14

The next few days were filled with excursions and adventures. Kelsey and Isabella went snorkeling, kayaking, bar hopping, and they tasted the local food. Sylvie set them up on Jeep tours and ATV tours. They even took a tour on a yacht to several of the surrounding islands.

"I can't believe we have the afternoon to ourselves," Kelsey said, holding the door to Peaches open for Isabella.

"Don't forget we're supposed to go on a sunset cruise tonight," Isabella said.

"I feel like all we've done since Christmas is go, go, go. What happened to hanging out at the resort?" Kelsey said.

"Hey there, we thought you two forgot about us," Liz said.

"Carmen has had us on the go every day," Isabella said, sliding onto a bar stool.

"We've had so much fun, but sometimes it's nice to sit and drink a beer with friends," Kelsey said.

Riley chuckled from behind the bar. "She wants you to experience as much as you can before you go back."

"We know that, but we *are* coming back. Let us do something new for our next visit in January," Isabella said.

"Don't you leave tomorrow?" Alex asked.

"Yes. We couldn't leave without seeing all of you one more time," Kelsey said.

"Do you have plans for tonight?"

"Of course we do," Isabella said.

"It's a sunset cruise," Kelsey added.

"You can do that in February for Valentine's Day," Riley said. "I'll explain it to Carmen. We have some ideas for your trips going forward."

Kelsey looked over at Isabella and raised her brows. "I wonder how receptive she'll be."

"We've known Carmen for a long time. She'll need everyone's help to make this work," Liz said. "Now, tell us what all you've been doing."

Kelsey and Isabella took turns giving them highlights from the last few days.

"We like to walk along the beach before we go to bed, but we've been so tired the last two nights we barely made it through dinner," Kelsey said.

"Yeah, we've learned a thing or two," Isabella said. "You don't have to be doing something all the time for it to be a vacation."

Liz chuckled. "Are you craving your everyday life back home?"

Kelsey and Isabella exchanged a look. "In two days I will be sitting in my own living room and I'm quite sure I'll be wondering what all of you are doing here at Peaches. It may be my everyday life, but I'll still remember my escape," Kelsey explained.

"We'll miss you, but it won't be that long until you're here again," Liz said.

A group of people walked into the bar and Liz seated them while Riley and Alex waited on the other tables.

"Will you really be thinking about Peaches next week?" Isabella asked.

"Won't you?"

"Yeah, I will. You know, I kind of feel bad for complaining to them. We have gotten to experience things that other people don't get to, but..." Isabella trailed off.

"But?"

"You know what I really missed the last few days?"

Kelsey smiled and waited.

"I missed sitting on your back deck and talking," Isabella said.

"I missed watching the sunset on the beach with you and taking selfies," Kelsey admitted. She chuckled when Isabella gave her a surprised look. "You take great pictures, Bella. My girls have loved receiving them every day."

"We have to document these memories," Isabella said. "Plus we may need to use them in posts throughout the year."

"I'm going to insist Carmen work in a lazy day for each trip," Kelsey said. "We can enjoy the resort or, if it's you and me, we'd come here."

"That's a great idea," Isabella said. "We have learned this week as well as played."

Kelsey thought back over the last few days. She and Isabella had been so busy they hadn't shared any intimate moments like when they first arrived on St. Thomas. It was probably a good thing because there were times when Kelsey wondered if they were developing feelings past friendship.

She smiled as she watched Isabella gaze at the crowd and drink her beer. Kelsey wondered what next week would look like without Isabella. Would they call each other? Text? No need to think about that right now when she had the opportunity for one more dance.

Kelsey got up and went over to where Riley was looking at her phone. She knew they controlled the music at Peaches from their phones. After a quick conversation, Kelsey walked back over to Isabella.

"One more dance?" Kelsey asked Isabella, holding out her hand.

The delight on Isabella's face went right to Kelsey's heart. "I'd love to," she replied.

Once they were on the dance floor Isabella smiled. "That's our song."

Kelsey nodded. "Yep. I hope if you hear it before we come back next month you'll think about us, right here at Peaches."

"Nope," Isabella said.

Kelsey furrowed her brow, not understanding Isabella's reaction.

"When I hear this at home, I'll be thinking of your Christmas gift to me, Kels."

Kelsey smiled with relief. "Our picture will be on my desk."

"We already have sweet memories of our time here. Just imagine what's to come," Isabella said.

Kelsey smiled and looked into Isabella's eyes. That little part of her simply asked *what if?*

* * *

Isabella and Kelsey settled into their seats and got ready for the plane to take them to Charlotte.

"I think you got your point across to Carmen." Isabella chuckled.

"I was ready for her to tell me she'd get someone else to do this with you," Kelsey said.

"I had your back, Kels. We're a couple. You keep forgetting that," Isabella said with a grin.

"Oh, I haven't forgotten. It's just that I'm not sure anyone else knows our secret."

Isabella laughed. "It's no secret we have become friends and we are the perfect people to pull off this grand adventure for Carmen, Sylvie, and our new friends in the Virgin Islands."

"Do you have a busy month ahead before our next trip?" Kelsey asked.

"I don't think so, but you never know what opportunities will come up." Isabella raised her brows. "If you would've told me when I landed here a week ago that we would be coming back every month…"

"Or that I would make a new friend whom I can't imagine not seeing tomorrow," Kelsey said.

"I know. Won't it be strange?" Isabella said. "What do we do this month while we're at home? I mean, are you going to call me or text me? Email, maybe?"

Kelsey chuckled. "You're asking me? I've never done anything like this either, Bella. We get to make the rules."

Isabella giggled. "I like that idea. Okay, texts, calls, emails—all forms of communication are open and accepted."

Kelsey smiled. "Look, Bella, you call or text me anytime. We're friends. There's no reason not to."

Isabella sighed with relief. "We'll need to talk about our next trip. We have to plan."

"I agree. When I fly into Charlotte next month and pick

you up, I want us to know what we're doing each day," Kelsey said.

"That sounded so funny." Isabella laughed. "When I pick you up next month," she said, mimicking Kelsey.

Kelsey laughed as well. "We'll be flying together just like we did last week. Only this time we'll know it."

"I had a great time, but I'm ready to see my kids," Isabella said.

"Me, too," Kelsey replied. "I'm looking forward to when we'll have them all here together."

"That will be fun, but we get Dana and Emma with their friends first," Isabella said.

"They are going to love you," Kelsey said. "You're the impromptu kind of fun they wish I was at times."

"Oh, I doubt that. If they're anything like you, we'll be fast friends, just like you and me," Isabella said.

Kelsey smiled and looked out the window.

"You look happy," Isabella said. "When I saw you looking out the window of the bus that day we met, you looked sad. Not anymore."

"I wonder why." Kelsey winked at her.

Isabella chuckled. "Hey, I just realized that I never saw you repeat outfits."

"Were you paying attention?"

"Yes I was!"

"We did so many things in our swimsuits that I was able to mix and match without you noticing," Kelsey explained.

Isabella narrowed her eyes. "I may have to try bringing one bag on our next trip."

"Bella," Kelsey said, reaching over and squeezing her hand. "You bring as many bags as you want. I will help you with your luggage. You have to be comfortable."

"Thanks, Kels," Isabella said. "That's sweet of you, but believe me, I'll bring what I need."

"I know you will." Kelsey grinned.

They talked, gazed out the window, and planned their next trip during the flight. Once they'd landed, Isabella helped Kelsey get her bag from the overhead bin and they deplaned.

"I'm glad our flight was on time. You shouldn't have to wait long to board your plane to Denver," Isabella said.

"Okay, I have to go this way," Kelsey said, reading the sign indicating her gate. "Baggage claim is through there."

"I feel like a bad host. You've flown into my city and I'm leaving you at the airport. I can wait until you get on your plane," Isabella said.

"You're not being a bad host. By the time you get your luggage my flight will be boarding."

"I'm walking with you to your gate." Isabella put her arm through Kelsey's. She had a strange feeling in her stomach. She knew Kelsey had to leave, but she hated to see her go.

They slowly walked to Kelsey's gate as other people hurried around them. "Here we are," Kelsey said. "Look, they're already pre-boarding."

"Take a picture and send it to me when you're in your seat," Isabella said.

"What?" Kelsey chuckled.

"Promise!" Isabella demanded.

"Okay. I promise."

"And don't forget to send me a pic of you and the girls in your T-shirts." Isabella was talking rapidly and couldn't seem to stop the anxiousness taking over her body.

"I will, Bella. I'll call you tonight when I get home," Kelsey said.

They heard the attendant over the loudspeaker announce that it was time for Kelsey's group to board.

Isabella threw her arms around Kelsey and hugged her tight. She kissed Kelsey on the cheek as her heart began to flutter in her chest. Then Isabella did something she'd never done before. She pulled her head back and stared into Kelsey's eyes. They were golden brown and looked at her so sweetly. That's when Isabella leaned in and quickly kissed Kelsey on the lips.

"Uh—are you sure you can get your bags," Kelsey stammered.

Isabella could see the shock on Kelsey's face and Isabella was just as surprised, but she also felt a kind of relief. She would sort that out on her way home.

"You're not carrying my baggage, Kels," she said. She smiled at Kelsey and let her go. "See you next month."

"See you next month," Kelsey replied with a smile.

Isabella watched her walk toward the entrance to the plane. At the last moment Kelsey looked over her shoulder and grinned.

What am I doing? Isabella thought with a little wave. Once Kelsey was out of sight, Isabella walked to baggage claim. She took her phone out of her purse to text Kelsey, but didn't know what to say.

As she walked up to the rotating table, her first bag made its way to her. Isabella easily reached down and pulled her bag off the table. She chuckled to herself, remembering how Kelsey had helped her in the Virgin Islands. Her other bag was just as easy to lift and she set it next to the other bag. She put her purse over one handle and her satchel over the other.

Before she began to roll them to exit the airport, she took a picture and sent it to Kelsey.

See you next month, she wrote under the picture.

A moment later Kelsey replied with a picture of her grinning into the phone, sitting in her seat on the plane. *See you next month.*

Isabella sighed. She didn't know what was happening. A sense of dread had settled over her as they got off the plane. Maybe it was the idea of going back to her everyday life, but she was excited to see her sons. Still, when she hugged Kelsey then looked into her eyes, she couldn't stop herself. The quick kiss was heartfelt and Isabella had immediately felt the dread leave her body. She would miss Kelsey; how could she not?

But then a thought came to her: Her heart was telling Kelsey's heart goodbye. Maybe that's why she had felt so unsettled, then after the brief kiss, it was as if she could breathe again. "How strange," she mumbled as she waited for her ride share.

Isabella wondered if Kelsey felt the same way. She saw the surprise on her face, but she didn't seem upset or angry. Kelsey was supposed to call her when she got to Denver. Should Isabella bring it up? She had to figure this out before it wrecked this year's travel plans.

15

Kelsey thought about Isabella for the entire flight home. That kiss had surprised her, but it wasn't unwelcome. Kelsey knew she needed to be careful with her feelings. So much had happened to her and Isabella in such a short time. They had been thrust into this marketing project and quickly became friends while they were working.

Since boarding the flight in St. Thomas that morning, Kelsey had felt like a cloud was descending over them. They were leaving paradise to return to their everyday lives. She and Isabella both missed their families, but there was also a type of grief from having to leave their new friends and each other. At least that's how Kelsey felt. She wondered if Isabella was feeling the same thing when she suddenly kissed her.

She had seen a change in Isabella the closer they got to Charlotte. Kelsey had felt it, too. She sighed as the plane landed and taxied towards the gate. She couldn't imagine her life going back to the way it was before this trip. Surely, she and Isabella would keep in touch. Yes, they had business to discuss as far as the resort account was concerned, but they were friends now. And friends shared their lives even if it was through texts, calls, or emails, right?

As Kelsey pulled her bag to the airport exit and toward the train station, she realized her light jacket was stuffed inside her satchel. Once outside she stopped, pulled it out, and quickly put it on. It must have snowed earlier because everything was covered with a fresh coat of white.

Kelsey grabbed her phone and took a selfie with the snow in the background. She sent it to Isabella with a simple message: *Brrrrr, I miss our paradise.*

Isabella quickly responded with a sad face and a heart.

Kelsey was reminded of her conversation with Liz at Peaches, when they talked about vacation life and real life. For people like Riley and Alex who chose to stay, their vacation lives had become their real lives in a way.

She got on the train and looked out the window as the fields outside the airport whizzed by. As they traveled further into the city, buildings came into view. Kelsey thought about her everyday life and how it included the cityscape of Denver. But now her and Isabella's everyday life would also include the Virgin Islands and their vacation life. The two were coming together.

"They had to," she mumbled. Isabella was now a part of her life, wasn't it natural to be sad when leaving a friend? Was that why she felt an emptiness inside?

Kelsey leaned back and smiled. Yeah, that must be it. She was glad to get that worked out in her head. *But that kiss?*

Once Kelsey was finally home, she walked into her house and left her bag in the living room. She looked around and felt such a feeling of loneliness. Tomorrow night would be a different story. Dana and Emma would be here, they'd open Christmas presents, and she'd tell them all about her trip.

She turned on a couple lights and got a bottle of beer from the refrigerator. She walked over to the couch, took out her phone, and sat down. The silence didn't usually bother her, but for whatever reason it did tonight.

Kelsey pulled up Isabella's number and connected the call.

"Hey, you," Isabella said cheerily.

"Hi," Kelsey said. "I made it home."

"It looks cold there," Isabella said.

Kelsey chuckled. "It's December and I'm in Denver, remember?"

Isabella laughed. "Doesn't it seem strange? It's cold here, too."

"Yes, it does. I had to find my jacket once I was out of the airport," Kelsey explained.

"Uh," Isabella murmured. "About the airport."

Kelsey smiled. "Thank you for that New Year's kiss. I'm sure you knew I would be alone, so that was very thoughtful of you."

Isabella giggled and Kelsey couldn't believe the feeling of happiness that washed over her at the sound.

"Yeah, that's me. Always the thoughtful one," Isabella said. "Listen, Kels. I was having the strangest feeling leaving you."

"I was, too, Bella. I get it," Kelsey said.

"You do?" Isabella paused then sighed. "Of course you do."

"Do you remember us talking about vacation life and everyday life?" Kelsey said.

"Yep."

"Well, I don't see how we can keep from living them both with these monthly trips," Kelsey explained.

"When we're not in St. Thomas, we'll be talking about the next trip," Isabella said.

"Yeah," Kelsey said. "And talking about the one we just came back from. It's like we'll be living the island life while we're home."

"That sounds like fun. I don't know about you, but it's too quiet at my house tonight," Isabella said.

"It's quiet here too." Kelsey gasped as realization struck her. "I know why! It's the water!"

"What?"

"We're used to hearing the waves lap onto the beach," Kelsey explained. "That's why it's so quiet."

"I think you're right," Isabella said. "Okay, I'm going to FaceTime you."

"What? Why?"

"Because I want to see your house and your face. Come on, accept the call."

Kelsey connected the call and Isabella's smiling face appeared on her screen.

"Happy New Year, Kels!"

Kelsey chuckled. "Happy New Year, Bella."

"Now, show me around," Isabella said. When Kelsey frowned she added, "Do you have anything better to do?"

Kelsey giggled. "No. I'm having a beer," she replied, holding up the bottle. "Do you have any?"

"No, but I have wine."

"Pour yourself a glass and I'll show you around," Kelsey said. She waited as Isabella went into the kitchen. Kelsey could hear her opening the door to the refrigerator and getting out a glass. It reminded her of their evenings on the beach at Coral Bay.

Yep, they were living an everyday life with their vacation life right alongside it. Kelsey smiled and thought she wouldn't want to do this with anyone else but Isabella Burns. Funny, she'd had that same thought a week ago when the idea was born.

"Okay, Kels. I'm ready. Let's go."

* * *

Isabella laughed as she watched Wyatt and Gus playing each other on a video game. Their characters were racing through a magical desert and Gus had just run Wyatt off the road.

"I'm coming for you, bro," Wyatt said with fake malice.

Gus giggled and Isabella relished the sound. There were times when Gus still laughed with joyous little boy glee even though he was getting older.

Her phone dinged with a text and Isabella smiled as she viewed it.

"Who's that?"

Isabella glanced at where her mother sat at the kitchen island next to her. Marti Raines had raised Isabella to be a confident woman and not be afraid to go after what she wanted. "Nosy, Rosy."

"I am not," Marti said. "If you could see the smile on your face you'd know why I'm asking."

"What does that mean?"

Marti gave her a smirk. "It means you're smiling. The boys are the only ones that make you smile like that anymore."

Isabella furrowed her brow. "I smile, Mom."

"Come on, who is it?"

"It's probably her friend Kelsey," Wyatt said from the living room.

Isabella looked at her mom and then to where her boys were battling it out with their game controllers in the living room. "How do you know that?"

"Duh," Wyatt said. "You've been talking about all the fun stuff you did with her since we got home."

"What kind of fun stuff?" Marti asked, leaning a little closer.

Isabella chuckled. "Beach stuff, Mom. Kelsey sent me a picture of her and her girls in shirts we bought them in St. Thomas," she explained.

"Let me see," Marti said.

Isabella held her phone where Marti could see it. In the photo, Kelsey was standing between the girls. Dana was taking the selfie and had her arm outstretched while Emma stood on the other side of Kelsey, pointing at their shirts. The smile on Kelsey's face reminded Isabella of the selfies they took while on the beach. She had told Kelsey to look into the phone and to imagine smiling at her girls or someone she loved. *Who are you smiling at, Kels?*

"Is that Kelsey in the middle?" Marti asked.

"Yeah. Her daughters look like her," Isabella murmured.

"Where's their father?"

"Mom!" Isabella snorted.

"What? I'm just asking. Is she divorced, like you?"

"No. She had both her girls via IVF," Isabella replied.

Marti raised her brows. "How brave."

"She is," Isabella said, staring at the pictures.

"What was your favorite part of the trip?" Marti asked.

"Mmm, let's see," Isabella said. "We usually took a nightly walk along the beach."

"That sounds nice."

"Oh, and there was this bar we loved over on St. John. We became friends with the owners," Isabella said.

"Show Gran the pictures of the boat, Mom," Gus said.

Isabella scrolled through her pictures while giving her mother a brief summary of the things they did.

"Is that the bar you liked?" Marti asked, looking at a picture of the patio at Peaches.

"Yes, that was Christmas Day," Isabella said. "They weren't open, but invited us to join them for the afternoon." She pointed to Carmen and Sylvie. "That is the CEO of the resort and her wife."

"Tell me about Kelsey," Marti said. "You're going to be spending a lot of time together."

Isabella smiled. "Yeah, we are." She paused for a moment, thinking, *how to describe Kelsey...* "She is very thoughtful. We met when she helped me with my luggage at the airport. We had no idea we were going to the same resort and ended up having dinner together that night."

"This is some undertaking, going back there every month," Marti said.

"I know. There's no one I'd want to do this with but her. Kelsey's so much fun and we've become friends. She's also really good with the website."

"You're really good at what you do, too," Marti said.

"Thanks, Mom," Isabella replied with a smile.

"Tell me something else you liked," Marti said.

"Um." Isabella furrowed her brow and thought back to all the activities they did, but one in particular came to the front of her mind. "We danced," she said softly.

"Danced?"

"Yeah, the bar played music and everyone got up and danced. It was fun."

Isabella could feel her mom studying her as she asked, "Did you dance with Kelsey?"

"I did."

Marti nodded and continued studying Isabella.

"It was no big deal, Mom. Everyone was dancing."

"I didn't say anything."

"It's the way you looked at me. *I* asked Kelsey to dance."

Marti smiled. "You did?"

"Yeah, a pretty song was playing and I felt like dancing. Kelsey was the lucky person." Isabella smirked.

"She certainly is." Marti smiled. "I'm proud of you for going on that trip alone. You've met someone who's now a friend and you have these big plans for the rest of the year. This is the woman I raised."

Isabella gaped at her mom and thought about the last couple of years with the divorce. There had been a lot of changes in her life that had made her less confident. But when she was in the Virgin Islands with Kelsey, she felt more like herself than she had in a long time. She was sure of the decisions she'd made and hopeful about this idea they'd come up with together.

Marti leaned in and quietly asked, "Is Kelsey gay?"

"Does it matter?"

"You were dancing in a bar with a gay woman. It might matter to her," Marti said.

Isabella scoffed. "It's not like that. We're friends." Her mom's comment made her wonder though. Kelsey hadn't done anything to make Isabella think they were anything but friends. After all, Isabella was the one who kissed Kelsey in the airport yesterday.

"Okay, guys. That's enough screen time for now." The boys groaned. "Take your gifts to your room and maybe we'll have another piece of this scrumptious pie Gran made for us."

That got a cheer.

Once they'd left the room, Marti turned to Isabella. "I wish you could hear how defensive you sound. Let me tell you something, honey. I'm not blind to the pressure you felt growing up. You have done what you thought was expected of you. You went to college, earned good grades, became successful at your profession, married a nice boy, had my beautiful grandsons, and things didn't work out. It's time you did something that you want to do. I haven't heard you talk about anyone the way you have Kelsey. Maybe you should think about a woman."

"What are you talking about?" Isabella couldn't believe her ears.

"Don't think I never looked at another woman twice," Marti scoffed.

Isabella stared at her mom with her mouth gaping open.

"I know you said Kelsey is your friend, but maybe she'd be more than that if you'd let her."

"Where is this coming from?" Isabella asked, confused.

"You've always been the perfect daughter when it comes to the major parts of your life. Be your spontaneous self and live a little, Isabella."

Isabella knew her mom was right. When it came to doing what she was supposed to do, Isabella did it. Yes, she could be impulsive and most of her friends would describe her as fun, but those were easy choices at frivolous parties or get-togethers. Thinking of Kelsey as more than a friend wasn't anything like that.

"What would Dad think?" Isabella said, the idea of doing something for herself swirling around her head.

"It doesn't matter what he thinks. He died five years ago," Marti said then smiled.

"Mom, I know that!"

"Well, it's true. It doesn't matter what anyone thinks, but you," Marti said.

"What about the boys? Have you forgotten about your grandsons? It does matter what they think."

"No it doesn't. You're not going to raise them any differently if you're by yourself, have a girlfriend, or a boyfriend," Marti said. "You're a good mother who teaches them to be open-minded, compassionate, and helpful."

"You're forgetting one thing. It makes a difference what Kelsey thinks."

"You'll have plenty of time to find that out on your next trip."

16

"I thought we were going hiking," Dana said, walking into Kelsey's office.

"We are. I need to finish one more thing," Kelsey said, staring at her computer screen and tapping the keyboard.

Emma walked in and picked up the framed picture sitting on Kelsey's desk. "This is a good picture of you and Isabella."

Kelsey gazed up at her and smiled. "That was a fun day."

"Weren't they all fun days?" Dana asked.

Kelsey tilted her head. "Yeah, they were."

"And to think you didn't want to go," Emma said.

Kelsey closed her laptop and swung around in her chair. "The idea of having Christmas at the beach meant that you two were supposed to be with me."

"I'll go with you next year. I promise," Dana said.

"You had a good time though," Emma said. "And scored a sweet deal for the rest of the year. Then there's Isabella."

"Yeah, what about Isabella?" Dana asked.

Kelsey could see the curious amusement on both their faces. "Bella is my friend," she stated calmly.

"Did you hear how she said, *Bel-la*?" Dana teased, drawing the word out.

"I did," Emma replied. She widened her eyes. "She's Isabella to us, but *Bella* to Mom."

"Okay, you two, that's enough. Bella and I will be doing this for a year. Anything more than friends would complicate things."

"So you're saying there might be a chance," Dana said.

"I did not say that."

"Come on, Mom," Emma said. "You've been texting and talking to her every day since you've been home."

"Yeah, and your face lights up when you talk to her. It doesn't do that with other clients," Dana added.

"She's not a client. We're collaborators," Kelsey said.

"Maybe you should try to collaborate on something else," Dana mumbled.

Kelsey smirked. "I heard that."

"What other friends do you dance with?" Emma asked, raising her brows and staring at her mother.

"I should've never told you about that," Kelsey said, shaking her head.

"I'm glad you did. The excitement on your face was adorable."

"You'll see in March when we go on the girls trip. We're just two friends who have fun together," Kelsey explained. "I will admit, I haven't connected with another person as quickly as I did with Bella. It feels like we've been friends a long time."

"Have a fling with her," Dana said.

Kelsey scoffed. "I'm not having a fling with Bella. Why is

this so important to you?" she asked, looking from Dana to Emma.

"It's time you had a girlfriend. We're not going to be around as much when we graduate. You sacrificed for us all these years. It's your turn," Emma said.

"I didn't sacrifice anything," Kelsey said, standing up. "I love our family. I wouldn't trade it for anything."

"We don't want you to trade it. Just open your eyes and your heart to what could be. You haven't been this interested or liked someone this much… ever," Dana said.

"You do things with Uncle Joel and Aunt Gabi and I know you've been on a few dates," Emma said.

"How do you know?" Kelsey said, narrowing her gaze.

"I just know, but you're different when you talk about Isabella," Emma said.

Kelsey sighed. She wasn't surprised the girls had noticed how happy she was since meeting Isabella, but it didn't matter. They had a job to do. Besides, she never had any inklings that Isabella thought of her as anything other than a friend. But there was that kiss at the airport…

"When we go in March, we'll take you to our favorite bar. The owners are gay and there's always women there. I'll open my eyes then. How's that?" Kelsey asked, trying to placate them.

"Fine," Emma said.

"But Isabella will be there, too. Your eyes should be looking in her direction," Dana said.

Kelsey shook her head. "So stubborn," she mumbled. "Are we going hiking or what?"

* * *

Isabella read the email from Carmen with their itinerary for the January trip. She reached for her phone and called Kelsey.

"Hey you," Kelsey said, answering the phone.

"Hey, Kels," Isabella replied. "What did you think of Carmen's email?"

"Hi, Isabella," a voice said through the phone.

Isabella chuckled. "Is that Dana or Emma?"

"It's both of them, actually. We just came in from a hike. I'm going to FaceTime you. It's time for you to meet these brats," Kelsey said.

"Okay," Isabella said, punching the button. She grinned when Kelsey's face appeared. "Hi." Isabella felt her heart skip a beat. *Where did that come from?* She talked to Kelsey just about every day, but those were texts. She watched as Kelsey flipped the camera around.

"This is Dana and that's Emma," Kelsey said, gesturing to the two young women waving into the camera.

"Hi," Dana said. "Give me the phone so we can see Isabella."

A moment later the screen was filled with the girls' faces. "We've been meaning to ask you," Emma began.

"Hey, hey, hey," Kelsey said in a warning voice.

"We want to know what you did to make our mom so happy. Whatever it is, keep doing it," Emma said, glancing up at Kelsey.

"You'll have to ask her because she did the same thing to me. Your mom knows how to have fun!" Isabella said. She wished she could see Kelsey's face because she imagined her cheeks would be red.

"It's easy to have fun when you're with the right person," Dana said. "We're looking forward to March."

"I am, too. I can't wait to show you the islands," Isabella

said. Just then Wyatt walked into the living room from the hallway. "Hey, come here, Wyatt. I want you to meet someone."

Wyatt walked over and plopped down next to Isabella. "This is Wyatt. He's my oldest," Isabella said into the phone. "This is Dana and that's Emma."

"Oh, you're Kelsey's daughters. We get to go on a family vacation with you," Wyatt said.

"That's what I heard. Do you like to snorkel?" Dana asked.

"I've only done it once," Wyatt said.

"Me too. We can learn together," Emma said.

Isabella saw a shy smile grow on his face. "Let me get Gus. You can meet him, too."

He hopped up and left the room and Isabella looked back at the phone. "Are you happy to be home with your mom?"

Dana and Emma exchanged a look and grinned. "Yes. She's sitting right there so we'll never hear the end of it," Dana said. "But we missed her."

Isabella laughed. "You missed a good time. Maybe you should've come with us."

"Told you so!" Kelsey yelled.

"This is my little brother, Gus," Wyatt said, pushing him down on the couch next to Isabella.

"Hi." Gus grinned. "Do you like turtles? I hope we get to see turtles when we go on vacation with you."

"I do like turtles," Emma said, chuckling.

"My mom saw turtles with your mom when they were there for Christmas," Gus said. "Mom brought me a turtle."

"She did?" Dana replied. "We got T-shirts."

"I got a cap," Wyatt said, squeezing next to Gus.

Isabella held the phone so the boys' faces were in view.

She could see Dana and Emma were smiling as they asked the boys about their Christmas gifts. A smile spread across her face. Why shouldn't their kids get along as well as she and Kelsey did? It shouldn't surprise her, but it certainly filled her heart with happiness.

The kids chatted and made plans for the vacation they would take together until Isabella finally took the phone back. "Okay, Kelsey and I need to talk business. Why don't you write down all the things you want to do when we get there?"

"It was nice seeing your face, Isabella," Dana said, handing the phone back to Kelsey.

"Did you hear all that?" Isabella asked as she got up and walked into the kitchen.

"Yes. They were so cute."

"They really were. Are you in your office?"

"I am now," Kelsey said, sitting down in her chair.

"Show me your computer," Isabella said.

"What? Okay."

Isabella waited for Kelsey to turn the camera around and saw their picture sitting beside Kelsey's computer. "I was just checking to make sure our picture was still there."

Kelsey chuckled. "Where else would it be? It's supposed to make me happy when I'm stressed."

"Has it worked?"

"It has. I had a lot to do yesterday and had to juggle several accounts. Your smiling face helped me through it."

Isabella grinned. "I'm glad. So Carmen sent an email with our itinerary for the January trip. I wanted to see what you thought, but if you just came in then you haven't had a chance to see it."

"I'll pull it up now. What did you think about it?" Kelsey asked.

"I think I'm looking forward to lazing on the beach behind our bungalows with you," Isabella said.

"Are you having a hard day?" Kelsey asked, smiling at Isabella.

"Sometimes Spencer is an ass," Isabella replied.

"Well, duh, he'd have to be to let you go," Kelsey said.

Isabella chuckled. Kelsey always knew how to make her smile. "That's right. What an idiot."

"Absolutely," Kelsey said.

"Thanks. That helped," Isabella said. "I think he must be dating someone new because I already made sure he would have the boys while we're gone in January and now he's trying to switch weekends."

"Oh no."

"It's okay. My mom will help out if need be, but I'm not letting him start this now. He knows how important this is for us and Coral Bay," Isabella explained.

"Do we need to switch weekends?" Kelsey asked.

"No, Carmen gave us dates for the first three trips. I sat down with Spencer and we put them in the calendar. He knows the deal."

Kelsey smiled. "Okay. Uh, does him dating someone bother you?"

"Not at all," Isabella said. "I think I've gone on maybe two dates since we've been divorced, but he's been busy in the dating realm. It's fine and I want him to be happy as long as he's thinking about the boys."

"Does he bring his dates around Wyatt and Gus?"

"He hasn't been serious with anyone yet. We agreed to be mindful of how new partners will affect the boys."

"Hey, look at me," Kelsey said.

Isabella looked away from her computer and into the phone.

"Listen," Kelsey said as music began to play through her phone.

Isabella's eyes widened. "That's our song!"

Kelsey chuckled. "Our song?"

"Yes. That's how I think of it now," Isabella explained.

"It won't be long until we're back in our vacation life," Kelsey said as the song continued.

"Will you dance with me when we get there?"

Kelsey nodded. "I can't wait."

"Thanks, Kels. You not only made my days in the islands better, but you're doing it from Denver now, too."

"You'd do the same for me."

Isabella smiled. *I'd do just about anything for you*, she thought.

"I'd better go find something to make us for dinner. These divas of mine can get bitchy when they're hungry," Kelsey said.

Isabella laughed. "I have a couple of those as well, but I call them princes."

Kelsey giggled. "I'll talk to you later."

"Okay. Bye, Kels," Isabella said and ended the call. She sighed and pulled up a picture of them on her phone. What was it about Kelsey Kenny that always managed to brighten her mood?

Isabella was looking forward to their next trip. It would be nice to see everyone again, but she couldn't wait to simply sit with Kelsey and do nothing.

"I like them, Mom," Wyatt said, coming into the kitchen.

"I think we'll have a good time together, don't you?"

"Yeah, they're cool and didn't treat us like little kids," Wyatt replied.

"That's because you're not a little kid, but you'll always

be my little boy," she said, grabbing him and pulling him into her lap.

Wyatt groaned, but let her cuddle him for a moment. "I love you, Mom."

"I love you, Wyatt."

17

Kelsey was looking forward to landing in St. Thomas and going back to the beach. That was where she could put all the work and the stress of this looming project behind her.

It had only been three weeks since she'd seen Isabella. Dana and Emma had stayed with her for almost two weeks, then Kelsey met with all her clients, whether it was via Zoom, phone, or email. She wanted to be sure no problems would come up while she and Isabella were on their first monthly adventure.

She leaned her head back against the airplane seat and smiled. Kelsey had taken extra care to pack for this trip whereas the month before she was content to throw her swimsuits, shorts, and T-shirts in her suitcase. She told herself that she chose particular outfits this time because they would be making videos, but she knew deep down Isabella was the reason she wanted to look nice.

Honestly, she couldn't wait to see her. She'd admitted that to herself this morning as she got ready to leave her house. They talked or texted most days, but she missed the way they walked arm in arm across the resort, and the little nudges they gave each other. Then there was Isabella's smile. She loved to tease Kelsey with what Isabella liked to call her winning smile, but it was the little smiles they exchanged when they shared a look that sometimes took Kelsey's breath away.

When she got on the plane that morning she'd decided to be more aware of the time she and Isabella spent together privately. They were simply good friends, getting to know more about each other and having fun spending time together. Did there need to be more than that?

Kelsey looked at her watch and found that they'd be landing in Charlotte soon. She didn't have to change planes and Isabella would be boarding for the flight to St. Thomas not long after they landed. They had plenty to discuss and planned to start with a video before they took off. Kelsey had things ready to upload to the website and had already posted several notices about the yearlong vacations to the Virgin Islands.

She was pleased to see several comments from people already following their journey. Kelsey checked a few other behind-the-scenes features of the website she'd built in to make sure it was ready to handle the traffic. Soon, the flight attendant asked her to put her laptop away as they prepared to land.

The scenery out the window kept getting closer and closer until the plane touched the runway. Kelsey felt her heart speed up at the thought of seeing Isabella.

It didn't take long for the plane to taxi to the gate and people who weren't continuing to St. Thomas began to get off. Kelsey took out her phone to check her email and texts.

There were texts from both Dana and Emma, then she saw a picture from Isabella.

She was standing at the gate, pointing to the sign that read St. Thomas with that winning smile. Kelsey chuckled at the message below the picture: *Can't wait to see you.*

"I can't wait to see you," Kelsey mumbled. She tried to tell herself she was excited to start this job, but really she was just as excited to see Isabella. Kelsey wondered if they hadn't come up with this idea if she and Isabella would be seeing each other again. She liked to believe they would, that their connection was that strong from the beginning.

"Excuse me ma'am, but you're in my seat."

Kelsey laughed and looked up into Isabella's smiling face. She wanted to play along but couldn't stop herself from jumping up and hugging Isabella. When she pulled away their eyes met and neither of them said anything for a moment. They simply smiled at each other.

"Uh, are you trying to claim the window seat?" Kelsey said, finally finding her voice.

"Come on, you had it all the way from Denver," Isabella replied.

Kelsey chuckled. "You always get your way." She held Isabella's upper arms and squeezed past her until she was standing in the aisle. Kelsey noticed a bag standing next to their row and recognized it as one of Isabella's from their Christmas trip.

"Isn't this yours?"

"Yep."

Kelsey picked it up and put it in the overhead bin. "Did you check your other one?"

"Have a seat," Isabella said, patting the seat next to her. Kelsey sat down while Isabella settled into the window seat.

"You're not going to believe this, but that's the only bag I brought."

Kelsey raised her brows and shook her head. "No way."

"Yep. We're going to show those folks traveling along with us that you don't have to pack a bunch of clothes to have a good time," Isabella explained. "Besides, we only need outfits for three days."

This trip was all about winter at the beach. They were leaving on a Monday, had plans for the next three days, and then would return home on Friday.

"We really only need swimsuits and shorts for this trip," Kelsey said. "The next one will require evening wear."

"Yep. We'll dress up for Valentine's Day."

"I'm so ready to be back at the beach," Kelsey said.

"I had no idea how much work it would take to get ready for this," Isabella said.

"But we're ready." Kelsey took out her phone. "Let's do the first video and I'll post it on the website before we take off. Have you seen all the comments so far?"

"I looked at them before I boarded. We have interest. Now, if we can keep it," Isabella said.

"Give them that winning smile," Kelsey said with a wink.

Isabella chuckled. "You know it."

"Ready?" Kelsey held the phone out so they would both be visible and pressed the record button.

Isabella welcomed their viewers and gave a quick summary of their yearlong fun beginning today. She promised to tell them more about her and Kelsey then gave a rundown of what was happening today.

Kelsey recounted how long the flight would be and what to expect when they got to St. Thomas. One thing they wanted to do was be open and transparent about every trip.

They wanted the public to know what to expect, so when others hopefully joined them in St. Thomas, there would only be happy surprises.

"As our creative director, do you approve?" Kelsey asked as she replayed the video.

Isabella chuckled. "I do. What are you?"

"Hmm," Kelsey said, tilting her head. "I'm the technical director." She quickly uploaded the video to the site and in a few moments it was live.

"Look!" Isabella said. "We already have a few comments."

Kelsey widened her eyes. "People really are watching us."

"That's the idea, Kels," Isabella said with a grin.

"I know, but..."

"But?"

Kelsey shrugged.

"Un-uh, don't do that. People are going to love you. Look how quickly I fell for you," Isabella said.

Kelsey whipped her head around and stared.

Isabella gave her a confused look. "Come on, you fell for me just as fast, right?"

"Right," Kelsey said, willing her heart to slow down. Isabella didn't mean she was in love with Kelsey, just that they'd become friends quickly.

"See!" Isabella grinned. She held her phone up and leaned in until her head was touching Kelsey's. "How can people not love us?" She snapped several selfies then put her phone in her lap. She looked into Kelsey's eyes and smiled.

"What?" Kelsey asked, not sure why Isabella was staring at her.

"I missed you," Isabella said softly.

Kelsey returned her smile. "I missed you, too. It seemed a little crazy since we talked nearly every day."

Isabella reached for Kelsey's hand and intertwined their fingers. "I think we needed each other and that's why we came into each other's lives."

Kelsey furrowed her brow and wasn't sure what to say. Did she need Isabella? More importantly, did Isabella need her?

"I don't care how it happened, but I'm glad it did," Isabella added.

Kelsey smiled. "I am too."

* * *

Once they made it to the resort, Carmen swept them into her office and went over the schedule. They barely had enough time to put their bags in their rooms before they started recording and uploading posts to the website.

For this trip they were staying in one of the hotel rooms that overlooked the beach. The view was incredible and Isabella and Kelsey made it the focus of one of their posts as the sun went down.

"Everything looks good," Kelsey said as she checked on the analytics of the site. They had more and more comments as well as traffic to the website and it was working exactly as Kelsey had designed it.

Isabella chuckled. "Are you surprised? I'm not. You designed it."

Kelsey smiled. "Thanks, Bella."

Isabella sighed. "This is more involved than I thought."

"We'll get better at it," Kelsey said. "For now, I think our content is good. People are commenting and that's what we want."

"I know, but I didn't really enjoy our meal because we were trying to record, eat, edit, and upload it. I was too worried about getting the right angle of the sunset instead of watching it with you," Isabella complained.

Kelsey closed her laptop and walked over to where Isabella stood at the balcony door, staring out at the water. "How about we take a quick walk along the beach before we go to bed?"

Isabella turned around and gazed into Kelsey's soft hazel eyes. "Just for us, no videos?"

"Just for us."

As they left the building and walked out onto the sand, Isabella put her arm through Kelsey's. "Our rooms are nice, but we don't have our little spot behind our bungalows where we talked every evening."

"Let's give our balcony a try," Kelsey said.

"Do you think we'll be able to hear the water?"

"Maybe."

"I sound like a spoiled little brat," Isabella said.

Kelsey chuckled. "We're tired and doing something neither of us has ever done. Tomorrow will be better."

"I'm sure you're right. Let's go sit on your balcony."

"You know, we don't have to do the same things every time we come here," Kelsey said.

Isabella led them back to the building. "I like sitting on the beach with you."

"I like it too, but it may be just as nice sitting on the balcony," Kelsey said. "I'm not sure it matters where we are."

They walked along in silence and Isabella thought about what Kelsey said. It was easy to sit in the dark, listen to the waves, and talk about anything with Kelsey. She wasn't so sure it would be the same someplace else.

"We're still going to Peaches, right?" Isabella said as they got on the elevator.

"Yes!" Kelsey exclaimed. "We're going to Peaches every trip, whether we record from there or not. Those people are our friends."

"Okay, just making sure," Isabella said.

They got off the elevator and walked back into Kelsey's room. Kelsey moved toward the refrigerator and asked, "Do you want something to drink?"

"I'll take a bottle of water," Isabella said, opening the sliding door to the balcony.

Kelsey handed her a bottle of water but not before she turned the light off in the room. "How's that?"

Isabella chuckled. "There's something about sitting in the dark at the beach, isn't there?'

"Yeah, it's soothing," Kelsey said.

"Thanks, Kels. I'm sorry I'm being so bitchy," Isabella said. "I promise I'll be better tomorrow."

"You're not being bitchy. Everything is going great, Bella. Because we're great. Where's that winning smile?"

"It's still here. I'm just resting it," Isabella said, taking a drink of her water.

"Is everything okay with you and Spencer?"

Isabella looked over at Kelsey. "Now what makes you ask that?"

"I don't know, you seem a little frustrated. The only time I've seen you like that is when Spencer is giving you problems."

Isabella sighed. "I'm not really frustrated with him. I just don't get how he goes out with a different woman every weekend."

"He does?"

"That's what my friends tell me. He never wanted to go out much after we had the boys. We had people over to our house or would go to friends' houses, but not very often. Since the divorce he goes out all the time."

"Hmm," Kelsey said. "We've already established that he's an idiot for letting you get away, but maybe he's not as dumb as I thought."

"What are you talking about?" Isabella asked, confused.

"Why would he want to go out when he could spend the evening at home with you? You can't make me believe any of your friends are more interesting than you."

Isabella chuckled. "Kelsey Kenny, you are something else."

Kelsey shrugged. "I've never been married, but if I'm in love with someone then that's the person I'd want to spend most of my time with."

Isabella stared at Kelsey through the darkness. She could see the lights from the resort reflecting in Kelsey's eyes. "Well that explains it then."

"Explains what?" Kelsey asked.

"Why we're a couple," Isabella said. "Don't tell me you've forgotten!"

Kelsey chuckled. "How could I forget that?"

"You make it sound so simple, but it's true. Why wouldn't you want to spend most of your time with the person you love? My next love is going to be like that."

"Next?"

"Yep. This will sound sappy, but I know my true love is waiting for me."

"That's not sappy," Kelsey said. "Maybe it's right here in the Virgin Islands."

Isabella stared at Kelsey as she looked out at the water.

Kelsey slowly turned her gaze to Isabella's and their eyes locked. Isabella could feel her heart beating with Kelsey's. She remembered having the same feeling when they danced together Christmas night on the deck of their bungalow. Isabella had never felt so close to another person and here they were again.

18

Their last day of vacation started on the ferry with a beautiful video of the water on the ride to St. John. They spent the morning riding bicycles around the island and stopped at Trunk Bay Beach to swim and snorkel. Kelsey and Isabella had advised Carmen to save the excursion to Honeymoon Beach for one of the summer weeks so they could highlight destination weddings or honeymoons.

"Well, look who's finally here," Liz said as Kelsey and Isabella walked into Peaches.

"We've got to plan better next time," Kelsey said, giving the older woman a hug.

"We have been so busy we've barely had time to sleep," Isabella said, hugging Liz as well.

"Who needs sleep on a vacation? You can do that when you get home," Liz said, laughing.

"Hey," Alex said, bringing them both a beer and showing them to a table on the patio.

"It's so good to see everyone," Kelsey said.

Riley walked up and joined them at the table. "I've been keeping up with your posts. You're doing such a good job."

"Oh, I hope so," Isabella said. "We're learning as we go."

"Are we being authentic to the islands?" Kelsey asked. "We want to show the parts we love, not just the tourist things."

"I think so," Alex said. "I haven't noticed any negative comments."

"Oh, there are a few, but not about our activities," Isabella said.

"There are always a few people that have to be assholes," Liz said.

"The ones I've seen are talking about affordability. We're going to focus on how to do these trips on a budget as well as more expensive dream vacation options," Kelsey said.

"You're doing just fine. Don't let comments influence what you're trying to achieve. You both know your stuff," Liz said with a smile.

"Thanks, Liz. We missed you!" Isabella exclaimed, putting her arm around Liz and squeezing her shoulder.

"Let's video the beach and the bar so we can put the phones away and enjoy our friends," Kelsey suggested.

"Great idea." Isabella turned to Riley and Alex. "Are you ready?" she asked.

"Us?" Alex asked, her eyes widening.

"Yes, you're the owners and Liz makes the history of the bar so interesting," Isabella said.

"Don't worry, Bella has a way of making it easy," Kelsey said.

"Okay, let's do it," Isabella said as Kelsey took her phone out.

Once they'd completed the videos, Kelsey did a quick

edit then handed the phone to Isabella. "What do you think?"

Isabella watched each video and smiled. Kelsey had captured Liz, Riley, and Alex perfectly. In the last video she and Kelsey explained that they were spending the afternoon at Peaches and would post later from the resort.

Kelsey watched as Isabella replayed the last video with just the two of them in it.

"Is something wrong with that one?" Kelsey asked. "We can do it again."

Isabella smiled and looked over at Kelsey. "There's nothing wrong with it. You look beautiful, Kels," she said softly.

Kelsey's mouth fell open in surprise and Isabella chuckled. "You do," she said. "You took your sunglasses off and your eyes are a sparkling blue-green."

"Your reply is 'thank you,' Kelsey," Liz said, teasing her.

"Uh—um," Kelsey stammered. "Thank you," she said as her cheeks reddened.

Isabella smiled and leaned over until their shoulders touched. "You're adorable when you blush."

"I'm just surprised," Kelsey said, reaching for her beer and trying to calm the butterflies that had erupted in her stomach. "We've been riding bikes and playing at the beach all day. How can I look anything but sandy and shaggy?"

"It's not always about the perfect hair or make-up," Isabella said. "You've got a happy glow about you and that makes you beautiful."

Kelsey smiled at Isabella. She wondered if Isabella had any idea she was the reason for Kelsey's happy glow. Just then two large groups walked into the bar.

"We've been busy this week," Liz said, getting up. "There's a wedding at the resort down the road from us and they've been coming in every afternoon. I'll be back once I get them settled."

Kelsey and Isabella sipped their beers as the volume of talking and laughter rose with the new customers. Riley turned the music up and several people stepped onto the dance floor.

"Maybe we should record some of this," Kelsey said to Isabella over the noise.

"Go ahead," Isabella said. "We'll need to get their permission to use it."

Kelsey nodded and began to video how deftly Alex and Liz worked in tandem at the bar mixing drinks for the newcomers.

"Excuse me," a woman said, walking up to their table. "Are you the women doing the vacation every month? I've been watching your posts."

"We are," Isabella said with a smile.

"I knew it!" the woman exclaimed. "I told my friend I thought it was you. We got here the day after you did and have been checking your posts for ideas on what to do in the islands. We took the same boat you did on your first day and loved it!"

Kelsey and Isabella exchanged a pleased look. "I'm so glad. That's why we're doing this. We want you to have the best time while you're here," Kelsey said.

"We are! What are you drinking? My friends and I want to buy you a round," she said.

Several other people came over to talk to them. Some asked questions, others had comments about what they were doing. Kelsey and Isabella explained why they loved Peaches so much. It turned into one big party.

"I can't believe this," Isabella said as she came back from

the dance floor. "People really are following our adventures."

"It's certainly brought us business this afternoon," Liz said, sitting back down next to Kelsey.

"Everyone is having a great time," Kelsey said, taking a sip of her beer.

"Isabella!" a woman called to her from the dance floor. "Come back and dance with us."

Isabella looked at Kelsey and shrugged.

"Have fun!" Kelsey exclaimed.

"You should come with me," Isabella said, urging Kelsey to join them.

Kelsey smiled and waved Isabella onto the dance floor.

"She wanted you to dance with her," Liz said.

"I think I need another beer or two," Kelsey said with a chuckle.

"Are you two going to admit your feelings for each other on this trip?" Liz asked.

"Excuse me?"

"Oh, come on, Kelsey. We can all see you and Isabella have feelings for each other," Liz said.

"We do. We're friends," Kelsey said.

Liz gave her a stern look. "You know it's more than that, but I get it. You're afraid."

Kelsey took a deep breath and stared at Liz. Was she afraid? Isabella had become such an important part of her life so quickly. She didn't want to lose her or their friendship.

"I have faith you two will figure it out," Liz said. "But right now, your friend needs you to rescue her."

Kelsey followed Liz's gaze and saw Isabella staring at her. She was pleading with her eyes while trying to keep a smile on her face. The woman she was dancing with was clueless, but Kelsey could read the distress in Isabella's eyes. The song ended and Kelsey hopped up and hurried to the dance floor as a slow song began to play.

She reached for Isabella's hand and said, "You promised me the next dance." Kelsey glanced at the woman Isabella had been dancing with and raised her eyebrows.

The woman smiled and walked away. Isabella put her arms around Kelsey's shoulders and gave her a grateful smile. "Thanks. I was getting a little uncomfortable."

Kelsey smiled and put her hands on Isabella's hips. It felt good to hold Isabella in her arms again. Kelsey was sure Liz was probably watching and would give her a smirk if their eyes met.

"I've missed dancing with you at night on the beach," Isabella said.

"I have, too," Kelsey replied.

"I learned something," Isabella said, running her hands across Kelsey's shoulders.

"What's that?"

"I don't want to dance with anyone but you," Isabella said.

Kelsey pulled her head back so she could see into Isabella's eyes. "Why? You looked like you were having fun."

"It was okay, but the only woman I want to put my arms around is you," Isabella said seriously. "I hope that's not weird, but I think you should know that going forward. You have to save me if I get in this situation again."

Kelsey stared at her. *What about me?* she wondered. Who was going to save her? Kelsey's feelings were shifting inside her heart. Yes, Isabella was her friend, but they were becoming more than that.

Kelsey knew Liz could see right through her even though Kelsey kept trying to deny they were more than friends. But she wondered if Isabella knew. Surely not or she wouldn't be dancing with Kelsey, holding her close and telling her things like that. Then Kelsey remembered Isabella said she didn't want to dance with another woman. *Of course!* Isabella was straight. She'd be fine dancing with a man like this.

"Hey," Isabella said, leaning back and looking into Kelsey's eyes. "Why are you so tense?"

"Oh, I was just thinking," Kelsey said.

"Well, stop and enjoy the music with me," Isabella said, squeezing Kelsey's shoulders.

Kelsey let out a deep breath and sank into Isabella's arms. She'd afford herself this moment and savor the memory. Later tonight she'd think all of this through and get control of her emotions.

* * *

They stayed at Peaches longer than they were supposed to and had to adjust their dinner plans once they were back at the resort. It was a good opportunity to show how flexible the islands could be. Instead of continuing the party at the resort, they decided to take a swim in the moonlight and eat a light dinner at the outdoor bar area next to the pool.

"This is so nice," Isabella said, floating on top of the water next to Kelsey. "Good call."

"Thanks," Kelsey said. "I couldn't drink one more beer or dance to one more song. I needed to wind down."

"I didn't want to eat a heavy dinner either," Isabella said.

"I think this will be okay. I guess we'll find out tomorrow when we meet with Carmen before we leave for the airport," Kelsey said.

"This area of the pool is so calming and inviting. It was

obvious in the video. I'm sure we'll have comments when we get out of the pool," Isabella said.

"I still can't believe we met people who have been watching the videos!" Kelsey exclaimed.

"I know! I mean, they were already coming to St. Thomas, but we must have done something right because they kept watching."

Kelsey felt Isabella's little finger graze against hers. She was immediately taken back to the dance floor and warmth spread through her body. *Oh, God!* She moaned to herself. Before, her heart would speed up and Kelsey could control that, but now her body was betraying her as she felt a tug low in her belly.

"I know, isn't this nice," Isabella said softly.

Kelsey pulled herself up as her feet reached for the bottom of the pool. Isabella had no idea what she was doing to Kelsey.

"Where are you going?" Isabella asked. "I thought you liked this."

Isabella had mistaken Kelsey's moan for pleasure when it was meant as a rebuke to her disloyal body. Kelsey sighed. "I'm one big wrinkle," she said, walking up the steps and out of the pool to where their towels were waiting on a nearby chair.

Kelsey began to dry off as Isabella climbed out of the pool.

"Can you believe we did it?" Isabella said, reaching for her towel. "We've made it through the first month. All we have to do is a video or two on the trip home tomorrow."

Kelsey continued to dry off.

"Kels," Isabella said, grabbing Kelsey's hand. "What's wrong? You've been quiet since we left Peaches."

Kelsey sighed. "I've been thinking about the women at

Peaches. When we come back on Valentine's Day, we should do videos from the bar here or maybe a bar in St. Thomas."

"Why?"

"Because those were gay women, Bella. It's great to be gay friendly, but we don't want to give the wrong impression about us."

"The wrong impression?" Isabella said. "We're two friends having a good time and we just happened to be dancing together."

Kelsey stared at her. "How many of your friends do you dance with, Bella?" She didn't want to upset Isabella, but she needed to be honest with her.

19

Isabella realized she was still holding Kelsey's hand. She could hear her mother's voice echoing in her head: *You were dancing in a bar with a gay woman. It might matter to her.*

Kelsey gave her a sad smile. "I know, Bella. You haven't danced with any of your friends. To you and me, we're just Bella and Kels, having a good time. But now we have to worry about how it looks for the resort."

"Are you saying you don't want to dance with me anymore?" Isabella asked. Why did the thought of that make her heart hurt? And why was there a burning sensation in her stomach?

"No." Kelsey shook her head. "I love dancing with you, but we should probably only do it at Peaches until we're through with this project."

Isabella nodded and searched Kelsey's eyes. They were golden brown and there was something else there that she couldn't read.

"Don't be upset, Bella," Kelsey said with compassion in

her voice. "You don't have to worry about things like this, but I've had to all my life."

"I'm sorry," Isabella said. "I never meant to make you feel uncomfortable."

"You didn't!" Kelsey exclaimed. She pulled them over to sit down in one of the lounge chairs.

Isabella looked into Kelsey's eyes once again. "Since the moment we met in the airport last month I felt a connection to you. I instantly felt comfortable with you, like we'd been friends forever."

Kelsey nodded. "I did, too."

"We were both here alone and no one knew us. I never thought twice about what other people thought of us."

Kelsey chuckled. "I didn't either."

"But now you're saying we need to," Isabella said.

Kelsey sighed. "Ugh, I'm not sure what I'm saying."

Isabella sat back in her chair. "Let's check the comments and talk to Carmen about it tomorrow. I don't want to stop going to Peaches."

"I don't either. They're our friends. We simply need to be more aware. That's all I'm saying," Kelsey said.

"Does that mean no more teasing about being a couple?" Isabella asked, raising her eyebrows. "What about walking around with my arm through yours? Friends do that." Isabella met Kelsey's eyes and wondered what she was thinking.

"I'm sorry, Bella. Did I just screw this up?"

Isabella could see Kelsey was frustrated. "You haven't screwed anything up. I understand what you're trying to say. At least I think I do," she said. "If it looks like we're in a relationship, then some people will tune out. We need to be two single moms going on a vacation. Right?"

Kelsey nodded.

"Okay, but we're also friends and we do work well together. Wouldn't you agree?"

"We do," Kelsey said.

"Next month is the Valentine's trip. We need to think about how we want to approach that."

"I think we need to do some things that friends would do and then also romantic things couples would do," Kelsey said.

"I've got an idea," Isabella said with a tentative smile. "Let's tell our followers that we'll choose two couples when we get here. One can go with us on a romantic excursion and the other can do the friends thing with us."

Isabella watched as Kelsey mulled over her idea. Isabella was the more spontaneous one and she'd come to love this contemplative part of Kelsey. She'd furrow her brow with concentration and then a smile would play across her lips. Isabella waited and kept looking for the smile.

"Well?" she finally asked.

"I think that might work. Do we get a straight couple and a gay couple?" Kelsey mused.

"We could." Isabella nodded. "Young or old?"

"Hmm." Kelsey stared at her.

"There's so many things to consider," Isabella said. "All because I like to dance with you."

Kelsey shrugged. "I like dancing with you, too."

Isabella smiled. That was a relief. She felt like there was something else going on between them. Something had shifted and Isabella wasn't sure what it was.

"Are we okay?" she asked Kelsey. At that moment Isabella had such a strong desire to reach for Kelsey. She wanted to hold her in her arms the way they did when they were dancing. That's where nothing else mattered and when she'd been the happiest during both of their trips to the

Virgin Islands. This realization stunned Isabella, but also amazed her. *My God, am I attracted to Kelsey?*

Kelsey smiled. "Yeah, Bella. We're okay," she replied.

Isabella couldn't tear her eyes away from Kelsey's. She could feel her heart pounding in her chest and she couldn't breathe. Isabella leaned over and slid her arms around Kelsey's shoulders, pulling her into a hug.

She felt Kelsey's arms tighten across her back and for a moment they stayed that way. Isabella closed her eyes and let Kelsey's warmth surround her. She could feel Kelsey's hot breath against her bare shoulder along with other sensations she hadn't felt since before her divorce.

A sudden feeling of panic raced through Isabella and she pulled away. "Sorry," she said breathlessly.

Kelsey scoffed. "For what? Giving me a much needed hug after I made things weird?"

Isabella tilted her head. "You didn't make things weird."

She could see the relief on Kelsey's face and was so confused. Her thoughts flew back to Peaches when she was dancing with the other woman. It was fun at first, but then Isabella didn't know what she'd do if the next song was a slow song. Kelsey was the only woman she wanted to dance close with. When her eyes met Kelsey's it was as if she knew the distress Isabella was feeling and came to her rescue. Isabella's fears were gone when Kelsey's arms went around her and the music began to play.

"I've heard that song we danced to at Christmas," Isabella said, not sure where the comment came from.

"I have too and I thought about you every time," Kelsey said with a smile.

Isabella studied Kelsey for a moment. "I think dancing to that song is how we should end our monthly trips. It's just for us, no one else."

Kelsey narrowed her gaze then smiled. "I like that idea. Let's go."

Isabella gathered their things and they walked to the elevator. It had been a strange end to their evening, but holding Kelsey and being in her arms would hopefully bring them back to their easy, laid-back friendship. She had all month to figure out these feelings for Kelsey she was suddenly very aware of. Every time she looked at Kelsey she couldn't help but wonder what she was thinking.

* * *

They got off the elevator and Kelsey caught Isabella staring at her once again. She had made things weird between them even though Isabella said she hadn't. But Kelsey was just thinking about the resort and the job they had to do, wasn't she? Oh, who was she kidding. She needed to put some distance between her and Isabella until she could get her emotions in check, yet the idea of saying goodbye to her tomorrow was already leaving a hole in her heart.

"Let me change out of my swimsuit and I'll be over in a minute," Isabella said, stopping at her door.

"Okay. I have enough wine left for each of us to have a glass," Kelsey said, unlocking her door.

She quickly changed and poured the rest of the wine into two glasses. Kelsey took a sip then looked into the mirror next to the door.

Her thoughts had been all over the place since they'd left Peaches. *Do I have feelings for Isabella? Does she have feelings for me? What is really going on between us? Does it matter? Would it ruin this friendship? Do we have a future?*

"Stop!" she said to her reflection. *Isabella.* Just the

thought of her made Kelsey smile. "Forget about all of this and enjoy the rest of the trip," she said quietly.

A knock at the door brought Kelsey's attention away from all the doubts and thoughts running through her head.

"Hey," she said with a smile as she opened the door for Isabella.

"Were you talking to someone?" Isabella asked.

"Yes, to myself," Kelsey admitted. She walked over and handed Isabella the other glass of wine. "I'm sorry things got a little strange earlier. Let's go back to you and me and enjoy the rest of this trip."

Isabella smiled. "I think we're both feeling the stress and pressure from this undertaking. We can do this if we stick together."

"To sticking together," Kelsey said, clinking her glass to Isabella's.

"I've got you, Kels," Isabella replied.

They both took a sip and Kelsey smiled. "We're a couple."

Isabella chuckled. "That's usually my line."

"I know, but you need to hear me say it."

"How do you do that?"

"Do what?" Kelsey asked, opening the door to the balcony.

"You're right, I did need to hear you say it. And you knew I needed your help on the dance floor at Peaches," Isabella said.

Kelsey shrugged. "You had a rather desperate look in your eyes."

Isabella smiled and sat down in one of the chairs. "You know, I forget that you're gay and someone might spark your interest at Peaches. I take up all your time."

Kelsey sat down next to her. "No you don't. What about you? I see heads turning in your direction wherever we go."

"I am not interested in turning heads," Isabella said.

Kelsey smirked. "Well, you do it quite well."

"What makes you so sure they're looking at me? You know who walks into those places right next to me. It's you," Isabella said, playfully slapping Kelsey's arm.

Kelsey chuckled. This felt right. They were back to their playful banter. When she glanced at Isabella her face was relaxed and a soft smile lit her sparkling blue eyes.

Isabella must have felt Kelsey staring because she looked over at her, and reached for her hand. "We're okay," she said quietly.

Kelsey squeezed her hand and they both gazed out over the water. They stayed like that as they finished their wine and listened to the surf gently meet the sand.

"How about that dance?" Isabella said as she set her wine glass on the table.

Kelsey got up, reached for her phone, and pulled up their song. She smiled at Isabella and opened her arms.

Instead of putting her arms around Kelsey's neck like she usually did, Isabella snaked her hands around Kelsey's middle and smiled. "We don't have to do everything the same way, right?"

Kelsey chuckled at her own words from the beginning of this trip and put her arms around Isabella's shoulders. She was a little taller than Isabella and ran one hand across her back. Before she realized what she was doing, Kelsey's other hand was gliding through Isabella's hair where it hung down her back.

Her hand stilled at the intimate gesture and Isabella didn't seem to notice. Kelsey took a deep breath and tried to relax in Isabella's arms.

"It's okay," Isabella whispered, pulling Kelsey a little closer. "It's just us."

Kelsey closed her eyes and rested her cheek against Isabella's hair as the song began to play again. They slowly moved to the music and their breaths began to come at the same time. Kelsey could feel her heart settle into a rhythm she was pretty sure matched Isabella's. With every beat the doubts from earlier, the fear Liz mentioned, and the uncertainty of the next few months washed away.

It was just them, the music, and the waves.

20

Kelsey glanced over at Isabella as she feverishly tapped her keyboard.

"Anything else?" Isabella asked.

"I think that's it," Kelsey said. "I'm glad Carmen changed next month's trip from Valentine's Day to the month of love."

"Yeah, I like the idea of keeping our trips to about the same week every month. Coming back for Valentine's Day would've been too soon," Isabella said.

"Does it make it easier for the boys' schedule?" Kelsey asked.

Isabella nodded. "Yeah, they're back and forth between mine and Spencer's house a lot as it is, but this makes it easier for me to schedule with Spencer."

"The boys will be happy to see you today," Kelsey said.

"Yeah, I miss the little terrors."

Kelsey laughed. "They're not terrors."

"That's because you talk to them on the phone when they want something."

"What do they want from me?" Kelsey asked.

"They are always asking about you and the girls. They want to know when we all get to go on vacation together."

"I'm looking forward to that, too."

"Are you sure you want to spend several days with two little kids? You've already raised yours," Isabella said.

"That doesn't matter. I suspect the boys are excited to spend time with Dana and Emma. They'll have someone to play with," Kelsey said.

Isabella chuckled. "I think we're fun to play with."

Kelsey smiled. "Do you think we could figure out a way to see Liz, Riley, and Alex more than just once each trip?"

"Oh, so that's where you want to play," Isabella said, wiggling her eyebrows at Kelsey.

"Ha ha," Kelsey deadpanned. "It's not that. If we were coming here on our own—"

"We'd be over there all the time," Isabella said, finishing her sentence.

"Yeah, we would."

Isabella tapped on her keyboard once again and closed her laptop just as the flight attendant asked her to put it away to prepare for landing.

Kelsey gazed at Isabella and frowned. "It's back to our everyday lives."

"Yeah. I know every trip won't be the same, but some things will. I'm walking you to your gate and waiting until you board your flight," Isabella said.

Kelsey grinned. "Okay. I'll send you a picture of me when I get to my seat."

"And you'll call me when you get home," Isabella added.

Kelsey nodded. Things between them were back to their casual playful ways since their dance last night. They'd had a meeting with Carmen that morning to go over the highs and lows of the trip. Kelsey and Isabella had each given her their concerns about next month's trip and how they wanted to portray the resort as well as the islands.

They had come to an agreement to wait until the week after Valentine's Day for the next trip. Carmen was very pleased with the first trip and the buzz Isabella and Kelsey had created so far.

Kelsey had begun to feel a cloud of melancholy descend over her the closer they got to Charlotte. She remembered feeling much the same the last time they'd done this. It surprised her in that she knew she'd be seeing Isabella again in a matter of weeks. They would talk and text just as they had the last month.

She was supposed to be feeling relieved to have the opportunity to put some space between them until she could figure out these feelings that kept getting stronger. But that was far from what she was feeling or wanted to do.

Kelsey reached over and squeezed Isabella's hand. "I'll miss you," she said quietly.

Isabella looked over at her and smiled. "I know."

Kelsey raised her eyebrows and chuckled. "You know!"

Isabella chuckled. "Yes, because I already miss you." She sat up and looked at Kelsey. "What is wrong with us?"

Kelsey stared into Isabella's bright blue eyes. "I know I can text or call you anytime, but there's something about seeing this pretty face." Kelsey reached over and grabbed Isabella's cheeks with her hands.

Isabella laughed and put her hands on Kelsey's, holding them there.

The plane landed and once they were through the walkway, Isabella fell into step next to Kelsey.

"You don't have to go to baggage claim this time," Kelsey commented as Isabella put her arm through hers.

"Nope."

"How was it only taking one bag?"

"It was okay. You're teaching me your laid back ways, Kels."

Kelsey chuckled. On this trip there were times when she'd felt anything but casual around Isabella. The woman could make her heart pound with a look or that soft smile.

"Here we are," Isabella said as they stopped at Kelsey's gate. "It looks like they're already boarding."

"I wonder how Carmen does that?" Kelsey said.

"I don't know." Isabella shrugged. "I'd stay with you until you're on the plane anyway."

Kelsey sighed. "You know you don't have to do that."

"But I want to," Isabella said then she gasped. "One of these days you need to stay an extra day with me and the boys."

Kelsey raised her eyebrows. "That sounds like fun. Maybe you and the boys can come out to Denver to visit us."

The gate attendant announced the next group to board.

"That's me," Kelsey said.

"Don't forget—"

"I'll text you a picture and call you when I get home," Kelsey said.

Isabella smiled and reached up to put her arms around Kelsey's neck. Kelsey closed her eyes and sank into the moment as they hugged.

They began to pull away and Isabella said quietly, "Some things stay the same."

Kelsey felt Isabella's lips touch hers. It was a brief kiss, yet it was soft and sure. The first time Isabella had done this Kelsey could feel the uncertainty and timidness. Not this time. It was over almost as quickly as it had begun, but Kelsey's lips tingled where Isabella's had touched hers.

"See you next month," Isabella said.

Kelsey watched a soft smile turn to a hint of a smirk on Isabella's face.

"See you next month," Kelsey replied with a smile of her own. She walked towards the tunnel to board the plane, but turned to get one more look at Isabella.

She was standing there, giving Kelsey her winning smile.

All Kelsey could do was smile back as her heart pounded in her chest and warmth raced through her body. *Good luck getting your emotions in check.*

* * *

Isabella stared at the picture Kelsey had texted her. She had just called to let Isabella know she'd made it home safely. Neither of them mentioned the kiss and Isabella didn't know what she would've said if Kelsey had brought it up.

She smiled and ran her finger along Kelsey's cheek in the picture. "What have you done to me?" she murmured. Isabella rested her head on the back of the couch and closed her eyes. She couldn't remember a single time when she'd been attracted to another woman. There had been friends growing up, in college and before she got married. She had been close to a lot of women at different times in her life.

But she'd never felt like this. The first time she'd kissed Kelsey it had been spontaneous. She had felt so uneasy and tense, but as soon as their lips touched all was in balance again. Isabella remembered thinking their hearts were having a moment.

This time Isabella knew she was going to kiss Kelsey. Although it was a little unfair to Kelsey, Isabella had to know what this attraction she was suddenly feeling was all about. She thought Kelsey would be surprised once again, but when she pulled away, Kelsey was smiling and her eyes sparkled.

Isabella scoffed. Is this attraction really all that sudden? She looked back at the picture and Kelsey's smile. "The bigger question is," she said quietly, "what's going on in your heart, Kelsey Kenny?"

Isabella sighed and put her phone down. *What am I doing?*

* * *

Three weeks later Isabella and Kelsey were back in the Virgin Islands. They had done the romantic Valentine's Day events with two lucky couples which earned them an afternoon to themselves and of course they wanted to spend it at Peaches.

Isabella lazed on the beach in a lounge chair with Riley next to her. They were watching Kelsey and Alex paddle board in the water behind the bar.

"I saw your posts about the day of romance yesterday," Riley said.

"It was something," Isabella replied. "Carmen surprised two couples who were staying at the resort. We took them for a day of fun at the beach, and then Sylvie took each couple on their own romantic tour of the island."

"Oh, I'm sure they loved that."

"It was challenging for Kelsey and me because we needed the videos, but we didn't want to infringe on their romantic day too much," Isabella explained.

"What did they do for dinner?" Riley asked.

"They each had a private beach dinner, complete with a serenade and music. It was so romantic," Isabella said.

"After that, one couple decided to go to the club at the resort and dance. The other couple stayed on the beach."

"Did you have to stay with them?"

"No. We took a couple of quick videos then Kelsey and I had a working dinner with Carmen. It was the longest day," Isabella said.

"Do you have everything figured out for your next month?" Riley asked.

"Yep. Sylvie took us around to several beaches. We're doing three days of parties at different beaches for the spring break trip. I hope I can last," Isabella said.

Riley chuckled. "Oh, come on. You can still hang with a bunch of twenty year olds."

"We're going to spend one day here. Kelsey and I plan to sit on the patio at the bar and watch them have fun."

"You'll have a good view with plenty to post and video," Riley said. "This part of the beach will be one big party."

"Perfect," Isabella said as she watched Kelsey. "We want to spend more time with all of you."

"Do you go back tomorrow?"

"Yeah, this was a quick trip. We did one day with the couples and today was for us to get everything planned for the next trip."

"You'll be here longer next month?" Riley asked.

"Yes, we're trying to make each trip a little different. Some are longer than others. This one is the shortest. We'll do one of these again later in the year," Isabella explained as she watched Kelsey paddle boarding. She couldn't keep from smiling at how easily Kelsey navigated the small waves bringing her back to the shore.

"Hey, Riley, have you always been attracted to women?" Isabella had decided to come on this trip and figure out this attraction to Kelsey. This was new for her. She had no idea what she was doing and had no one to talk to about it.

"Yeah. It took me a minute to figure it out when I was a teenager," Riley replied. "How about you?"

Isabella sighed. "I've never thought about another woman that way..."

"Until Kelsey?"

Isabella looked over at Riley and widened her eyes. "Am I that obvious?"

"No, but you have been watching her rather closely all afternoon." Riley chuckled.

"I mean, look at her!" Isabella exclaimed.

"The woman paddling with her caught my eye," Riley teased.

Isabella chuckled. "Alex is a beautiful woman, but Kelsey..." She sighed. "I don't know when or how it happened. One minute we were laughing and having a good time as friends and the next my heart was pounding and I was weak in the knees."

"I'm sure she feels the same way," Riley said.

Isabella whipped her head around and stared. "What?"

"Have you talked to her about it?" Riley asked.

"No!" Isabella exclaimed. "I wouldn't know what to say. Besides, I don't think she feels the same way."

"Why do you think that?"

Isabella shrugged. "I don't know. The last time we were here she said we had to be more careful of the impression we gave our followers. I hadn't even considered it, but she's right. We're two single moms showing folks how wonderful the resort is and how to vacation in the islands."

"Hmm, I can see how that's important, but..." Riley trailed off.

"But what?"

"You look and act like a couple and Kelsey knows that," Riley said with a smile. "Maybe she is feeling the same and doesn't know how you feel."

Isabella gasped and looked at Riley in surprise. "You think? Oh my God!"

21

Riley chuckled and shook her head. "Don't you remember when we first met you? We thought the two of you were together."

Isabella sat back against her chair. "If Kelsey feels the same way then she must be thinking about the resort and the trips we've planned for the year. Just imagine how we could mess that up!"

"Why would it mess things up?"

"It could make things awkward. Our followers might not trust us since we didn't say anything in the beginning. We didn't tell Carmen. I could go on and on," Isabella said, panic rising in her voice.

"You could also show folks how romantic it is here and how things happen," Riley said suggestively.

"Do you mean a fling? Oh no," Isabella protested. "Kelsey is not a fling type of person." She paused then added, "I may be the spontaneous one, but I'm not like that either. There has to be more."

Riley raised her eyebrows. "Are you trying to tell me there's not already something there? You're lying to yourself, my friend. You dance together every time you come to the bar and you're always walking arm in arm."

Isabella narrowed her gaze. "Kelsey mentioned the same thing. She asked me if I had danced with my other friends."

Riley gave her a knowing smile. "There's only one person I slow dance with."

Isabella nodded. "Alex."

"Talk to her," Riley suggested.

"I'm so afraid it will make things weird," Isabella murmured as she watched Kelsey. Then she remembered Kelsey thinking she'd made things weird on their last trip. They'd talked things through then danced to their song and everything felt right. *Their song!* Did friends have a song?

"What is it?"

"I was just remembering something from our last trip. I think I know what to do and it's not talking," Isabella said to herself more so than Riley.

* * *

Kelsey and Isabella walked arm and arm back to their bungalows after dinner.

"I guess since this was such a quick trip Carmen let us have our bungalows this time," Isabella said.

"I'm glad. My favorite part of our trips is sitting and talking with you at the end of the night," Kelsey said.

"Really? I thought you liked Peaches and our friends," Isabella said.

"I do, but this is my favorite."

"Well," Isabella said and squeezed Kelsey's arm a little tighter, "my favorite is our last dance of the night with the ocean providing background music."

Kelsey opened her front door. "Let's do our favorite thing."

They went inside and Kelsey poured them each a glass of wine. On this trip they hadn't had much alone time and Kelsey had been able to control her feelings. She was very aware of every time she and Isabella touched or exchanged a look and nothing seemed out of the ordinary.

Kelsey handed Isabella her wine and they went out on the back deck. A breeze was blowing off the water and the sound of the waves greeted them.

"This feels like home," Kelsey said.

"I know you don't mean Denver." Isabella chuckled.

"It's too quiet at my house without the girls now. I don't know what it is about being here with you, but it feels more like home than Denver does."

"I know what you mean, Kels. When the boys are at Spencer's my house feels empty," Isabella said.

"I never feel empty when I'm here," Kelsey said.

Isabella smiled and set her glass on the table. "Let's dance."

When Kelsey met Isabella's gaze her heart immediately began to speed up. She licked her lips and found her mouth had gone dry. It only took a moment for Kelsey to pull up their song and put it on repeat. She held out her arms and waited.

Isabella gasped. "Are you letting me lead?"

Kelsey dropped her chin. "You always do."

Isabella chuckled and put her arms around Kelsey's neck. That little chuckle had become one of Kelsey's favorite tunes. She put her hands on Isabella's hips and pulled her close.

How many times had they done this? They tried to

convince each other that this was just two friends enjoying a dance, but that had never been true.

The last notes of the song wafted around them. Kelsey knew they'd start again, but then she felt Isabella's fingers playing with the hair at the nape of her neck. It sent delicious shivers through her body and Kelsey choked back a moan. She could feel Isabella's breath just below her ear followed by the softest touch of her lips.

This time Kelsey couldn't stop the low moan from escaping her throat. Isabella pulled her head back and their eyes met. She cupped Kelsey's face with both her hands and they simply stared into each other's eyes.

Isabella looked down at Kelsey's lips then back into her eyes. Kelsey saw Isabella's eyes start to flutter closed just as their lips touched ever so softly.

This wasn't one of their airport kisses. This kiss was soft yet firm. Any uncertainty Kelsey may have felt before was gone. Isabella was kissing her and Kelsey was kissing her back.

Kelsey kept her lips pressed to Isabella's, assuring this wasn't a brief encounter like the ones before. She took the time to sink into Isabella's pillowy lips and marveled at how perfectly they fit together.

Then the kiss came to life. They caressed, they nibbled, they nipped each other's lips. Their breaths added to the symphony the music and waves created around them.

Isabella's arms slipped around Kelsey's shoulders, pulling her closer and keeping their lips locked together. Kelsey groaned and heard the sweetest sigh bubble from Isabella.

Before Kelsey could think about what she was doing, her tongue slid across Isabella's lower lip and an electric charge shot through her.

Isabella immediately parted her lips and when their tongues touched Kelsey melted into Isabella's arms. They may have started out dancing, but their tongues now took this intimate dance to another level.

"Mmm," Isabella moaned.

"Bella," Kelsey whispered as she trailed kisses over Isabella's jaw and down her neck. But she wanted Isabella's lips. She crushed her lips to Isabella's bringing on another round of moans and groans.

Their tongues tangled as their lips caressed and their arms once again tightened around each other. Kelsey could hear her own pulse pounding in her ears and felt Isabella's staccato beat when her lips once again kissed her neck.

Isabella tangled her fingers in Kelsey's hair then rested her hands on her cheeks once again. She stared into Kelsey's eyes. "Don't say anything," she said softly. "Just keep kissing me."

Kelsey knew doubts would flood in eventually for both of them, but Isabella was simply saying not yet.

With a soft smile, it was Kelsey's turn to cup Isabella's beautiful face with her hands. She tenderly touched her lips to Isabella's then deepened the kiss to a chorus of moans from them both.

Kelsey tried to keep all thoughts out of her head and simply feel, but she couldn't escape the idea that these were the lips she'd been waiting to kiss all her life. That was a little grand, but she couldn't chase the thought away.

Isabella's arms tightened around Kelsey's middle and once again Kelsey had the most overwhelming feeling of being home. She kissed Isabella with all the feelings she'd been trying to hide.

When their lips finally parted, Isabella put her finger

over Kelsey's lips. "Don't say anything," she whispered. "I can't talk about this yet."

Kelsey nodded. She still had her hands on Isabella's upper arms and kept them there.

"I know I've complicated everything," Isabella began.

"Bella, you may have kissed me first, but I kissed you back," Kelsey said.

Isabella exhaled. "Yeah, you did," she said dreamily, with a hint of a smile. "I'll see you in the morning."

Kelsey felt a sudden emptiness as Isabella stepped away from her.

"Promise me something, Kels," Isabella said, turning around.

"What's that?"

"Don't quit."

"Quit?" Kelsey asked, confused.

"I know you were unsure about this marketing project from the beginning, but promise me you won't give up on it," Isabella said.

Kelsey nodded. "I promise. I won't quit the project and I won't give up." She watched Isabella leave her deck and walk through the back door of her own bungalow.

Kelsey had never considered quitting the project, but what Isabella didn't know is that she wasn't giving up on them. Yes, they both had a lot to think about and Kelsey wasn't sure what this meant for them, but one thing she was sure of was that she wanted Isabella Burns in her life.

The next morning they rolled their suitcases into the lobby of the resort and were discussing breakfast when Carmen cornered them.

"I've made some arrangements for next month. I want

the girls to stay together in one room like most of the young people who come here for spring break do. Very few of them can afford their own room for the week and it's one big party anyway."

"Okay," Kelsey said. "The girls will like that."

"I have a couple of other things to show you," Carmen said, leading them to her office.

Kelsey looked over at Isabella and she smiled then shrugged.

By the time Carmen finished with them they had to leave for the airport. She walked them out the front door just as Sylvie drove up.

"I'm your ride," she said with a smile. "I have to pick up some folks at the airport."

"Thanks," Kelsey said, getting in the back of the Jeep. She'd hoped to talk to Isabella on the way to the airport, but not now.

Isabella met Kelsey's eyes and smiled at her as she climbed into the front of the Jeep. Kelsey was trying to keep her anxiety at bay and wondered if Isabella felt the same way. She hadn't noticed Isabella having any trouble meeting her gaze that morning so she took that as a good sign. Honestly, Kelsey wasn't sure what to think, but knew she would give Isabella whatever time and space she needed.

Once they made it to the airport they said their goodbyes to Sylvie and Kelsey turned to Isabella. "Coffee?"

"Yes, please," Isabella said with a hint of desperation.

Kelsey gave the barista their orders and they found seats at their gate along with the other travelers.

"This isn't the ideal place to talk, and honestly, Kels," Isabella began, "I'm not ready."

"Okay," Kelsey said quietly, taking a sip of her coffee.

"I want to say one thing though."

Kelsey raised her eyebrows and listened.

"I've never danced with any of my friends and I've never been attracted to another woman."

Kelsey winced. "But you are now?" she asked tentatively.

Isabella playfully smacked Kelsey on the arm. "Yes! To you! I wouldn't have been kissing you like that last night if I wasn't."

Kelsey sighed in relief.

"My mom pointed out something to me when I got home from our Christmas trip," Isabella said. "I've always done what was expected of me. I did all the activities in school, went to college, and made good grades. I married a man and had kids." Isabella took a deep breath. "She said it was time for me to do what makes me happy."

"That's good advice," Kelsey said.

"I know I have complicated everything, Kels."

"You said that last night and no, you haven't," Kelsey said. "You do remember that I kissed you."

"Yeah you did," she said, a little breathless. Isabella smiled. "I don't know if this is our vacation life and our everyday life coming together. I want to go home and think all this through."

"Okay," Kelsey said. "But it's my turn to say one thing. Since I got home from our trip at Christmas I haven't been able to get you out of my mind. I look forward to our trips each month and can't wait for the family trip this summer."

"You do?"

Kelsey nodded. "Will you do something for me?"

"Of course," Isabella replied.

"Don't make your mind up about anything until we get to talk again."

"I won't," Isabella said.

The gate attendant announced it was their turn to board and as they got in line Isabella put her arm through Kelsey's.

On the flight home they discussed the trip and took notes as they'd done before.

The melancholic cloud descended the closer they got to Charlotte, but Kelsey reached for Isabella's hand, holding onto the last minutes of their island time until the plane landed.

"I'm walking you to your gate," Isabella said as they deplaned.

"I'll send you a picture when I'm seated and call you when I get home," Kelsey replied.

As they stopped at Kelsey's gate, she noticed her group was already boarding. She led Isabella away from the line of travelers and next to a wall. No one bothered to give them a look.

"Some things stay the same," Kelsey said. She opened her arms and Isabella walked into them.

"I'll miss you," Isabella said softly. She pulled away and kissed Kelsey on the cheek.

This time Kelsey kissed Isabella. It wasn't their usual brief airport kiss. She pressed her lips to Isabella's and gave their hearts time to whisper goodbye. When she pulled away she watched Isabella open her eyes then smile.

"See you next month," Isabella said.

"See you next month," Kelsey replied.

She walked to the attendant and showed her boarding pass, then turned to smile at Isabella one more time. *What are we going to do now?*

22

Isabella nervously waited to board her flight to St. Thomas. She knew Kelsey was on the plane waiting for her, but so were her daughters with a couple of friends in tow.

They had texted and talked on the phone nearly every day since returning from the Valentine's trip. Kelsey was patient and never asked Isabella if she was ready to talk. A couple of times things felt a little awkward as they planned the next month's trip, but Kelsey found a way to ease them right back to their easygoing friendship. She told Isabella that what had happened between them was too important to talk about on the phone. It needed to be a face-to-face conversation so nothing could be misunderstood.

Isabella agreed with her and they hoped to find time to be alone that evening after they got the girls settled. Her greatest fear was losing Kelsey. If all they could be was friends then that would have to be enough for Isabella. In a few short months Kelsey had become the most important person in her life aside from her boys.

She sighed and shook her head as she laughed at

herself. Isabella had envisioned getting back to her everyday life and the thought of that kiss would fade. Part of her thought she and Kelsey had just gotten caught up in the occasion. After all, they were at a romantic resort and celebrating a month of love.

Forget that kiss? She couldn't stop thinking about their kisses. If it wouldn't get them kicked off the plane, Isabella would grab Kelsey and kiss her as soon as she laid eyes on her!

There was no doubt in Isabella's mind or heart that she wanted Kelsey Kenny, but there was so much more to it than that. How did Kelsey feel? Isabella had never been with a woman. What did this mean for their big marketing strategy and the resort? The questions kept coming.

Isabella sighed. All she wanted was to see Kelsey. Somehow she knew just being with her would make everything manageable.

"Finally!" she murmured as she showed her boarding pass and walked down the tunnel to the plane. She smiled at the flight attendant and started down the aisle.

When she made it to her row she stopped. The aisle seat was vacant and Kelsey sat in the middle seat, leaving the window seat for her. Isabella could see an anxious look on Kelsey's face, but before she could say anything, Kelsey looked up with anticipation.

The most beautiful smile grew on her face as Kelsey stood up. Isabella grabbed her and hugged her like her life depended on it.

"Uh, I hope you're Isabella," a woman said from the row across from them. "Or my mom has a secret girlfriend she hasn't told us about."

Isabella laughed but didn't immediately let Kelsey go.

She winked then turned to the woman. "It wouldn't be a secret if you knew."

The woman raised her eyebrows while her seatmates began to laugh.

"Duh, Dana. I know you recognize me from our phone calls and pictures," Isabella said. "Where's Emma?"

"Right here!" she exclaimed, coming up the aisle from the restroom.

Kelsey shook her head and chuckled. "These are my girls."

Isabella chuckled. "I'm so happy to finally meet you in person." Isabella gave each of them a quick hug.

"The flight attendant is giving us looks," Kelsey said in a quiet voice. "I saved the window seat for you."

Isabella smiled at Kelsey and felt her heart speed up. From the moment they'd met, Kelsey Kenny had been doing nice things for her.

"Wait!" Dana exclaimed. "Isabella, this is Lily and this is Grace," she said, pointing to the two girls sitting next to her.

"Hi." Isabella shook each of their hands and smiled. "We're going to have so much fun."

Kelsey took Isabella's bag and placed it in the overhead bin. "Is this the only one?"

"Yep," Isabella said, plopping down in her seat. "I learned from the best."

Kelsey chuckled and sat down next to her.

"Surprise, surprise. We only brought one bag each, too," Emma said, sitting down next to her mother.

"Don't be fooled, girls. Your momma is full of surprises," Isabella said, looking into Kelsey's eyes.

"Ha!" Dana said sarcastically. "I'll believe it when I see it."

"Rule number one," Isabella said, leaning over so she

could see all four girls. "I'm the only one who gets to tease your mom. We're partners and we stick together."

"Okay, okay," Dana said with a grin.

"Yes ma'am," the other girls replied in unison.

Isabella leaned in and quietly said to Kelsey, "We're a couple."

Kelsey nodded and squeezed her hand.

Isabella sat back in relief. So far, so good.

* * *

It had been such a strange day. Kelsey was relieved when she was able to look into Isabella's eyes and that giant hug on the plane certainly helped. She had no idea what their relationship looked like going forward, but there wasn't any awkwardness between them for now.

The strange part was having someone else with them. They usually traveled alone and experienced these trips together, just the two of them. But not just anyone was with them this trip: It was Kelsey's daughters and friends. It made Kelsey tentative. Where she usually didn't hesitate to reach over and squeeze Isabella's hand or bump her shoulder, now she was aware of every time they touched.

As they were walking through the airport Kelsey glanced over at Isabella and smiled.

Isabella put her arm through Kelsey's, "Relax, this is going to be fun."

Kelsey sighed. "I hope so."

Once they'd made it to the resort everything happened quickly. They were whisked away to their rooms which were on the ground floor and poolside. Carmen's kids, Tanner and Mia, were waiting to greet them at the pool. After quick introductions they made plans to meet at the pool bar once they'd unpacked.

Kelsey left her room and was about to knock on Isabella's door when it opened.

"Hey," Isabella said.

"Hey." Kelsey felt her heart begin to hammer in her chest. "Maybe we could sneak away for our beach walk after dinner and talk."

"I'd like that, Kels," Isabella said with a smile.

The way Isabella said her name and the look in her eyes sent warmth through Kelsey's body. All she wanted to do was kiss her. It was as if their kisses last month had opened some kind of gate and all the feelings Kelsey had been trying to tamp down were now free.

"Hey, Mom," Dana said excitedly, walking over to them. "This place is amazing. Thank you so much for bringing us."

Kelsey smiled. "You're welcome."

"Come on Isabella." Dana grabbed her hand. "I want one of those fruity drinks you're always showing in your posts."

Isabella looked back at Kelsey with a grin. "Come on, *Mom*," she implored her.

Kelsey chuckled and followed behind them.

As everyone got their drinks Tanner and Mia were quick to tell Kelsey's girls how much fun they'd had with her at Christmas.

"Yeah," Dana said. "We messed that up."

"We thought we wanted to do our own thing at Christmas, but we were wrong," Emma added.

"What?" Kelsey exclaimed. "I can't believe you're admitting it."

"It wasn't so great for you either," Dana said.

Kelsey looked over at Isabella. "We had a wonderful Christmas, didn't we, Bella?"

"Yeah we did. It would've been nice to have our families with us, but we made new friends," Isabella said.

"And family," Mia added. "The Peaches crew loves you both."

"That's the bar on the other island, right?" Dana asked.

"Yeah, you're going to love it over there. My mom has a business on St. John," Tanner said.

"I thought your mom ran the resort," Emma said.

"She does." He chuckled. "I have two moms."

"Oh! Did you tell us that?" Emma asked, turning to Kelsey.

"I did," Kelsey replied and shook her head. "You can see how well they listen to me."

Isabella chuckled. "You'll get to meet Sylvie tomorrow," she said. "She'll be jetting us from island to island and party to party."

"Wow!" they exclaimed.

"Let's go have dinner and we can talk about what's to come," Kelsey suggested.

Tanner and Mia entertained them with their favorite things about the islands while they had dinner.

"Isn't this strange?" Kelsey said, leaning closer to Isabella where they sat at the end of the table.

"What?"

"We know people here," Kelsey said. "I'm so used to looking around the dining room and smiling at the servers, but we actually know guests this time."

Isabella chuckled. "That's true. Do we still look like a couple?"

Kelsey shrugged.

"What do you mean?" Emma asked.

"If you look around the restaurant you see families and couples," Isabella explained.

"Okay," Dana said.

"The first time we were here our server thought we were a couple and suggested a nice walk on the beach after dinner." Isabella chuckled. "Remember, Kels?"

"I remember the look on your face when you figured it out," Kelsey said.

"I was surprised. That's never happened to me," Isabella said defensively.

"Did it bother you?" Dana asked.

"Not at all," Isabella said. "Look who I was with."

Kelsey scoffed. "I look like a mom surrounded by her kids now."

"No way!" Tanner exclaimed. "You look too young."

"Yeah," Lily said. "You and Isabella look like you're here with all these other people for spring break. Look around the room."

Kelsey gazed around the room and sure enough it was a different crowd than usual. The tables contained groups of people, most around Dana and Emma's age. She wondered if their posts leading up to this week had helped fill the resort. Carmen had mentioned they were booked.

"I think people are watching your posts, Mom," Emma said with a grin.

"How about that," Isabella said.

"We're doing something right," Kelsey said quietly.

Isabella winked at her and just like that Kelsey's heart began to pound. She couldn't wait to talk to Isabella later this evening, alone.

After dinner they went back to the pool. Music filtered from the bar and if they weren't dancing they were swimming. Everyone was having a good time and the kids seemed to hit it off.

"Do you think we can slip away to the beach?" Isabella asked quietly from behind Kelsey.

Shivers went through Kelsey just as they had the night Isabella kissed her. "Let's go," she said, getting up.

They started to walk away.

"Hey, Mom," Emma called to her. "Where are you going?"

"Bella and I are going for a walk on the beach," Kelsey explained.

"Can I come with you?" Emma asked.

"Oh, I want to go." Grace jumped up from her chair.

Kelsey looked at Isabella and sighed. "Sure, come on."

Isabella chuckled, put her arm through Kelsey's, and led them to the beach.

"This is so nice," Emma said.

"Listen to those waves," Grace commented.

Kelsey chuckled. "Bella and I take a walk on the beach every night before we go to bed."

"Yeah, it's our way to end the day," Isabella said. "And dancing," she muttered so only Kelsey could hear.

Kelsey smiled and noticed Emma glancing her way. "What is it, Em?"

"You two have become close friends," she said.

"We have," Isabella replied. "I don't know what I'd do without your mom."

"But what about when you're home?" Grace asked. "Are you just friends when you're here?"

"No," Kelsey said. "Don't you still have friends in your hometown, Grace?"

"Yeah, but they're not close like you two are."

"We text and call each other when we're home," Isabella

said. "This is also part of our job. We have to plan and get ready for these trips."

"I can't wait to hit the beach tomorrow!" Emma exclaimed.

"Pace yourself, Em," Isabella warned her. "We have several days ahead of us."

"Gotcha, Isabella. Thanks," Emma said.

Isabella chuckled as they made their way back to their rooms.

Kelsey was about to tell Isabella she would come to her room once the girls were settled when Emma turned to her.

"Mom, can I stay with you tonight? I know Dana and Lily are going to be up for hours talking and I'm tired. I'm taking Isabella's advice," Emma said.

"Sure, honey," Kelsey replied and stole a glance at Isabella. She could already tell finding time to be alone was going to be a challenge.

Isabella gave her a sweet smile and pulled her away from the others. "I know we can't dance tonight, but we will at Peaches. Okay?"

Kelsey sighed. "Okay. I was hoping to talk after they were in their room."

"We'll find time. Don't give up," Isabella said.

Kelsey smiled and remembered those were her words to Isabella on their last trip.

23

Isabella looked out at the beach and watched her group playing volleyball with other people enjoying the spring break party. She and Kelsey still hadn't had an opportunity to talk about what was growing between them. There were times when she wanted to grab Kelsey, pull her behind a tree, and kiss her until they both couldn't breathe. Then there were the times she wanted to reach over and simply hold her hand. They were running out of time because it was the last day of spring break and they'd fly home tomorrow.

Isabella sighed and wondered if this was how it felt for people in the closet. At the moment she felt like she couldn't be her authentic self and had to hide her feelings for Kelsey. She kept things in the friend zone, but the longing she felt to simply sit and talk to Kelsey was growing to the point she might explode. Maybe she could come up with some excuse about work that they had to deal with so they could be alone.

"Are you keeping up with the twenty-year-olds?"

Isabella turned to find Riley sliding in the seat next to her. "Barely," she replied. "This is our last day."

"I've been watching your posts and everyone seems to be having a great time," Riley said.

"They are. The kids get along well. Kels and I have had fun with them."

"Then why don't you look happy?" Riley asked.

Isabella glanced over at her. "I don't?"

"You seem to be watching a certain dark-haired beauty. We've done this before," Riley teased.

Isabella chuckled. "I do like watching her. Kelsey and I haven't had a moment to ourselves and there's something important we need to talk about."

"I see." Riley nodded. "Can I help with that?"

"I don't know, can you?" Isabella looked at her friend and the slightest feeling of hope danced in her chest.

"Riley," Dana said, running up to them. "Alex needs the air pump for the volleyball."

"I'll be right back." Riley got up and went into the bar.

Dana sat down next to Isabella, put her arm around her, and gave her a side hug.

Isabella chuckled. "What was that for?"

"For making my mom happy. She is having so much fun."

"We always have fun," Isabella replied.

"Mom has given up a lot for us. She says she hasn't, but I know she has."

"Your mom didn't do anything she didn't want to."

Dana looked over at Isabella. "She's talked to you about us?"

Isabella nodded.

"She rarely dates. Besides, who would want to have a

relationship when she has a couple of kids?" Dana said. "At least now we're out of the house and she has more privacy."

"She just hasn't found the right woman yet," Isabella said, watching Kelsey hit the ball.

"It doesn't mean she won't."

"I hope so. Emma and I will be moving when we graduate."

"You won't mind sharing her with someone else?" Isabella asked, raising her eyebrows. "You're both pretty protective of her."

"Hey, maybe she'll find someone on these trips!" Dana exclaimed.

Isabella smiled. She wondered if maybe Kelsey already had.

"Here you go," Riley said, walking up and handing Dana the air pump. "Can you take your mom's place? I need her up here to help me with something."

"Sure. I'll tell her. Thanks," Dana said and started to walk back to the beach. "Hey, Isabella, I'd share my mom with you." Then she ran off the patio.

"What was that?" Riley asked.

Isabella shook her head. "I'm not sure."

Kelsey walked up to the patio and Isabella noticed the fine sheen of sweat on her shoulders. *Why is that so hot?*

"Come with me, you two," Riley said, leading them into the bar. "I have something I want to show you."

Isabella and Kelsey exchanged a look and followed Riley into Peaches. She led them through a door at the end of the bar and up a flight of stairs. She opened another door into a large room that took up the space over the bar.

"This is lovely," Isabella said.

"Alex and I love it up here. She keeps asking me if I want

to live in a house, but this is where we fell in love and I don't want to leave it."

"It's beautiful," Kelsey said.

"We have everything we need. This is the living area and kitchen. That door leads to the bathroom and this is our bedroom," Riley said, walking into the other room. "Come on."

They followed her into the bedroom and out a door that led to a patio.

"Oh my God!" Isabella exclaimed.

"Just wait," Riley said. "One more flight."

They walked up a set of stairs that opened up to a rooftop deck.

Kelsey gasped. "You can see forever up here."

"Now you know why I don't want to move," Riley said. "Okay, I will take care of the kids while you have a moment of peace. There's beer in that little refrigerator."

Isabella took a moment to look around the space. There was a couch with tables and lounge chairs that looked out over the water.

"This is incredible," Kelsey said.

"Yeah, and so are you," Isabella said.

Kelsey turned around and smiled at Isabella.

"I told Riley we had something important to talk about, but we haven't had a moment alone the entire trip," Isabella said.

"I know and it's been killing me," Kelsey said.

"Let's sit," Isabella suggested.

They settled on the couch and Isabella looked at Kesley. "You are so beautiful." She ran her fingers through Kelsey's hair. "I see a few strands of gray."

"You put them there."

"Me?"

"Yes, by saying things like that."

"I can't tell you that you're beautiful?" Isabella asked softly.

"You are such an important part of my life now, Bella. You keep saying things like that and what's going to happen? We have a fling in the islands and after our year is over we go back to our lives."

"Who says it has to be over?"

Kelsey closed her eyes. "I don't want to lose you," she whispered.

"What if we made it?"

Kelsey's eyes popped open and Isabella looked at her seriously. "I don't want to go back to my life the way it was before. The time we've spent here is the best part of my year. Why can't we have it all month long?"

Kelsey sighed. "This wouldn't just be a fling for me."

"It wouldn't be for me either. I can't stop thinking about you. And when I think about you, my next thought is of kissing you. I miss you when we're not here."

"I miss you, too," Kelsey said.

"But what do you think, Kels?"

Kelsey let out a breath and reached for Isabella's hands. "I think this is the best thing that's ever happened to me, yet I don't know how to make it happen."

Isabella scoffed then smiled. "Aren't we a couple."

That got a small smile from Kelsey.

"I want our next trip to be just us. We'll do some kind of relaxing vacation theme where we won't have to video and post as much. We'll have time to figure this out."

Kelsey raised her eyebrows. "Figure this out? You've never been with a woman. We can walk this back and still be friends, Bella."

Isabella felt heat rise to her cheeks and a sinking feeling in her stomach. "Can we, Kelsey?"

Kelsey sighed in frustration. "I'm afraid if I tell you everything that's swirling in my heart it'll scare you away."

"That's what next month's trip is for. We can talk about all our fears, doubts, hopes and what it means to this job we're doing—"

"And our families," Kelsey said. "It's not such a big deal for my girls, but your boys are younger."

Isabella smiled. Of course Kelsey was thinking of her. "They won't always be that way."

Kelsey smirked. "You know what I mean. This is different from just going out with someone new."

"Because you're a woman?"

Kelsey nodded. "Yes. Unfortunately, that adds another layer to the other things we have to consider."

"Do you want to date me, Kels?" Isabella asked.

Kelsey grinned. "Date you? We live in different states and see each other once a month."

"If you think about it, we've been dating pretty much since the moment we met," Isabella said.

Kelsey tilted her head. "Hmm, that's one way to look at it."

Isabella leaned over and cupped the side of Kelsey's face with her hand. "I know who you are, Kels. I want to know more and I think you do, too," Isabella said, staring into her eyes. "I'm falling in love with you and I think you're in love with me." Isabella smiled softly.

Kelsey opened her mouth to speak and Isabella reached over and put her fingers over her lips. "Don't start with the what ifs. Kiss me. Then you'll know we can make it work. Because how could we not."

Kelsey crashed her lips to Isabella's in a steamy kiss.

They both moaned and Isabella felt Kelsey's fingers fist in her hair, holding their lips together.

All the waiting, all the anticipation, all the hidden emotions erupted into that searing kiss. Isabella reached around Kelsey's middle and pulled her closer.

After several moments Isabella felt Kelsey loosen her hold and they began to softly caress each other's lips in the most luxurious of kisses. Heated breaths with quiet moans were the build-up to another scorching kiss. When their tongues touched, once again Isabella felt her heart open grasping for more of Kelsey. If this was how she felt kissing this incredible woman, Isabella couldn't imagine what would happen next.

They pulled apart, both heaving for needed breaths.

Isabella looked into Kelsey's eyes with amusement. "Go back to being friends. Are you fucking kidding me!"

Kelsey chuckled. "I wasn't sure how you felt."

Isabella tilted her head. "Let me show you."

She grabbed Kelsey's face and pressed their lips together in a long, soulful kiss. Isabella took her time, gently touching her tongue to Kelsey's, softly exploring her sumptuous mouth and ever so slowly pulling away.

With her lips just touching Kelsey's, she whispered, "That's how I feel."

Kelsey smiled and Isabella could see the emotion in her eyes. *Too soon, too soon, too soon*, she chided herself. Oh, who was she kidding, she could see love in Kelsey's eyes.

"I don't want anyone to know yet," Kelsey said. "I want to keep this for just us."

Isabella nodded. "You know, right before you walked up, Dana told me she'd share you with me."

Kelsey's eyes widened. "She did?"

"Those girls love you and want you to be happy. They also don't want you to be alone."

"I'm not," Kelsey said with a smile and a sweet kiss to Isabella's lips.

"I know we have more to talk about, but while we're alone," Isabella said, wrapping her arms around Kelsey's shoulders and crawling onto her lap, "all I want to do is keep kissing you."

Kelsey smiled and kissed Isabella on the cheek then below her ear. Isabella melted into Kelsey's arms when she ran her tongue along the pulse point in her neck.

"Oh, God, Kels," Isabella moaned.

She felt Kelsey pull her even closer until her center was flush against Kelsey's stomach. Isabella found Kelsey's lips once again and as she slid her tongue in Kelsey's mouth, she ground her hips into Kelsey.

"Fuck, Bella," Kelsey groaned.

"Hey, Dana. Where's Mom?" They heard Emma yell down on the beach.

Isabella pulled her lips from Kelsey's and widened her eyes.

"Ignore them," Kelsey said, capturing Isabella's lips once again.

Isabella giggled. "I guess we've been missed. What is it with your girls? They like you."

Kelsey laughed. "They like you, too."

Isabella took Kelsey's face in her hands and smiled. "I know we won't get to dance tonight, but I'll play our song and think about you."

"Don't give up, Bella. Maybe I can sneak out of my room," Kelsey said, wiggling her eyebrows.

Isabella couldn't keep from laughing. "They're supposed to be sneaking away from us!"

Kelsey shrugged. "We're having more fun."

"Mmm, we definitely are now," Isabella said in a sultry voice as she kissed Kelsey again.

A few moments later she pulled away, stood up, and offered her hand to Kelsey. "We'd better go."

"I can't wait for next month," Kelsey said.

"We'll figure this out," Isabella replied. She led them down the stairway to Riley and Alex's bedroom then out of their apartment.

"Can you imagine living here?"

"Maybe someday," Kelsey said, putting her hand on the door that led to the bar before Isabella could open it.

Isabella turned to her and smiled, then she pressed her lips to Kelsey's for one more tender kiss. What was it about Kelsey's kisses? They lit Isabella on fire at times and at others soothed her soul. She reluctantly pulled away, but placed her hand over Kelsey's heart.

"My heart is talking to your heart," Isabella said.

"I know," Kelsey whispered and smiled. "I hear it."

Isabella groaned. "Fuck," she mumbled and opened the door.

24

Kelsey closed her eyes and leaned her head back against the seat rest. She was in the middle seat, but she didn't care because Isabella was sitting right next to her, their legs pressed together. Her thoughts drifted back to last night. They had danced at Peaches with the rest of the spring break revelers then returned to the resort for dinner.

The group continued the party outside their rooms at the pool. Kelsey and Isabella took their regular evening walk on the beach, this time joined by Dana and Mia. After they returned to the party Kelsey and Isabella explained they had a work issue to take care of and went into Isabella's room. They had their last-night dance, as they had begun to call it, after all.

Kelsey remembered holding Isabella in her arms as they swayed to the music. She couldn't wait until their trip next month.

"You have a very pleased look on your face," Isabella whispered. "What are you thinking about?"

Kelsey opened her eyes and gazed over at Isabella. "Your

eyes are a beautiful sparkling blue right now," she said quietly.

Isabella smiled, but raised her eyebrows in question.

"I was thinking about our dance last night," Kelsey replied softly. She reached over and touched her little finger to Isabella's where it rested on her thigh. "Have you noticed how perfectly our bodies fit together when we dance?"

She was rewarded with a big smile from Isabella. "I have noticed," she whispered.

Kelsey straightened up and turned to her. "I was surprised at how receptive Carmen was to our idea of rejuvenation next month."

"I think she knows we need a little break," Isabella said. "I'm glad it's only three weeks until our next trip, but..." She leaned in closer and lowered her voice. "What are we going to do for those three weeks?"

"We're going to talk and text about everything we're going to do next month," Kelsey said with a sexy smile.

"God, help me." Isabella sighed. "I have no idea what I'm doing."

"Yes, you do," Kelsey whispered.

Dana leaned towards them from where she sat on Kelsey's other side. "What are you whispering about?" she asked in a faux whisper.

"Wouldn't you like to know," Isabella said. "Nosy."

Dana had a shocked look on her face, making Isabella and Kelsey chuckle. "We're not talking about anything special," Kelsey said. "Just the trip."

"When do we get to hang out again, Isabella?" Dana asked.

"Not next month," Isabella said. "Your mom and I need to relax."

"Oh, it must be so hard going to the Virgin Islands every month," Dana said sarcastically.

"You'd be surprised," Kelsey said.

"Yeah, I didn't see you planning any of the videos or pictures to get the best views or writing any of the copy for the blog or other posts," Isabella said.

Dana shrugged. "I admit, there's a lot more to this than I thought," she said. "Thank you again for having us for spring break."

"You're welcome. Don't forget we have the family vacation this summer," Isabella said.

"I can't wait to actually meet Wyatt and Gus. It'll be fun showing them around. Is Mia coming back for that?" Dana asked.

Isabella raised her brows. "I don't know," she replied. "We can ask."

Dana nodded and smiled.

"What about Tanner?"

"Sure," Dana said. "It'd be nice to see him again, too."

Isabella winked at Kelsey as Dana looked away.

The flight attendants came around to prepare for landing and it wasn't long until they were on the ground. Once they made it through the walkway and into the airport they stopped.

"Is this where we say our goodbyes?" Emma said with a pout.

"Nope," Isabella said. "I always walk your mom to her next flight."

Dana and Emma led the group through the airport to their gate. Kelsey and Isabella followed at the rear, arm and arm, just like always.

"Hey, perfect timing, we're about to board," Emma said.

"It usually works out that way," Kelsey said.

Isabella held out her arms. "Okay, I need hugs."

Lily and Grace each hugged her and thanked her once again for the trip.

It was Emma's turn and she quietly said, "I'm sad to leave you. This was so much fun."

Isabella pulled away and smiled at her. "You'll see me again before you know it."

Dana grabbed Isabella and hugged her tightly. "Now we know why our mom talks about you so often. You're our friend now."

"Aw, I am your friend," Isabella said. "This wasn't just a job to us. It was a girls trip."

The gate attendant called their group and the girls got in line to board.

"Mom, aren't you coming?" Emma asked.

"Yes. You go ahead. I'll be there in a minute."

Emma furrowed her brows and shrugged. "Okay. Is this another one of the things you two do every trip? Like walking on the beach?"

"Yep," Isabella said. "Kelsey will take a pic of you all when you're in your seats on the plane."

"And I'll call when we get home tonight," Kelsey added quietly.

"That's so cute," Lily said, smiling at them.

Kelsey and Isabella watched them wheel their bags down the walkway then they stepped over towards the wall.

"I'm going to miss you even more this time," Isabella said, putting her arms around Kelsey's neck.

"Why more?"

"Because I know you feel this, too, and we have so much to look forward to," she replied.

Kelsey leaned down and kissed Isabella softly then

pulled her into a tight hug. "I'll miss you, Bella. More than you know."

Isabella leaned her head back and kissed Kelsey firmly. "Are you ready for all the questions when you get on the plane?"

"Did you notice them watching us?"

"Mm hmm, they kept stealing glances our way. They know we're more than friends," Isabella said.

"I'll be fine," Kelsey said. She kissed Isabella one more time and groaned as she pulled her lips away. "It's so hard to leave you."

"You'd better go before one of them gets off the plane and comes looking for you." Isabella chuckled.

"Wait," Kelsey said, reaching for her phone. "One more pic of us."

She held her arm out and wrapped the other one around Isabella. "Ready?"

Just before she hit the button she put her lips to Isabella's cheek.

"Let me see!" Isabella exclaimed. She took Kelsey's phone and smiled at the photo. "I'm sending this to myself right now."

Kelsey chuckled.

"I have another idea," Isabella said. She held Kelsey's phone out and grinned at her. "Kiss me."

"What?"

"Come on. We don't have much time."

Kelsey pressed her lips to Isabella's and heard her push the button to take the photo.

They looked at the picture and saw that Isabella had captured them in a sweet kiss.

"Okay, when we're missing each other, which will be all

the time," Isabella said as she sent the picture to her phone, "we can look at this and feel each other's lips."

Kelsey giggled and smiled at Isabella. She couldn't help but think they were acting like a couple of kids, but she didn't care.

"See you next month," Isabella said, pecking Kelsey's lips one more time.

"See you next month," Kelsey replied.

She walked over, showed her boarding pass to the attendant, and turned to smile at Isabella one more time before she disappeared down the walkway.

Kelsey sighed and couldn't believe how happy her heart felt. There was a hint of sadness leaving Isabella, but she knew next month it would just be the two of them. They'd told Carmen to put them in one bungalow, explaining that they were together most of the time anyway.

"I thought you were going to miss our flight," Dana said, taking Kelsey's bag and putting it in the overhead bin.

Kelsey looked up and down the aisle as several people were still finding their seats. "Right," she said sarcastically.

"Okay, Mom," Emma said, patting the middle seat. "You're sitting between me and Dana. We need to talk."

Kelsey raised her eyebrows at both her daughters and sat down. "Hold it. Picture first," she said, taking out her phone. She handed it to Emma. The three of them leaned in with Lily and Grace waving from their seats across the aisle.

"Smile at Bella," Kelsey said, grinning at the phone. She sent the pic to Isabella and said: *Miss you already.* Kelsey quickly put her phone away before either of the girls decided to grab it and snoop.

Once they were in the air Dana turned to Kelsey. "So do you do the same things every time you go on one of these trips?"

"Some things. We take a walk on the beach, go to Peaches and do a little dancing—"

"Let's talk about dancing," Emma said, narrowing her gaze.

Kelsey wanted to laugh, but held it in. *This should be fun, she thought.*

"It isn't strange dancing with Isabella?"

Kelsey scoffed. "Did we look strange? We've been dancing together since we met."

Dana gasped. "I knew it! What's really going on, Mom?"

Kelsey raised her brows and looked from one daughter to the other. "Excuse me?"

Emma huffed. "Why aren't you and Isabella together? You're perfect for each other!"

Kelsey smiled.

"Sorry, Mom. What Emma is trying to say is that we can see how the two of you look at each other. What's holding you back?" Dana asked softly.

"Duh, Isabella isn't gay, right?" Emma exclaimed.

"That doesn't matter," Dana replied.

Kelsey felt like she was watching a tennis match as each of her daughters fired off comments.

"Mom," Emma said, taking a deep breath. "Isabella is into you and I know you're into her."

"Am I?"

"Yes," Dana said. "You may not have dated much, but I know when you care for someone and you love Isabella."

"Whoa! Slow down," Kelsey said.

"Why?" Dana asked. "It's obvious. You're both in love with each other."

Was it obvious? They were friends and laughed a lot. But with each day and each trip they got closer and closer. Did she love Isabella? There was so much to consider.

"Come on, Mom. What's really going on?" Emma asked softly.

Kelsey sighed. "Isabella and I became friends instantly," she began. "We were at the resort alone, both feeling a bit sad about that and had dinner together the first night we met. We didn't know we were both working for the resort."

"You didn't?" Dana asked.

Kelsey shook her head. "Not that first night. The next day, the idea for the monthly trips was brought up and it took off. Carmen wanted us to do it instead of a paid influencer because she thought it would be more believable."

Kelsey paused to take a breath and smiled at Dana and Emma. "Isabella and I have grown closer and closer. We've talked about our families, our hopes, lots of things," she said, beginning to squirm in her seat. She didn't want to share their private moments with anyone. Those were hers and Isabella's to cherish.

"Talk?" Emma said, raising her eyebrows. "You've been dancing, too. What else?"

Kelsey glared at them. "That's not your business. But I will tell you this," she said a bit testily. "We tried to find a moment alone during this trip because we'd just realized our feelings for each other, but couldn't get away from the two of you to have a conversation!"

"Oh," Emma said with an apologetic wince.

"Why didn't you just say so?" Dana said defensively.

Kelsey's eyes widened then she laughed. "Really! What would you have done?"

"Uh..."

"You wouldn't have given us a moment's peace. You would have been asking questions or teasing us the entire time."

"Guilty," Emma said, raising her hand.

"Mom, we want you to be happy," Dana said. "Isabella told me you hadn't found the right woman, but you would."

Kelsey smiled. "She did?"

"Yeah, I think you've found her," Dana said with a smile.

"OMG, Dana!" Emma exclaimed. "We're going to have another mommy!"

Kelsey thought her eyes would pop out of her head.

Dana and Emma burst out laughing. "We're kidding," Emma said, trying to catch her breath.

"Oh, you two are so funny," Kelsey said with a smirk. She reached for their hands, gave them a squeeze and smiled.

25

Kelsey was about to call Isabella and let her know they'd made it home when the girls sat down on the couch with her.

"Uh, Mom," Dana began nervously. "We need to tell you something."

"Okay," Kelsey said, raising her brows.

"You know when I graduate I'll be moving," Emma said. "I've applied for several positions in DC and I'm sure to get one of them."

Kelsey nodded. "That was your plan all along. I'm happy for you, honey." She reached over and squeezed Emma's hand. This wasn't news to her. Emma had been planning to make this move since she started college.

"But she's not the only one moving," Dana said.

"Oh." Kelsey nodded.

"I'm going to be a traveling nurse. I've been thinking about it for a while now. It's time for me to live somewhere besides Colorado."

Kelsey smiled. "Good for you." She looked from Dana to

Emma and furrowed her brow. "Why are you both so serious? This is exciting news!"

"It means you'll be here all by yourself," Emma said.

"I've been by myself since you both went to college. I think I'm doing okay, don't you?" Kelsey said, amused.

Dana sighed. "What we're trying to say is that we know we were diva bitches growing up."

Kelsey laughed. "What?"

"You never had a girlfriend for long when we were growing up and we had a lot to do with that," Emma said.

"No, you didn't," Kelsey said.

"Oh, yes we did," Dana said. "Isabella mentioned to me that we're protective of you and she's not wrong."

"Yeah, if you'll remember, you couldn't get away from us to talk." Emma winced.

"I guess what we're trying to say is, don't let us keep you from being with Isabella," Dana said.

Kelsey smiled and patted both their knees. "Next month our trip is just for us," she said. "We've kind of been dating this whole time, but just now realized it. We'll talk about everything and see where we go after this year. I hope Isabella will always be in my life, but this is all new to us. Okay?"

"Okay," Emma said.

Dana nodded then chuckled. "She's so into you, Mom."

Kelsey sighed. "She isn't the only one."

"Let's call her," Emma said.

Kelsey connected the call and chatted with Isabella for a moment before the girls took over the conversation. They switched to a video call so they could both talk to her. Then the boys decided to join in the fun. Kelsey got up and went to the kitchen and watched as Dana and Emma animatedly told Wyatt and Gus about all the things they were going to do when they were together on the summer vacation trip.

Kelsey opened a beer and knew she'd call Isabella back later after everyone was in bed. She could hear the boys' excitement on the other end of the call from their gasps and laughter. They sounded like one big happy family.

Kelsey sighed. "Now who's getting ahead of herself," she mumbled, taking a sip of her beer.

* * *

"You seem especially excited for this upcoming trip," Marti said as she watched Isabella pack.

"I am," Isabella replied. "I took your advice, Mom."

"Oh?"

"I'm doing something for me, something that makes me happy," Isabella said with a smile.

"Would it have anything to do with Kelsey?" Marti asked.

Isabella smiled. "She does go with me on every one of these trips."

Marti chuckled. "Yes, but there's something different about you."

"I know," Isabella said. "I have feelings for her and she feels the same way."

"I see," Marti said with an amused smile. "I'm guessing these feelings are more than friendship." She chuckled. "Because I wouldn't want to assume anything since you dance with her every month just as you would your other friends."

Isabella looked over at her mother and smirked. "Very funny." She sat down on the bed next to her mom and sighed. "I have no idea what I'm doing. Kelsey is the most incredible person and at first I didn't realize how attracted I was to her."

"Because she's a woman?"

"Maybe, but there's something about her, Mom. When we're together I feel so settled and safe and at the same time very..."

"Excited?" Marti asked with raised eyebrows.

Isabella chuckled. "Yeah, you could call it that."

Marti laughed. "I may be old to you, but I know what it feels like to be hot for someone, Isabella Burns."

Isabella laughed with her. "Yes ma'am." She giggled. "I'm so hot for Kelsey."

Marti giggled with her.

Isabella put her arm around Marti and hugged her. "I'm so glad I can talk to you like this. If I told any of my other friends I was falling for a woman they'd look at me like I've lost it."

"If they'd look down at you because of that then they aren't your friends," Marti stated.

Isabella looked over at her and tilted her head. "You're right. I think that's why Kelsey and I became friends so quickly. We needed each other, in a way."

Marti patted Isabella's knee. "Okay. Here's one more bit of advice. Don't let anyone or anything scare you away from this because it's different."

"What do you mean scare me away?"

"Unfortunately some people will not be as happy about this as I am. They will try to make it hard for you," Marti said.

Isabella nodded. "You're happy for me?"

"I haven't met Kelsey yet, but she has to be worth something to put this kind of smile on your face. My confident, vibrant daughter is re-emerging before my eyes and that makes me very happy. Don't think the boys haven't noticed because they have."

Isabella tilted her head.

"They told me that you are always happy when you come back from one of your trips with Kelsey."

Isabella smiled. "I am. They've talked to her and her daughters on the phone several times. I'll be happy when they finally meet."

"Listen to your heart, Isabella, and you can't go wrong."

"Oh, Mom, I hope so."

"I know so. I know your heart." Marti got up and went to Isabella's closet. "Now, let's see if we can find something sexy for you to wear when you have dinner with Kelsey."

Isabella chuckled. "Never in a million years did I think you would be helping me pack to impress a woman."

"Oh, honey. You look lovely in this blue dress," Marti said, holding it up for Isabella to see.

"The blue one it is," Isabella said.

* * *

Kelsey kept peeking down the aisle in hopes of catching a glimpse of Isabella as she boarded the plane. It had been the longest three weeks impatiently awaiting their reunion. They talked every day, but Kelsey couldn't wait to put her arms around Isabella.

She rested her head against the seat, closed her eyes, and took a deep breath. *When have I felt this kind of anticipation to see another woman?*

"Hey, sexy. Have you got room for me?"

Kelsey opened her eyes and felt such relief then excitement when her eyes met Isabella's. Her smile couldn't get any bigger as they wrapped their arms around each other.

"Mmm," Isabella murmured in Kelsey's ear. "I missed you, too."

Kelsey pulled back and softly kissed Isabella's lips. She didn't immediately pull away, but tried to be respectful of the passengers around them.

Isabella quickly put her suitcase in the overhead bin and plopped into the window seat. Kelsey sat next to her and reached for her hand.

"Do you have any idea how good it feels to hug and kiss you right now?" Kelsey grinned.

"I do," Isabella replied, raising a brow. "Because I hugged and kissed you right back."

They both giggled like a couple of kids.

"Let's do a quick post," Kelsey said, getting her phone out. "I've got this, just go with me."

"Okay," Isabella said, grinning at the camera.

"Hey, everyone. It's Kelsey and Isabella coming to you for another wonderful trip to Coral Bay on St. Thomas. First, I want to thank you all for coming along on these adventures with us every month. In January we did winter at the beach followed by our love vacation in February. Last month we spent spring break at the beach. So much fun," Kelsey said, glancing at Isabella.

Isabella grinned. "I'm still dancing," she said, moving her arms.

"This month is for all of you workaholics out there and you know who you are," Kelsey said, pointing at the screen. "Some people actually go on vacation to rest and recharge. We're going to show you all the amenities at Coral Bay that will help you rejuvenate and reset. You're now on island time. We'll see you there!"

Kelsey winked and ended the video. She quickly posted it to the website before they took off.

"You did have that ready. Way to go, babe," Isabella said, watching over Kelsey's shoulder.

Kelsey stopped what she was doing and looked at Isabella with a grin. "Babe?"

"Yep." Isabella kissed her cheek.

Kelsey giggled and couldn't believe how full her heart felt with that simple term of endearment from Isabella. She finished posting the video and turned back to Isabella.

"What would you think about having dinner on the beach tonight outside our bungalow?" Kelsey asked.

"Like our Valentine couples did?"

Kelsey nodded. "Sort of, but it would just be us. I thought we could dress up and actually have a date tomorrow," she said. "If that's all right with you," she quickly added.

"That sounds lovely, but I'd like to ask you for something."

"Okay."

"It feels to me like when we get on this plane, we are on island time. We leave our cares and problems behind and it's just us. Yes, we're doing a job, but we're still on island time."

"Yeah, I feel that way, too," Kelsey replied.

"I know we have things to talk about, but this trip feels special. We're doing these things together as a real couple. Can we stay on island time and not let real life creep in?"

Kelsey smiled and stroked the back of Isabella's hand with her thumb. "Yes, but..."

"But?"

"Bella, I don't want to just explore us on island time. I want real life, too," Kelsey said earnestly.

"I want that," Isabella said with a sweet smile. "But honestly, all I want right now is to put my arms around you and kiss you into tomorrow."

Kelsey grinned.

"We have a lot to explore when we get there," Isabella said in a low voice.

Good God! Kelsey felt warmth rush through her as she stared into Isabella's eyes. Her heart was thumping in her chest.

"Breathe, Kels," Isabella whispered.

"We may never get out of that bungalow," Kelsey said softly.

"That's fine with me." Isabella winked.

Kelsey chuckled and leaned over to quickly kiss Isabella. When she sat back and glanced at the man sitting next to her he had a smirk on his face as he stared at his phone. He briefly looked up at her and nodded.

Kelsey knew he couldn't hear their conversation but she was relieved to know he didn't mind their kiss.

"Do you remember the first time we went to Peaches?" Isabella asked.

"Of course I do. We danced together for the first time to our song."

Isabella nodded. "They thought we were a couple. Liz told me that day that she could see us together."

"Really?"

"Yep. She encouraged me to bring us back to Peaches." Isabella chuckled. "I told her we'd be back because we liked it and them so much. But she wanted us to come back because the island has a way of making you see things clearly."

Kelsey smiled. "Can you see us together?"

Isabella nodded. "We're a couple."

Kelsey chuckled and squeezed Isabella's hand. This was going to be their best trip yet.

26

"Oh, Kelsey. Look," Isabella said, opening the doors onto the deck. "We have time for a quick walk on the beach before dinner. Let's get our feet wet."

Kelsey took Isabella's hand and they ran towards the beach. They kicked up water as they splashed into the sea.

"Oh, that feels so good," Isabella said.

"Let's walk." Kelsey took Isabella's hand as they walked along the shore with the waves lapping at their feet.

"Here we are, holding hands and not hiding our feelings," Isabella said, bumping her shoulder to Kelsey's.

"You were hiding your feelings?" Kelsey teased.

"Don't think I didn't see you stealing looks at me on our various adventures," Isabella said.

"Oh, God," Kelsey groaned. "I couldn't help it."

Isabella chuckled. "I was doing the same thing, Kels."

"But now?"

Isabella dropped Kelsey's hand and put her arm through hers. "You know my boys come first just as your girls do, but I'm doing what makes me happy from now on. And you make me happy. These trips with you have made me see things differently, important things."

"They have?"

"Yes. You've shown me things, like how you didn't let other people determine your happiness. You had Dana and Emma on your own when it wasn't easy."

Kelsey smiled. "I remember when I told my mom what I wanted to do and she shook her head. We'd had several conversations about it already and she said, 'I can see you have your heart set on this, so I'll be here to do whatever you need.'"

"Your daughters are not only beautiful girls, they are good people," Isabella said.

"Thank you. My mom helped me along with my brother and sister-in-law. We raised our families together."

"What about your mom now?"

Kelsey chuckled. "She is living her best life with her sister in Florida. I don't talk about her much because she is so busy doing things in her retirement community I can't get her to slow down and have a conversation. She does stop to check in with the girls often."

"You know, island time has us slowing down and seeing things differently, but that started with you and your more laid-back attitude."

"Bella, you need to stop and see what you've done. Just look at what you've accomplished," Kelsey said.

"I know that and I'm proud of what I've done so far, but there's more to life than being successful in your career and raising kids." Isabella stopped them and turned to Kelsey. "You make me feel such possibilities right here." She took Kelsey's hand and put it over her heart.

Kelsey smiled. "Oh, babe. I feel it, too. My heart has never been this open and happy. You have done that to me."

Isabella leaned up and gently pressed her lips to Kelsey's. "Let's go have dinner and put a little more happiness in our hearts."

They turned around and walked back to the bungalow. As they stepped onto the back deck they found Luis setting up a feast.

"Luis!" Isabella exclaimed. "What are you doing working so late?"

"I'm helping at the restaurant this evening," he said, pouring two glasses of wine. "It's a beautiful night for a beautiful dinner."

"Thank you," Kelsey said, taking the glass from him.

"Enjoy," he said.

As Luis left, Isabella turned to Kelsey. "Let's drink to island magic," she said, holding up her glass. "I think some kind of magic has been working on us since we stepped off the plane back at Christmas."

Kelsey clinked her glass to Isabella's. "I don't know what's been working on us, but I don't want it to stop."

Isabella chuckled. "It won't. Our hearts are involved now and it's up to us."

"I believe in us," Kelsey said, sipping from her glass.

"Me, too." Isabella sat down at the table. "Look at all this."

"You said earlier that I helped you see things differently, but you've done the same for me, Bella. Do you remember our first dinner together?"

"Of course I do. That's when our server suggested a romantic walk along the beach." Isabella giggled.

"Yes, but you ordered the sampler for us and I tried several types of seafood that I wouldn't have if it weren't for you. From then on I've tried new things because of you." Kelsey took a bite and moaned with delight.

"So, what you're saying is—"

"What I'm saying is, our hearts connected that day at the airport and we can't ignore what they've been telling us," Kelsey said.

Isabella took a bite of her food and thought about what Kelsey said. "I know I've felt something for you from the beginning. The way you so casually rolled your one bag to the shuttle with your small purse."

Kelsey laughed. "It was my luggage that caught your eye?"

"No, babe. It was the way you moved and the confidence that radiated from you. God, it was hot." Isabella grinned and continued eating.

Kelsey raised her eyebrows. "Even though I'm a woman?"

Isabella tilted her head and swallowed. "I never really thought about that until much later." Isabella chuckled. "What did you see in me? A woman who brought too much stuff and couldn't handle her luggage."

"Not at all. I was amazed at how together you were. Once those bags were off that table, you had everything under control," Kelsey said with a grin.

"Hmm, so we connected over luggage."

"No," Kelsey said quietly.

Isabella looked up into Kelsey's eyes. They were such a golden shade of brown with flecks of green, but she could see a fire building.

"You were so beautiful," Kelsey said. "We'd just flown for hours, you were having trouble with your luggage, but when you stopped and smiled at me, my heart skipped a beat."

Isabella set her glass down and stood up. She reached out her hand to Kelsey and once she took it, Isabella pulled her to standing. She wrapped her hands around Kelsey's neck like she had many times before and smiled. "The first time I put my arms around you like this, my heart fluttered."

* * *

Kelsey smiled down at Isabella and could feel the familiar feeling of warmth flowing through her. Isabella could do that with a look, a touch, or a kiss. She pressed her lips to Isabella's and felt such a sensation of home. They were exactly where they should be at this particular moment in their lives, in the world. It all felt so right. Kelsey had never experienced anything like it. She let the feeling blanket them for several moments and hoped Isabella felt it, too.

"Let's go inside," Kelsey whispered.

"Mmm, yes," Isabella replied softly.

Kelsey led them through the back door.

"Let's leave them open," Isabella said. "I love the sound of the waves and there's no one around us."

Kelsey smiled and butterflies took flight throughout her body. She felt Isabella's hand stroke her cheek and, as if reading her mind, Isabella said, "It's just us, Kels."

"I know, but..."

"I'm not nervous," Isabella said, staring into Kelsey's eyes. "I trust you."

"Bella," Kelsey whispered and ran her fingers through Isabella's hair.

"Your kisses drive me wild, Kels. I want to feel your lips all over me. I want you to touch me everywhere," Isabella said softly.

Kelsey stared into her dark blue eyes. She thought she'd seen every possible shade of blue in Isabella's eyes, but tonight they were the color of the night sky.

"You are so beautiful," Kelsey whispered. She began to

unbutton Isabella's shirt as she softly pressed their lips together. The butterflies were gone and desire raced through Kelsey with every quickened beat of her heart.

Kelsey pulled her lips away and slowly slid the shirt over Isabella's shoulders. It was dark in the room, but the moonlight reflected off the water and cast just enough light for Kelsey to see the sparkle in Isabella's eyes. She dropped the shirt on the floor and reached for the waist of Isabella's shorts. Kelsey could feel Isabella's hands tighten on her shoulders as she kneeled to push the shorts down her legs.

Kelsey waited for her to step out of the shorts then put her arms around Isabella's middle and kissed her belly. She felt and heard Isabella's sharp intake of breath.

"So beautiful," Kelsey murmured against Isabella's skin. She could feel Isabella's fingers combing through her hair and all the sensations made her dizzy for a moment. Isabella's sweet scent, her soft skin under Kelsey's fingers, the waves crashing against the sand and the moonlight all added up to make this the most romantic moment Kelsey could remember ever having.

Kelsey kissed Isabella's stomach once again and as she stood up, she placed kisses at the top of Isabella's breasts and up her neck along the way. She could feel Isabella shiver under her hands.

Isabella moaned, leaning her head back as Kelsey's lips nibbled her ear lobe.

"Do you have any idea how many times I wanted to kiss you here when we danced," Kelsey whispered.

Isabella groaned. "I love it," she panted.

Kelsey reached around and unhooked Isabella's bra, dropping it to the floor. She stared at Isabella's breasts and couldn't stop both her hands from cupping them. "Bella, I can't stop saying it. You are beautiful," Kelsey said.

Isabella smiled. "You don't have to stop saying it."

Kelsey looked into her eyes and smiled. She took Isabella's nipples between her fingers and thumbs. Isabella's eyes shut and her head fell back in pleasure.

"God, Kels. That feels so good."

Kelsey gently pushed Isabella back until her legs were against the bed. She brought their lips together in a deep kiss as Isabella sat down on the bed. Kelsey kneeled between her legs and pulled her close as their tongues ignited the kiss to scorching.

They groaned and tried to catch a quick breath, but their lips never parted. Finally Kelsey pulled away and eased her hands to Isabella's hips. She hooked her fingers in the sides of Isabella's undies and pulled them down her legs.

Isabella climbed further onto the bed while Kelsey quickly began to take her own clothes off.

"Slow down," Isabella said.

Kelsey grinned and tossed her shirt and bra into the pile with Isabella's clothes. She raised her eyebrows and slowly slid her shorts and undies down her own legs then stood in front of Isabella.

"Exquisite beauty. That's what you are, my Kelsey," Isabella said.

"You're not nervous and I'm not the least bit hesitant to stand naked in front of you." Kelsey shook her head. "I've never felt so sure of anything, Bella."

Isabella smiled. "I've seen enough for now. I need you, Kels."

Kelsey could feel her own wetness and see Isabella's in the moonlight. She climbed up the bed and eased her body on top of Isabella's. Once again they both groaned then their lips took over.

Kelsey's leg was between Isabella's just as her tongue slid

into her mouth. She ran her hand down Isabella's side, over her belly, and cupped her breast. Isabella's moans were in harmony with the waves, creating a passionate tune.

As much as Kelsey wanted to keep kissing Isabella she couldn't wait any longer to taste her. She tore her lips away and kissed down Isabella's neck across her collarbone and down to her breast. Kelsey swirled her tongue around Isabella's hardened nipple then took it into her mouth.

Isabella's fingers immediately tangled in Kelsey's hair and she moaned when Kelsey's teeth bit down gently.

"Oh, God," Isabella moaned.

Kelsey kissed her way across Isabella's chest to her other breast while her hand cupped the other. She could feel the desire building inside Isabella with every touch, stroke, and lick of her tongue. It had been a while since Kelsey had had sex, but this was different.

She felt like Isabella's body was speaking to her through her heart. Yes, Kelsey knew how to pleasure a woman, but she felt Isabella's heart talking to hers from deep inside them. She'd never felt anything like it.

Kelsey kissed down Isabella's body and settled between her legs. She looked up and found Isabella staring down at her.

"God, I want you, Kels," Isabella said. "Make me yours."

Kelsey smiled then kissed across the sensitive skin just below Isabella's belly. She could smell Isabella's musky scent and couldn't wait any longer. Kelsey ran her tongue up Isabella's wetness and felt such passion erupt in her own body.

Isabella's hips shot off the bed and Kelsey could feel the vibrations from Isabella's groan through her tongue.

"Kelsey!" Isabella shouted.

27

Isabella's fingers were fisted in Kelsey's hair and she was trying to catch a breath. Kelsey's tongue was doing magical things to her center and Isabella thought she might just float away.

"Breathe," Kelsey said softly.

"I'm trying," Isabella replied, holding Kelsey's head between her legs. "Don't stop, baby, please don't stop."

Kelsey moaned and Isabella felt her tongue slide up and around her clit until she moaned with her. Then Kelsey sucked Isabella into her mouth and Isabella's hands hit the bed. *Good God, what is she doing to me?*

Isabella gulped in a deep breath and raised her hips even higher. She felt Kelsey's hands push her back down on the bed as her tongue started to swirl round and round again.

"So good," Isabella moaned.

"Mmm," Kelsey replied with a moan of her own.

Isabella was in a sexual haze of bliss when she felt Kelsey's finger circle her entrance. When she slipped it inside, Isabella reached for Kelsey's head. "I need your lips up here."

She pulled Kelsey to her just as Kelsey put another finger inside her. Isabella groaned as she and Kelsey started a slow, sexy rhythm.

Isabella cupped Kelsey's face in her hands and stared into her eyes. Even in the sliver of light from the moon Isabella could tell they were dark now, but also sparkling. "Kiss me," she whispered.

Kelsey's lips were on hers and their tongues tangled. Isabella wrapped her arms around Kelsey's neck and their rhythm quickened.

The fire inside Isabella was building, getting hotter and hotter. It all felt so good. She moved her hips in perfect rhythm to Kelsey's now deepening strokes. She felt Kelsey's fingers touch her in her most sensitive spot then still inside her.

Isabella tore her lips away from Kelsey's and squeezed her arms around Kelsey's neck, holding on as the orgasm began to take her.

"Look at me, Bella," Kelsey said.

Isabella's eyes flew open and she shared the most intense yet beautiful stare with Kelsey as she went over the edge. She expected music to play and fireworks to go off as a wave of ecstasy flowed through her.

When her body shuddered one last time she smirked at Kelsey. "My God, we could've been doing this the whole time."

Kelsey chuckled. "Oh, Bella. You are amazing."

"Me? You did this!"

"We did this," Kelsey said.

Isabella took a deep breath and sighed. "Oh Kelsey, Kelsey, Kelsey." She moved to get off the bed.

"Where are you going?" Kelsey asked, alarmed.

"I'm closing the door. We may get a little noisy."

Isabella closed the door and got a bottle of water from the refrigerator. She set it on the night stand and crawled back onto the bed. "My turn."

"Uh, Bella. I don't want you to feel like you have to do anything..."

Isabella hovered over Kelsey and looked into her eyes. "Oh, Kels. I've wanted to touch you for so long. I'm counting on our hearts to show me the way, but you have to tell me if I do something you don't like."

"I will," Kelsey said. "Was everything okay..."

Isabella grinned. "You don't even have to ask that."

Kelsey nodded. "I wanted it to be as amazing as you are."

"Oh, baby." Isabella softly kissed Kelsey. She ran her fingers through Kelsey's hair and stared into her eyes. "This feels right." There had been something missing in Isabella's marriage and she had just found it. At this point she wasn't sure if it was being with a woman or if it was Kelsey. It didn't matter. Kelsey had her heart and she hoped Kelsey would keep it.

"I want you, Bella," Kelsey whispered. "All of you."

Isabella wanted to show Kelsey that this was more than just sex to her. She was giving her her heart and it started with a deep, luscious kiss.

"God, when you kiss me like that," Kelsey said breathlessly, "I melt."

Isabella began to kiss down Kelsey's neck. She wanted to find every little sensitive spot on Kelsey's body then revisit it again. She raised up and ran her fingers from Kelsey's shoulder across her chest and between her breasts.

Isabella smiled as her fingers left a trail of goosebumps. Then she noticed Kelsey's nipples harden before her eyes.

She did that! She had that effect on Kelsey's body. It emboldened Isabella, but also amazed her. Kelsey's body was talking to her and Isabella loved it.

Isabella took her finger and drew circles around Kelsey's nipple, getting closer and closer until the pad of her finger gently rubbed the tip.

Kelsey sucked in a breath, drawing Isabella's attention back to Kelsey's beautiful face.

"I'm sorry," Isabella said. "This is all new to me and it's amazing."

"It's okay," Kelsey said softly. "I'm watching your eyes light up in wonder."

"I—I," Isabella stammered. "This is special, Kels. It's our first time, my first time."

"I know," Kelsey said, stroking the side of Isabella's face. "Look what you do to me. If only you could see inside my heart right now."

Isabella smiled. "I intend to try." With that she passionately pressed her lips to Kelsey's. She wanted Kelsey to feel inside her heart. A fresh wave of desire swept through Isabella with urgency.

Her hand cupped Kelsey's breast and her finger and thumb sought her nipple. Isabella pulled her lips from Kelsey's and gave her a sultry smile.

"God, you're beautiful," Isabella said softly. "I can see the anticipation in your eyes. I won't make you wait too long."

"I'm yours," Kelsey whispered.

Isabella nuzzled Kelsey's neck then traced a path with her tongue along her collarbone and over to her other breast. She circled Kelsey's nipple with her tongue then sucked it into her mouth. As good as it felt to have Kelsey's mouth on her, Isabella thought this might be even better.

Kelsey's pebbled nipple begged to be nibbled and caressed.

"Oh, Bella," Kelsey moaned.

Isabella smiled against Kelsey's breast as her hand roamed along her stomach. She could feel Kelsey's muscles flex with every touch.

Kelsey gasped and inhaled. "Bella."

Isabella ran her hand down Kelsey's thigh then up the inside until she felt Kelsey's wetness. She glided her finger between Kelsey's lips and marveled at the feel of her slick, warm folds. *God this is heavenly!* Isabella circled Kelsey's rigid clit as she once again bit down on Kelsey's nipple.

"Fuck, Bella!" Kelsey exclaimed, holding Isabella's head in her hands.

Isabella slid her finger down and around Kelsey's opening. She was so wet and Isabella's finger easily slipped inside. This brought another loud moan from Kelsey, but before Isabella could marvel at the feel of Kelsey on her finger, she heard Kelsey whisper, "More."

Isabella slid another finger inside Kelsey and pushed a little deeper.

"Oh, yes," Kelsey moaned.

Isabella loved the feel of Kelsey around her fingers. The velvety softness was warm, wet, and oh so inviting. She pulled her lips away from Kelsey's breast and looked into her eyes.

"Ready?" Isabella asked softly.

"Mmm," Kelsey moaned. "Let's go."

Isabella began to move her fingers in and out to the rhythm of Kelsey's hips. *Oh, this is fun!*

"Kiss me, babe," Kelsey said with a little desperation in her voice.

Isabella claimed Kelsey's lips and their tongues began to dance to the same rhythm.

Kelsey's groans grew louder and more insistent, so Isabella increased their pace. She pulled her lips away and looked into Kelsey's eyes. Isabella could see the intensity and knew Kelsey was close. How she knew was beyond her, but she knew.

Isabella thrust her fingers a little deeper then curled them to find the elusive spot Kelsey had so easily found inside her. She felt Kelsey clamp down around her fingers and Isabella held them there.

A beatific look passed over Kelsey's face as the orgasm ran through her in waves. Isabella could feel it in her fingers as it flowed from Kelsey through her. *This is incredible!*

Isabella gasped as she felt the orgasm race through her as well. Then there was no sound, no breathing, just their eyes locked on each other. Isabella was inside Kelsey and looking into her heart. For a moment Isabella felt an aura around them. It had to be love.

When their tense muscles eased, they took a breath and exhaled.

"Good God, Bella," Kelsey said softly. "I've never felt anything like that."

Isabella raised her eyebrows and smiled. "Me either," she said almost reverently. "That was truly amazing."

Kelsey reached up and kissed Isabella softly and smiled.

"What was that?" Isabella said.

"You're asking me?"

Isabella tilted her head. "You are the gay one, here."

Kelsey chuckled. "I think you looked inside my heart and now it's yours."

"Oh good." Isabella sighed with relief. "You already have my heart."

She plopped down on the bed and pulled Kelsey into her arms. Neither of them said anything for several moments.

"This is perfect. My arm around you, your head on my shoulder, and my fingers interlaced with yours. This is the way it should be," Isabella said.

"The way what should be?"

"Life, babe. Our life."

"Mmm, it is rather perfect," Kelsey said.

"But?"

"I didn't say but," Kelsey replied.

"I could hear it in your voice."

Kelsey sighed. "I'd rather not talk about buts right now. I'd rather have a drink from that water bottle and do this all over again."

Isabella took the top off the water and handed it to Kelsey. She watched her take a deep drink from it then hand it back. Isabella took a drink as well.

"We should tell Carmen," Isabella said.

Kelsey nodded. "We can in the morning."

"What do you think her reaction will be?"

"I think she'll be happy for us," Kelsey smiled over at her. "But I'm not sure what it means for the marketing campaign."

"We can figure it out, Kels."

"We will," Kelsey said.

"You once told me that you wouldn't give up on us," Isabella said. "I'm not sure you meant this."

"I did mean this," Kelsey stated. "I didn't say more then because I wasn't sure you were ready to hear it."

Isabella put the water bottle back on the table then pushed Kelsey back down on the bed. She held Kelsey's hands on either side of her head and smiled. "You may not be ready to hear this, but I have to tell you."

Kelsey raised her brows.

"I'm falling in love with you, Kels," Isabella said. "If I wasn't sure before I am now. No one has made me feel what you just did. I've never felt so close to another person."

"Our hearts have been talking to each other and tonight we listened," Kelsey said.

Isabella nodded. "Something has been missing in my life for a long time. Now I know, it's you."

Kelsey furrowed her brow. "Really?"

"Yes."

"I've been waiting. I hoped my person was out there. I finally found her." Kelsey reached up and kissed Isabella's lips.

"Oh, Kels. I want to be the person you can count on and share all the girls' successes with," Isabella said.

"Bella." Kelsey smiled. "I remember sharing that with you not long after we met."

"I listened, babe."

Kelsey reached up and cupped the side of Isabella's face. "I'm definitely more than just your friend."

Isabella chuckled. "You were listening, too."

"I think we can talk more later," Kelsey said, pulling Isabella down for a kiss that quickly became heated.

"Mmm." Isabella pulled her lips away and began to kiss down Kelsey's body. "I want to talk to your heart again."

Kelsey gasped as Isabella kissed lower and lower.

28

"Who knew a shower could be this much fun?" Isabella chuckled and wrapped a towel around Kelsey.

"It's so big, it would be a waste not to use it," Kelsey said with a smirk.

"Absolutely." Isabella gave Kelsey a quick kiss.

"Okay, the plan this morning is to go see Carmen and then to the spa, right?"

"I guess," Isabella said as she slowly got dressed. "Are you sure we can't just stay here?"

"I'm sensing something, Bella," Kelsey said. "You sound a little desperate, like this is the only time we'll get to be alone on one of these adventures. This is just our first trip, babe."

Isabella sighed. "It's just that... Who knows about us right now?"

"Well, Dana and Emma do and I imagine Riley has figured it out since she let us talk at her place last month," Kelsey said.

"I just told Riley we had something important to talk

about and couldn't get away from the group," Isabella explained.

"Don't you think she has a pretty good idea what we needed to talk about?"

"Yeah, and if Riley knows then Alex and Liz do, too."

"Okay, so does it matter who knows?" Kelsey asked.

Isabella sighed. "It's just us. We're in our perfect little world with no problems. It's nothing but you and me right now and I want to keep it like that as long as I can. I'm not naive, Kels. I know we'll have challenges and things will come up, but do we have to have them now? I want to put them off as long as I can."

"We will have challenges, but there's no reason to put them off. We'll face them together and as long as we do that everything will be all right. I believe in us, babe. You believe in us, right?"

"Yes, I do."

"We have to think about this and prepare. That doesn't mean we can't do all the things you want to do. We simply need to talk, that's all, nothing more than that."

"I've never been in a shall we say *different* relationship," Isabella said.

Kelsey raised her brows.

"The only reason our relationship is different is because it's two women," Isabella added. "I've always done what everyone expected, so I don't know what is going to be coming at us."

"Okay, I get that, but we'll face the challenges together," Kelsey said again.

"I think I understand now. We have to be prepared. This is not a time to be spontaneous," Isabella said.

Kelsey walked over and pulled Isabella tightly against her. "There's nothing wrong with being spontaneous."

She crushed her lips to Isabella's in a deep, passionate kiss.

"Oh," Isabella said, catching her breath. "I like the way you're spontaneous."

Kelsey smiled, but still held Isabella close. "We never danced last night."

"Uh, we were kind of busy doing another kind of dance." Isabella giggled.

"How about now?" Kelsey said, reaching for her phone.

"We have to go out on the deck then."

As Isabella opened the back door, Kelsey brought up "STRINGS" by MAX. As it began to play, she opened her arms. Isabella smiled and put her arms around Kelsey's neck as she'd done many times before.

"The first time we danced to this song I felt like I was in a dream," Kelsey said. "Your boldness never surprises me now, but it was a different story then."

Isabella chuckled. "Something came over me when I heard that song and looked at you."

"Oh, Bella," Kelsey said softly. She inhaled to slow the emotions that suddenly raced through her body. "When I started to listen to the words, I realized they were true." She smiled and began to sing along with the song. "'Make my heart beat double time when you're on me. Don't you know that's what you do?'"

"I didn't know what was happening to me," Isabella said, gazing into Kelsey's eyes. She cupped the side of Kelsey's face. "I thought it was the island magic Liz had been telling us about. But I couldn't keep from thinking or talking about you after I got home and I knew there was more going on."

Kelsey softly pressed her lips to Isabella's and felt tears sting the back of her eyes. She couldn't quite believe this incredible woman was falling in love with her.

As the song ended Kelsey pulled away. "I love you, Bella," she said, her voice thick with emotion.

"Oh, Kels. I love you, too," Isabella said, pressing her lips to Kelsey's. It was a tender kiss putting an exclamation point on the poignant moment.

Kelsey rested her forehead against Isabella's and sighed. "I didn't mean to get so emotional, but the song and this place…"

"It's the perfect time for me to hear and say I love you," Isabella said with a smile. "It's us."

"It's so us." Kelsey chuckled. She nuzzled Isabella's neck and they held each other for a moment.

"Mmm," Isabella murmured. "I'll remember this moment for the rest of my life."

They pulled away and smiled.

"Okay, let's go see Carmen. I can handle anything with you." Isabella winked.

Kelsey smiled and hoped Isabella would remember that when issues began to surface because she knew they would.

They walked through the resort holding hands and Isabella grinned at Kelsey. "I like this."

Kelsey chuckled. "Is it different than when we walk arm in arm?"

"Yep," Isabella said. "There's a sign flashing over heads that says we're a couple."

Kelsey chuckled. "Oh, my God," she said under her breath. "Here we go."

Isabella laughed as they walked into the lobby and down the hall to Carmen's office.

Kelsey knocked on her open door. "Hi, Carmen."

"I could hear you laughing down the hall. Aren't you

both in a good mood," Carmen said with a smile. "Have a seat. Are you ready to rest and rejuvenate?"

"We are," Isabella said, sitting in one of the chairs across from Carmen's desk.

"There has been a development," Kelsey said, sitting next to Isabella.

"A development? There have been tons of positive comments on your post from the flight yesterday."

"Oh, good," Kelsey said.

"There's also been another uptick in reservations this month. More people are following you two than all the other months combined."

"Really?" Isabella said. "I'm telling you, people want to slow down. They need to recharge."

"So what's this development?" Carmen said, steepling her hands on the desk.

Isabella smiled at Kelsey and reached for her hand. "Kelsey and I are under the island's magic spell. We've fallen in love," she said, looking over at Carmen with a wide grin.

"Oh!" Carmen exclaimed, sitting back in her chair.

"Is that a good oh or a bad oh?" Kelsey asked after a moment. She could see the wheels turning in Carmen's head as she looked from Isabella to Kelsey and back.

Carmen took a breath and let it out then smiled. "Well, first, good for you. That's wonderful." She tilted her head. "You know, Sylvie thought there might be something going on between you two."

Kelsey smiled. "It just kind of happened. Neither one of us was looking for anything—"

"But our hearts had different plans," Isabella finished.

Carmen smiled and sighed. "I'm not sure what this means for us. You two have had chemistry from the beginning and your friendliness is what attracts followers."

"But," Kelsey said, "you're not sure what will happen if they find out we're more than two single moms who've become friends."

Carmen nodded.

"We didn't have many negative comments about our Valentine's trip when one of the couples we highlighted was gay," Isabella said defensively.

"Yes, but they weren't the hosts. It was advertised as a trip for couples to celebrate love in February," Carmen stated. "I wish you nothing but the best, honestly I do. Please understand I have to look at this from a business standpoint as well."

Kelsey nodded. "I get that."

"Couldn't it possibly bring in more queer followers?" Isabella said. "Every month we've mentioned how LGBTQ+ friendly the islands are."

Carmen nodded. "Maybe, but we could also lose as many or more. We've already invested a lot of money in this."

"It isn't like we did this on purpose," Isabella said heatedly.

Kelsey squeezed Isabella's hand and could feel her temper rising.

Carmen smiled. "We don't choose who we fall in love with. I know that as well as anybody. I'm sorry if I offended you, Isabella."

Isabella sighed. "I've never been this happy in my life, Carmen. I'm not about to let you or anyone else question the love Kelsey and I have for each other."

Kelsey raised her eyebrows and held back the grin trying to spread across her face. She knew Isabella could be fierce, but to hear her defend their freshly proclaimed love filled her heart.

"This trip isn't nearly as involved as the ones in the previous months," Kelsey began. "Why don't we take a breath and do a little research?"

"That's a good idea," Carmen said. "I can have our marketing team go over the previous comments and also look into how this could affect the campaign both ways."

"We were going to video in the spa this morning," Kelsey said.

"Then we planned to go to Peaches this afternoon. Could you and Sylvie join us?" Isabella asked.

Carmen stared at them both. "I feel like I've fucked this up with my reaction to this news."

"We're in your office. You're the CEO of this resort. Of course you're thinking of business first," Kelsey said.

"However," Isabella said, glancing at Kelsey then looking at Carmen, "you are the one who threw us together in this lovely resort and have shown us the time of our lives. Perhaps you share some responsibility here, Madame CEO."

Carmen's brows shot up her forehead then she burst out laughing. "Oh, Isabella, I knew you were good. Well played turning this right back on me."

"Seriously, Carmen, why does this have to be a problem?" Isabella said. "We can continue to do the posts and videos just as we've done."

"Let me think this through," Carmen said. "And I would love to meet you at Peaches later this afternoon."

"We'll go do our thing in the spa," Kelsey said, standing up. It was time to give Carmen her space before their words became heated again. Kelsey knew they would be put in a defensive position, but she was surprised by Isabella's reaction.

Carmen came around the desk and hugged them both.

"I really am happy for you. This fucking job gets the best of me sometimes. Thank God for Sylvie."

"She calms you, I take it," Isabella said. "Like Kelsey does me."

"Yes," Carmen said. "Believe me, we were the most unlikely couple when we first got together, but it's worked for almost thirty years."

"Bella is the best thing that has ever happened to me. I may be the more laid-back one, but I won't let a job, or nasty comments, or an account threaten our love. It's new, but it's strong," Kelsey said, gazing over at Isabella.

"It is." Isabella put her arm around Kelsey's shoulder.

"Good, it will have to be," Carmen said. "I'll see you later."

They walked out of Carmen's office and headed towards the spa.

"What did she mean by that last comment?" Isabella asked Kelsey.

"We're two women in love, babe. Not everyone will be happy for us."

"Oh, well. Fuck them." Isabella grinned.

Kelsey chuckled. "I think we could use a couple's massage. What do you say?"

"Hmm, that's a tough one," Isabella said, narrowing her gaze. "I know something else that would take the edge off."

Kelsey giggled. "We can do both!"

Isabella leaned over and quickly kissed Kelsey on the lips. "Oh, I like how you think, love."

29

"This view is more beautiful today than I've ever seen it," Isabella said, leaning on the rail of the ferry. Her arm was looped through Kelsey's and they both gazed out at the beautiful blue water as the breeze blew through their hair. "Aren't you going to ask me why, Kels?"

Kelsey glanced over at her. "I'm sure it has something to do with the couples massage we enjoyed then the fun we had in our bungalow afterwards."

"The fun we had?" Isabella said. "That was some of the absolute best sex I've ever had, babe. Let's call it what it is."

Kelsey giggled. "God, I know. It was amazing."

"Really?" Isabella asked, turning to face Kelsey.

"Yes!" Kelsey assured her. "There's sex and then there's what we did. It felt like you were holding my heart and loving it, but there was more. It's hard to explain. Your love was wrapped around me, inside me, then swirled around us."

"I felt it, but it wasn't just *my* love. It's *our* love." Isabella smiled. "I've never felt anything like this, Kels. When I kissed you, the love inside me exploded and grew. And when you told me you felt the same way, my love had a place to go and that was even better. It was like the icing on the cake."

"Are we being over the top?" Kelsey asked.

"If we are then who cares. I plan to tell you and show you how much I love you every chance I get," Isabella said.

"It may have taken us a while to get here, but once we made it, things really did speed up," Kelsey said.

"Does that bother you?"

"No, I think I've been in love with you since that afternoon we spent on the beach after we met with Carmen the first time. We drank, we swam, we planned these adventures, and we talked. Remember?"

Isabella nodded. "It amazed me how easy it was to talk to you. I felt safe and didn't hesitate to be honest. That's when I should've known something was going on."

"It was friendship, but already so much more."

Isabella took out her phone. "Let's take a pic and send it to Riley so she'll know we're on the way."

They stood next to the railing with the gorgeous blue sky meeting the sparkling water as their backdrop. Their smiles were bright and love shone in their eyes.

As they left the ferry Kelsey said, "Let's walk to Peaches. We can take the beach route and surprise them."

"It's such a beautiful day," Isabella said, grabbing Kelsey's hand.

"It's not as beautiful as my girlfriend," Kelsey said, kissing Isabella's cheek.

"Your girlfriend?" Isabella teased. She stopped and looked at Kelsey. "You're my girlfriend. I've never had a girlfriend."

Kelsey raised her brows. "I promise I'm worth it."

Isabella melted. "Oh, babe." She wrapped her arms around Kelsey and held her close. Isabella hadn't really thought about what it meant to be in a relationship with another woman. She realized problems would arise, but they did in all relationships, right?

After a moment Kelsey pulled back. "Is everything okay?"

Isabella nodded. "I can't imagine my life without you now and I don't ever want to."

Kelsey smiled and they began to walk again. "We're on island time, remember? Real life can wait until we get back on the plane."

Isabella furrowed her brow and wondered what would happen after this trip. Being away from Kelsey had become harder and harder, but they were together now and that's what mattered.

"I can almost taste my favorite fruity drink Alex makes," Kelsey said as Peaches came into view.

"There's Riley," Isabella said, waving to the woman on the patio.

"Hey!" Riley shouted.

When they got closer Riley put her hands on her hips and smirked. "Is there something you need to tell us?"

Isabella laughed. "Let's just say that our talk last month went well."

"I was wondering." Riley laughed. "I'm happy for you both."

"Thanks," Kelsey said, grinning at Isabella and kissing the back of her hand.

"Oh, you've got it bad," Riley said.

"If you mean being in love, then yes we do," Isabella said, smiling back at Kelsey.

"Wow, things change quickly around here," Riley said.

"You're one to talk," Liz said, joining them on the patio. "You and Alex fell in love in less than two weeks." She gave Kelsey a hug then turned to Isabella. "You see what I see now, don't you?"

"Yep." Isabella grinned, hugging Liz. "I'd give your island magic the credit, but it was our hearts." She put her arm around Kelsey and gazed into her eyes. "They knew from the beginning."

"Yeah, we finally listened to them," Kelsey said.

"We need to celebrate," Liz said. "Alex is inside making your favorite drinks."

"Perfect," Isabella said.

Riley led them to a table. "Sit down and tell us what happened."

"I think we know what happened. You two could no longer deny your feelings," Liz said.

"Here we go." Alex set a tray down on the table and passed everyone a drink. "Welcome back."

They all clinked their glasses together and drank.

"I almost said welcome home." Alex chuckled. "Have we convinced you two to move here yet?"

"Oh gosh, could you imagine?" Isabella said, looking at Kelsey.

"You never know." Kelsey shrugged. "Maybe someday."

"I could tell your girls loved Isabella," Liz said. "Were they surprised you became more than friends?" She wiggled her eyebrows.

Kelsey chuckled. "They couldn't understand why we weren't together from the beginning. But you're right. They love Isabella and are happy we're together."

"I haven't explained it to my boys yet," Isabella said. "This trip was for us to figure it all out."

"What's to figure out?" Liz said.

"Well, we live in separate states. I have two boys still in school and Kelsey and I are in the middle of this big marketing campaign."

"Not to mention this is a brand new relationship that comes with issues simply because you are both women," Riley said.

"Yeah, this is all new to me," Isabella said. "But I love Kelsey. I don't see why that should be a problem for anyone else."

"You're right, hon. But it's surprising how people you don't even know will have an opinion about who you love," Liz said.

"Have you told Carmen?" Alex asked.

Kelsey nodded. "We talked to her this morning. She's supposed to meet us here later."

"She was happy for us, but it could affect the project," Isabella said.

"You never know how people online are going to react," Alex said. "It gives them a sense of anonymity."

"Yeah, and people can be awful," Riley said, reaching for Alex's hand. "We deal with assholes from time to time."

"I hope you don't mean me," Sylvie said, walking onto the patio with Carmen right behind her.

"Hey," Liz said. "You're only awful when we need you to be."

Sylvie laughed. "I have had to play bouncer a few times."

"I think I'm the awful one today," Carmen said, sitting down across from Kelsey and Isabella.

"I'm sure you were surprised by our news," Kelsey said.

"I shouldn't have been, but I don't think you're going to like what I have to say," Carmen replied.

Isabella raised her brows and reached for Kelsey's hand under the table. "Why's that?"

"For now, we think it's best for you two to remain the friendly single moms in front of the camera," Carmen said.

"I don't know why it has to be such a big deal," Isabella said softly then sighed.

"It won't be any different than what you've been doing," Carmen said.

"I understand that," Kelsey said. "But what if we run into people at the resort that are here because of the earlier posts we've done? Are we supposed to act like nothing is going on between us while we're in public?"

Carmen nodded. "I know it's a lot to ask, but for now I'd rather you keep your relationship between us."

"It might be a good thing." Riley shrugged. "You won't have anyone staring or approaching you with questions."

"I'm not sure why you want to keep it a secret," Liz said. "It was obvious from the beginning that the two of them have chemistry. Don't you think your followers can see that?"

"That's just it. We never mentioned anything about them being a couple. If it comes out, I think it could be a shit show," Carmen said.

"Some people won't like that you're gay," Alex said. "Some people will think you were keeping secrets."

"And others may not give a shit," Isabella said, exasperation in her voice. She had no idea this would be such a big deal. While she had concerns about how her boys might react, she never dreamed it would be such a problem for the resort.

"I know you think we're making a big deal out of this when we shouldn't, but you and Kelsey are reaching more people than you think, Isabella. And you of all people know how a blemish on our brand could affect us going forward," Carmen said.

"Of course I understand all that," Isabella said. "In my experience, honesty works so much better in the long run. Trying to spin things often times leads to more problems."

Carmen studied them for a moment. "Give me more time to think this through. I'm listening to what you're saying, but I also know there are more haters out there than you think."

Isabella looked over at Kelsey. She didn't want to hide her feelings. The last couple of days had felt magical. They had openly expressed their love for each other whether it was through a look, a touch, or simply a smile. It felt wonderful and freeing. And now Carmen wanted them to rein it in.

Kelsey gave Isabella a sad smile. "I guess that messes up our first date."

"It's okay." Isabella squeezed her hand.

"What are you talking about?" Riley asked.

"We realized all this time we were kind of dating," Kelsey said.

"Yeah, we just didn't know it." Isabella chuckled. "Anyway, we were going to get dressed up and have our first official date at the resort."

"I'm sorry," Carmen said with an apologetic look.

"You can have it here," Riley said. "I know a place that is very romantic as well as private." Riley looked at Alex and raised her brows.

"What a great idea," Alex said. "We'll take care of everything."

"You don't have to do that. We can stay in our bungalow," Isabella said.

"Absolutely not," Liz said. "Let us show you a little island hospitality."

"You've been showing us that since we've met," Kelsey replied.

"Then let your friends do something special for you," Riley countered.

"Besides, you've been bringing us business," Sylvie said. "This may have started with highlighting the resort, but it's helped me and other businesses, too. Come on, I'll be your private water taxi."

Isabella looked at Kelsey and widened her eyes. "What do you think?"

Kelsey smiled. "I think we have a date tonight."

30

Kelsey was standing on the deck of the bungalow and couldn't wait to see Isabella. They had stayed at Peaches and had another drink with their friends before Sylvie took them back to St. Thomas to get ready for their date.

Riley, Alex, and Liz had planned a special evening for them and Kelsey couldn't quite believe it. She knew the islands could be magical, but she'd attributed that to the beautiful surroundings and how the people catered to tourists. But this was more than that. These were their friends and they were happy she and Isabella had found their way to each other.

Kelsey decided to stop questioning everything and just enjoy it. She took a deep breath, closed her eyes, and let the sounds of the waves along with the breeze give her a moment of calm.

"Hey there, sexy," Isabella said from the back door.

Kelsey turned around and with one look at Isabella, she lost her breath. "Bella," she gasped. "You're so beautiful."

"Do you like it?" Isabella held the hem of her dress out and twirled in a circle.

She was wearing a short dress that hugged her waistline as the skirt flowed around her thighs. The spaghetti straps were hidden under her loose blond curls that rested on her shoulders. The azure color of the dress made Isabella's eyes sparkle an even deeper blue.

"I love it," Kelsey said. "I can't stop staring at you."

"Oh, honey. Look at you! I won't be able to take my eyes off of you all night," Isabella said.

It was Kelsey's turn to do a little twirl with a shy smile. She was wearing a soft floral print dress with a high-low hem and flowy skirt. It was a sleeveless V-neck, also with spaghetti straps, and an open back. It was more revealing than anything Kelsey had ever purchased for herself, but when she saw it she knew she wanted to wear it for Isabella.

Kelsey remembered Isabella commenting on their first trip how much she liked it when she wore her hair down. So Kelsey decided to let her curls hang loose just above her shoulders.

Isabella walked over and reached for Kelsey's hands. Kelsey watched as Isabella gazed up and down her body then met her eyes. "You are the most beautiful woman I've ever seen, Kels."

Kelsey grinned. "We are a stunning couple."

Isabella leaned up and gently kissed Kelsey's lips. "Mmm, are we sure we want to do this? Our bungalow is pretty inviting right about now."

Kelsey chuckled. "Oh no, we're going out for a romantic evening, my gorgeous love."

They heard a knock at the door and Kelsey furrowed her brow. "I wonder who that could be?"

"We're not supposed to be at the dock to meet Sylvie for another twenty minutes," Isabella said.

Kelsey opened the door to find Carmen smiling at them.

"Hi," she said. "Oh, my. You both look absolutely incredible."

"Thank you," Isabella said. "We never get to dress up on these trips and it's fun."

"Is something wrong?" Kelsey asked with a flutter of uneasiness in her stomach.

"No, no. Everything is fine. I wanted to drive you to the dock to meet Sylvie," Carmen said.

"You don't have to do that."

"I want to," Carmen said. She looked at Kelsey then Isabella. "I feel bad about the whole situation. I really want you to have a special evening."

Kelsey glanced at Isabella and gave her hand a squeeze. "I know you have to do what's best for the resort. We understand, right, babe?"

Isabella nodded and smiled. "We do. It's been a bit of a whirlwind when you think about it. When Kelsey and I came here we never thought about making a new friend, much less falling in love. Here we are in the middle of a huge, dare I say, successful marketing campaign. We've fallen in love and now what do we do?" Isabella chuckled. "We'll figure it out together."

"Thank you for understanding. But tonight is all about your special first date. Shall we?" Carmen said, walking out the front door.

They walked down the path that led to the front of the resort. Kelsey felt Isabella put her arm through hers and smiled over at her.

"Hey, Kelsey. Hey, Isabella," someone called from the pool.

They stopped and two women approached them. "We've been following your trips and can't thank you enough for this one. When you announced this month was to relax and recharge, my friends and I couldn't make reservations soon enough."

"Oh, wow," Isabella said. "I'm so glad you're making time for yourselves."

"We did massages this afternoon after we saw your post this morning," the other woman said.

"Weren't they amazing?" Kelsey said.

"Oh, yeah," the two women said in unison.

"Tomorrow is a beach day," Isabella said. "The resort has the best attendants that will bring you anything you need."

"This is Carmen Oliver," Kelsey said. "She's the CEO of the resort and will make sure you have a wonderful time."

Carmen shook each of the women's hands and smiled.

"We don't mean to keep you. It was nice meeting you all," the woman said.

"Wait," the second woman said. "Could we get a picture with you?"

"Of course," Isabella replied.

"Let me take it," Carmen offered.

Kelsey gently put her arm around Isabella's waist as the women stood on either side of them. They all smiled and Kelsey couldn't imagine that these women would care if they knew they were a couple.

"Thank you," the woman said. "We'll post this in the comments and tag you both."

"Have a wonderful evening," Kelsey said.

"You, too," the second woman said. "You both look lovely."

As they walked away Carmen looked over at them but didn't say anything.

"Maybe we should just ask them," Isabella said.

"Ask them?"

"Yeah. Hey, thanks for coming to the resort," Isabella began. "You'll never guess what happened. Kelsey and I have fallen in love. Does that make you want to stop following us?"

Kelsey chuckled and played along. "Why no, Isabella. We're all about the rest and relaxation this trip. By the way, you both look amazing."

Carmen smirked and started towards the lobby. "You both do look amazing. Let's forget about all the other stuff and have a lovely evening."

Kelsey smiled at Isabella and put her arm through hers. "I already am."

Sylvie was waiting at the dock and whisked them over to Peaches. It was such a beautiful night and the stars were beginning to come out. The moon was shining bright and lighting their way across the calm water.

Once they were on shore, Sylvie drove them to Peaches where they walked in to find Liz, Riley, and Alex waiting for them.

"Welcome," Riley said. "We have a special table for you. If you'll follow me."

"Wait, what about all of you?" Isabella asked.

"We'll take you back when you're ready. No hurry," Sylvie said.

"Liz and Alex are taking care of the bar and I'm taking care of you," Riley said with a grin. "Now, please follow me."

Kelsey held out her arm to Isabella and they followed Riley through the door and up to their apartment.

"I know you've been up here before, but it's quite the romantic spot when the moon is out and the stars are shining," Riley said.

They went through the bedroom up to the rooftop where a string of lights adorned the sitting area. There was a table set off to one side and Riley reached into the small refrigerator for a bottle of wine.

"Riley, this is beautiful," Isabella said.

She poured each of them a glass of wine. "Take a little time to enjoy your drink and I'll be back up with dinner shortly."

"Thank you," Kelsey said.

"It's our pleasure," Riley said with a wink then left them alone.

Isabella raised her glass. "To our first date of many."

Kelsey smiled and touched her glass to Isabella's. She took a sip of her wine, but her eyes never left Isabella's. "Are you sure about all this?"

Isabella raised her brows then her face relaxed into the most beautiful smile. "I am. I know we'll have challenges to overcome along the way, but I'm sure about you and me."

Kelsey grinned. "I wanted to give you one more chance because I'm never letting you go, Bella." She reached for Isabella's hand and led them over to the edge of the deck. They looked out over the water, a blanket of stars above them.

"I don't like this idea of hiding our relationship," Isabella said. "I know I haven't been in your shoes, Kels, or faced the things you have, but I don't think I can hide this happiness I feel. People are going to know."

"I don't like it either," Kelsey replied. "I'm not sure hiding it is the right thing to do. I agree with you that honesty would be the best way to handle it."

"Maybe we could drop little hints here and there and see what happens," Isabella said, taking a sip of her wine.

"Hmm," Kelsey murmured. "Why would we act any

differently than we have? I mean, I'm not going to post that picture we took last month of us kissing. That's for us. Let's do our regular thing tomorrow on the beach and see how it goes."

"We'll see if we act any differently," Isabella said.

"Good plan." Kelsey leaned over and kissed Isabella softly.

"I was thinking," Isabella said. "Do you have to go back to Denver once we land in Charlotte?"

Kelsey tilted her head. "I guess I don't. Why?"

"Well, if you're not letting me go, don't you think it's time you met Wyatt and Gus in person?" Isabella said, raising one eyebrow. "Stay with us a few days before you go back to Denver."

Kelsey widened her eyes. She had talked to the boys regularly since starting this marketing campaign. They had all done video calls and the boys were often in the background when she talked to Isabella.

"Is that fear in your eyes, babe?" Isabella asked, amused.

"No, it's just that my girls love you and..."

"And my boys are going to love *you*. They ask you about the family vacation every week."

"Are you sure?" Kelsey said

"You keep asking me that," Isabella said. "Maybe I need to ask you?"

Kelsey reached for their glasses and put them on a nearby table. She put her hands on Isabella's hips. "I've told you that I want you here and also in our real life. We haven't talked about what's next, but I love you and what I see is our big happy family."

Isabella put her hands on Kelsey's cheeks and cradled her face. "Oh, Kels. I love you, too. That's exactly what I want."

Kelsey pressed her lips to Isabella's in a heated kiss. She pulled her closer and deepened the kiss as Isabella's arms wrapped around her neck.

"Mmm," Isabella moaned, gasping for a breath.

They heard Riley coming up the stairs and Kelsey quickly kissed Isabella again.

"There will be more of that later," Isabella said softly.

Kelsey giggled and handed Isabella her wine. "Much more."

"Hey," Riley said, stepping onto the deck with a bag of food. "Dinner is served. I've brought a variety of seafood."

"Oh wow, Riley," Kelsey said, helping her set out the food.

"That's what we had the first time we had dinner together," Isabella said.

"There is a Wi-Fi speaker over on that table if you want to play music. Do you need anything else?" Riley asked.

"I don't think so," Kelsey said, looking over the spread before them.

"If you need anything, text me. Other than that you're welcome to stay up here as long as you want," Riley said.

"Thank you, Riley. You're spoiling us," Isabella said.

"Nonsense. You're our friends and we're happy to do it. One of these days we'll visit you in the states and I know you'd do the same for us."

"We'd love that!" Kelsey exclaimed.

Riley smiled. "Enjoy the rest of your evening."

They watched her go down the stairs then turned to their feast.

31

"Oh, babe," Isabella said. "Taste this." She forked a piece of conch into Kelsey's mouth.

"Mmm," Kelsey moaned. "This is so good."

"I know," Isabella replied. "All of it is. Riley must have gotten this from the restaurant next door."

Kelsey topped off their glasses as her phone began to ring. Isabella reached for it and handed it to Kelsey. "It's Dana. They just can't leave us alone," she teased.

Kelsey chuckled as she answered. "Hey, kiddo."

"Mom, I'm not a kid anymore," Dana droned.

"You'll always be my kid," Kelsey replied.

"Hold on while I connect Emma," Dana said.

Kelsey put them on speaker and waited. "This ought to be good."

"Hey, Mom," Emma's voice echoed from the phone. "Is Isabella with you?"

"Hello to you, Em." Kelsey chuckled.

Isabella laughed. "I'm here. Hi you two!"

"Isabella," Emma said. "Dana and I want to invite you to our graduation next month."

"I graduate on Friday and Emma on Saturday," Dana explained. "We really hope you can be there."

Isabella beamed a smile at Kelsey in excitement. "I'd love to!"

"Great. If you want to bring Wyatt and Gus let me know and we'll find some fun things to do with them," Dana said.

Isabella shrugged. "But this is your special day. Are you sure you want them tagging along?"

"Of course we want them there," Emma said. "Make sure Carmen doesn't plan your next trip for that weekend."

"I've already told her," Kelsey said.

"Okay. What are you two doing?"

"We're on our first official date," Kelsey said.

"Let me take a picture and send to you," Isabella said. She quickly snapped a picture and texted it to them.

"Aww, you both look so nice. You're all dressed up," Dana said. "Mom, is that a new dress?"

Kelsey smiled shyly. "This is a special occasion."

Isabella smiled and kissed Kelsey on the cheek.

"Okay, we need to leave you alone now," Emma said. "Have fun, see you next month."

"Bye, Mom. Bye, Isabella," Dana said, ending the call.

Kelsey chuckled. "Those two."

"I love them. I can't believe they invited me to graduation."

"I'm so glad they did," Kelsey said. Then she gasped and put both hands on her cheeks.

"What's wrong, babe?" Isabella asked.

"I just realized I have someone to share this with," Kelsey said as tears pooled in her eyes. "I remember our conversation that day on the beach. I didn't realize how much it meant to me until right this moment." Tears spilled down Kelsey's cheeks.

Isabella moved closer to Kelsey and took her in her arms. "Oh babe, we'll be celebrating so many successes together."

Kelsey's head rested on Isabella's shoulder. "I hope so." She pulled away and looked into Isabella's eyes. "It won't be easy."

"I don't know what all you've been through and what you've faced as a gay single mom, but you're no longer alone, Kels. I will fight for us. I will fight for our kids. I will protect you."

Kelsey smiled. "I got that idea in Carmen's office this morning. You were fierce and defended our love even though it's so new."

"It may be new, but I know in my heart that we belong together. We have so much love to give and it will only grow. Just imagine how wonderful it's going to be. Our kids will feel it and it will make them strong, too."

Kelsey kissed Isabella softly.

"I know you're worried, but I'm strong and I believe in us. Trust me, baby," Isabella said.

"I do trust you," Kelsey said. "But it's like Alex said earlier today. People can be awful."

"Believe me, I know that. Is there anyone nastier than a snobby Southern woman who thinks she knows best and her kids do no wrong?" Isabella said with an exaggerated Southern drawl.

Kelsey raised her eyebrows and stared.

"I've grown up with those women and my kids go to school with their kids. I know hate, Kels."

"But what if they direct it towards your kids, babe? That's different from you and me," Kelsey said. "I don't want to put a damper on our lovely evening, but I'm worried for Wyatt and Gus."

Isabella smiled and caressed Kelsey's face. "We'll take care of the boys. I'll try not to murder anyone because you know how I can be. Wyatt and Gus know love and it's stronger than any of the shit people will throw at us."

"For someone who's never been on this side of things you're very sure of yourself," Kelsey said.

"It breaks my heart that anyone would mistreat you because you're gay, but I have to be smart, not lose my temper, and be an example for the boys and your girls," Isabella said. "I may yell and scream with you and talk a big game, but throwing hate at hate isn't going to help anyone."

"My God, my girlfriend isn't only beautiful and smart, she's also fucking amazing," Kelsey said with pride.

Isabella grinned. "You bought a new dress to wear for me?" she said, lifting her brows.

Kelsey nodded. "I remember the picture you took of me on the beach that first day. You said I was beautiful and didn't know it."

"I remember," Isabella said softly.

"I feel beautiful when you look at me, Bella. When I saw this dress I could imagine the look in your eyes."

Isabella raised her brows. "What did you see in my eyes when I looked at you?"

"I saw love."

"Oh, there was more than love in my eyes," Isabella said, leaning over and capturing Kelsey's lips in a passionate kiss.

Kelsey giggled. "I may have seen a little lust."

Isabella laughed. "Oh, honey. There was a lot of lust and there still is."

Their lips met again in a playful kiss that quickly became much more. Isabella pulled Kelsey closer and moaned with desire. She ran her hand up Kelsey's thigh and under her dress.

"Mmm," Kelsey groaned. "Babe," she whispered breathlessly.

"I love you," Isabella said softly. She could feel Kelsey's wetness through her panties. It amazed Isabella that she could do this to Kelsey, but she couldn't think about that right now.

Isabella slipped her hand inside Kelsey's undies and her fingers were covered in slick warm wetness. Kelsey groaned a little louder and Isabella covered her mouth with her own in another heated kiss.

She pressed her finger up and through Kelsey's folds then circled her clit. God, she loved touching this woman and the way her groans vibrated through Isabella's body.

"So good," Isabella moaned. She slipped her finger inside Kelsey and felt her arms tighten around her shoulders. Isabella pushed her finger even deeper.

"Oh, God, babe," Kelsey said, tearing her lips away from Isabella's.

"Let go," Isabella whispered, stroking her finger across Kelsey's most sensitive spot. She felt Kelsey clamp around her finger as her whole body tensed.

The orgasm was fast and intense. A moment later Kelsey took a deep breath and groaned. "Bella!"

Isabella giggled. "Oh, that was fun."

Kelsey exhaled another breath then chuckled. "You!"

Isabella shrugged. "It's you! And that new dress."

Kelsey smirked and reached for her wine.

"We've never walked on the beach over here at night. What do you say?"

"I'd love to. We can dance when we get back to our bungalow," Kelsey replied.

They went downstairs, waved at Riley, and slipped out

through the patio to the beach. The wind was cool coming off the water and the waves were playing their song.

Isabella held Kelsey's hand and they walked right on the edge of the water. "Walking on the beach with you is one of my favorite things."

"I picture these moments in my head when I'm home," Kelsey said.

"I know you worry about what's to come and you especially worry about me, but I assure you, babe, I've thought about this."

Kelsey squeezed her hand.

"Since we met at Christmas, I've been thinking about us and what it would mean to be with you," Isabella said.

"You have?" Kelsey looked at her in surprise.

"Yep. I asked myself a lot of questions. Why did it feel so good to be in your arms when we danced for the first time? From there I knew we were more than friends. I thought about what that could mean for me and the boys." Isabella paused for a moment to take a breath.

Kelsey patiently waited and that's one thing Isabella loved about her.

"Before I met you, I was just going about life. I got married, had kids, and worked on a career. Like I've said, doing what was expected. But after Spencer and I split up I knew I wouldn't do that again. My heart kept telling me there was more to life. I wasn't living; I was just doing. When I met you it all started to come together. There were many nights when I couldn't sleep and stared at the ceiling, but it all clicked into place when I let myself think of you and me together."

Isabella stopped walking and turned to Kelsey, taking her hands.

"My heart was singing with happiness whenever I

simply thought of you. It felt settled and the uneasiness was gone. I know this will be hard. I'm not naive. I know people will not approve and the boys will bear part of that. I hope not, but I'm prepared. I know my heart, Kels, and it's yours. Don't be afraid to take it. Let me tell you the same thing you told me. I'm worth it. We're worth it."

"Bella," Kelsey said with tears in her eyes. "You've had my heart from the beginning. Our love *is* worth it. I surrounded my girls with love and it's gotten us through. We'll do the same for Wyatt and Gus."

Isabella smiled in relief. They would face all of these challenges together. "One other thing," she said. "We'll finish this trip, but after that I'm not hiding. Our relationship is beautiful and we fell in love in a beautiful place. If that isn't the ultimate advertisement then Carmen doesn't know marketing."

Kelsey laughed. "We'll find a way to tell our followers. We'll lose a few, but you never know what we'll gain."

"So we're doing this," Isabella said as they began to walk back towards Peaches.

"Yep. We're doing real life with a little island time sprinkled in."

"You'll come back to Charlotte with me and meet the boys. It'll be a look at our real life. Then I'll come to Denver with you and the girls. We'll take it a step at a time."

"Our real life now is us together," Kelsey said. "I miss you so much when we're apart."

"I know, babe," Isabella replied. "I miss you, too. We'll figure that step out sooner rather than later."

"When things get hard," Kelsey said, stopping and facing Isabella.

"And they will," Isabella added.

"Look up," Kelsey said.

They both looked up to see millions of stars twinkling in the sky. "Our love is this big and this beautiful," Kelsey said. "We'll remember this moment, when we were both happy, strong, and so in love."

Isabella looked back down into Kelsey's eyes. "So in love," she said softly, pressing her lips to Kelsey's. "I'm ready to go back. This has been lovely, but I need to be naked in your arms," she said. She kissed Kelsey again knowing they wouldn't always be this happy, but they would be in love.

32

"I know I've talked to Wyatt and Gus several times, but I'm nervous," Kelsey said as they pulled into Isabella's driveway.

"They already love you, Kels."

"But you didn't warn them," Kelsey said.

"Yes, I did," Isabella said with a grin. "I told them I'm bringing a big surprise."

Kelsey sighed.

Isabella reached over and squeezed her hand. "Come on, babe."

They got out of the car and walked to Isabella's front door. She opened it and before she could say anything Gus exclaimed. "Mommy!"

He jumped up, ran to the front door and stopped. "Kelsey?"

"Hi, Gus," Kelsey said with a big smile.

He ran to her and hugged her tightly. Kelsey raised her brows at Isabella and put her arms around the little boy. Isabella thought her heart would melt in her chest.

Gus looked up into Kelsey's face and grinned. "Are you our surprise?"

Kelsey chuckled. "I hope you're not too disappointed."

"Yippee!" he said, letting her go. "Wyatt! You'll never guess who's here." He took off down the hall and disappeared.

"That shows you how much they miss me." Isabella shrugged.

Gus came running back into the room with his older brother behind him. "See!" Gus said, running up to Kelsey.

"Hold it, mister," Isabella said. "How about a hug for your mom?"

Gus giggled and threw his arms around Isabella.

"Hi, Wyatt," Kelsey said with a smile.

"You're really here," he replied. "Are Dana and Emma with you?"

"Not this time. They graduate from college next month so they're back in Colorado studying, I hope."

He nodded and hugged Isabella. "Hi, Mom."

Isabella hugged her oldest son and smiled over the top of his head at Kelsey. "He'll be as tall as me by the end of the summer."

Wyatt pulled away and grinned, then he put an arm around Kelsey and gave her a side hug. "Are you going to be here tomorrow after school?"

Kelsey smiled and looked at Isabella. "Yes, I'm staying a couple of days."

"I have a baseball game tomorrow night. Mom always comes and you're invited, too," Wyatt said.

"I'd love to watch you play."

He smiled shyly and nodded.

"Okay, boys. Out of the way. It's my turn," Marti said as she came into the room.

"Mom, I'd like you to meet Kelsey Kenny," Isabella said.

Kelsey stuck out her hand. "It's nice to meet you."

Marti took her hand and pulled her into a hug. "We're huggers around here. Isabella speaks of you so often that I feel like I know you."

Kelsey hugged the woman back.

"Please, call me, Marti," she said, letting Kelsey go. "How was the trip?"

"It was great," Isabella replied, looking over at Kelsey.

"Yeah it was," Kelsey said with a shy smile.

Isabella watched this play out and couldn't believe the emotions that flowed through her. Kelsey belonged with them. She knew it and now her family did too.

"Can we have pizza tonight?" Gus asked.

"Yeah, Mom," Wyatt added. "We promised Kelsey we'd get Santini's when she came to see us!"

Isabella turned to her mother. "One evening when we were talking to Kelsey on the phone, our pizza arrived, which led to quite the discussion on the best toppings."

"That's right," Kelsey agreed. "What toppings are you going to get, Wyatt?"

He gave her a sly look. "Sausage and...onions."

"Oh, yuck," Kelsey said, making a face. "Not for me."

Wyatt laughed. "I was just kidding. I know you don't like onions, neither does Mom. How about sausage and olives?"

"Ohhh," Kelsey exclaimed. "I'm in."

"Wait," Gus said. "Let's get one with pepperoni, too."

"I love pepperoni, Gus," Kelsey said. "It's my favorite!"

The little boy beamed a smile at Kelsey. "Do you want to play a video game with me?"

"Oh?" Kelsey narrowed her gaze. "Do I? Are you going to kick my you-know-what?"

Gus giggled. "Yep. I'm gonna dominate!"

"Come on, let's set the game up," Wyatt said, putting his arm around Gus's neck and pulling him towards the TV.

And just like that Kelsey made her place in this family. Dana and Emma were all they were missing.

The next day Kelsey went with Isabella to take the boys to school. Isabella needed to check in with a couple of clients and Kelsey tagged along. They met Marti for lunch then went home to work on the marketing campaign.

After they returned from a trip they usually waited a day before looking back over their posts and reading over all the comments. Now, they sat side by side on Isabella's couch, both staring at their computers.

"These are all okay," Kelsey said. "There's nothing negative. Several have asked what we're doing in May."

"Since we're doing the trip at the end of the month we could make it a graduation trip," Isabella suggested.

"Or a school's out celebration," Kelsey said.

Isabella nodded. "Either would work. I'll email Carmen and let her choose."

Kelsey closed her laptop and leaned back on the couch. Once Isabella hit send, she set her computer on the coffee table and turned to Kelsey. She leaned in and softly kissed her.

"Mmm," Isabella murmured. "Do you have any idea how much I loved waking up this morning with you in my bed?"

Kelsey smiled. "I could get used to waking up with you every morning."

"Is that so," Isabella said, pushing Kelsey down on the couch. "You were afraid to make a sound last night."

Kelsey smirked. "I didn't want the boys to hear us."

"They wouldn't have heard us," Isabella said. "We're

going to have sex while the boys are in the house, Kels. We are."

Kelsey raised her eyebrows.

"You'll be more comfortable tonight."

"I'm comfortable right here with you on top of me," Kelsey said.

Isabella propped her head on her hand and gazed into Kelsey's eyes. "This is better than I imagined. We are here, together, in the same house, and it's real life."

Kelsey smiled and smoothed her hand over Isabella's hair. "Can you imagine being together every day, just like this?"

Isabella answered by touching Kelsey's lips softly with her own. "I want you with me all the time. Every day, all day."

Kelsey put her arms around Isabella and pulled her down for a heated kiss.

"Mmm," Isabella moaned and slipped her hand under Kelsey's shirt, cupping her breast.

"Right here?" Kelsey asked breathlessly.

"You have awakened something inside me, baby," Isabella replied, kissing Kelsey's neck. "Sex was never like this before. I've never wanted to touch someone like I do you." Isabella raised up to look into Kelsey's eyes. "That's why I've always got my arm through yours when we're simply walking. That's why I can't stop looking at you when we're in the same room. That's why I often FaceTimed you instead of texting or calling."

"But we only had sex for the first time this trip," Kelsey said.

"We were loving each other and touching each other long before we had sex." Isabella smiled. "And now I have all of you."

"I'm yours, Bella," Kelsey whispered.

Isabella softly kissed Kelsey's lips, her cheek, and just below her ear as her fingers unbuttoned and unzipped Kelsey's jeans. She slid her hand inside her pants and her undies. Her fingers were greeted with wetness and she smiled.

"That's what you do to me," Kelsey moaned. She pushed her pants down her thighs, giving Isabella more room. "God, I want you, Bella."

Isabella's fingers slid through Kelsey's wetness then she slipped two fingers inside.

Kelsey groaned with pleasure and Isabella pushed a little deeper.

"You are so beautiful," Isabella whispered. She began to move her fingers in and out as her lips found Kelsey's. Their tongues tangled in a sensual dance of love.

Isabella had found that she loved to take the lead in their lovemaking. Just like now, when desire began to build with a single look or an innocent kiss, Isabella didn't want to hold back. She wanted to show Kelsey how much she wanted her and loved her.

"Oh, baby," Kelsey moaned. "Right there," she gasped.

Isabella focused her efforts where Kelsey most needed it and felt the orgasm race through her.

Kelsey's hand covered Isabella's as she held it in place.

"Holy fuck," Kelsey said breathlessly.

Isabella smiled. "That's how much I love you."

"Oh, God," Kelsey said, opening her eyes. "I'm the luckiest woman in the world."

Isabella chuckled. "Yeah, you are. Right along with me."

Kelsey grinned and caressed Isabella's cheek with her hand. "I love you, too."

"Let's hold each other for a few minutes then we'll get the boys, have a snack, and play some baseball."

"Mmm," Kelsey replied, pulling Isabella closer. "That sounds perfect."

* * *

They climbed up the bleachers to the left of home plate and sat near the third base dugout. Isabella had already introduced Kelsey to several of the other mothers before sitting in their seats.

"Mom, can I go play with my friends?" Gus asked Isabella.

"Why don't you sit with us for a minute and watch your brother," Isabella replied.

"Okay," Gus said, plopping down next to Kelsey. "I wish you could stay longer and see me play, too."

"I know," Kelsey said. "I'll come back and watch you this summer. I promise."

Gus smiled up at her. "Hey, there's Gran," he said, waving at Marti.

Kelsey had grown to like the boys through their conversations and the stories Isabella told her, but she had no idea how quickly they would steal her heart. She didn't seem to upset their routine by being there and Kelsey felt comfortable being in the middle of everything.

Marti made her way up the bleachers and sat in front of Isabella and Kelsey. "I saw your daddy in the parking lot, Gus," she said.

Isabella bumped Kelsey's shoulder with hers. "I'll introduce you to him after the game. He usually stands down at the end of the dugout with a few of the other dads."

Kelsey was curious about Spencer Burns. She couldn't imagine how he could ever let Isabella go.

"Wyatt is playing third base today and Spencer will be down there in his ear," Isabella said despairingly. "I think it makes Wyatt nervous. I've told Spencer to ease up but he doesn't listen to me."

"Yeah," Kelsey replied. "Wyatt mentioned that to me once before. We'll encourage him from here." She smiled at Isabella.

"Hey, Gus," a man called from the walkway in front of the bleachers. "Come stand down here with me." He waved at Isabella and waited.

"That's Spencer," Isabella said.

Kelsey made eye contact with the man and smiled. She'd seen pictures of him on Isabella's phone and could just make out his short blond hair under his baseball cap. He was dressed in a T-shirt and shorts much like the other dads down by the dugout.

"I'll come down in a minute!" Gus said.

When their eyes locked, Kelsey could tell Spencer didn't particularly like that response. She knew Isabella had told him about her and the job they were doing for the resort, but that was it. When he walked away, Kelsey let out a breath. Spencer Burns did not give off good vibes.

"You don't have to go down there if you don't want to, Gus," Isabella said. "You can sit with us."

"Can I go play now?" Gus asked.

"Watch your brother bat, then you can go play. Make sure you stay where I can see you," Isabella said. "Wyatt bats second," she said to Kelsey.

The game started and Kelsey saw Wyatt look up into the stands for them while he waited to bat. He smiled when he saw them and Kelsey gave him a stealth wave. She noticed his smile brighten then he turned away to take a few practice swings.

"If I did that, he'd roll his eyes at me," Isabella said quietly, leaning closer to Kelsey.

"The newness of me will wear off," Kelsey replied.

"Oh, I don't think so," Isabella said in a low voice.

Kelsey cut her eyes towards Isabella and mouthed, "Stop."

Isabella chuckled.

The game started and Wyatt's team ended up winning, but it was close. He made several good plays on defense and drove in the winning run to end the game.

Isabella, Kelsey, and Marti walked down the bleachers and waited for Wyatt while the coach talked to them in the dugout.

33

Isabella took Kelsey's arm and led her over to where Spencer was waiting as well. "Spencer, this is Kelsey Kenny," Isabella said. "Kels, this is Spencer."

"Hi, Spencer," Kelsey said with a friendly smile.

"So you're the one Isabella parties with every month on these vacations," Spencer said in a less than friendly tone.

"I wouldn't call them parties." Kelsey narrowed her eyes. "Have you seen our posts on the website? The Virgin Islands are magical."

Spencer scoffed. "Yeah, it's kind of hard to take a vacation with the expenses of the boys and all."

"I know what you mean," Kelsey said. "I have two daughters in college. They graduate next month along with some of the expenses." Kelsey could feel Isabella smirking next to her.

"Oh. You do know, then," he said.

"Great game, Wyatt," Isabella said as he walked up to them.

"There he is," Spencer said. "The man with the winning hit."

Kelsey held up her hand for a high five. "Your defense saved it for your team."

"Thanks," Wyatt said, slapping her hand.

"Good job, son," Spencer said, putting his arm around him.

Kelsey noticed Spencer made sure to catch her eye as he squeezed Wyatt's shoulder possessively.

"I liked how you stayed calm even when the other team caught up," Marti said, winking at him.

"Thanks, Gran," he replied. "And thanks for coming, Kelsey. I'm glad you finally got to see me play."

"I am, too," Kelsey replied.

"She'll be back to watch me when my season starts," Gus said. "Right, Kelsey?"

"That's right. I'll be here." She smiled at the boy's exuberance.

"Okay, team. I see ice cream for the win," Isabella said, holding up her arms.

"Yay!" the boys exclaimed.

"It was nice to meet you, Spencer," Kelsey said with a nod.

"You, too," he replied. "Bye, Isabella."

"Bye," Isabella said, turning to walk towards their car. She put her arm around Wyatt and Gus ran up and grabbed Kelsey's hand.

"Talk to you tomorrow," Marti said, veering away from them.

It wasn't lost on Kelsey that they looked like a happy little family going for ice cream. She could feel Spencer's gaze on her back and she knew it wasn't friendly. *Here we go.*

. . .

Isabella drove them to the ice cream shop and once they'd all gotten their preferred flavor they found a table in the corner of the outdoor patio.

"Congrats on your win, Wyatt," Kelsey said, taking a lick of her ice cream cone.

"Thanks," he replied. "Do you have to go back tomorrow?"

"Yeah, you don't have any kids at home," Gus said.

Isabella chuckled. "No, but Kelsey does have things to check on at her house."

"Actually, there was something I wanted to ask you boys," Kelsey said. She waited until they both looked up at her. "Would you want to come to Denver for Dana and Emma's graduation?"

"Can we, Mom?" Wyatt asked excitedly.

"I don't know," Isabella said. "Can you sit still long enough to watch a bunch of people walk across a stage?"

"Yes!" they both yelled.

Kelsey laughed. "We can take you to the mountain where Dana works during the winter."

"I'm sure we'll find plenty to do," Isabella said.

Kelsey looked over at Isabella and grinned. She couldn't wait for Dana and Emma to meet the boys. At first she had been surprised by their interest in Wyatt and Gus when they'd happened to be home during one of Kelsey and Isabella's phone calls. But they seemed to genuinely like them and were looking forward to the family vacation at the resort.

"Okay, finish up," Isabella said. "You still have homework, baths, then bed when we get home."

It didn't take long to finish their ice cream and the boys immediately went to their rooms when they got home.

"Would you look at that," Isabella said.

"What?"

"They actually did what they were supposed to," Isabella replied. "I think they are on their best behavior because they want you to stay."

Kelsey chuckled. "I doubt that."

"I don't," Isabella said, slipping her arm around Kelsey's waist. "I want you to stay, too."

Kelsey groaned. "You know I want to, but..."

"I know," Isabella said softly. "We'll figure it out."

Kelsey nodded.

"Tomorrow night I'm going to tell the boys we're more than friends," Isabella said.

Kelsey raised her eyebrows and waited.

"I didn't like introducing you as my friend at the baseball game," Isabella said, making air quotes with her fingers. "We're more than that and I'm not hiding it."

"This has to be your call, Bella," Kelsey said.

"I know. This will surprise you," she said in a sarcastic tone, "but there are no gay people in our friend group."

Kelsey chuckled.

"However, the boys have a few kids in their classes that have same-sex parents. They already love you, so I think they'll be happy about it."

"And Spencer?"

"Yeah, I didn't get good vibes from him tonight, but that's not unusual," Isabella replied. "I'm sure he noticed how much Wyatt and Gus like you and that probably didn't sit well with him."

Kelsey sighed.

"I'll tell him because it's the nice thing to do. Plus, I'm sure the boys will say something about it the next time they're with him," Isabella said.

"Should I stay?" Kelsey asked. "If it doesn't go well I want to be here for you and if it does go well..." Kelsey shrugged and grinned. "I want to be here for you."

Isabella chuckled.

"Does it feel real?" Kelsey asked.

Isabella tilted her head and grabbed Kelsey's hand. "Since the day we met, it's felt magical."

"Yeah." Kelsey nodded. "It doesn't matter if it's island time or real time, it's always magical. I don't see that ever changing."

"Me neither," Isabella replied.

Kelsey looked down the hall then quickly kissed Isabella on the lips. "I love you," she whispered.

"I love you, too." Isabella winked.

"Hey Kelsey," Gus said, walking down the hall with a book under his arm. "Can I read to you? I have to read a few pages out loud for homework."

Kelsey looked over at Isabella and she nodded. "I'd love that, Gus."

They settled on the couch while Isabella went down the hall to check on Wyatt.

A short time later Isabella and Wyatt walked into the living room. "We have time for one episode of *House Hunters*," Isabella said, turning on the TV.

"You watch *House Hunters*, too?" Kelsey exclaimed.

"Yep," Wyatt said, plopping down on the end of the couch. "We guess which house they're going to pick at the end."

Isabella sat down on the other side of Gus. She put her arm around the back of the couch and squeezed Kelsey's shoulder. "You wanna play?"

"Heck, yeah," Kelsey said. She looked over at Wyatt and gave him a playful shove on the shoulder.

He grinned at her as the show began.

"Okay," Isabella said, pausing the TV at the end of the show. "They should choose number two, but I think they'll choose number three."

"Nope," Wyatt said. "They'll pick number one."

"I'm with Bella," Kelsey said. "They'll choose three."

Wyatt chuckled. "It's funny you call our mom Bella."

"Why?" Kelsey asked.

"She doesn't like people to call her Bella. She always corrects them," he said.

"Yeah," Gus said. "*My name is Isa-bella*," he said, imitating his mom.

Isabella laughed. "You know, I don't mind Kelsey calling me Bella. It sounds nice the way she says it."

"Well, *Bella*," Kelsey said. "Are you going to show us which house they choose?"

"Gus, what's your pick?" Isabella asked.

"I think number two," he replied.

Isabella started the show again and the couple chose number one.

"Yes!" Wyatt yelled, jumping up. "I knew it!"

"It's your night to win, Wyatt," Kelsey said.

"Okay, it's bedtime," Isabella said, getting up.

Gus got up as well and started to his room. He turned around and looked at Kelsey. "Aren't you coming?"

"Sure," Kelsey said, jumping up. She couldn't believe how quickly she'd grown to love Wyatt and Gus, but she shouldn't be surprised. They were a part of Isabella and she didn't know how it was possible, yet she loved her more every day.

She stood next to Isabella at the side of Gus's bed. "Good night, Gus," Kelsey said.

Isabella leaned down and kissed his forehead. "Sweet dreams, sweetie," Isabella said.

"Night," Gus said.

Next they walked to Wyatt's room and Kelsey stood in the doorway. "I'm glad I got to see you play today," Kelsey said.

"Me, too. I wish you didn't have to go home tomorrow," he said. "Mom's really happy when you're here."

Isabella raised her eyebrows at him. "Is that right? I thought I was happy most of the time."

He shrugged. "I guess so, but you're happier now."

"Good night, buddy," Isabella said.

"Night."

Isabella pulled his door almost closed. She put her arm around Kelsey as they walked down the hall. "Even they know how happy you make me."

"Let's go to bed and I'll *show* you how happy you make me," Kelsey said with one eyebrow raised.

"Oh, yeah?"

They walked into Isabella's bedroom and closed the door.

"I know you wanted to check on a couple of your clients today. I'm sorry we never got to it," Isabella said as she kicked her sandals off.

"I'm not," Kelsey said, reaching for Isabella's hand and spinning her around. "I had the best day."

Isabella smiled and put her arms around Kelsey. "I did, too."

Kelsey narrowed her gaze. "You have jumped right in," she said. "I know you had doubts."

Isabella led Kelsey over to the bed and they sat down. "There were several times when I wondered what I was doing," she said, widening her eyes. "Am I gay? What would this do to my life and especially Wyatt and Gus's?" She smiled and took a deep breath. "But every time I had those thoughts, something made me pause. In those spaces I noticed how wonderful my heart felt with you in it. My life was already different. With you everything felt right. It all made sense. This is how it's supposed to be, Kels. When we walked into the house the other day and Gus hugged you and Wyatt came rushing in from his room, I thought my heart was going to explode with love. They have never taken to anyone the way they have you and your girls. I don't know if I'm gay and it doesn't matter. You are the person I'm supposed to live my life with. I truly believe our two families were meant to be one."

"Oh, babe," Kelsey said and squeezed her hands. She leaned in, but Isabella stopped her.

"Hold up. You had to have doubts too," Isabella said, raising her brows. "Why in the world would you want to take on me and my two young sons when your girls are about to graduate?"

Kelsey chuckled. "Well, *I* realized," she began, "Dana and Emma may be graduating and starting their lives on their own, but they're never completely without me. The idea of getting to be part of Wyatt and Gus's lives never gave me doubts." She paused and took a breath. "I thought about the choices I made with the girls in mind. This choice would be for all of us, but especially for me, Bella. This is happily-ever-after stuff, forever stuff. How can I not choose us?"

Isabella cradled Kelsey's cheeks between her hands. "Oh, Kels."

"It's not a choice. It's our hearts demanding to be together," Kelsey said with tears in her eyes.

"Kelsey Kenny, you have my heart," Isabella said. "I promise to always take care of yours."

"Isabella Burns, my heart is yours. I promise to cherish yours always."

Isabella smiled. "Now that we have that settled, didn't you mention something about showing me how much you love me?" she said seductively.

"Oh, honey," Kelsey replied. She pressed her lips to Isabella's and they fell on the bed in a tangle of arms, legs and love.

This feels a lot like home, Kelsey thought.

34

Isabella could feel Kelsey's arm around her middle. She didn't know which was better, to wake up with Kelsey's arm around her or her arms around Kelsey.

After their impromptu commitment 'moment' last night, their hearts were on fire. Isabella could feel Kelsey's love in every touch. Whether it was her lips, her hands, her tongue, or her body: it was all love. She had never felt desire like that nor had she ever felt so loved. It was incredible and Isabella knew it was only the beginning.

She sighed contentedly and pushed back into Kelsey, wanting to get closer. This was what she imagined being in love was supposed to feel like. With Spencer she had thought she was being foolish and that her ideas of love were those of the romances in novels or in the movies. What they had was real life and not like that. But was she ever wrong! She had found that fairytale kind of love with Kelsey. She was her person. She was love.

Isabella felt Kelsey's arm slide away and she grabbed her hand and grumbled, "Mmm, where are you going?"

"I'm going to make breakfast for the boys," Kelsey said softly, kissing just below Isabella's ear.

Isabella quickly rolled over. "We could give them a PopTart and do something a little more fun." She pulled Kelsey's lips to hers and hungrily kissed her.

"Good morning to you, too." Kelsey chuckled as she pulled away.

Isabella smiled. "God, I love kissing you."

"Mmmm," Kelsey murmured and pressed their lips together again. "I love it, too."

"But..." Isabella sighed. "You're going to get out of this bed to make breakfast, aren't you?"

"You don't have to get up yet," Kelsey said. "Pancakes or waffles?"

"They love waffles." Isabella smiled and ran her fingers along Kelsey's cheek. "I'm spending every second I can with you today." She kissed Kelsey again and threw the covers back. "We could shower together," she suggested, getting out of the bed.

Kelsey shook her head. "You know I can't resist you, but..."

"Okay, okay. Let's make breakfast." Isabella grinned.

Kelsey went into the kitchen to start breakfast while Isabella woke the boys. It didn't take them long to get ready for the day.

As she walked down the hall, Isabella couldn't help but think that this is how it would be every day, someday. She didn't know when or where they would end up, but she and Kelsey were already making a life together.

Once the boys found out Kelsey was making waffles they quickly got ready for school and joined them in the kitchen.

"Thanks for making us waffles," Wyatt said, stuffing a big bite in his mouth.

"You're welcome," Kelsey said. "You know, waffles aren't as good when they're reheated, so here's one more." She plopped the last waffle on Wyatt's plate and grinned.

"I'm so full," Gus said, draining what was left of the milk in his glass.

"That has to be the best milk mustache I've ever seen," Kelsey teased him.

He grabbed his napkin and wiped his mouth. "How long until we get to see you again?"

"It's not that long," Kelsey said. "The time will fly."

Isabella frowned at her. "I doubt it."

"It's less than two weeks away," Kelsey said. "Dana and Emma can't wait for you to get there."

"Okay," Isabella said. "Finish up so we can get to school on time."

Kelsey began to clear the plates away and put them in the sink while the boys got their backpacks.

"I have a request," Kelsey said. "Can I get a hug from each of you before we get to school? I won't be here when you get home."

Gus wrapped his arms around Kelsey's middle and smiled up at her.

"Thanks, Gus. You give great hugs," Kelsey said.

Kelsey held out one arm to give Wyatt a side hug, but instead he put both arms around her. "I'm glad you came to visit."

It was clear to Isabella that both Wyatt and Gus loved Kelsey. They had to figure this out sooner rather than later because Kelsey made them all happy.

Isabella drove the boys to school and Kelsey went along. Once they'd dropped them off, Kelsey turned to Isabella. "Did you see Wyatt give me a hug?"

"I did." Isabella smiled.

"I couldn't believe it. I thought side hugs were the thing now with teenagers," Kelsey said.

"He loves you, Kels. So does Gus. I can already tell."

Kelsey sighed. "I love them."

"It's a good thing because they come with me," Isabella teased.

Kelsey chuckled. "I have a couple that come with me."

They got back to the house and cleaned up the kitchen together.

"I've got an idea. We'll use the island as our work space," Isabella said, getting her computer out of her bag.

"I only have a couple of things to do. It won't take long."

"We both work from home so we'll have to be disciplined about our jobs," Isabella said. "You can have this end and this side of the island."

"Okay." Kelsey got her computer out and opened it.

"I'll be at this end across from you. I'll work, but it will be nice to look up and see you down there. No kisses. If we start that we won't get anything done."

"My, oh my," Kelsey said. "So many rules."

Isabella chuckled. "Get to work so we can play before I have to take you to the airport."

They both got to work and a short time later the doorbell rang.

"Oh," Isabella said, walking towards the front door. "It's Spencer."

"Hey," he said, walking into the living area. "Wyatt left his hoodie at my house and I thought he might need it."

Isabella furrowed her brow. The boys had clothes at both of their houses.

"Hi, Kelsey," Spencer said, walking further into the room. "You're still here."

"Hi, Spencer," Kelsey replied with a friendly smile. "Yep."

Isabella could feel the annoyance building inside her. Spencer rarely came by her house and his nonchalance was irritating.

"I wondered if I might talk to you for a minute," Spencer said, turning to Isabella.

"I have a call I need to make," Kelsey said. "I'll be out on the patio."

Isabella smiled at Kelsey and almost stopped her, but knew it would be better to talk to Spencer alone and send him on his way.

"Uh, I thought we had agreed to check with each other before the boys met someone new," Spencer said.

"Do you mean Kelsey? She's not new. The boys know her. They talk to her every week and have since this marketing project began. This is the first time they've met in person, but they know her."

"Hmm," Spencer murmured.

Isabella had an uneasy feeling in her stomach. "We're all going on a family vacation in a couple of months, Spence. I've given you the schedule. We've talked about this. Kelsey's daughters are going with us."

He nodded. "I remember, Isabella," he said testily.

"Then what's the problem?"

"I don't know," he said. "She seems nice, but I hadn't thought about her being around the boys. That's all."

Isabella furrowed her brow. "Why would that be an issue?"

"She's gay, right?"

"And?" Isabella said.

"I don't know," he said, frustrated. "I'm not sure I want the boys around gay people."

"Excuse me?" Isabella said, the hair on the back of her neck beginning to stand up. "Since when?"

"Since we don't have any gay friends," Spencer said.

"Yeah, we do. The boys do," Isabella said.

"Who? Kids from school? We don't hang out with those people."

"Spencer," Isabella said, taking a deep breath. "Wyatt has a friend with two moms and Gus has a kid in his class with two dads. They have been in school together since the first grade. You know this. What's going on?"

Spencer sighed. "I guess I didn't realize the boys would be spending this much time with Kelsey. I don't really know why it's bothering me. She seems nice."

"She is nice," Isabella said. "The boys like her and she likes the boys. What is the big deal?"

Spencer shrugged.

Isabella looked through the window and could see Kelsey on the patio. This wasn't the time to tell Spencer about them, but she wasn't going to let him talk shit about Kelsey either.

"Thanks for bringing the hoodie by. I'll be sure and let Wyatt know," Isabella said, hoping Spencer would get the hint.

"Sure."

"Is there someone you need to tell me about?" Isabella asked, deciding to turn things around on him. She couldn't keep up with all the women Spencer had dated since the divorce and didn't want to.

"No," he said, walking towards the front door. "She just doesn't seem like your other friends."

If he only knew.

"She's not," Isabella replied, opening the door.

"See ya," he said.

Isabella closed the door and stood there for a moment. She wondered if he could feel the love between her and Kelsey. Or was he jealous because the boys liked Kelsey? She let out a deep breath. It was time to explain things to Wyatt and Gus. She wasn't about to hide her love for Kelsey, but then again, they couldn't hide it anyway.

"You can drop me off," Kelsey said.

"Nope," Isabella said, pulling into a parking space. "I told you, I'm coming in with you."

Before they got out of the car Kelsey reached for Isabella's hand. "I think I should stay."

Isabella smiled at her. "Are you my protector now?"

"No." Kelsey shook her head. "You don't need a protector. But you are going to have a couple of hard conversations. What if you need me to hold you?"

"I always need you to hold me," Isabella said. "It won't be hard with the boys and if I need a hug they will do the job until we're in Denver."

Kelsey sighed. "I know you need to do this on your own and in your own way, but you're not alone."

"I know that," Isabella said, leaning over and kissing Kelsey softly. "I'll never be alone again."

Kelsey nodded.

They both got out of the car and Kelsey took her bag from the back seat.

"I'll walk you to security then maybe we'll make out and cause a scene," Isabella teased.

"I know what you're doing," Kelsey said, reaching for Isabella's hand as they crossed the street.

"What am I doing? Am I trying to find my courage so I won't cry when you walk through that security gate?"

"Just know that if you cry then I'll cry and it will be an even bigger scene," Kelsey said.

Isabella chuckled. "We are so fucking sappy."

As they neared the security checkpoint Isabella said, "I put something in your suitcase for when you get home. Don't forget to take a picture when you get to your seat."

"And I'll call you when I get home," Kelsey added.

They faced each other and Isabella smiled. "I love you."

Kelsey swallowed the lump in her throat. "I love you, babe."

They pressed their lips together in a tender kiss and held each other for a moment.

"See you next month." Isabella smiled.

"See you next month," Kelsey replied.

* * *

Kelsey went into her bedroom and sighed. It was so quiet. She'd just gotten off the phone with Isabella and the boys.

Isabella had recounted how she had explained to the boys that Kelsey was her girlfriend. She said the biggest smile grew on Wyatt's face and his response had been, "That's so cool, Mom."

Gus had asked her if they held hands and kissed sometimes. Isabella had answered yes, as she held in her laughter.

The other thing they wanted to know was if that meant they'd get to see Kelsey more often. She and Isabella agreed that from now on Kelsey would be spending a few days in Charlotte around their monthly trips.

Kelsey couldn't believe all the emotions of the day. Leaving Isabella at the airport had been one of the hardest things she'd ever done.

That was followed by what had to be one of the happiest moments of her life so far. The boys wanted to know if Dana and Emma were part of their family now since Kelsey was.

Tears stung the back of Kelsey's eyes as she opened her suitcase. She blinked a few times unsure of what she was seeing.

There, on top of her clothes, was the shirt Isabella had slept in last night.

"Oh, baby."

Kelsey picked it up and pressed it to her face, inhaling deeply. She could smell the sweet scent of Isabella. Her heart clenched in her chest as the happy tears began to fall, but then a sharp pang of longing almost took her breath away.

At that moment Kelsey realized what she had to do.

35

Isabella heard a knock at the front door before her mom's familiar voice called out, "Knock, knock."

"Hi, Mom," Isabella replied. "Come on in."

"I'll be sure to knock from now on out of respect for you and Kelsey," Marti said, pulling out a stool and joining Isabella at the island.

"In just a couple of days she made her place in this house and now it feels like it's missing something," Isabella said, setting a mug of coffee in front of her mom.

Marti smiled and sipped her coffee.

"I am head over heels in love with her."

"It feels incredible, doesn't it?"

Isabella narrowed her gaze. "Why didn't you tell me it was supposed to feel like this? I don't remember ever feeling this way with Spencer."

Marti shrugged. "You had to find out for yourself, honey."

Isabella smirked and took a sip of her coffee. "I never understood the love of my life or soulmate thing until I fell in love with Kelsey. I always thought that was in the movies or unrealistic. I get it now."

"But now is the hard part," Marti said. "You can't let what people say or do scare you away."

Isabella nodded. "I wish you could've seen the boys when I told them. They were so happy. It didn't seem to faze them."

"That's because they see how happy you are," Marti said.

"Spencer is coming over and I'm planning to tell him," Isabella said.

"Why? He never warned you about any of the women he's been seeing since you moved out," Marti said with a bite to her voice.

"I'm a nice person, that's why," Isabella said, widening her eyes. "I'd rather tell him and talk about it instead of having him find out because the boys say something to him. You know they will."

"Uh oh," Marti said, gazing towards the front door. "He's here."

Isabella got up to answer the door and Marti followed her.

"I can stay," Marti offered.

"Thanks, Mom, but I've got this," Isabella said confidently and opened the door.

"Oh," Spencer said when he saw Marti. "Hi."

"Hi," Marti replied, walking onto the front porch. "I'll see you later."

"Bye, Mom," Isabella said with a smile.

Spencer walked into the house and took a quick look around the room.

"Would you like a cup of coffee?" Isabella asked.

"No thanks," he replied. "Is your friend still here?"

"No, Kelsey has gone back to Denver," Isabella said.

"Have a seat." She sat down on the end of the couch and waited for him to join her.

"What's up?" he asked, sitting in a chair perpendicular to her.

"I wanted you to know that Kelsey is not just my friend. She's my girlfriend," Isabella began.

"What?" He shrugged. "Your girlfriend? Like best friend or something?"

"No. Well, yes," Isabella said. "She is my best friend, but we're also in a relationship, Spencer."

He stared at her. "I told you the boys shouldn't be around her," he said, pressing his lips together in anger. "She's gay, Isabella, and now you're telling me you are too?"

Isabella took a breath. "What I'm telling you is that Kelsey and I are making a life together."

"You are not taking my boys to Denver!" he exclaimed, hitting his hands on his thighs.

"That's not what I'm saying," Isabella said calmly. She sighed and tried to choose her words carefully, but finally she blurted out, "I love Kelsey. Wyatt and Gus love her, too. She's part of our lives now and I thought you should know."

"Where is this coming from?" he asked. "You couldn't be like the other wives and stay at home, raise the boys and go to the fucking country club or whatever they do?" He stood up, waved his arms, and began to pace in front of the couch. "Oh, no! You had to work and then start your own business. I didn't say anything when you started these monthly trips and now you're telling me you're gay." He stopped in front of Isabella and stared down at her. "I won't have my boys around her."

"Are you finished?" Isabella asked as she stood up and stared at him.

He exhaled loudly and sat back down.

"Our sons live with me and we share custody," Isabella said, sitting back down. "I'm telling you about my relationship with Kelsey out of courtesy, Spencer. We agreed not to introduce the boys to anyone new in our lives until it was serious. We also agreed to have a conversation if either of us want to move out of North Carolina. Do you remember?"

"Yes, Isabella. I remember," he replied acerbically.

"The boys are happy here. There's no reason to change that right now. They come first and I will always do what is best for them," Isabella said.

"People are going to gossip about you and that will affect Wyatt and Gus," Spencer said.

Isabella scoffed. "They aren't going to gossip about me any more than they did when we split up. I have to hear about every one of the women you date."

Spencer squirmed in his chair. "The boys haven't met any of them."

Isabella simply looked at him.

"All your friends will drop you," he said.

"What friends?" Isabella said. "You've made it so awkward that most of them don't talk to me anyway." She stood up and walked back to the island. "I've got work to do."

"So that's it," he said, following her into the kitchen. "No discussion."

"We just talked about it," Isabella replied. "There's nothing else to discuss. I love Kelsey, she loves me, and we're together from now on."

She walked to the front door and opened it. Spencer stared her down one more time then stopped in front of her. "We'll see how long this lasts."

"It's a forever thing," Isabella said with a smile.

Spencer left and Isabella shut the door. She walked over to the island and was still smiling when she called Kelsey.

* * *

"This is going to take us up the mountain," Dana said, stopping in front of a four-seater ATV.

Gus squealed and hopped into the front seat on the passenger side. "Let's go!"

"Uh," Wyatt said, holding up a finger. "There are six of us and four seats."

"It's okay, Wyatt," Kelsey said, resting her hand on his shoulder. "Your mom and I will stay down here."

"If you'll follow that trail just into the woods, there's a bench with a nice view. We won't be long," Dana said. "Buckle up, buttercup," she said to Gus as she went around to the driver's side.

Gus giggled then he leaned over towards Dana. "I know what they'll be doing."

"What's that?" Emma asked, getting into the back seat with Wyatt.

"They'll be holding hands and kissing the whole time we're gone," Gus said.

"Yuck!" Emma exclaimed.

Gus turned around and laughed. "You didn't mean that."

Kelsey couldn't keep from smiling at their playful banter. As soon as Isabella and the boys had landed in Denver, Dana and Emma had made sure the boys were having a good time.

"Be careful, Dana. You're hauling precious cargo, including yourself," Kelsey said.

"Precious cargo?" Wyatt asked.

"We are precious to our moms," Dana explained.

"Oh, we're the cargo," he replied and chuckled.

"Have fun!" Isabella said.

"Bye Moms!" Emma yelled over the roar of the engine as Dana drove away.

Kelsey rolled her eyes and shook her head.

Isabella chuckled. "She loves saying that."

"Yes, she does."

"Sitting on a bench kissing you sounds like a great idea to me," Isabella said.

Kelsey put her arm through Isabella's and led them to the trail. "This has been the best weekend. I'm so glad you're here."

"It's been fun meeting your family. Your mom is adorable," Isabella said.

"She is a go-getter."

"Are you sure she doesn't mind staying with your brother?"

"No, she stays with both of us when she comes to visit. She was with me for three days before you and the boys got here and she'll finish her visit with my brother's family," Kelsey explained.

"Oh, this is beautiful," Isabella said, sitting down.

Kelsey sat next to her and reached for her hand. She intertwined their fingers then gazed out at the view.

"It's so beautiful here," Isabella said. "How could you ever leave it?"

"You're not here," Kelsey replied, looking over at her.

"What?"

"You asked how I could leave Colorado. I could because you're not here." Kelsey turned so she could face Isabella. "I want to be with you, Bella. I don't mean long distance or just when we're in the Virgin Islands."

Isabella furrowed her brow. "Are you saying you'd move to Charlotte?"

Kelsey nodded. "I have nothing keeping me here."

"What about your family?"

Kelsey smiled and cradled Isabella's face between her hands. "You're my family." She leaned in and softly pressed her lips to Isabella's. "Emma will be in DC and that's a lot closer to Charlotte than Denver. And Dana has accepted a job at a hospital in Richmond, Virginia for the next six months."

"That's only four hours from Charlotte," Isabella said with a hopeful look.

"I know you have to stay in Charlotte because of the custody agreement. I want to be with you," Kelsey said.

"It's not set in stone," Isabella said. "Spencer and I just have to discuss it if either of us wants to move."

"Do you want to move?" Kelsey asked, furrowing her brow.

Isabella smiled. "I want to live with you," she whispered, then brought their lips together again in a sweet kiss. "I didn't know how to ask you to move in with me. I wasn't sure you liked Charlotte."

Kelsey chuckled. "What's not to like? The woman I am madly in love with lives there along with her incredible sons."

"Oh, Kelsey," Isabella said, holding her close. "Will you move in with us?"

"Should we ask Wyatt and Gus?" Kelsey asked, raising a brow.

"I think they will be so excited." Isabella grinned.

"We should still ask them," Kelsey said. "I haven't told the girls because I wanted to talk to you first."

Isabella narrowed her gaze. "Our real life is beginning to look a lot like our island life."

"How about we have one big happy life?" Kelsey grinned. "With four kids," she added.

Their lips met in another kiss that quickly turned passionate. Kelsey pulled Isabella closer and her heart pounded with love.

"At times I wondered if I would end up alone in this life, but Bella," Kelsey said, her voice thick with emotion, "the love we have is so much better than I ever imagined."

"Oh, baby," Isabella said softly, touching her lips to Kelsey's. "You are stuck with me for life."

"God, I love you," Kelsey said, pressing her lips firmly to Isabella's. She ran her tongue across Isabella's lips and then slipped it inside. They both moaned and tightened their arms around each other as their tongues danced with delight.

The drone of an engine could be heard in the distance. It grew louder as it neared.

"Those pesky kids," Isabella whispered.

Kelsey giggled. "They aren't here yet." She captured Isabella's lips in another passionate kiss.

"I love you, Kels," Isabella said softly. "We're going to have a great life."

Kelsey smiled as the buzz got closer and closer.

Dana steered the ATV into the clearing where Kelsey and Isabella sat on the bench.

"I knew it!" Gus said. "They've been kissing."

Kelsey and Isabella laughed.

"Hey, Gus, let me ask you something," Isabella said. "Does it really bother you when I kiss Kelsey?"

"Nah," he replied. "I just like to tease you."

"Did you know that Dana and Emma are moving?" Kelsey asked.

"Yeah, they're moving closer to us," Gus said with a grin. "And they're coming to visit."

"Oh, they are," Kelsey said, raising her eyebrows at her girls.

Dana shrugged. "I thought you might be visiting Isabella and I could come down and see you."

"That means Kelsey will be in Colorado all by herself," Isabella said.

"Wait a minute," Wyatt said, eyeing them both. "You work from home just like Mom does, right, Kelsey?"

"That's right."

"Why can't you move, too?" Wyatt asked.

Gus gasped. "You could live with us!"

Kelsey looked at Wyatt and Gus. "Are you sure you want me around all the time?"

"Yes!" Gus exclaimed.

"Don't you want to be with Mom?" Wyatt asked with a serious look on his face.

"I want to be with you and Gus, too," Kelsey replied.

"What do you say, guys?" Isabella said, putting her arm around Kelsey. "Should we invite Kelsey to move in with us?"

A chorus of 'yes' echoed through the woods.

"Can we come back and visit Colorado?" Wyatt asked. "Dana said she'd teach me to ski."

"We're having a summer family vacation in the Virgin Islands," Emma said. "Why not have a winter vacation on the mountain?"

"I like how she thinks," Isabella said with a grin.

Kelsey gazed over at the ATV and saw happy smiles. She

looked into Isabella's eyes and saw joy there as well. "I can't believe this is happening," she said.

"Believe it, babe," Isabella said, grabbing her cheeks. "We have a whole life to share."

Isabella pressed their lips together as whoops of happiness echoed from the ATV.

36

"I think this calls for a celebration," Isabella said as they started back to the car. "We have two brand new college graduates who are heading east and we've convinced Kelsey to come with them."

"I don't think you had to do much convincing." Emma chuckled.

"When you know, you know. Right, babe?" Kelsey said.

"Right," Isabella replied, squeezing Kelsey's arm.

"Oh my God, Dana. Did you hear mom call Isabella *babe*?" Emma teased.

"I think it sounds fucking awesome," Dana said then immediately covered her mouth. "Oops, I mean friggin'."

Wyatt and Gus giggled. "We've heard Mom say that before."

Isabella smirked. "Real life here."

"Wyatt and Gus treated me to their favorite pizza place while I was in Charlotte. I think we should go by Angelo's and show them our favorite," Kelsey said.

"I'll buy the beer," Isabella added.

Kelsey ordered the pizza as they drove down the mountain. They picked it up on the way home and settled in for dinner and a movie.

After dinner Isabella helped Kelsey clean up the kitchen while the kids tried to decide on a movie. "Dana and Emma have been so good with the boys."

"I think Emma is enjoying this calm before she hits the stormy world of politics in DC," Kelsey said. "Dana has always enjoyed helping kids learn to ski and enjoy the mountains."

"Yeah, but I thought they'd be partying with their friends since graduating," Isabella said.

"That's what they did the week before," Kelsey explained. "All their friends' families were coming in for graduation so they were busy with them."

Isabella leaned her elbows on the island and gazed into the living room.

Kelsey sidled up next to her and bumped her shoulder. "What are you thinking?"

Isabella glanced over at Kelsey. "I'm almost afraid to say."

"Why?"

"I don't want to jinx anything," Isabella said.

Kelsey chuckled. "You said I was stuck with you."

"Oh, you are, but still," Isabella said, arching an eyebrow. "Everything is going so well."

"Spill it," Kelsey said, leaning against Isabella.

"I was thinking... They look like a happy blended family," Isabella said, gazing back at the living room.

Kelsey rested her head on Isabella's shoulder. "Mmhmm."

"Too much?" Isabella asked.

"Just right," Kelsey replied.

A phone began to vibrate at the end of the island.

"That's yours," Isabella said, reaching for it and handing it to Kelsey.

"It's Carmen," Kelsey said, connecting the call. "Hey."

"Hi, have you seen the latest comments on the website?" Carmen asked.

"Uh, no," Kelsey replied. "The girls graduated this weekend and Isabella and the boys are here. I haven't looked at them today."

"Isabella's with you? Can you put me on speaker?"

"Yeah, hold on a sec," Kelsey said. "She wants to talk to both of us. Let's go in here."

Isabella followed Kelsey into her office. It was also the extra bedroom where the girls were staying and clothes were scattered everywhere.

Kelsey sat in her desk chair and powered up her computer while Isabella dumped clothes out of a chair and put them on the bed. She pulled the chair over next to Kelsey and smiled when she saw the picture of them on the beach at Coral Bay. She'd given it to Kelsey for Christmas with instructions to put it next to her computer at home. The idea was to look at it and remember that wonderful day along with those happy feelings when things weren't going so great at home. Isabella had a feeling they were about to need it.

"Hi, Carmen," Isabella said.

"Hi, Isabella. Something is going on with the site. Look at these comments."

"Uh," Kelsey mumbled. "Give us a sec—I'm pulling them up now."

"What is that?" Isabella asked, squinting her eyes at the screen.

"'It looks like the single moms vacationing their way around the Virgin Islands aren't so single after all,'"

Carmen read. "'Why are they pretending to be just like you and me when they're really lesbians in a gay relationship? Who are they trying to fool? Why pretend? Is this just another scam to get honest people to spend their hard-earned money on one-star vacations pretending to be five-star accommodations? Couldn't this resort get better spokespeople?'"

"Oh, fuck," Isabella murmured. "Can you take it down?"

"Yeah, but there are a couple of comments under it," Kelsey said.

"'Why would they lie?'" Isabella read.

"There's another," Carmen said. "'What's the big deal?'" she read.

"I can take it down," Kelsey said.

"Wait," Isabella said, sliding the keyboard over. She began to type a comment on the website. "I'm going to tell our followers to prepare for a surprise next week when we get to St. Thomas."

"What surprise?" Carmen asked.

"We're going to tell the truth," Isabella said. "Don't worry, Carmen. Kelsey and I will come up with something you and our followers will love. I never felt right about hiding this in the first place."

"I've got it," Kelsey said. "How can you not fall in love in the Virgin Islands? That's what happened to us and our followers were along for the ride. We can do this honestly and still save the campaign, Carmen."

"Let me think about it," Carmen said.

"I'll keep an eye on the website and see if anyone notices we took the comment down," Kelsey said.

"Okay. I'll get back to you," Carmen said, ending the call.

"Are y'all coming to watch the movie?" Emma asked from the doorway.

"Uh, we have a work issue. Go ahead and start it," Kelsey replied.

"We'll be right there," Isabella added.

Emma walked away and Isabella looked at Kelsey. "Can you tell where or who left the comment?"

"Maybe."

"I can't believe I'm saying this, but I think it might be Spencer," Isabella said.

Kelsey looked over at her with surprise on her face.

"I haven't told anyone but him about us," Isabella said. "Think about it, who says 'gay relationship?' It has to be him, Kels."

Before Kelsey could say anything Emma once again appeared in the doorway. "You know my education is in politics and how to spin things," she said. "I didn't mean to overhear, but it sounds like I might be able to help."

"When we told Carmen about our relationship, she asked us to keep it to ourselves for now," Kelsey said.

"We both thought it was a bad idea and wanted to be honest, but we agreed to wait," Isabella continued. "Now someone has made a comment about us not being honest on the website. We always say we're two single moms showing the benefits of Coral Bay and what it offers."

Emma nodded.

"I just posted a comment that we have a big surprise to announce on our trip next week," Isabella said.

"I think we need to simply tell the truth," Kelsey said. "We fell in love on these trips and our followers were right there with us."

"Okay. There are good ways and bad ways to tell the truth," Emma said. "I think you need to show your followers how it happened. Didn't it start when you were both there at Christmas?"

Isabella smiled at Kelsey. "Yeah, it did."

"Did you do anything on that trip that you haven't done on any of the vacations yet?" Emma asked.

"Yes!" Kelsey said excitedly. "We haven't shown them Honeymoon Beach yet. That was a magical day."

Isabella reached for Kelsey's hand and held it between hers "That was the first day we danced together. I remember telling Liz that I'd never been with a woman." Isabella smiled. "She said everyone had a first."

Kelsey chuckled. "That's true."

"But I told her you weren't a first, you were a forever."

"Oh, Bella," Kelsey said, her face softening with emotion.

Emma smiled at them. "Focus, please."

They both looked at her. "Isn't it obvious we're in love?" Isabella said.

"I think you take us, as followers, to Honeymoon Beach and then to Peaches where you danced," Emma said.

"Okay, we can do that."

"Isabella, I hate to do this to you," Emma began, "but you may need to tell your coming out story. You never thought of another woman until you met my mom, isn't that correct?"

"Yes, and then I met the people at Peaches and saw the possibilities," Isabella replied.

"There may be a lot of women who are divorced and in a similar situation," Emma said. "You could help them, be a role model for them."

Kelsey looked at Isabella and smiled.

"And Mom, you need to tell your story. You made decisions for yourself with your two daughters in mind. Now we're about to embark on our careers and you can do something for yourself," Emma said.

"So you're saying we might help others by telling our stories?" Kelsey asked.

Emma nodded. "Neither one of you told the other about your feelings for months, so you weren't being dishonest or trying to hide your relationship. You were trying to figure out your feelings. That's honest. And now you want to share this with your followers. You've got to make them want to see what happens next."

"We should ask them to go along with us on this trip and to give us one more trip the next month," Kelsey said. "We should move up the family vacation. They need to see how our family has come together and if they don't like us after that then we can stop the trips. It's indulgent, but it's open and honest."

"That's a great idea," Emma said. "School will be out for the boys and Dana and I already told our employers about this trip when we were hired."

"Now that I think about it, we've never been dishonest or hidden anything," Isabella said. "We had to figure this out for ourselves first, and then as a couple."

"I still say the islands are a magical place and we're the perfect example of what can happen," Kelsey said.

"I'd be happy to work up a statement or two for this upcoming trip. I could give you some ideas of what to include when you get there and then build up Honeymoon Beach. The next day your followers get to experience it with you. I can outline the points you need to make at each place. Then you can invite them to meet us next month. It would just be a guide," Emma said.

Kelsey smiled. "Bella, would you listen to my smart daughter?"

"I hear her." Isabella put her arm around Kelsey. "I don't know about you, but I'm very proud at this moment."

Emma chuckled. "Stop it, Moms. You'll make me blush."

Kelsey and Isabella laughed.

"We're missing the movie," Emma said, getting up and walking to the door.

"We'll be there in a minute," Kelsey said.

"I had a feeling something was going to happen when Carmen asked us to keep this quiet," Isabella said.

"I did, too," Kelsey said.

"After I told Spencer, I got the same feeling. But I didn't think he'd do something like this," Isabella said.

Kelsey swung around and faced Isabella. "I don't care what comments are made or if we finish these trips. Spencer can try to undermine us all he wants, but I won't leave you, Bella. I love you and my life is with you. I've waited a long time to find my person and here you are. I'm holding on tight and I won't let go."

Isabella felt her heart overflow with love. With Kelsey's promise to hold on to, how could anyone or anything stop them? "I'm not letting go," she said softly and touched her lips to Kelsey's in a tender kiss.

When they pulled away Isabella raised her eyebrows. "Do you think we could sneak into your room while they finish the movie?"

Kelsey giggled. "What ever would we do there?"

"We'd go here," Isabella said, reaching for the picture next to Kelsey's computer.

"That was such a good day," Kelsey said.

"This day is, too." Isabella wrapped her arms around Kelsey's neck and pulled her in for a long, slow kiss.

Kelsey pulled away and took a deep breath. She reached for her phone and began to type.

"What are you doing?"

"I'm sending Emma a text telling them we'll see them after the movie is over." Kelsey smiled.

Isabella chuckled and stood up. "Kelsey Kenny, I love you more every day."

Kelsey took Isabella's hand and led them to her bedroom.

37

Isabella parked her car and looked up at the office building in front of her. She'd decided to pay Spencer a visit at work. Isabella thought it might be better to talk to him at his office in hopes of controlling her temper.

After discovering the comments on the website, Isabella thought her anger would dissipate, but it had seemed to grow the closer she got to Charlotte. She'd almost gone to his house when they'd gotten in from Denver last night, but had thought better of it.

"Deep breaths," she murmured as she got out of the car. She marched up to the building and every step seemed to fuel her fury.

Isabella walked into the reception area and smiled. "Is he in his office?"

The woman behind the desk nodded as her eyes widened. Isabella didn't give her time to say anything. She walked down the hall and opened Spencer's door.

"What the fuck, Spencer?" she said angrily after closing the door. "What were you thinking!"

Spencer jumped up and started to come around from

behind his desk. He held up his hands and stopped. "I was angry!"

"I get that, but why did you have to post that comment on the website?"

"What makes you think it was me?"

"Really?" Isabella said, putting her hands on her hips and staring at him. "You're going to try and deny it?"

Spencer sighed and sat back down. "Why couldn't you be like the other wives? I'm supposed to make the money and you run the house. I'm the protector."

"So that's what this is about? You wanted me to be dependent on you? I'm supposed to go to the country club and to charity events? You wanted me to be a trophy wife! When are you going to get it? I don't need protecting!" Isabella said, raising her voice. "I've got myself!" She pointed to her chest. "I'm going to make my own happiness with our sons. If you want to be part of that, fine. If you're going to be an ass and a dickhead, then they won't be with you. Don't tell me I can't do that because, by damn, I can and will!"

Spencer sat in his chair and sighed.

"Spencer, you don't have to be jealous."

"I'm not jealous!" he fired back.

"Yes, you are. You're jealous of Kelsey's relationship with the boys. Wyatt and Gus can like you, they can like me, they can like Kelsey, and they can like whomever you choose to be your girlfriend someday. It's not a competition. They love your parents. They love my mom and dad."

"Oh..." Spencer said quietly. "Your dad was the best."

Isabella closed her eyes and took a deep breath. "Yes, he was, but stay on task, Spencer."

"So now you're going to talk to me like I'm one of the boys," he said.

Isabella smirked.

"Okay, I probably deserved that," he said. "I get it. Our boys can love everybody. It's not a contest."

"Exactly," Isabella said with a sigh. "We want to co-parent and to do that we need to get along."

"You're right. The boys come first," Spencer said.

Isabella sat down in the chair across from his desk. "The boys do come first, but they're not everything."

Spencer raised his eyebrows.

"There has to be more and I've found that with Kelsey. We will always be there for our kids, but they'll be on their own someday."

Spencer nodded. "It's hard to be divorced around here, Isabella. You know that, but add to it being gay. It won't be easy for you."

"I know." Isabella winced. "But I won't be alone."

"Let me guess? Kelsey's moving here," he said evenly. Then he chuckled and looked at the ceiling. "Well, of course she is."

"You might actually like her," Isabella said.

Spencer nodded. "Maybe."

They stared at each other then both smiled. "I'm an old Southern boy," Spencer said with an exaggerated accent. "And you're a progressive badass. What a combination. No wonder we didn't make it."

"But we have two amazing kids," Isabella said.

"That we do," he agreed. "I'm sorry about the comments. I shouldn't have messed with your business."

"No, you shouldn't have. I came here in hopes that I wouldn't yell at you, but that didn't work," Isabella said with a shrug.

Spencer laughed. "You always liven things up around here. That hasn't changed."

"Don't forget to pick the boys up from school on Thursday," Isabella said, getting up and walking to the door. "I leave for St. Thomas that day."

"It's on my schedule," Spencer said, walking around his desk. "Safe travels."

"Hmph," Isabella muttered. "It almost sounded like you meant that."

Spencer smiled. "I do."

"See there? It's not so hard to get along." Isabella grinned and walked out the door.

* * *

"It won't be long now," Isabella said, looking out the window as the plane descended.

Kelsey reached for her hand and held it in her lap. "I had a long talk with Dana and Emma after you and the boys went home. I wanted to be sure they were okay with my move."

Isabella furrowed her brow. "I thought they were excited about it."

"They are, but I'm not sure they realized we were leaving their childhood home," Kelsey said.

"Oh, babe. I didn't think of that. Are they okay?" Isabella said.

Kelsey nodded. "I'll only be bringing my clothes and a few other things to Charlotte."

"Wait a minute," Isabella said, looking into Kelsey's eyes. "You're moving in with us, but this has to be your home, too. We have to fix this."

"Can we fix one thing at a time, please?" Kelsey smiled. "Let's focus on saving this marketing campaign for the next few days. We can talk about the move later."

"You moving in with us is more important than anything on this trip," Isabella said.

"I agree, but I'm moving no matter what. We have time to talk about that, but we only have a few days to make people fall in love with us as a couple."

"Little do our followers know we've been a couple the entire time." Isabella grinned.

"I'll keep my house for a while because Dana doesn't have a place for her things since she'll be traveling. We'll figure it all out."

"That's a good idea." Isabella stared at Kelsey and nodded.

Kelsey could see the wheels turning in her head. "What are you thinking, babe?"

"Kels, we're beginning a life together and that means we share everything. We need to look at our finances and make *our* home. As I said, you're moving here to be with us, but we don't have to stay in that house or sell yours. We need to look at all of it."

Kelsey shook her head in amazement and gazed into Isabella's beautiful blue eyes. She would never get tired of that view. "We will, babe. But right now, I'm excited to relive how we started. Our first meeting at the luggage carousel, our first dinner together, but mostly I'm looking forward to Honeymoon Beach."

"Not our dance at Peaches?"

Kelsey shook her head. "I can stare at you all I want while we're on the beach. I don't have to worry about you catching me." She chuckled. "And I can kiss you and hold you under those leaning palm trees. Mmhmm, I can't wait."

Isabella giggled. "You're making me very hot right now," she whispered. "We may have to sneak to the restroom."

Kelsey chuckled. "We're about to land."

"Be ready when we get to our room," Isabella said, wiggling her eyebrows.

"Oh, I will be." Kelsey winked. "But first, are you ready to tell everyone how we met?"

Isabella nodded. "I love you, baby."

"I love you," Kelsey whispered. "We can do this."

As soon as they got off the plane they went to baggage claim and shot a video of how they met. Next, they got on the shuttle and rode to the resort.

"Let's go by Carmen's office and explain our plan. We need to record on the beach before it gets dark," Kelsey suggested.

"I'm right behind you," Carmen said.

They turned around and Carmen smiled at them.

"We talked to a political strategist and have come up with a good plan," Isabella said.

Carmen raised her eyebrows.

Kelsey smiled at Isabella and shook her head. "Emma just graduated with a degree in political science and she specialized in public relations," Kelsey said to Carmen. "She gave us some good points to bring up and explained the best ways to present them."

"I was very impressed with Emma on the spring break trip. I don't doubt her abilities or the two of you. Are you beginning your posts today?"

"Yes, we're starting off by the beach outside our bungalow. We want it to be authentic and that's where we've spent a lot of time," Isabella explained.

"Then go," Carmen said. "We can catch up later."

"Wait," Kelsey said. "Give us a few minutes to set up, then come to the beach and do the post with us."

"You don't have to be on camera," Isabella added. "You can help us edit it if we need to."

"You've always done these on your own. I don't want to get in the way," Carmen said.

Kelsey raised her eyebrows. "You're just as nervous about this as we are. It is your resort."

"We did a quick post from the airport when we left Charlotte," Isabella said. "We promised another when we got here."

"I saw the first one and there have already been several positive comments," Carmen said. "Go do your thing, I'll check in with you later."

Kelsey and Isabella grabbed their bags and wheeled them out of the resort past the swimming pool just like they'd always done. Once inside their bungalow, Isabella went to the bathroom and ran her fingers through her hair.

"You look beautiful," Kelsey said, putting her arms around her from behind. She kissed her neck then met her gaze in the mirror. "I don't think anyone is going to be surprised by our news."

"What do you mean?"

"Our followers have been with us the whole time. We've had a comment or two that we'd make a cute couple, remember?"

"Hmm, maybe you're right. They've had a front seat to our little romance," Isabella said, turning in Kelsey's arms.

"Little? We've been meeting in the Virgin Islands for six months. I wouldn't call that little." Kelsey smiled and kissed Isabella softly.

"Mmm," Isabella moaned and pulled Kelsey closer.

The kiss may have started softly, but Kelsey's lips were hungry for Isabella's once they touched. Their breaths and quiet moans were the only sounds echoing in the bathroom as their tongues did a dance of love.

When they finally pulled apart Kelsey gulped a breath. "Our romance is big, just like our love."

Isabella put her hand on Kelsey's cheek. "Let's shoot this video and celebrate our big love the rest of the night."

"You always have the best ideas." Kelsey kissed Isabella again then playfully tapped her on the ass.

Isabella laughed. She walked out of the bathroom and opened the back door onto the deck. "Aww, our happy place," she said, holding out her arms.

Kelsey grabbed her hand as she walked by and led them to their favorite table and chairs on the beach. There were a few people sprinkled here and there down the beach, but no one nearby.

"Are you ready?" Isabella asked as she sat in a chair next to Kelsey.

"Action," Kelsey said in her best director's voice.

38

Isabella chuckled, held up her phone, and began recording. "Hi everyone, thanks for joining us on another magical trip to Coral Bay. We usually have a theme for these trips, but this one is a little different. Last month on our recharge and reset trip, some things happened that we felt compelled to share with you." Isabella smiled over at Kelsey.

"This month we'd planned to do a bachelorette or bridesmaids vacation, but instead we're calling this trip: magic," Kelsey said, taking up the conversation. "If you'll remember, we originally started these trips as two single moms who wanted to show you all that Coral Bay had to offer along with the magic of the islands. We're not influencers or spokespeople, we're just working moms like many of you."

"Right now we're sitting outside our bungalow," Isabella said. She panned the phone around to show the back deck, the beach, then the water. "We're still Kelsey and Isabella. We're still moms, but we're no longer single."

"Is that a gasp I heard from the crowd?" Kelsey teased.

Isabella laughed and rolled her eyes. "We've been telling you all along that it's magical here and wow, has it worked on us." Isabella smiled at Kelsey. "Kelsey and I have fallen in love," she said, then looked back at the camera.

"Some of you may have seen it coming, but we certainly didn't." Kelsey grinned.

"We want to take you with us once again and show you how it happened," Isabella said. "It began at the airport where we first met—"

"Neither of us knowing we were both going to Coral Bay, but we ran into each other there and quickly fell into a friendship," Kelsey said. "We haven't shown you everything we discovered on that first trip at Christmas, but tomorrow you're coming with us to a place that is truly magical."

"We'd been saving Honeymoon Beach over on St. John for a special trip, but decided it's time to share it with all of you," Isabella said. "If you'll indulge us and come along with us tomorrow I think you'll feel the magic we're always talking about."

Isabella smiled at Kelsey then looked back at the camera and tilted her head. "Have you ever had a friend who just gets you?" she asked. "That's Kels for me. The very first time we met was at the baggage claim. I was trying to wrangle two big suitcases, a satchel for my computer, and a very large purse. All Kelsey had was a small suitcase and little purse. She helped me get my bags, but more than that she showed me I didn't need all this stuff."

Isabella smiled at Kelsey and handed her the camera. "I'd been carrying around all these expectations." She held her hands up by her shoulders as if she was holding something heavy. "Much like my suitcases, I let all that stuff go. Guess what happened?"

Isabella paused, looked over at Kelsey, then back to the camera. "Letting go gave me room to be me. Not the me everyone thought I should be, but the me I want to be. That's the magic you bring back with you after you visit the islands."

Kelsey smiled as Isabella reached for the camera. She raised her eyebrows. "It must be my turn." She looked over at the water and back to the camera. "I came here because I always wanted to spend Christmas at the beach. However, I thought my daughters would come with me. If you've been following us, then you met Dana and Emma in March on our spring break trip. They had other plans at Christmas, though. My expectations were very low when I got off the plane. I planned to stay to myself, enjoy the beach with a few cocktails, and work."

Isabella leaned into the frame and smiled. "Kelsey has spent the last twenty-five years doing things for her girls. It was time she chose herself."

"So I agreed to join Bella and show you Coral Bay and the Virgin Islands." Kelsey swept her hand towards the water. "I chose to open myself to something new and Isabella flew right into my heart," she said as she smiled into the camera.

"We're not saying come here and you'll fall in love," Kelsey continued, holding her arms out wide. "We are saying, come here and do something for yourself. That's what I needed and what Isabella helped me see."

"How many of you are divorced out there?" Isabella paused. "Kelsey showed me how to let all that go for a while. Real life will be waiting for you when you get back home. When you're on island time, you can let real life go. You've heard us speak of that in earlier posts."

"That's how this magic works," Kelsey said. "But then it

winds its way into your heart and before you know it, you've brought island time into your real life."

"That's when the real magic begins." Isabella grinned.

"You'll have the time of your lives at Coral Bay—"

"We certainly have," Isabella said.

"But what you take with you will last a lifetime," Kelsey added.

"Okay, I hope you're still with us. I promise, tomorrow will be worth it," Isabella said.

"See you on Honeymoon Beach."

Isabella stopped the video and sat back in her chair. "What do you think?"

Kelsey shrugged. "I thought we were honest. It does feel like there's magic here, but every time I went back home, I took part of you with me."

"Let's post this and let Carmen know," Isabella said, getting up from her chair. "She can watch the comments tonight. I want to spend the evening loving my girl."

Kelsey chuckled. "Let's order a combination plate and eat here."

"Like we did our first night?"

Kelsey nodded. "After dinner we can dance on the deck and..."

Isabella grinned. "Oh, we're definitely going to *and*."

Kelsey laughed as they went inside. They replayed the video and decided not to edit it. Kelsey sat down in the desk chair, opened her computer, and posted the video while Isabella rested her chin on her shoulder. "There it goes."

"Did you see my winning smile?" Isabella teased. "It convinced you to begin this little—" Isabella stopped when Kelsey raised her eyebrows. "I mean, big adventure with me."

Kelsey spun the chair around and put her arms around

Isabella's middle. She picked her up and carried her the two short steps to the bed. They fell down in a heap, both giggling.

"Oh!" Isabella exclaimed when Kelsey raised up and stared into her eyes.

"I could never say no to your winning smile." Kelsey pressed her lips to Isabella's in a passionate kiss. Talking earnestly to the camera and reliving those early moments when they met filled Kelsey's heart with gratitude. The one thing she had done for herself by going on that Christmas trip had brought her to Isabella. This love was like nothing she'd ever felt and was only getting bigger.

Kelsey pulled her lips away and started to raise up. "Oh no you don't," Isabella said, pulling her back down into another heated kiss. Isabella's arms were tightly wrapped around Kelsey's shoulders as their lips slammed together.

Their breaths came faster and louder as the kiss became white hot. This time when Kelsey pulled away she tore her shirt from her body. They couldn't get undressed fast enough. When their clothes were strewn across the room Kelsey once again loomed over Isabella. She had never felt this much desire and passion for another person. The love in her heart for Isabella was coursing through her veins.

Kelsey could see the fire in Isabella's eyes daring her to let go and take her.

"Who do you belong to?" Isabella smirked.

"You," Kelsey said in a loud whisper.

"Show me," Isabella said firmly.

Kelsey crashed her lips to Isabella's. All the uncertainty of their situation, all the challenges they knew they'd face, all the negative comments they were sure would come were kissed away. There was only love. Their passion and desire in this almost frenzied moment was driving them.

Kelsey had to be inside Isabella. As her tongue explored and wrestled with Isabella's, she ran her hand down and over Isabella's stomach, into her wetness.

Isabella tore her lips away and groaned loudly. "Yes!"

Kelsey slid one then two fingers inside. They both groaned when she pushed them in deeper.

"Fucking take me, Kels. I want to be yours," Isabella groaned.

Kelsey looked into Isabella's eyes and could see a dark blue storm. She would take her through this fierce desire and bring her to an island of intense pleasure. "I've got you, baby," Kelsey said, crushing her lips to Isabella's again.

Kelsey began to move her fingers in and out with purpose. She felt Isabella's arms tighten around her shoulders and she picked up the pace.

Isabella moaned with pleasure as Kelsey's hand moved even faster. "Yes, baby, yes!"

When Kelsey could tell Isabella was close she pulled her lips away and looked into her eyes. She pushed her fingers deeper and curled them up to find Isabella's velvety center. "Let's go," she said, urging Isabella over the edge. "Together."

Isabella struggled for a deep breath and Kelsey felt her clamp down on her fingers. Just then the most amazing jolt of sensation leapt through Kelsey's fingers and into her body. She could see sparks fly through Isabella's eyes as the current passed back and forth through them both.

When Isabella's muscles finally went slack, Kelsey fell down on top of her. They were both panting and gulping in air when Kelsey felt the rumble of a giggle begin in Isabella's chest.

Kelsey raised up and couldn't keep the smile from her lips.

Isabella grabbed her face and stared into her eyes as the giggle escaped her lips. "My God, Kelsey!"

"My God, Bella," Kelsey replied.

They stared at one another for a moment.

"I belong to you," Isabella whispered.

Kelsey smiled and softly caressed Isabella's now swollen lips with her own.

"I've never felt anything like that," Isabella said.

"I had to touch you. I had to love you," Kelsey said.

Isabella smiled. "Maybe you need to take the lead more often."

Kelsey chuckled and rolled over next to Isabella. "Once I move to Charlotte we get to do this all the time."

Isabella raised up on her elbow and rested her head in her hand. "Promise?"

"All I need is that winning smile," Kelsey replied.

Isabella laughed and crawled on top of Kelsey. "You've got all of me."

* * *

The next morning Isabella woke up nestled in Kelsey's arms. She could feel and hear Kelsey's rhythmic breathing and it made her smile. Isabella's mind drifted to the previous night. She had never felt so close to another person. Yes, she'd had that same thought about Kelsey before, but last night was different. She had felt the emotions pumping through Kelsey's body through every touch, sound, and look. It wasn't just love, it was lust and desire, devotion and adoration.

Isabella took a deep breath as those same feelings began to build inside her once again.

"Mmm," Kelsey murmured. "Good morning, love," she

said in a hoarse whisper. "Are you thinking about last night?"

Isabella raised up and looked into sleepy yet mischievous brownish-green eyes. "How did you know?"

"Your body tensed and your arms tightened around me," Kelsey said. She furrowed her brows. "Were you thinking of dinner or something else?"

Isabella gave her a sexy smile. "I was remembering how the breeze felt on my skin after you lit me on fire before dinner."

After they'd made love, they'd texted Carmen and finally ordered dinner. While they waited on the back deck they enjoyed the breeze and the sound of the waves. Once they'd eaten they'd gone back to bed and didn't fall asleep until they were both spent.

"Wouldn't it be nice if we could come on one of these trips just for us? We wouldn't have to worry about posting or lighting or backdrops or any of that," Isabella said.

Kelsey stifled a yawn. "Do you mean we could stay in bed all day and listen to the waves if we wanted to?"

"That's exactly what I mean, but I think we'd be doing more than listening to waves."

Kelsey pulled Isabella down and kissed her with intent. "I know we would. Let's do it. Let's come and do a vacation just for us."

"We can do our favorite things."

"That would be a great trip for November," Kelsey said.

Isabella raised her brows. "Do you think we'll still be doing these trips in November?"

"If we're not then we'll come on our own. I've been thinking and I don't see what the big deal is. We didn't deceive anybody. We didn't keep anything from anybody. We fell in love and have shared it with our followers. I don't see the problem. If some of our followers don't like it because we're gay then, bye. Go find another vacation site. For those followers that want to stay with us, we'll keep showing them this wonderful resort and how to play with magic." Kelsey grinned.

"Mmm, I love your magic," Isabella said, pressing her lips to Kelsey's. "Hey, let's ask Liz, Riley, and Alex to go to Honeymoon Beach with us today."

Kelsey raised her brows. "Maybe Carmen and Sylvie could come too. We could have our own beach party after we do the videos."

"You know, babe, these islands will always be a part of us. It's where we fell in love. We'll be back whether Coral Bay is our client or not."

"Let's go to Honeymoon Beach," Kelsey said with a grin.

39

It didn't take long for the beach party to come together. Riley offered to bring the drinks while Kelsey ordered a picnic basket from the resort. Sylvie would be waiting for them at the dock on St. Thomas. Liz, Riley, and Alex agreed to meet them on St. John with transportation to the trailhead.

Kelsey and Isabella picked up the picnic basket and met Carmen in the lobby of the resort.

"Have you looked at the website?" Carmen asked as they walked to her car.

"Nope," Isabella replied. "We told you last night that we weren't checking it."

Carmen chuckled as they got in her car.

"I'm guessing the comments are good or you wouldn't be taking the day off to go to the beach with us," Kelsey said.

"You would be correct," Carmen replied as she pulled the car out of the resort. "There have been a few haters, but we expected that. The majority of them were positive." She chuckled. "Several proclaimed they saw it coming or they already knew."

"I'm not surprised," Isabella said.

"We couldn't keep this a secret if we wanted to," Kelsey said. "It's the way we look at each other."

"I agree," Carmen said. "I look at Sylvie that way."

"Maybe we'll get to keep doing these trips," Kelsey said.

"I hope so," Carmen said. "What's the plan for today?"

"We have several posts we want to do with the leaning palms, snorkeling, that cute beach bar, and simply lounging by the water," Isabella said. "But we really want to enjoy the beach with our friends."

Carmen smiled. "Thanks for thinking of this. I think it'll be good for all of us."

They pulled into the parking lot and saw Sylvie waiting at the boat. She gave Kelsey and Isabella a hand as they stepped aboard. Isabella looked up in time to see Carmen take Sylvie's hand and pull her in for a kiss.

Isabella grinned. "Love is in the air," she murmured.

Off they went towards St. John and what they hoped was a day of fun with friends.

Later that afternoon, after Kelsey and Isabella had done their last post, they snuck away for a walk on the beach. There were other vacationers spread out across the sand, but it wasn't crowded. Isabella took Kelsey's hand in hers as they wandered along, letting the water lap at their feet.

She stole a glance at Kelsey and thought of the picture she'd taken on their first trip all those months ago. Kelsey had no idea how beautiful she was and Isabella pointed that out when she later showed her the picture. Isabella's heart was full. This is what it was supposed to feel like all along. Being in love with Kelsey gave her a sense of totality. Their love was absolute. She knew in her heart that they were supposed to live this life together. The feeling of searching and wondering was over.

Kelsey kissed the back of Isabella's hand. "I feel like we're walking down this beach with a kind of shield of love surrounding us and it feels so damn good."

"Like you're protected?"

"Yes, our love will protect us from anything anyone wants to throw at us," Kelsey said.

"Spencer thought he was my protector and I finally made him understand I didn't need anyone to protect me. But now, I think I know what you mean. Loving you gives me a kind of strength I didn't have before because I know you're with me."

"I suppose this is like the honeymoon phase," Kelsey said. "But I can't imagine not feeling your love in my heart and what it does to me. It's hard to explain."

"You don't have to explain," Isabella said. "I get it. I feel it, too."

Kelsey stopped and turned to Isabella. "We may have to change some things to keep coming back here every month."

Isabella smiled. "It will be much easier because I don't have to say 'see you next month' anymore."

Kelsey sighed and led them back towards the others. "God, I know. I felt like I was leaving a part of myself in Charlotte each month. At first I didn't understand it, but it didn't take long to figure it out."

"Hey!" Carmen yelled to them and waved.

"What's wrong?" Isabella asked as they walked up to her.

"The website is full of positive comments," Carmen said. "People want to book trips to Coral Bay and come to Honeymoon Beach."

"How about that," Riley said with a grin. "That's what we've wanted them to do all along."

"It sounds like sharing your story was a great idea," Sylvie said.

"I remember when you came to Peaches the first time," Liz said. "I could see the spark between you two that day."

"Oh, I remember," Isabella said. "You made me think about the possibilities."

Liz chuckled. "And look what happened."

"Isabella pulled me onto the dance floor and I didn't know it then, but it was the best Christmas gift I've ever received," Kelsey said, taking Isabella in her arms and twirling her in a circle.

"I hope you'll be back for Christmas," Alex said. "We'd love for you to spend it with us again."

Memories of last Christmas on Honeymoon Beach and dancing with Kelsey at Peaches flooded Isabella's brain and her heart. This wasn't only what love was supposed to feel like—this is what being married was supposed to feel like. A smile grew on her face as she said, "I think we should do the wedding trip this Christmas."

Kelsey raised her eyebrows. "I guess we could. We don't have it planned for a specific month yet."

"Are you going to have an actual couple get married or just show your followers the options?" Riley asked.

"I know a couple who could get married here this Christmas," Isabella said.

Kelsey turned to her and widened her eyes when Isabella sank to one knee.

Isabella grinned and took Kelsey's hand in both of hers. "This is where we first met and I found my best friend," Isabella began. "We connected so quickly and so deeply. It was like you knew me from the beginning.

When I realized what I felt was more than friendship, it didn't freak me out that you were a woman. My heart said thank God you're gay because then what would I have done."

There were chuckles as well as gasps heard around them.

"All this time I had this idea of what love and marriage were supposed to feel like, but I was wrong. My heart knew and when I finally listened, look what it gave me. I've found my person." Isabella took a deep breath. "I don't want to just be your girl, Kels. I want to be your wife. Will you marry me?"

Kelsey dropped to the sand and took Isabella's face into her hands.

"You know I'm the spontaneous one," Isabella said with tears in her eyes.

"I don't have to think about this, Bella," Kelsey said as a tear rolled down her cheek. "I want to be your wife. Yes, I'll marry you!"

Isabella brought their lips together in a tear-filled kiss while their friends applauded.

"Uh, excuse us."

Isabella pulled away and looked up to see two women standing there.

"We don't mean to intrude," the woman said. "We've been following your travel blog since you started it in January. We could feel the magic that you both speak about so often. It inspired us to come see for ourselves." She smiled at the woman standing next to her who began to speak as Kelsey and Isabella got to their feet.

"We've watched you fall in love through these trips. When we saw your post yesterday about coming to Honeymoon Beach, we had to see it, too. We've been married thirty years and this magic reminded us of what's most important and that's us."

"So, you can fall in love or fall *back* in love here," the woman said with a smile. "Your posts and these trips are reaching people. I hope you'll keep going."

Kelsey smiled at Isabella and nodded.

"Uh, we posted the picture we took of you earlier," the first woman said, turning the phone around so they could see.

She had captured Isabella and Kelsey strolling along the beach. "I hope you don't mind, but it was so sweet and captured the winding down of this wonderful day."

Isabella looked at Kelsey and smiled. "Thank you. We don't mind."

"We also took this video when we saw what was happening," the woman said with a sheepish grin. "I'd like to send it to you and then I'll delete it. This was a beautiful private moment between you and your friends and you should have it."

The woman handed Isabella her phone so she could type in her phone number. After she took the phone back the woman sent Isabella the video then deleted it.

"Have you been to Peaches yet?" Kelsey asked them.

"No, that's our next stop," the woman replied. "We were gathering our things when we saw Isabella kneel."

"Please join us there," Kelsey said. "We were about to leave as well."

"We're going dancing," Isabella said, putting her arm around Kelsey's shoulder.

They packed up their things and headed towards the trail. Kelsey and Isabella were behind everyone else when Kelsey tugged at Isabella's hand. She turned to look back at the beach.

"We fell in love here and now we've gotten engaged here. I know where we should spend our honeymoon." Kelsey grinned.

"How could we not?" Isabella reached up and kissed Kelsey tenderly. "I know where I want to get married."

"I do, too," Kelsey replied. "On the beach outside our bungalow."

Isabella smiled and kissed Kelsey again. "Wait a minute," she said. "I didn't give you a ring. So much for spontaneity."

Kelsey chuckled. "I don't need a ring. I've got you."

"We'll get matching rings tomorrow in the gift shop," Isabella said, leading them down the trail to catch up with the others. "Something really tacky and fun."

Kelsey laughed. "To always remember this day."

40

Seven Months Later

"It's almost time," Kelsey said.

"After twelve months of trips," Isabella began. "We've done winter on the beach, Valentine's Day, spring break, family vacations, bridesmaids getaway, honeymoons, and…"

"We did self-care, girls trips, fall vacations, holidays, and just because," Kelsey added.

"Did you ever see us ending up here?" Isabella asked, raising her brows.

Kelsey nodded and put her arm around Isabella's shoulder as she gazed out at the people gathered on the beach outside their bungalow. "I hoped," she said softly.

"Me too, love," Isabella murmured, resting her head on Kelsey's shoulder.

Several chairs had been arranged looking out over the water. In the front row were both their mothers and all the kids. Behind them sat Carmen and Sylvie with Tanner and Mia along with Riley and Alex. They had asked Liz to officiate. A few of the friends they'd made at the resort were also there, but it was a small intimate group just like they wanted.

Liz stood up from where she'd been sitting and took her place facing the others. They saw her smile and Kelsey held out her arm to Isabella.

"Will you marry me?" Kelsey asked with a grin.

Isabella leaned up and kissed Kelsey softly. "Anytime," she said, putting her arm through Kelsey's.

They didn't have an aisle to walk down because they were already one big family and wanted them to sit that way. Arm in arm, just like they usually walked together, they made their way around the small group and stood in front of their kids.

"We're doing this together," Kelsey said.

"Will you stand with us?" Isabella asked.

Kelsey reached for Emma and Wyatt's hands while Isabella took Gus and Dana's.

"One year ago today these two women came to our islands. I think their hearts had been searching and waiting for that chance moment when they met. Then the magic took over," Liz said, raising her brows. "If you'll join hands."

Kelsey and Isabella faced each other and clasped hands.

"Kelsey, do you take Isabella to be your wife?" Liz asked simply.

"I do," Kelsey said, staring into Isabella's bright blue eyes with a huge smile.

"Isabella," Liz said. "Do you take Kelsey to be your wife?"

Isabella returned Kelsey's smile with an even bigger grin. "I do," she said firmly.

"Okay," Liz said cheerfully. "It's your turn, Kelsey."

Kelsey took a deep breath and swallowed. "One year ago today was the best day of my life. That was the day I met you and every day since has been even better. Yes, having my girls were wonderful days, but finding the woman I am meant to live this life with made me a new person with a full heart." She took another breath and struggled for words. "Your love has made me a better mom, a better partner, and a better person. It's amazing what you can do when you feel the *true* love from the one you're meant to be with."

Isabella smiled with tears in her eyes. She took a breath and said, "Your love, our love, has made everything better. When I felt your love enter my heart it was like my eyes were opened." She held Kelsey's hands to her heart. "I thought I knew what love was about but oh, it is so much more. Your love protects me even though I didn't think I needed it. But knowing you love me makes me invincible. It's a feeling I can't put into words. There is an aura around us that's pure love. It's magical and I know it's everlasting."

Kelsey smiled with tears in her eyes. She didn't think her heart could hold the love she was feeling from Isabella. She quickly glanced at Liz because she had to kiss Isabella right then.

"It is my honor to pronounce you married," Liz said with a smile. "You may kiss."

Kelsey pressed her lips to Isabella's as her arms curled around her shoulders, pulling her even closer.

After a moment she could feel Isabella's lips smile against hers. That's when Kelsey heard their family and friends clapping. She pulled away and the happiness on Isabella's face made Kelsey's heart overflow.

"I love you so much," Isabella said and kissed Kelsey again.

"Party at Peaches!" Liz shouted.

After everyone congratulated the couple Riley said, "We'll take your moms and kids with us. Why don't you ride with Carmen and Sylvie?"

"Okay, thanks," Kelsey said,

"I'll grab our purses," Isabella said, starting towards the bungalow.

"Wait—" Kelsey grabbed her hand and pulled her in for a quick kiss. "Hurry."

Isabella giggled and dashed to the deck.

"Congrats," Carmen said. "I can't believe a year ago I welcomed you to the resort and the next day we came up with this plan."

"I wasn't kidding," Kelsey said, watching Isabella hurry back towards her. "It was the best day of my life."

"Excuse me, do you remember us?" a woman said, walking up to them holding another woman's hand.

"You were on the beach the day Isabella proposed to me," Kelsey said.

Isabella walked up and slid her hand into Kelsey's. "Oh, hi."

"We had to come back to Coral Bay to experience Christmas," the woman said.

"We have the photo you took of us in our office at home," Isabella said. "It's where we both can see it when we're at our desks."

"Congratulations," the other woman said. "We've met several people at the resort who are your followers."

"We plan to do a post tomorrow closing out the year," Kelsey explained.

"But we'll be checking in from time to time," Isabella added.

"It was nice to see you again," the woman said.

"How many offers have you had from other resorts?" Carmen asked as they waded the short distance to the boat.

"We've had a few from other Caribbean islands," Kelsey said.

"But we've just moved into our new house and want to stay at home for a while," Isabella said.

Sylvie had arranged for two boats to whisk them away from the beach over to Peaches. They got in the boat and could see their family waving as their boat started towards St. John.

"Have you had any problems since you moved there?" Sylvie asked Kelsey.

"There have been a few things said here and there, but nothing we couldn't handle or didn't expect," Kelsey said, smiling at Isabella.

"I think fear of the unknown is what drives some people. Once they get to know us, how can they not like us?" Isabella chuckled.

"I can't imagine." Carmen laughed with her.

They settled back and enjoyed the ride to St. John as a married couple. Once they'd made it to Peaches, several of the locals who had become friends were already there. The party was in full swing.

"We'll give you a minute," Carmen said as they reached the beach.

Kelsey and Isabella watched as Carmen and Sylvie walked away hand in hand.

"We've made it through a year of vacations," Kelsey said, gazing at Peaches.

"Did you ever doubt us?" Isabella asked, stepping in front of her.

"Once I said yes to you, I never doubted," Kelsey said honestly.

"That's my girl," Isabella said, cupping her cheek. "And my wife."

"God, I love the sound of that: my wife," Kelsey said. She leaned in and softly touched her lips to Isabella's. She wrapped her arms around her, pulling her closer and deepening the kiss. Their lips caressed, nibbled, and expressed the love bubbling from their hearts.

After several moments Isabella moaned. "I've been wanting to kiss you like that since we said I do."

"I know," Kelsey murmured, touching her forehead to Isabella's. Suddenly she gasped. "Listen! They're playing our song."

Isabella smiled. "This is a beautiful song, we're in a beautiful place. Let's be beautiful. Will you dance with me, babe?"

"Aww, that's what you said the first time we danced," Kelsey replied. "Always," she whispered with tears in her eyes. She put her hands on Isabella's hips and pulled her close.

Isabella put her arms around Kelsey's neck and they slowly moved to the music.

Kelsey glanced up and saw their family and friends on the patio watching them. There was happiness radiating from all the people they loved.

"This is everlasting love," Isabella said softly, pressing her lips to Kelsey's.

With their favorite song playing and their family and friends around them, this was more than a dance. Kelsey could feel all they had built month after month, a life full of romance, but also with challenges. It was all coming together to make a big life full of their big love.

FIFTEEN YEARS LATER

"It feels good to be home," Isabella said, opening the door to Peaches.

Kelsey chuckled and walked inside. "Yeah, it does."

"Hey!" Riley exclaimed when she saw them. "You didn't tell us you were coming in."

"How long do you get to stay this time?" Alex asked, coming around from behind the bar to hug them both.

Kelsey grinned at Isabella. "We're here for good."

Riley gasped. "Really?"

"Yep." Isabella smiled. "The rest of our things will arrive next week."

"Grab a table," Alex said. "I'll bring the beer. We're celebrating!"

They chuckled and went to their favorite table on the patio. Alex brought the beer and once they'd all sat down, Riley held up her glass.

"To our dear friends who are finally home," she said.

They clinked their glasses and everyone drank.

"Oh, that's so good," Kelsey said. "I swear you serve the best beer."

Alex chuckled. "You say that nearly every time you come here."

"It's true!" Isabella exclaimed.

"Where's Liz?" Kelsey asked, looking around the bar.

"She'll be here a little later," Alex replied. "She doesn't stay here all day like she used to."

"Did you know she'll be eighty this year?" Riley said.

"Wow," Isabella said. "I knew she was getting close."

"We're all in our sixties, except for my young bride," Kelsey said, winking at Isabella. "I have a thing for younger women," she teased.

"Your thing had better be with this younger woman *only*," Isabella warned.

Kelsey chuckled. "You know it is."

"Catch us up," Riley said. "I didn't think you were making the move until next year."

"Well," Kelsey began. "Our son just happens to be a financial genius."

Isabella chuckled. "Wyatt may have followed in his father's footsteps as far as going into finance, but he has a gift for finding great investments."

"When I moved to Charlotte and we found our new home, I sold my house in Colorado and we saved a good chunk of that money. We invested it, but while Wyatt was in college he found a couple of opportunities and we gave him a sum to invest for us," Kelsey explained.

"Let's just say that it did quite well," Isabella said.

"Anyway, we were able to buy our sweet little bungalow near yours," Kelsey said.

"Without stairs," Liz said, walking onto the patio.

"Liz!" Isabella exclaimed and hugged the older woman.

Alex hurried to the bar to get Liz a beer while Kelsey pulled up another chair.

"I remember Riley and Alex buying their house down the beach because they were tired of climbing those stairs above the bar several times a day," Liz said.

"We appreciate you keeping an eye out for us," Isabella said. "We couldn't believe it when the place next door to you became available."

"There are some perks to owning a bar." Riley winked. "People like to talk, especially after they've had a drink or two."

"I told Riley we needed to call you immediately when we heard the couple who had it was moving back to the states," Alex said.

"It all worked out perfectly," Kelsey said. She looked over at Isabella and smiled. "Like our lives have since we came here all those years ago."

Isabella grinned and squeezed her hand.

"I saw your oldest daughter today," Liz said.

"You did?" Kelsey raised her eyebrows. "Were you at the hospital?"

"I had to go in for a routine scan," Liz said. "I'll tell you, since she became Director of Nursing, that hospital runs smoothly."

Isabella smiled. "We are very proud of Dana. It still amazes us that she and Mia got married and moved back here."

"That was another reason we came back sooner than expected," Kelsey said. "Carmen and Sylvie get to spoil our grandkids more than we do!"

Liz chuckled. "That family is good for the islands. As principal, Mia has turned the elementary school around."

"Have you talked to Ellie and Allie lately?" Alex asked. "They want to take over the bar when they get to high school."

Kelsey and Isabella laughed. "I'm not surprised," Kelsey said. "Whenever we talk to them they have to tell us about going to see the aunts."

"They come over just about every week," Riley said. "Dana and Mia are raising two very smart young girls."

Kelsey beamed a smile at Isabella. Not long after Kelsey and Isabella got married, Dana and Mia began dating. They fell in love, got married, and had twins. When the girls were old enough to start school they decided to move to St. Thomas because Mia's parents were already there and Kelsey and Isabella had plans to move there eventually.

"What about Emma and Gus?" Riley asked.

"Emma has decided to run for Congress," Kelsey said with a proud smile.

"Really?" Alex said. "She will be wonderful. I'm guessing her focus is on equal rights."

"It is," Isabella said. "You'll never guess who is helping run her campaign."

They all shrugged then Riley said, "Wait a minute. Could it be the young civil rights attorney, Augustus Burns?"

Isabella chuckled. "That's right. Her baby brother, Gus, is her biggest supporter and does that man have ideas."

Kelsey chuckled. "Believe me, they are a force!"

"I know you're proud of them," Liz said. "So are we."

"What about you two? Are you officially retired?" Alex asked.

"We have kept a few clients," Isabella said.

"That monthly thing you did with Carmen made you the vacation queens of the Caribbean." Liz chuckled. "What a genius marketing play."

"There were times when it didn't look so genius," Isabella replied.

"But it all worked out," Kelsey said and smiled at Isabella.

"Yeah it did." Isabella leaned over and gave Kelsey a sweet kiss. "Besides, we won't need to vacation ever again. We are finally where we've wanted to be since the first time we came here."

"That's right," Kelsey said. "We're surrounded by love and magic all the time."

Isabella finished her beer and turned to Kelsey. "Are you ready?"

Kelsey nodded. "We're going to do one of our new favorite things."

"What's that?" Riley asked.

Isabella grinned at Kelsey and took her hand. "We can walk home along the beach."

"Let's go," Kelsey said with a smile.

They hugged everyone, promising to see them tomorrow, then walked off the patio onto the beach. Isabella turned to grasp Kelsey's hand as they walked towards their new home.

"Can you believe that fifteen years ago we came to this place to simply meet with a client?" Kelsey said.

"If we've learned anything, it's that those simple things are the ones that matter most," Isabella said.

Tears stung Kelsey's eyes as emotion washed over her. She reached up to brush away a tear and Isabella stopped them.

"Baby," she said with concern, taking Kelsey's other hand. "What is it?"

Kelsey smiled as another tear rolled down her cheek. "Simple things like these." Kelsey held up her left hand and wiggled her ring finger. She wore a simple silver band inlaid with coral gemstones.

"These were supposed to be fun little rings that day I proposed," Isabella said, looking at her matching ring. "We were going to get better rings, but neither one of us could take these off."

"I remember the day I got off the plane I sarcastically muttered, welcome to paradise. I had no idea moments later paradise would embrace me and change my life forever."

"Oh, my love," Isabella said, kissing Kelsey tenderly.

"And here we are again—this time, living in paradise."

"I don't think that's quite accurate," Isabella said, starting down the beach again. "We've been living in paradise since that day fifteen years ago. It may not have always felt like it, but…"

Kelsey chuckled. "It did to me. There were sad times and hard times, but at night when I laid down with you and we held each other, I knew everything would be better in the morning."

"And then there were those nights when everything was paradise." Isabella giggled as they neared the stretch of beach in front of their humble bungalow.

Kelsey stopped them once again, looked into those familiar blue eyes, and ran her hand along Isabella's hair. "My Bella," she whispered. She softly touched her lips to Isabella's and thought, *this is paradise.*

The softest moan from Isabella caused Kelsey to deepen the kiss and warmth spread through her. This woman was everything and Kelsey knew this next phase of their life would be even better than the last.

Isabella pulled away slightly and began to softly sing the song they first danced to fifteen years ago. "I hear strings play, every time you look my way…"

"Don't you know that's what you do, feels like ooh," Kelsey sang along.

Isabella pressed their lips together again in a passionate kiss and Kelsey lost her breath.

"Take me inside," Isabella whispered as she pulled away.

Kelsey grabbed Isabella's hand and they walked onto their back deck, both humming their song.

ABOUT THE AUTHOR

Jamey Moody is a bestselling author of sapphic contemporary romance. Her characters are strong women, living everyday lives with a few bumps in the road, but they get their happily ever afters.

Jamey lives in Texas with her adorable terrier Leo.

You can find Jamey's books on Amazon and on her website: jameymoody.com

Join her newsletter for latest book news and other fun. Join here.

Jamey loves to hear from readers. Email her at: jameymoodyauthor@gmail.com

On the next page is a list of Jamey's books with links that will take you to their page.

Jamey has included the first chapter of CeCe Sloan is Swooning. When CeCe Sloan's favorite client comes to her new salon's open house a sexy, flirty banter begins. Alexis is so far out of her league, but what happens in the back room doesn't count, right?

Come along on this sexy, romantic adventure and find out why CeCe Sloan is swooning.

ALSO BY JAMEY MOODY

Stand Alones

Live This Love

One Little Yes

Who I Believe

* What Now

See You Next Month

The Your Way Series:

* Finding Home

*Finding Family

*Finding Forever

The Lovers Landing Series

*Where Secrets Are Safe

*No More Secrets

*And The Truth Is …

*Instead Of Happy

The Second Chance Series

*The Woman at the Top of the Stairs

*The Woman Who Climbed A Mountain

*The Woman I Found In Me

Sloan Sisters' Romance Series

*CeCe Sloan is Swooning

*Cory Sloan is Swearing

*Cat Sloan is Swirling

Christmas Novellas

*It Takes A Miracle

The Great Christmas Tree Mystery

With One Look

*Also available as an audiobook

CECE SLOAN IS SWOONING
PROLOGUE

"What are we looking at?"

"It looks like a shopping center to me."

"Oh, it's not just any shopping center," Cory replied. "It's ours. You are gazing upon the Sloan Sisters' Shopping Extravaganza."

At forty-four years old, Corrine Sloan was the oldest sister. She had thick blond hair and clear blue eyes that saw a vision of what this property could be.

"What are you talking about? I think I would remember buying a shopping center," CeCe remarked.

Cecilia was the quintessential middle sister of the Sloan siblings. Her fiery red hair and crystal blue eyes matched her personality. She was a forty-two-year-old good time ready to happen and was usually responsible for the fun.

"We didn't buy it," Cat Sloan said. "Explain yourself, Cory."

The youngest and therefore the baby sister, Catarina was thirty-seven. Her rich dark chocolate hair set off her blue eyes that matched her big sisters'. She was the quiet, reserved one, but not to be overlooked.

"Do you remember when Dad's rich uncle died and gave us all that money?"

"Of course I remember," CeCe scoffed. "He took us out to dinner and told us not to get any ideas about spending it."

"Yeah, as far as I can remember that's the only time he spent any of it," Cat added.

"Well, Daddy set aside part of that money for us," Cory said. "He left explicit instructions for us to do something with it together. This shopping center includes three stores, one for each of us."

"Why are we just now finding out about this?" CeCe asked, giving her sister a measured look. "And why isn't Mom telling us about it?"

"You know since Dad died Mom gave over all the financial stuff to me," Cory said.

"Yeah, Dad's been gone a year, Cory. What took so long for us to find out about this?" CeCe demanded.

"Dad had this in an investment that didn't mature until now. Mom told me about it last month," Cory replied.

"Why didn't you tell us!" Cat exclaimed.

"Because I had to be sure there was plenty of money for Mom to live comfortably going forward," Cory said defensively.

"I thought Dad made sure of that with his life insurance," CeCe said.

Cory nodded. "He did, but there were other things we had to do to get the money. It was all documentation bullshit and as you've both told me numerous times, neither one of you cared to be bothered with that. Right?"

CeCe and Cat looked at each other and smirked. "So, tell us what happened," CeCe said with a dramatic sigh.

"Mom told me about the investment. I contacted the company and they gave us an option of monthly disbursements or a lump sum." Cory took an envelope out of her pocket and handed it to CeCe. "This is what Dad wanted."

CeCe opened the envelope and held it so Cat could read over her shoulder. Tears welled in both their eyes as they scanned the handwritten letter.

CeCe looked up at her sisters with fire in her eyes. "I don't know why he couldn't have enjoyed this money instead of saving it for us! He kept working at that damn factory, building planes, when he could've retired and spent time with Mom or us!"

Cat put her arm around her sister. "He loved building those airplanes. Can you imagine him sitting around? No, that wasn't who he was. The man was always building something. And did you ever hear Mom complain? Did any of us ever really want for anything growing up?"

CeCe sighed loudly. "We weren't poor, but we damn sure weren't well-off either!"

"This is what Dad wanted," Cory said, taking the letter from CeCe's hands. "Can you imagine how proud he would be if we owned our own stores, side by side? This is the place!"

"It's not even finished yet," CeCe observed.

"That's the beauty of it. CeCe, you have always wanted to open your own salon. You can customize this space and make it yours. How many chairs do you want?" Cory asked.

"Hmm." A smile grew on CeCe's face. "I can see three on each side as you walk in and then two or three stations in the back to do nails and facials."

"Okay, so CeCe gets her salon. What kind of store are you going to open, Cory?" Cat asked.

"There's not a liquor store within ten miles of this area. Look at the storefront at the end. That's about to become The Liquor Box," Cory said proudly.

"What!" Cat laughed.

"That's right," Cory replied with a laugh. "I'm a lesbian and that's what we do. We lick—"

"Stop!" CeCe and Cat yelled in unison.

"We know what you do. You've told us over and over," CeCe said.

"We get it. The Liquor Box," Cat added.

"I've already lined up my first big customer."

"Who?" CeCe asked.

"You know that sapphic resort at the lake where the Hollywood gays go?"

"Yeah, Krista Kyle owns it with Julia Lansing. I've done their hair and they've brought several of their clients in over the last couple of years," CeCe said.

"Didn't you go out there for a party last summer?" Cat asked.

CeCe wiggled her eyebrows. "I certainly did. Those Hollywood folks know how to have a good time."

Cory and Cat both chuckled.

"So CeCe opens a salon and you're opening a liquor store. What do you have in mind for me?" Cat asked.

"Well, little sister. I have an idea, but if you could open any store you wanted, what would it be?"

"Hmm," Cat murmured as she stared at the building.

"Oh, I know!" CeCe exclaimed. "It has to have something to do with books. You love to read!"

"That's what I was thinking." Cory nodded.

Cat glanced at her sisters with a sly smile on her face. "I'd love to open a bookstore, and in the back I'd have an exclusive toy store."

Cory and CeCe gazed at their little sister with confused looks on their faces.

"A private, clandestine adult toy store," Cat stated.

"Oh!" CeCe exclaimed as her eyes widened.

Laughter bubbled from Cory as she said, "Oh my God, Cat. That's perfect!"

The three sisters gazed at the building as ideas flowed through their heads.

"What do you think? Will you join The Liquor Box?" Cory asked.

"I can see it now," CeCe said, holding her arms out wide. "Salon 411. You'll not only get the perfect hairstyle, but you'll know everything that's going on in town."

"Oh, I like it," Cory said. She turned to Cat. "Your turn."

"Hmm, let's see. How about Your Next Great Read?"

"Yes!" CeCe exclaimed.

"Do you have a name for the room in the back?" Cory asked Cat.

"Yeah, I think I'll call it The Bottom Shelf." Cat grinned. "But let's not tell Mom about that part."

Cory chuckled. "You have to watch out for the quiet ones."

"So, little sister. Do we get a discount?" CeCe asked.

Cat laughed. "Do you think this is what Dad had in mind?"

"I can see it now!" Cory exclaimed. "Our clients can stop by and get a drink, a book, and get their hair done."

CeCe held out her hand. "I'm in."

"I'm in," Cat said, placing her hand on top of CeCe's.

"Watch out," Cory said, placing her hand on top. "Here come the Sloan Sisters!"

CHAPTER 1

Three Months Later

"Are you ready?" Cory asked her sisters.

"Hold it!" CeCe exclaimed. She went over to a table where glasses of champagne were poured and waiting. She balanced three flutes in her hands and held them so each of her sisters could take one. "We should have a toast to kick off this open house."

"To the Sloan Sisters," Cory said, holding up her glass.

"May we bring joy to this little piece of our city." Cat held her glass next to Cory's and looked at CeCe.

"And…may we live happily ever after." CeCe chuckled and clinked her glass to her sisters'.

"What?" Cory laughed.

"I couldn't think of anything and I want us all to live happily ever after, so why not drink to that?" CeCe shrugged.

"How can we not? We'll be working side by side most days and doing something we love. Drink up," Cory said, "it's time to unlock the doors."

"Wait," Cat said. "Let's drink to Dad. This may not be what he had in mind, but he'd still be proud."

They clinked their glasses together again and drank.

"I think this is exactly what he wanted. We're together, doing our own thing, but still supporting each other," CeCe said.

"Remember to encourage people to walk through to the other stores," Cory said.

"It was a good idea to build these extra large openings in the walls so clients can move easily from store to store," CeCe said.

"We've got plenty of champagne in each store and other drinks if anyone prefers. Okay?" Cory looked at her sisters.

"Got it. I'll come by later to see you both. Now, get out of here. Salon 411 is ready to open," CeCe said, unlocking her front door.

Cory and Cat went to their respective stores and CeCe turned to face the other stylists.

"Everyone is going to come here to get their hair and nails done," Amber said, smiling at CeCe.

"Oh, I hope so." CeCe was barely able to contain her excitement. "I want to thank each of you once again for taking a chance and coming with me."

"It was a no-brainer," Ryan said. "We have brand new equipment, reasonable booth rent, and the best group of coworkers anywhere."

"And you let me put up my Nails by Nora sign," Nora said, clapping her hands. "Kerry wouldn't let me at my other shop."

CeCe laughed. "It's fine, Nora. I know we are all self-employed, but I hope we can be a team and help spread the word about *our* salon."

"We're more than a team." Heather gestured at everyone. "Everyone come closer." She put her arm around CeCe and the rest of them formed a circle, arm in arm. "We're a family," Heather said, smiling at everyone.

"Let's welcome our clients, family. Here they come," Ryan said, nodding towards the door.

For an hour a steady stream of customers came in the front door as well as through each entrance to the adjoining stores. CeCe and her stylists showed off the new salon and encouraged people to check out the other stores. The champagne and wine flowed along with snacks offered in each store.

"I love how this turned out," Marina Summit said, walking up to CeCe.

"Hey, if it isn't the best realtor in town." CeCe grinned. "Thank you again for helping us get such a good deal on the property. I know you're in residential real estate now, so I appreciate you looking into this as a favor to us."

"It's the least I could do for the best stylist in the entire metroplex," Marina said.

CeCe beamed. "Where's that beautiful wife of yours? I want to show her how the shampoo area turned out. She had the best suggestions to give us more room and stage the area."

"Dru is on her way."

"Have you been next door to Cat's bookstore?"

"Not yet. I stopped by to say hello to Cory before I came in here," Marina said, taking a sip of champagne.

CeCe leaned in and quietly said, "Be sure and ask Cat to show you the bottom shelf. Tell her I sent you." CeCe winked.

"Okay." Marina drew the word out. "That sounds deliciously secretive."

CeCe grinned. "Oh, it is. Take Dru with you. And tell Cat whatever you choose is on me."

Marina raised her brows and clinked her glass to CeCe's. "Okay, thank you. Congratulations, CeCe. I know you'll be very successful here."

"Thanks, Marina."

CeCe watched as Marina made her way through the entrance to the bookstore. Her attention was quickly drawn to the front door of the salon. A beautiful woman with rich brown hair the color of dark chocolate and sparkling chestnut eyes sauntered just inside the doorway and stopped.

CeCe couldn't stop the smile that grew on her face. This was one of her favorite clients and she was surprised she'd taken the time to come to the open house. She snagged a flute of champagne and met the woman as she started her way through the salon.

"Doc! I'm so glad you made it." CeCe handed the woman the glass of champagne.

"I couldn't miss this. You're one of my favorite people, CeCe Sloan," the woman said.

CeCe smiled shyly. "You say that because I make you look even more gorgeous while you're fighting off all the doctors and nurses and probably a few patients."

Doctor Alexis Reed was one of the premier, most sought after surgeons in the area. Her schedule was jam-packed and CeCe knew her free time was precious. For her to take time out and come to the salon's opening warmed CeCe's heart.

"Oh, I don't fight off all of them." Alexis smiled seductively and sipped her champagne.

CeCe raised her eyebrows and looked into Alexis's eyes. "Is there something you need to share with me?"

Alexis chuckled. "You're the one I've heard stories about."

"Oh, please!" CeCe scoffed. "Those were from a decade ago and have been greatly embellished."

"Hmm, I'm not so sure," Alexis said, raising one eyebrow. "Show me around your new place and I'll be the judge of that."

CeCe shook her head. "I'm telling you, Doc. They aren't true. Right this way."

They strolled around the salon and CeCe pointed out each of the new stylist stations. Towards the back on one side were several shampoo bowls and on the other side was CeCe's station which was separate from the others.

"Oh, I like this," Alexis said, walking over to CeCe's chair. There were strands of shiny silver beads hanging vertically from the ceiling to the floor, creating a wall of sorts. It gave the space a bit of seclusion from the rest of the shop.

Alexis sat down in the chair and spun around to face CeCe. "This gives us a little privacy for you to catch me up on all your shenanigans... Or are they dalliances?" She crossed her legs and stared up at CeCe.

"Could you be any sexier?" CeCe asked, putting one hand on her hip and looking Alexis up and down. She paused for a moment, hoping to deflect the attention away from her, but Alexis's stare never wavered. "What in the world are these stories you've heard?"

Alexis giggled and took another sip of her champagne. "Is this the end of the tour or is there a back room? I heard that's where the fun happens."

CeCe laughed. "How long have I been doing your hair?

You know there's always a back room. You've *been* to the back room."

Alexis got up and followed CeCe down a hallway where the restrooms were located along with a supply room. A door opened into a larger area that was mainly for storage. But in one corner, CeCe had arranged a little seating area complete with a couch, several chairs, a coffee table and a rug that gave it a homey feel. Over to one side was a refrigerator with a small table beside it. There was also a larger table with chairs around it where the stylists could eat and gather.

"Isn't this cute." Alexis walked over and ran her hand along the back of the couch. She looked around the room then nodded towards the back door. "Is that where you park your cars or is it for sneaking in?"

"What is with you? All of a sudden you act like I have all these trysts in some secret room," CeCe said, walking over next to Alexis. "This is the break area. You've had a glass of wine with me in the back room of the other salon. This isn't any different."

Alexis walked around and sat down on the couch. She looked up at CeCe and raised her eyebrows, silently inviting CeCe to join her.

"I heard that you may have fooled around a time or two in the back room of the shop when you needed to be discreet."

CeCe narrowed her gaze. "Is someone talking shit about me since I opened my own salon?"

Alexis smiled. "No. I ran into Krista Kyle and her wife, Melanie. We got to talking about the shopping center and they told me Cory was their new supplier for spirits. They particularly loved the name."

CeCe laughed. "Cory is quite proud of The Liquor Box."

"I mentioned that you were the talented stylist that keeps me looking my best."

CeCe smiled. "It doesn't take much."

Alexis returned CeCe's smile. "Thank you," she said softly. "But they mentioned you'd been to a party or two at their place at the lake."

"I have. They needed a hairstylist for a photo shoot they were doing. At the last minute, the stylist who was supposed to come with the photographer couldn't make it, so I helped out. They asked me to stay for the party afterwards."

"Those women know how to party," Alexis commented.

"They take karaoke and dancing to another level." Wide-eyed, CeCe laughed. "Have you been to one of their parties?"

"I've been to a couple."

"Why, Doc. I didn't know you have a soft spot for the ladies," CeCe teased. "Or is it just those Hollywood starlets?"

"You should know me better than that by now, CeCe. Much like you, I never walk the straight and narrow. Why do you think we get along so well?" Alexis chuckled.

CeCe grinned. "That leads me to believe my little back room, as you like to call it," she said in a low, deep voice, "must be a lot like the supply rooms or doctor's respite rooms at the hospital."

"I never kiss and tell." Alexis winked at her.

CeCe studied Alexis as she finished her glass of champagne. She'd harbored a little crush on Alexis since the first time she'd done her hair. There could never be anything between them because Alexis was way out of CeCe's league and CeCe never messed around with her clients. That had been a hard and fast rule from the beginning. But a little harmless flirting never hurt anyone, did it?

Alexis gave CeCe a genuine smile. "Do you have any idea how much I value my appointments with you?"

"I think so. I know how busy your days are," CeCe said earnestly. She tried to make all her clients feel special, but she took extra time with Alexis. There were times when she could feel the stress leave Alexis's body as she massaged her scalp or gently rubbed her shoulders.

"I can come here and put everything aside. You not only take good care of my hair, but you also ease my mind when I need it. Plus, you entertain me with all the craziness that surrounds a good salon."

CeCe laughed. "I don't know how it happens, but you're right. Craziness abounds at times."

"I love it and most of the time I need it!"

"I'm glad, Doc. I do have one other place I need to show you," CeCe said with a twinkle in her eyes.

"Oh?"

"Yeah, we can pick you up another glass on the way. You'll need it." CeCe winked.

CeCe led them back inside the salon and waved to a couple of clients as they walked through the threshold to Cat's bookstore.

"I love the name!" Alexis exclaimed. "If only I had time to read anything other than medical journals."

CeCe handed Alexis another glass of champagne as she waved to her sister.

"Are you going to drive me home?" Alexis asked as she took the drink from CeCe.

"Nah, I'm going to insist you hang around with me until you can drive yourself." CeCe grinned.

"Hey," Cat said, walking over to them.

"Hi, sis. I'd like you to meet...probably my favorite client." CeCe smiled at Alexis. "This is Doctor Alexis Reed."

"Oh, CeCe," Alexis scoffed. "It's nice to meet you," she said, holding out her hand to Cat, who took it and smiled.

"Listen Doc, you've worked hard and earned your title. Everybody would be calling me doctor if I'd gone to school that long and accomplished the things you have. You're a big deal," CeCe said.

Alexis shook her head and smirked, but CeCe could see her praise was appreciated.

"This is Cat, my little sister," CeCe said, finishing the introduction.

"Hi, Alexis. It's nice to meet you," Cat said. "I've heard CeCe mention you."

"Uh oh. Am I one of her problem clients?" Alexis asked.

"Not at all. She's always happy after your appointments," Cat explained.

CeCe looked over at Alexis and shrugged. "What can I say, I'm glad I'm your stylist."

Alexis smiled at CeCe and sipped her champagne.

"I gave Alexis a tour of the salon, but I saved the best for last. Do you mind?" CeCe asked, nodding towards the back of the store.

Get CeCe Sloan is Swooning

Printed in Great Britain
by Amazon